The Library Room

The Library Room

KIMBERLY LOVING ROSS

TATE PUBLISHING
AND ENTERPRISES, LLC

The Library Room
Copyright © 2014 by Kimberly Loving Ross. All rights reserved.

No part of this publication may be reproduced, stored in a retrieval system or transmitted in any way by any means, electronic, mechanical, photocopy, recording or otherwise without the prior permission of the author except as provided by USA copyright law.

This novel is a work of fiction. Names, descriptions, entities, and incidents included in the story are products of the author's imagination. Any resemblance to actual persons, events, and entities is entirely coincidental.

The opinions expressed by the author are not necessarily those of Tate Publishing, LLC.

Published by Tate Publishing & Enterprises, LLC
127 E. Trade Center Terrace | Mustang, Oklahoma 73064 USA
1.888.361.9473 | www.tatepublishing.com

Tate Publishing is committed to excellence in the publishing industry. The company reflects the philosophy established by the founders, based on Psalm 68:11,
"The Lord gave the word and great was the company of those who published it."

Book design copyright © 2014 by Tate Publishing, LLC. All rights reserved.
Cover design by Carlo nino Suico
Interior design by Jake Muelle

Published in the United States of America

ISBN: 978-1-63122-810-0
1. Fiction / Spiritual / General
2. Fiction / General
14.05.20

Acknowledgments

A special thanks to Michael P. Sanderson for your constant words of encouragement and support during this entire process. I love you more than words could ever express.

Additional thanks and recognition go to Michael Dobies, Rhnee Kincaid, Reverend William and Virginia Norman, Jennifer Gasche Labate, and Associate Pastor Jason Humble.

Debbie Shannon, your kindness in giving is beyond measure. You inspired me to push myself up out of a pity-party when I was penniless and near a dark bottom. I love you, sister.

To all of my family and friends, I thank you for your feedback, support, and positive words.

One

Loren's long hair had tangled and pulled as she tossed her purse and laptop onto the table at the library. Her blue eyes reread the assignments on her pad and willed a different assignment. Unfortunately, it didn't work.

Her flat tummy growled a soft complaint. She'd full intentions of making a smoothie for lunch before going to her part-time apprentice job at Samson Marketing. If only she hadn't argued so long with her professor over the assignment.

She inhaled the musty smells of books, the cedar planked walls, and decades of wood polishing chemicals. It was one of her most treasured sensations, the smell of "her library." When she needed to unwind, she could recall Hersche Library's aroma to be calmed. Today, it was being called upon to help with the apprehension of her assignment.

She huffed and thought, *Toad warts! Where do I start? Okay, Loren, focus...Books...Um, I'll assume a Bible and whatever Jewish people read and...who do I know? Who can I call? Who can I hire to do this and how much would it cost?*

As she stared at the ornate crown moldings tying together the cedar walls and tin ceiling, a familiar figure walked in front of her lower peripheral vision.

The librarian wore a bright fuchsia dress with a black scarf. She kept her nappy hair short, displaying random touches of silver. Her slender and nearly six foot height commanded respect along with her proper posture; however, kindness resonated in her soft voice. Loren was always impressed by her knowledge of the different reference books and authors throughout the library. Although Loren had never bothered asking the woman's name, they were kindred spirits brought together by books and a building. As she busied herself returning books to shelves, her black scarf fluttered around her shoulder.

Loren snapped out of her trance and brushed a long strand of brown hair out of her face. Surely, she'd know what resources would be most helpful for completing this project. "Excuse me," Loren interrupted.

"Ah, yes, Loren. How are you today?" Amida asked looking down at Loren's five foot one slender frame.

"Oh, uh, okay, I suppose. But I'm stuck on a project Professor Finkel assigned me. I mean, I'm not even sure where to start or what I'll need to know or worry about. I haven't attended church since I was about fifteen years old with the exceptions of weddings or when Mom dragged us there for Grandmother's birthday."

"Oh," the librarian said. "He picked you this year. Well, there are a few books that have been helpful over the years on this assignment. It'll be interesting knowing your conclusions with such an unbiased analysis. You have little Christianity and no Judaism background to sway you one way or the other... Interesting choice for him. He must like you."

"I thought he liked me," Loren said. "I've had him for different classes. I must have ticked him off. I begged him for a different assignment since I know nothing of either religion, but he wouldn't back down. I explained I relate to air, water, plants, and animals as a form of meditation. He's normally an understanding professor. He's even met me before or after class answering questions about lessons I didn't understand. Are religious projects allowed to be assigned?"

"Loren, don't panic," Amida said in a soothing tone. "Read up on both religions. I'm sure Professor Finkel will be happy to

The Library Room

help fill in blanks." She guided Loren to the religious section and handed her a book from the top shelf while explaining, "Professor Finkel's been assigning this project for about fifteen years. The assignment's been challenged numerous times as to being allowed. To answer your earlier question, Professor Finkel's a licensed attorney who loves arguing. I don't suggest bringing up the legality of the issue. It's a private college, not a government-funded institution."

"Yes, I'd assumed that was the case." Loren lowered her head as if she was defeated. She took the first book from Amida and read the title. *The Torah Revealed* by Avraham Yaakov Finkel. She looked up at the librarian through her thin brown bangs. "Oh no. Did he write this book?" She tried to recall Professor Finkel's first name. *Jack, Jacob, Jeffery...Jeffery! That's it!*

Reading Loren's face, Amida saw she'd figured the correct answer. "No, and when I asked him if they were related in any way, he replied, 'Not to my knowledge.' So you don't have to worry about offending him on any views you write," she reassured.

Further down the aisle, the librarian handed her a book called *The Contemporary Torah: A Gender-Sensitive Adaptation of the JPS Translation* by Revising Editor, David E. S. Stein, consulting editors, Adele Berlin, Ellen Frankel, and Carol L. Meyers. Without commenting, Amida went down another aisle, grabbed and handed Loren the *Holy Bible: The New International Version* and then the *Believer's Bible Commentary* by William MacDonald.

The weight of the hard covered books, totaling over nine inches in height and weighing around ten pounds, felt like a whole universe in Loren's hands.

Amida sensed Loren was overwhelmed by her pile. She winked. "This'll get you started. I'd ask search engines pointed questions and follow up with the books for the honest answers. Form your own opinions, as you've done all of your life. Don't let others influence or intimidate you from finding the truth. Promise me that, will you?"

Loren nodded and thanked her with all the enthusiasm she could muster and returned to her study table.

She looked up at the clock and quietly sighed to herself. "Six o'clock already! No wonder I'm starving!"

She glanced at her notepad again hoping it would miraculously change this time but it didn't. It was still the same assignment.

She texted her friends, asking if any were coming to the library. While waiting for replies, she pulled her laptop from her backpack. Looking at the pile of books in the center of the table she wondered how she'd fit everything into her backpack. And as she placed her hand in the center of her back she imagined how her back could handle such a load.

She wondered if her boyfriend, Giles, would be joining them tonight. On one hand, if he did come, he'd bring her something to eat from the four-star Italian restaurant he worked. On the other hand, being an atheist, he'd have his share of commentary on her project. She didn't need the added pressures of his opinions telling her she shouldn't do it to prove a point. He was passionate against people forcing religion on him or others. She envisioned his short black beard showing signs of a reddened face as he'd take it personally and somehow shame her into not doing the project.

She was relieved when his text read, "Stuck here 2nite. Relief chef didn't show."

Her phone vibrated with more texts. They were all on their way: Amy, Collin, Drew, Jessica, Rachel, and Sarah.

They'd decided dinner already. This meant, since it's Thursday night, Chinese closing special—again. She texted them back with a sense of urgency: "I'm starving!"

After a few minutes of browsing online, she logged off, pouted, and called her mother. Loren was sure she'd know the answer since she loved all that churchy stuff which occasionally came between the two of them getting along nicely.

Her mother, Diane, was short and struggled maintaining a healthy weight; although, she didn't look obese. Her blue eyes and blond hair kept her looking younger than her actual age.

"Hello?" Diane sung.

"Hi, Mom, I'm checking in on you and Dad."

"Hi, sweetie! We're well and getting ready for dinner. Is everything okay?"

"Oh, yeah, everything's fine here. I've a lot of research and won't be making it home this month."

"Oh, sweetie, it's okay. Your father and I understand assignments are important. What's this assignment you sound so excited about?"

"I must prove Jewish people are making a mistake for not accepting Jesus as their Messiah *or* prove they're right in not considering him. Any suggestions on how I go about doing that? It's unfair, Mom! You know how I feel about organized religion. I don't want this assignment. It's a waste of my time and energy. It won't help either cause. How's this helping me with my degree in marketing? Sometimes, I think colleges scam students into paying for classes they don't need!"

Diane rattled plates and pans. "Hold on, sweetie. I'm finishing a couple of things so I can talk." She turned the stove off and signaled her husband to take up his dinner.

Loren's dad, Mitch, could tell by the scowl on Diane's forehead it was a serious conversation that couldn't be tossed aside. After thirty years of marriage, he knew that look.

Diane carried the phone into the study while Loren had continued talking.

"College extortion mandating expensive elective classes! Plus, out of all the students in Professor Finkel's class, why me? Why didn't he choose a theologian student?"

Once Loren stopped ranting, Diane spoke. Her heart was heavy with Loren's dilemma, yet she was excited she was being challenged in her beliefs or lack of them. "I hear what you're saying. I understand you're annoyed. However, there must be a reason for all this to be happening to you. Did he assign this to everyone in your class? Is someone taking the same class on a different day or time? Maybe you could pair up and use each other's notes?"

Loren expected sympathy instead of questions. She calmed down before responding. "He only teaches this class once a year. He assigns a different project to each person in the class. We've strict instructions not to contact nor use any notes or students from prior years. We're encouraged to interview, ask for help from friends or relatives to gain different views, use traditional reference materials—like Bibles or study guides—and the Internet." Perhaps, if she laid out all the work, she'd get sympathy from her mother?

"Loren, I know you don't like attending church. I know you've different ideas about God. I'm not even sure what you believe in anymore. Frankly, it frightens me. You've fallen away from God and how you were raised. However, I agree with you. This might not be the best assignment for you at this time in your life. You're not ready to handle some of the truths you uncover. You're on a path where you're confused about life, your passions, and your beliefs. I'm not convinced you believe all the babble that comes out of your mouth, nor do I feel you're at peace with your convictions."

"Mom, I didn't call to argue religion or get your opinion on my current life path. I called to find out what you know about these two religions and if you'd help shed some light on the subject so I can find the information, write it down, hand it in, and get a passing grade." Loren scowled through the phone.

"Ha! If life and religion were that simple, my dear. Good luck on that grade thing if that's all you intend to do." Her mother was smiling. She knew once she added the challenges of not handling the results, combined with not pursuing it all with the fullest effort, she'd increase Loren's desire to prove Momma wrong, and in this case, Momma might win…or lose based on what she discovers.

The Library Room

Diane longed to see her child know the truth. Prayers would be sent up daily on her church prayer chain. Diane continued, "Aw, don't feel bad, sweetheart. I didn't get it until I was in my mid-thirties. It's what we old people do. We settle down, become still enough to listen to God, figure out our purpose, and then we work on God's plan for us. You can't have a purpose if you don't believe in God who put you here for a purpose. Understand?"

"Mom, I don't have time to figure out my so-called purpose as well as solve a two-thousand-year-old mystery all within a few weeks! I gotta go. I'll give you a call after the weekend unless I've a specific question for you."

The conversation was quickly turning into a typical one between Loren and her mother where her mother tried telling Loren what to think or do or whom she should date or not live with until her wedding vows were made. She was done listening and needed to get working on the research. "I love you, Mom. I hate to cut this short, but I've only a few weeks to cram all this stuff together. Based on the books the librarian gave me to use, it's going to take a lot of my time." She loved her mother and knew she wasn't deliberately aggravating her.

"I understand, honey. I'll pray the answers come to you. I love you too." Diane felt satisfied by Loren's determined tone. Diane longed to somehow keep Giles from having such a strong influence on her daughter. She asked God to deliver undisputable evidence to Giles of God's existence.

Diane climbed out of the recliner to go eat her cold meal. She knew the professor had chosen the right student this year. She thanked God for his divine intervention.

Loren placed the warm phone next to her laptop. She was determined to prove to her mother her toughness in handling whatever scandals or epiphanies she discovers.

She stared at the time on her phone, lifted her hair up and placed the still warm phone on an aching neck muscle.

Why do I always fight Mom and Dad on attending church? She remembered her mother arguing about her part-time coffee shop job interfering with church services. Until then, she'd enjoyed going as a child without issues.

While waiting for the others to arrive, she allowed herself to daydream about her church. It was a welcoming church with padded pews instead of folding chairs she's seen in other churches. The bright white steeple could be seen for miles before the actual low-ranch structure of the building came into view. It wasn't as ornate as the Catholic Church her friends Collin and Jessica attended every Sunday on campus. Nor was it without character like the new church Amy made her attend when it first opened…although they served food, so it turned out to be nice.

She'd always felt welcomed in her childhood church. She recalled the different Sunday school teachers she'd had over the years. Some were more memorable than others. She remembered paper figures sticking to felt cloth sceneries as teachers told stories from the Bible. She could still recall the smell of crayons and glue as they made a craft about the lesson they'd learned. Perhaps it was time to stop in and see what it looks like today. The thought sent a pang of homesickness.

Amy showed up with a backpack, a suitcase-sized purse hanging off of her right shoulder, a laptop hanging off of her left shoulder, and her cell phone held to her ear while finishing up a conversation. She wore navy blue scrubs with her sandy blond hair pulled back into a ponytail. Her hard day was evident by the smeared makeup under her brown eyes. She plopped her laptop onto the table. Her purse dropped to the floor with a thud while she wiggled the backpack off and set it in the chair next to her.

Loren stated, "I see you're packed to run away soon," waving her arm across the table referring to Amy's bags.

"Ha, funny! I see you're still working on your witty lines," Amy responded back in kind. "So we're the first to arrive? What's with

The Library Room

all the books? I thought you were down to labs and easy electives this year?"

Loren rolled her eyes. "Yeah, it sounded good in theory. Apparently, Mr. Finkel assigns impossible projects every year to each student in this class, confirmed by our librarian who helped me pick out my books. Oh, and this report will count for 100 percent of my grade—no homework, no quizzes, only checking on notes, and then the final report. After that, we get to go on field trips at the cost of the college for the rest of the quarter. Thankfully, they're not mandatory. I thought it'd be an easy credit. I was wrong."

"That sounds cool! So what are you researching?" Amy picked up the Holy Bible. "Are you getting churchy?"

"Um, no! It's part of my assignment, which I know nothing about. I'm hoping your churchy wisdom can add some insight." Loren slouched in her chair. She hated asking friends for help. She didn't mind helping others but hated asking for help.

"Okay, I'll help if I can. What's it about?" Amy offered.

Just then, Collin and Drew walked around a bookshelf, laughing and bumping each other trying to get the attention of the girls. Both were grinning and trying to outdo the other in a game only the two of them understood. Drew saw Loren and Amy looking in their direction. He puffed his chest out and flexed his arms showing them his rugby jersey could stretch quite a bit. Not to be outdone by Drew, Collin flexed his pectoral muscles beneath a tight white T-shirt.

"Well, I see you've both had your testosterone levels elevated by playing football today," Loren remarked at their antics.

They sat down, grinning from ear to ear. Amy and Loren kept looking from one pasted smile to the other.

Finally, Amy asked, "Are you two goofs going to start studying something or keep pretending to be cheesy mannequins all night?"

Collin piped up, "I was thinking about going to grab the chow for everyone first. What's your order?" He extended his hand, knowing it'd be four dollars from each since it's a Thursday night.

Loren handed four dollars to Collin. "I'll have the usual Chinese Thursday night special whatever it may be this week. I'll place odds it'll be bourbon chicken, fried rice, lo mein, and a rock-hard egg roll."

"Shouldn't we wait for Jessica, Sarah, and Rachel?" Amy said as she searched her purse for her wallet.

Drew answered, "No, they already texted me to let me know they were stopping there first before showing up at the library. They wanted to know if you two had sent us 'beefy boys' out to fetch the chow yet."

"Beefy boys?" Amy and Loren exclaimed at the same time and laughed. Now, they understood why the boys were acting up earlier.

"Yes." Collin lifted his chin. "That'd be us."

Laughter busted from everyone as they looked around to see if they were disturbing anyone in their area. Luckily, they were the only ones studying at this hour.

Money in hand, Collin headed across the street to meet the girls.

One of Loren's books caught Drew's eye. "*The Torah Revealed*," he read out loud. "Are you changing your faith to Judaism?"

Loren smirked. "Yeah, right. No offense, I mean, I don't see myself wanting to be subjected to any organized form of religion right now. I'm only reading up on it so I can write a paper for Professor Finkel's class. However, maybe you could help me?"

Drew looked her in the eye. He loved how Loren didn't try candy-coating her opinions for anyone. She was honest to a fault. "Not sure I can help. What do you need help with?"

"I know nothing about Judaism or what you do in your church. Do you even go to church?" She felt uncomfortable asking Drew about his religious beliefs.

"When I was younger, our family attended the synagogue. Some people call it temple. However, don't call it temple in front of my grandfather. He doesn't like that term. My grandfather calls it *beit k'nesset*, which, means house of assembly. They cut my dad's pay at the firm, and the annual membership became too expensive for us. After that, it became embarrassing for us to hang around the synagogue all the time. Everyone knew."

Amy asked, "You pay an annual membership? Why don't they pass a plate around to collect a tithe each week like they do at our church? Most don't even tithe, yet they're still welcomed."

Drew answered, "We aren't allowed to carry money into the synagogue on holidays or Sabbath. You're allowed to worship there without being a member. However, if you want a seat for Rosh Hashanah or Yom Kippur, you'd better be a member and have paid for a reserved seat since they draw a packed service."

"So why didn't you go if you didn't have to be a member to the worship part?" Amy was curious.

Loren took notes as fast as her fingers could write.

Drew explained, "My father still made a decent living, but with three kids, it seemed we always lived paycheck to paycheck. I suspect my mother's spending habits didn't change with his lower pay. My dad never complained. Husbands live to please and accommodate their wives. It's the Jewish way." Drew didn't seem bothered by it or annoyed at his mother. It was stated as a matter of fact.

Loren stopped writing. "Drew, that's the first thing anyone's ever said about any religion that appeals to my liking! The men live to please and accommodate their wives!" She reread her notes and asked, "Why do you suppose your grandfather doesn't like the synagogue being called temple?"

Drew answered, "There's no supposing. He doesn't like it because he feels there's only one temple, the one in Jerusalem, which will be restored once the Messiah or, as we say, Mashiach comes."

Loren fired another question. "So it needs to be restored? Why don't they just do it? Certainly, there are architects and builders there."

Amy answered for Drew, "The spot where the temple's supposed to be is now occupied by a Muslim mosque called The Dome of the Rock."

"Very good, Amy. You're correct." Drew further explained, "The original temple was built back in Solomon's time. During the Babylonian exile, it was partially destroyed and then rebuilt, making it the second temple destroyed."

Sarah, Jessica, Collin, and Rachel arrived with their dinners. Loren placed her notes under her laptop for safekeeping. The noise caused the librarian to poke her head around the corner, making the "sh" sign to those facing her. Loren and Collin raised their hands to quiet everyone.

When they'd finished eating, Jessica said, "Well, it's not the greatest-tasting stuff, but it does the job when you're starving." Everyone agreed.

"Rachel," Drew addressed, "Loren's been quizzing me on our Jewish synagogues and the temple. Her project's due in a few weeks. It's been a while since I've attended any of the *beit midrash* or *beit tefilah*. Perhaps you can help too."

Loren pulled out her notes and held up her hand to stop the conversation. "Wait! Okay, what were those two places you mentioned? Beit rashes and beit teflon?"

Drew corrected her, "*Beit midrash*, a house of study, and *beit tefilah*, a house of prayer, are both inside our synagogue."

Amy worked on her homework while listening.

Jessica, being a newcomer to the conversation, welcomed learning about Judaism without having to do the prodding. She was slightly overweight with a muffin top over the sides of her jeans which she did her best to keep hidden with long, loose fitting tops. Her short, thin, dark hair curled under naturally at her chin and drew attention to her face. Her full cheeks gave her the appearance of always smiling.

Sarah prayed for a different topic. Religious topics always made her uncomfortable due to her strict Baptist upbringing. Her red hair cascaded down to the middle of her back in large ringlets. She worked out daily to maintain her curvy yet firm body and liked to accentuate it with fashionable style.

Rachel sat straight up in her chair as if she were ready to play her piano. Since she worked at the high-end art gallery she was always dressed in the latest glamour fashion. Her constant proper posture and slender frame made her seem taller than her five foot two height. She missed attending synagogue. She loved volunteering at the social welfare agency, the social center, participating in prayers, and instructing educational classes.

Collin sat defensively, waiting for Drew to make an offhanded Christian remark. He was the taller of the two men. He'd started shaving his head in high school when his hair began thinning. The look on him was natural and clean looking. His eyes reflected the intensity of concern or fun he was instigating. He often used his eyes to convey his message without using a word.

Drew, like Collin, always maintained a clean looking image by keeping his light brown hair very short and spiky. Although he had a perfect body like Collin, his dimples were his greatest feature. When he smiled, his whole face became a chiseled piece of masculine art.

They were a diverse group, from different cultures, income levels, and beliefs. They were friends, the best kind of friends you find in college that last a lifetime.

Two

"So, Loren," Rachel questioned, "what's the assignment? Is it about the Jewish culture, race, synagogues, or the Talmud?"

Loren looked up from her laptop where she'd asked a search engine "Is there proof Jesus is the Jewish Messiah?"

"Yes, no, well…maybe. Sort of…Okay, probably all of the above," she answered the entire group. "But I'm not sure where to start. Professor Finkel wants me to prove or disprove Jesus is the Jewish Messiah."

Everyone stared at her. Loren thought, *Was I louder than I thought?*

Each mind had been triggered with the answer they'd been taught. Each knew there'd be controversial views.

As tension entered their small group, Loren cowered in her seat.

Amy spoke first, "Well, that should be easy enough to prove. He is. All prophecies were fulfilled, proving he's the Messiah."

Drew folded his arms across his chest and showed his attorney face. "Now, wait a minute. Nothing's ever been proven. I've been taught Jesus was a great teacher, but he's not the Messiah or Mashiach, the Anointed One!"

Sarah interjected, "I've gone to Sunday school all of my life and learned Jesus is the Savior of all and whoever believes in him shall not perish in hell but will obtain eternal life in heaven. I say why take the chance and deny? No one else comes close to doing what Jesus did and how he did it. I mean, why should anyone sacrifice their life so we could all be saved from our sins and go to heaven? I don't know about you, but I've yet to hear of any other person rising from the dead three days after being killed and then ascending to heaven. There are tons of miracles he performed in the name of God, our Father. How do you explain it as just a *teacher* thing, Drew?"

Rachel came to Drew's defense. "Judaism doesn't believe in human blood sacrifices. We don't believe a person can sacrifice himself for another's sin. God would be appalled over the sacrifice of a human, which Jesus was, because God is God and humans are humans."

Collin tried lightening up the mood by exclaiming, "Ouch! Seriously? What'd you do to tick that professor off? I mean, come on! This topic's been debated for over two thousand years! He thinks you can come up with an undisputable answer? Did he give you a deadline of say…two thousand years from now?" He chuckled to try to get everyone on the same laugh at poor Loren's dilemma page.

"Oh, Collin, I don't know what I'm going to do!" Lauren exclaimed, exasperated. "You know me; I'm not on either side. I don't like organized religion. I don't like bickering. I want to run to a beach or meadow where I can't hear any pounding in my brain about who's right and who's wrong. And what's the answer? Should I lean left or look harder to the right? I don't think it's to fair to assign this to someone not in theology classes. I wish I could drop the class. But I've never backed down from anything. I'm not a quitter. I must prove to my mother I can do this and handle whatever I might uncover…whatever she meant. And look, just telling everybody caused arguments. Drew's spiky hair grew another half inch from standing on end! Whoa! Turn around so we can see the hair on the back of your neck too."

Jessica laughed the hardest while rubbing the palm of her hand over the tips of Drew's spiked hair. She said, "We've various opinions. What if everyone helps Loren out by bringing her information on what we've been taught to believe? She can compile it all together and see where the dice lands. Wow! I just thought of something! Have you told Giles yet?"

Loren turned white. "No, he's going to freak out. You know how he reacts over talks about God. That's one thing I'm not sure how to get around either."

Everyone agreed Giles will be furious. Furthermore, each was relieved he was working late and wasn't at the library throwing a tantrum although, no one would say it out loud.

Loren's laptop gave a soft chirp indicating a new e-mail. It was from Professor Finkel. Praying it was a reassignment to a different project, she opened it.

"Ugh!" she sighed. "A reminder of the assignment along with the rules and due date. Gee, thanks, Professor Finkel, for making sure I understand your impossible project."

Jessica was selling the others into helping with Loren's project. "Everyone comes from a different background. Drew and Rachel are Jewish. Collin and I are Catholic. Amy, Loren, and Sarah… what are you three anyway?"

Amy responded with, "I'm Methodist."

Sarah added, "I'm Baptist, which is also Protestant, and y'all are sinners and going to hell." She giggled over her own joke. Everyone else smirked or chuckled to humor her.

All eyes rested on Loren. For all the years they've known her, she'd always been elusive regarding her faith or what she believed. After careful consideration, she answered, "I'm nothing I guess, although if I'd label myself, I'd say I'm spiritual. I mean, I believe in a Higher Power despite Giles trying to convince me otherwise. I'm sure going to a Pentecostal Protestant Church as a kid influenced my believing in God. However, some days, I question if he exists."

Jessica began again, "Okay, we're quite a diverse group. How can we help? What do you want or need from us?"

"I guess the best approach is to,"—Loren wrote on her notepad—"figure out the differences between Judaism and Christianity. Understand why Christians feel Jesus is the Messiah. Then understand why Jewish people feel Jesus isn't the Messiah. And finally, examine evidence proving one way or the other." Loren's phone vibrated. Seeing it was Giles, she excused herself to take his call.

"Hi! How's life in the hot kitchen?"

"Oh, just great. We had a retirement party, and I swear each person who attended had a special request added to their order. What are you up to tonight? Are you still at the library, or are you home now?" he asked.

"I'm still here at the library, working on my newest assignment," Loren replied. "The whole gang's here. They said hi." She lied about the later part. Sometimes, she felt they were all right with him working long hours and not being able to meet at the library.

"Oh yeah? Are you hungry? Have you eaten yet? I'll be off in about an hour once the kitchen's cleaned."

Loren was relieved he didn't ask about her assignment. "Yes, we had our Thursday night cheap-eat Chinese—"

"Ew, I'm glad I worked," Giles barked. Then he changed his tone to sweet and sexy. "But I miss you. What time do you think you'll make it home? Or do you want me to swing by to pick you up so you're not walking home alone in the dark?"

"I'm not sure yet. I've a lot of research to do, so I might stay a bit late. Don't worry about me walking in the dark. I could use some alone time. Just go on home. I'll sneak into bed when I get home. I miss you too. It seems we never see each other between my classes and our work schedules. We need a date night."

"Date night? What's a date? It's been so long since we've had the funds or time to go on a date, I'd forgotten that word." He laughed and then cussed as a pan clanged against something.

"Are you all right?" she asked.

"Yeah, I need to get off of the phone. The pasta boiled over and made a mess."

"Okay, I'll see ya," Loren said, "when I see ya, even if you don't see me with your eyes shut."

"Yep, gotta go now. Love ya."

"Love you too. Bye," she finished, but he'd already hung up before she could finish her good-byes.

She didn't have time to analyze her relationship or conversation with Giles. She knew their relationship had been disintegrating; however, she didn't want to deal with it at the moment. She knew he wasn't going to marry her since he didn't believe in marital vows written on paper. And she wasn't too keen about signing on a dotted line and tying her to one person for the rest of her life either since people change over time.

As she walked back to the table, she could hear the gang chatting. This was *her* long-term relationship in life. Her friends, her support system, her strength when she felt weak, and her uplift when she felt down. They could make her laugh when she needed to laugh even, if she was already happy. They made her a happier person. She almost hated stepping into view for fear their excited commotion would end.

Amy was the first to spot her and announced, "Loren! Look what we've found on the Internet! We've come up with an idea for your project, which, by the way, we've now claimed as *our* project. Thank you very much. Here's where we're at."

Loren walked over looked at Collin's laptop. On it was a four-column sheet with a title "Messianic Prophesies" at the top. A header for each column was subtitled "Prophesy/Covenant," "Scriptures," "Fulfilled by/how," and "Scriptures."

Drew and Rachel were excited at the other end of the table to show her their find: *What Hebrews Believe*, which they found at www.whatHebrewsbelieve.org

Loren realized it would become a race between the Christians and the Hebrews to find the correct answers.

Jessica examined Drew and Rachel's site after she'd studied Collin's spreadsheet. After reading a few topics on the main page, she announced, "We've pro-Christian and pro-Judaism. Both can't be wrong, and both can't be right. Both have valid points from what I've glanced at. Nonetheless, we'll need to verify the validity. Or at least see if it makes sense to someone who isn't a scholar. Agreed?"

Everyone nodded.

Jessica continued, "Team Christians, split up the verses and find out if all or any are true. Team Hebrews, you've information disputing Christianity. Research and verify your findings. Everyone needs to ask God to guide your work and reveal what we need to believe."

Again everyone nodded.

Drew and Rachel looked at each other; two against five didn't seem fair.

"Do we ask Loren or Jessica to be on our team?" Rachel whispered to Drew. "We can't ask Collin based upon his reactions to your Christian jokes; he's too biased."

Drew agreed with her assessment and whispered back, "Right and Amy's too churchy. She'll only see things her way. Sarah seems bitter by her telling us we're all going to hell. Yes, ask both Loren and Jessica. Take the one who accepts the fastest."

"Hey, Loren or Jessica, which of you will help us with our research, so it's more even keel?" Rachel requested.

"Oh, me! I'd love to!" Jessica bounced over to the other side of the table excited to start her new adventure studying Judaism.

"Loren, when is this due?" Drew asked.

"Before sunset on September twenty-fifth. I find that to be an odd requirement. Don't you?"

Drew answered, "Not at all. It's the eve before the Day of Atonement this year."

"Day of Atonement. What's that, Drew?" Sarah inquired.

"Yom Kippur, tenth day in the seventh month," Drew explained.

"Isn't that July tenth?" Jessica asked.

"No, a Jewish year is different than the American and Western year. Our years start in the spring. A month revolves around the lunar and sun cycle, which takes about twenty-nine and a half days on the lunar for a month. Some months have thirty days, and some have twenty-nine days. The year is three hundred sixty-five and a quarter days. Some years we've twelve months, and some years we've thirteen months due to leap year."

"Yom Kippur's the most important Jewish holiday to me," Rachel continued. "It's a complete twenty-five-hour period of fasting from food and even water if you can. I spend a lot of time at the synagogue praying. As your professor indicates, it starts at sundown the day before the tenth and ends after nightfall. It's a day to atone for the sins of the past year. No bathing, sex, makeup, work, deodorant, food, water, or leather."

"No leather?" Jessica questioned.

"Yes, no leather." Rachel explained, "Most men wear canvas tennis shoes under their dress clothes. Women wear plastic, clothe, or any other fashionable shoe as long as it doesn't contain leather. In Exodus, the second book in the Torah, Moses removes his leather sandals before entering a holy place. It's a form of being humble before God. It's nothing to do with being a fashion statement or not wearing animals as I've heard a speaker say while comparing Christians to Hebrews. Moses's leather shoes protected his feet. If you're uncomfortable, you're humbled. You need to be humble when atoning."

Rachel loved teaching others about Judaism. She's served on different types of welcome committees at the synagogue mentoring women who were either marrying into the faith and/or were interested in converting.

"Does Professor Finkel observe the Jewish holidays? Do we write the paper slanted as Jesus isn't the Messiah so he'll give Loren a passing grade?" Collin sneered.

"You know, Collin, there are those of us who believe what you just said, and look, we're not running around killing people because we believe differently," Drew defended.

"Drew, I didn't mean any offense when I said that. It's just I remembered someone writing a paper slanting an opinion toward supporting a deist theory to get a great grade on a paper. I don't think I could stomach writing a report against something so intimately close to my beliefs. It'd be denying God. I can't do it even if it's for a grade," Collin answered Drew.

"You're right, Collin. I actually atoned for that deceptive act. It wasn't right of me to do that. I know there's a God who wants a personal relationship with each person and community as it teaches in the Tanakh, our Bible. I wouldn't expect you to give up your beliefs without sound proof nor would I."

Drew reached his hand out to Collin in a gentleman's shake. Drew felt sorry for his friend Collin. He knew once he learns Yeshua isn't the Mashiach, he'll be devastated.

Collin shook his hand and patted him on his shoulder knowing it will be hard for Drew and harder for Rachel to discover the truth after being brought up so deeply in their faith.

At the end of the night, everyone went over the notes Loren had written on her laptop. As each added their input and different findings, the report began taking shape.

To the team, the notes needed to tell the whole story, not highlights you hear in church, see in a movie, or read in a condensed article. The report had to prove it was all real. God is real in order for the Mashiach to be real or not, needed or not, fulfilled prophecy or not, for Hebrews and Gentiles or not. So the report begins.

Three

Loren's Notes Part I—Lineage

The group migrated to the beginning of time to gain better knowledge of when, why, how, and where.

The first few chapters of Genesis point out there's a God. Without a God, we wouldn't exist. Without a God, there'd be no breathable air, vegetation, water, trees, fish, fowl, animals, humans, etc.

Amy and Rachel feel you don't have a purpose in life if you don't believe in God. There's no accountability for being good, honest, moral, or righteous, if you don't believe in God. You're a part of his plan. You must believe in God in order to know why you're here and what you're here to do.

This sounds nice, but too preachy for me. I feel like I'm the only one on our team who isn't convinced of this concept. I've known God growing up as a child, yet today, I feel distanced. Doesn't that happen to everyone who grows up at some point? As I read the beginning stages of earth and life, I can't help but think, 'Really?' The rest of the team accepts the readings as truth.

Rachel read Tanakh Torah Bereshit Genesis 1:1–2, NIV: "In the beginning God created the heavens and the earth. Now the earth was formless and empty, darkness was over the surface of the deep, and the Spirit of God was hovering over the waters."

Amy says she loves how Moses, the writer of Genesis, gave us a vision of God drafting earth. The Spirit of God, the Holy Spirit, was there all along "hovering" over earth. From the moment God created earth, the Holy Spirit knew it'd be special. I feel the Holy Spirit hovered over earth like a mother to a child when I read that passage.

Collin sees it more like a hen on an egg.

I read and summarized, "Tanakh Torah Bereshit Genesis 1:3–26 NIV: The first day, God created light. He separated light from darkness. God called the light 'day,' and the darkness He called 'night.' And there was evening, and there was morning. The sixth day, God created land creatures: livestock, creatures that move along the ground, and wild animals. Then God said, 'Let us make man in our image, in our likeness, and let them rule over the fish of the sea, the birds of the air, over the livestock, over all the earth, and over all the creatures that move along the ground.'"

Rachel pointed out, "Notice the 'let us' in His command? Who was God talking to when all the other times prior he says, 'let there' or 'let the' to make a command?"

Collin guessed, "God was speaking to the Holy Spirit."

Jessica guessed, "To angels?"

Drew suggested, "To himself, as a king would declare in third person."

Rachel read, "Tanakh, Nevi'im. Job 38:4–7 NIV: 'Where were you when I laid the earth's foundation? Tell me, if you understand. Who marked off its dimensions? Surely you know! Who stretched a measuring line across it? On what were its footings set or who laid its cornerstone—while the morning stars sang together and all the angels shouted for joy?' The angels were beside God as he laid the foundation of the earth."

Jessica asked how dinosaurs fit into God's plans? "Was God's day equivalent to years or even millions of years? Were the dinosaurs his first form of amusement on earth before he decided to create man? And who were the cavemen? Were they fallen angels sent to earth before he created Adam and Eve? Perhaps Mr. Finkel should make that one of his future projects."

Rachel summarized God's sixth and seventh days after reading, Tanakh Torah Bereshit Genesis 1:27–2:4 JPS: "God created man in his own image. Then, my favorite day of the week, the seventh day, God was happy and satisfied, so he rested from all his works of creation. He determined it to be a Holy Day and blessed it, Sabbath."

Drew summarized Tanakh Torah Bereshit Genesis 2:5–25 JPS: "God placed man with a helpmate, woman, made from the side of man so as the two are together they're of one flesh and bone in charge of the garden of Eden. They were naked and felt no shame, and they were equals to each other. In this garden of Eden they were to guard, till, work the land, eat the plants, fruits, seeds, care for the beasts and name everything."

I'm curious from whom they were guarding it from? Or what were they guarding it from? No one addressed my question. I was told to move forward since it's not relevant to the task."

Jessica read and then summarized Tanakh Torah Bereshit Genesis 3:1–24 NIV: "There were two trees in the garden of Eden. God forbade Adam and Eve to touch or consume these— the Tree of Life located somewhere within Eden and the Tree of Knowledge of Good and Bad located in the center of the Eden. The serpent convinced Eve that God wanted to keep her stupid, she wouldn't die if she touched or ate the forbidden fruit, and she'd become like the divine beings in knowing the difference between good and evil. She trusted the serpent and ate the forbidden fruit. Then, she took it to Adam and fed him. Once both had partaken of the fruit, their eyes were opened to knowledge of good and bad. When God breezed into the garden to visit with them, he knew what they'd done since they were hiding their nakedness from him. Adam and Eve pointed fingers. Adam blamed Eve, and Eve blamed the serpent. God punished them by first cursing the serpent to slither on its belly. Prior to this, the serpent stood upright."

I picture the serpent to be an outer space creature looking thing.

Rachel explained the Jewish Talmud teaches the serpent desired Eve and wanted her as his wife. He was jealous of Adam. Satan wanted to plant his own seed in Eve.

Collin said, "Here's the very first Messianic prophecy. God addresses Satan in Tanakh Torah Bereshit Genesis 3:15–19 KJV (Collin's summarized interpretation): 'I'll put hatred between you and the woman, And between your seed and her seed; Her offspring shall bruise you on the head, and your offspring shall bruise Him on the heel.' Next, God punished Eve by informing her of future labor pains for all women during birth, yet she'd still have sexual urges towards her husband, and husbands shall now rule over their wives instead of being equals. (Insert inappropriate high-five from Collin and Drew here.)Then, God punished Adam. God cursed the ground by allowing weeds to sprout, making it harder to grow food. When God said, "For you'll die if you eat of the forbidden fruit." 'He meant humans will die over a time period instead of being immortal on earth.' "From dust you were taken. For dust you are, and to dust you shall return."

"Lastly, God banished everyone from the Garden of Eden so no one could touch or taste the Tree of Life, which is now guarded by cherubim with a fiery ever-turning sword."

Amy explained this one event became the whole purpose of needing a Messiah. This was the introduction of sin. Prior to this fall from grace, there was no sin, no good and bad, and no sinful desires.

Rachel had learned eating of meat didn't happen until after Noah and the Ark. So when God told Adam he'd have to eat grass, or grain, while fighting the weeds, Adam argued about eating like his livestock! God gave him relief. "You'll eat bread," he said. Processing grains into bread were then put into their minds.

Sarah feels it was mean of God to send them out of paradise for disobeying him.

Amy defended God saying that since they'd disobeyed they had acquired sinful hearts. They'd always be tempted to disobey. Additionally, God created libido, which would result in having children who'd turn into sinful kids too. To be left in a paradise with The Tree of Life would've been catastrophic for all humankind! Someone, possibly Adam, or Eve, or one of their kids could've succumbed to the temptation from the Tree of Life, which means mankind would've lived forever with infirmity and degenerative conditions while continually populating Earth.

Drew summarized Tanakh, Torah, Bereshit, Noach, Lekh Lekha, Genesis 4:1-15 JPS: Adam and Eve went from the Garden of Eden. They "knew" each other. Eve birthed Cain and then later Abel. Over the years, the two sons had been instructed on the condition in which the only way you can approach the Holy God is on the ground of the blood of a surrogate sacrifice. Cain didn't accept these teachings. Cain looked after the fields. Abel looked after the animals. Cain offered harvested food to God for his sacrifice. Abel offered a firstborn lamb, thus showing God his belief and faith in the divine instruction. God accepted the lamb and not the harvest. Cain became jealous and angry even after God lovingly warned him that "sin's crouching at your door and ready to destroy you." Cain didn't repent. Nor did he try to find a better sacrifice. Instead, he took out his jealous anger on his brother by killing him in a field. God was angered by this action! He sent Cain out to the land of Nod, east of Eden, to never work the fields again.

This is where the lineage begins. Tanakh Torah Bereshit Genesis 4:25–5:32 KJV: [I'm *italicizing* and summarizing the fathers and omitting text not relevant this part of the task to skim though the lineage information faster.] *Adam* and Eve then bore another…son named *Seth*. Seth fathered *Enos*[1] who fathered *Cainan* [2] who fathered *Mahalaleel*, who fathered *Jared*, who fathered *Enoch*, who fathered *Methuselah*, who fathered *Lamech*, who fathered *Noah*, who fathered *Shem*,

Rachel found the lineage skips down to Tanakh, Torah, Noach, Genesis 10:22 KJV: Sons of Shem: *Arphaxad.*

Amy found Tanakh, Torah, Noach, Genesis 11:12 KJV: Arphaxad, the father of *Shelah.*[3]

Jessica found Tanakh, Torah, Noach, Genesis 11:14–26 KJV: Shelah fathered *Eber*, who fathered *Peleg*, who fathered *Reu*, who fathered *Serug*, who fathered *Nahor*, who fathered *Terah*, who fathered *Abram*."

Drew summarized Tanakh Torah Lech Lecha Genesis 15:2–21 JPS: "Abram and Sarai hadn't produced a child. Sarai was past child-bearing years.

When Abram won a war, he didn't take any war treasures offered by the King of Sodom. Instead, Abram gave the credit for the success to God. God rewarded Abram by assuring him, 'A son coming from your own body will be your heir.'

As the sun was setting, Abram fell asleep, and a thick and dreadful darkness came over him. God spoke, "Your descendants will be enslaved for four hundred years. But I'll punish the nation they serve as slaves, and afterward, they'll come out with great possessions. However, you'll go to your ancestors in peace and be buried at a good old age. In the fourth generation, your descendants will come back here, for the sin of the Amorites hasn't yet reached its full measure."

When darkness had fallen, a smoking firepot with a blazing torch appeared and passed between the pieces. On that day, the Lord made a covenant with Abram and said, "To your descendants, I give this land, from the river of Egypt to the great river, the Euphrates—the land of the Kenites, Kenizzites, Kadmonites, Hittites, Perizzites, Rephaites, Amorites, Canaanites, Girgashites, and Jebusites."

Amy points out he was in a "deep sleep" while this was happening, and yet he knows it's happening as a dark shadow came over him, and he heard God's voice.

Jessica feels his "deep sleep" was like a temporary paralysis.

Everyone agrees God didn't allow nor expected him to walk between the sacrifices like a typical Eastern tradition pact as God knew Abram would never be able to keep his part. It was a one-party covenant. Thus, the unconditional covenant was made to Abram from God. God's free grace.

Rachel then summarized Tanakh Torah Lech Lecha Genesis 17:1–15 JPS: Abram was ninety-nine years old when God presented another covenant. This time, it was conditional to not only Abram but all of his descendants after him forever. God ordered, "You [Abram] and every male among you shall be circumcised as a sign of a covenant between us. For generations to come, every eight days old male must be circumcised. My covenant in your flesh is to be an everlasting covenant. Any uncircumcised male, who hasn't been circumcised in the flesh, will be cut off from his people. He's broken my covenant." God then changed Abram's name to Abraham and Sarai's name to Sarah.

Jessica points out the obvious of looking for Abraham's son(s) in the lineage task which is Abram. Then she reads Tanakh, Torah, Lech Lecha, Genesis 17:19–21 NIV: Then God said, "Sarah will bear you a son, and you'll call him Isaac. I'll establish my covenant with him as an everlasting covenant for his descendants after him...But, my covenant I'll establish with Isaac, whom Sarah will bear to you by this time next year."

Sarah says, "Imagine Sarah in her nineties, overhearing the conversation. When she heard she was going to have a child, she laughed. Tanakh, Torah, Vayeira, Genesis 18: 13–15 NIV: Then the Lord asked Abraham, 'Why did Sarah laugh and say, "I'll really have a child, now that I'm old?" Is anything too hard for the Lord? I'll return to you at the appointed time next year and

Sarah will have a son.' Sarah was afraid, so she lied and said, 'I didn't laugh.' God said, 'Yes, you did laugh.'"

Amy feels she laughed from shocked joy and a lot over the idea of her old husband's *plumbing*. God called her out on it since God has a sense of humor. God, knowing the frailty of man's ego, didn't point that out making Abraham feel less of a man than what he'd appeared to be to his wife. Instead, for the sake of *romance*, he turned it around by asking the question, making it sound like she was laughing at her *own* abilities as an old woman or God's great abilities to open a closed womb.

Sarah agreed and said she pictures God winking at her when he says, "Yes, you did laugh."

Drew told us the Talmud teaches when Isaac was being weaned, Abraham threw a feast and invited all the important people of his time, and Sarah invited their wives. Skeptics accused them of finding and adopting an abandoned boy. Each of the wives brought their children without their wet nurses. Sarah's breasts miraculously opened like two wells. She nursed all the children who'd needed nursing, thus putting to rest the validity of Isaac being Sarah and Abraham' son.

Jessica felt God provided proof to the skeptics because God knew the lineage needed to be clear and indisputable for the Messiah to be born according to his covenants and Messianic prophecies.

Amy added, "God proved he could open closed wombs and perform miracle births which was popular with old mythological stories too."

Collin insisted we look at this next part instead of moving forward with the lineage because it also contains seeded prophecy in his opinion. So, he summarized Tanakh, Torah, Vayeira, Genesis 22:1–18 NIV: "God tested Abraham by asking him to sacrifice Isaac in a burnt offering. As they approached the spot, Isaac asked, 'The fire and wood are here, but where's the lamb for the burn offering?' Abraham answered him, 'God, himself,

The Library Room

will provide the lamb for the burn offering, my son.' And once they arrived to the place, Abraham placed him on the altar, and prepared to slay his son. Just then, the angel of the Lord cried out to him, 'Abraham! Don't do anything to him. Now I know you fear Me, because you haven't withheld from Me your son, your only son.'

Abraham saw a ram caught by its horns. He sacrificed it as a burnt offering instead.

The angel of the Lord called out a second time to Abraham. 'I swear by Myself, declares the Lord: Because you've done this and haven't withheld your son, your favorite one, I'll bestow My blessing upon you and make your descendants as numerous as the stars of heaven and the sands on the seashore; and your descendants shall seize the gates of their foes. And through your offspring all nations on earth will be blessed because you obeyed Me.'"

Wow! What a test! My heart breaks for the quandary God placed him in that day.

Amy agrees with Collin there are two seeded prophecies: 1.) .God, himself will supply the sacrificial lamb, and 2.) all nations on earth will be blessed through Abraham's offspring.

Rachel told us about Isaac praying to the Lord because Rebekah, his wife was barren. The Lord answered his prayer, and Rebekah became pregnant with twins. The first to come out was Esau. Jacob came out with his hand grasping Esau's heel.

Amy told us how one day, Esau came in starving, and Jacob had made a stew. Esau demanded some stew. Jacob replied, "First, sell me your birthright." Esau answered, "Look, I'm about to die. What good is the birthright to me?" But Jacob insisted, "Swear to me first." So Esau swore an oath selling his birthright. Jacob gave Esau bread and stew.

Rachel told us the story about Jacob's wives and concubines before quoting Jacob's first wife, Leah after conceiving her fourth child, "This time, I'll praise the Lord" So she named him Judah... Tanakh, Torah, Yayetzei, Genesis 29:35 JPS.

Collin feels the blessing to Judah was prophetic. Jacob, who was renamed Israel by God, blessed all of his sons before he died. Tanakh, Torah, Vayechi, Genesis 49:8–12 NIV: "Judah, your brothers will praise you; your hand will be on the neck of your enemies; you father's sons will bow down to you. You're a lion's club, O Judah; you return from the prey, my son. Like a lion he crouches and lies down, like a lioness—who dares to rouse him? The scepter won't depart from Judah, nor the ruler's staff from between his feet, until he comes to whom it belongs and the obedience of the nations is His."

The Mashiach will be born in the bloodline of Judah. God keeps giving prophecy to the prophets so they don't forget there'll be a Mashiach from this one bloodline.

Amy found another account of the genealogies. Tanakh, Ketuvim, 1 Chronicles 1:1–4 KJV: *Adam, Seth, Enosh, Kenan, Mahalalel, Jared, Enoch, Methuselah, Lamech, Noah*. The sons of Noah, *Shem*...

Tanakh, Ketuvim, 1 Chronicles 1:19 KJV: The sons of Shem... *Arphaxad*...was the father of *Shelah*, the father of *Eber*. Two sons were born to Eber. One was named *Peleg*...

Tanakh, Ketuvim, 1 Chronicles 1:25–27 KJV: *Reu, Serug, Nahor, Terah, Abram* [Abraham.]

Tanakh, Ketuvim, 1 Chronicles 1:34 KJV: Abraham...father of *Isaac*. The sons of Isaac: *Israel*, who was known as Jacob until God changed his name.

Tanakh, Ketuvim, 1 Chronicles 2:1 KJV: sons of Israel... Judah..."

Drew and I agree that so far, we've the descendants to Judah.

Sarah read the next paragraphs which follow the bloodline from Judah to David. Tanakh, Ketuvim, 1 Chronicles 2:4–15 KJV:...*Perez* [son of Judah.]...*Perez*...*Hezron*...*Ram*,...

Amminadab,...Nahshon,...Salmon,...Boaz,...Obed,...Jesse,... David.

The son of David, Tanakh, Ketuvim, 1 Chronicles 3:17 KJV:... *Solomon...Rehoboam,...Abijah...Asa...Jehoshaphat...Jehoram... Ahaziah...Joash...Amaziah...Azariah* (4)*...Jotham...Ahaz... Hezekiah...Manasseh...Amon...Josiah...*Josiah...Jehoiakim... Jehoiachin...Shealtiel,* and then, it seemed to end there.

Amy used a search engine to find Tanakh, Nevi'im, Haggai 1:1 NIV: The word of the Lord came through the prophet Haggai to *Zerubbabel*, Son of Shealtiel, governor of Judah.

Jessica found supporting information on that too. Tanakh, Ketuvim, Ezra 3: 2 NIV: Then Jeshua and his fellow priests and Zerubbabel, son of Shealtiel and his associates.

Collin then found Tanakh, Ketuvim, 1 Chronicles 3:19–20 KJV: The sons of Zerubbabel: Meshullam and Hananiah. Hashubah, Ohel, Berekiah, Hasadiah, and Jushab-Hesed.

This shows seven different sons of Zerubbabel instead of nine. It's unclear if Abiud hadn't been born yet to Zerubbabel during the time of recording. Obadiah's also missing.

We'll rely on Matthew's genealogical records from this point. In the days of Jesus, if you belonged to the line of David, you'd know the names of your grandfathers all the way back to David. I'm confident in Matthew's genealogy since it'd have been disputed at the time of the writing. I'm not finding any disputes. Also, during the mandated census, Joseph had to report to Bethlehem as David's descendant.

New Testament, Matthew 1:12–16 KJV: Zerubbabel...*Abiud... Eliakim...Azor...Zadok...Akim...Eliud...Eleazar...Matthan... Jacob...Joseph,* the husband of Mary, of whom was born *Jesus...*

It's important to note God was technically Jesus's father. God placed his seed in the Virgin Mary who was betrothed to Joseph. Joseph is Jesus's earthly father by adoption. Joseph was a patrilineal descendant of King David.

Drew feels Joseph doesn't count because he wasn't an heir to the throne of King David. He was only in the bloodline.

Collin questioned if Joseph needed to qualify as an heir to the throne?

Upon thorough investigation of different prophecies, we've concluded no. The prophets state the Messiah would be born a descendant or come from the House of David. An heir to the throne was not required.

Amy reread Tanakh, Torah, Bereshit, Genesis 3:15 KJV: "I'll put enmity between thee and the woman, between thy seed and her seed; He shall bruise thy head, and thou shall bruise his heel."

See, it backs up the need for Mashiach to be born of a virgin. The key is "her seed." Everyone knows a woman doesn't have seed—only men. It won't come from the seed of a man, but, from a virgin whose egg is inseminated thus becoming the seed of the woman.

Matthew traced the lineage back to David. It'd be impossible to substantiate a bloodline of anyone claiming to be the Mashiach today because genealogical records of the Jewish people were destroyed during various Tefutsot—dispersions—of Jews after Yeshua.

Although, this lineage holds legitimacy, Rachel and Drew aren't convinced Yeshua's the Mashiach.

---

1. Some biblical versions spell his name as Enosh
2. Some biblical versions spell his name as Kenan
3. Some biblical versions spell his name as Salah
4. Some biblical versions spell his name as Uzziah

Four

The team had been so eager to finish the lineage research; they didn't leave the library until after midnight. They were exhausted.

It was left up in the air as to what they'd do Friday night. Rachel talked about taking a trip home for her parent's anniversary. Amy didn't know if she'd have to pull her usual double shift at the nursing home from someone calling in sick. Giles would probably be working at the restaurant; which, left the rest to find something to do together.

When they first became friends, they'd spend Friday nights finding fraternity parties to attend for free drinks, free munchies, socializing, and free entertainment. It fit their budgets.

They were too tired to think and agreed to contact each other to see who comes up with the best plan.

Loren crept into the apartment and went to the kitchen. She didn't want to disturb Giles's sleep. She was hungry again.

"That's what I get for eating Chinese," she whispered to the empty refrigerator. "Giles didn't bring home any goodies to eat. Boo-hiss, Giles, you're slacking."

As she shut the door of the refrigerator, she stepped into someone standing behind her. She let out a startled scream. Then she realized it was Giles who'd snuck up behind her.

She pounded him in the arm for sneaking up on her. "What are you doing? Are you trying to give your girlfriend a heart attack or make me pee myself?" she yelled louder than his boisterous laughter as she ran to the bathroom.

Upon her return, she yawned after seeing his yawn. His brown eyes twinkled at her as he stroked his well trimmed black beard.

"Why does another person's yawn make me want to yawn too?" she asked him. He came over and put his arms around her as she stretched. When she finished she put her arms around his thin back and placed her head on his bare chest. He wasn't a tall man; but, he was a head taller than her and he liked the feeling of rest his chin on top of her head when they embraced.

"Did you have a nice time out with the friends?" he asked.

"Actually, it turned out to be a fun night researching together. Haven't you been to bed yet?" she asked. She then noticed his tussled hair, which meant he'd been to bed already but woke when she came home. She reached her hand up and finished messing up his hair to let him know she'd figured out the answer.

"Oh? Everyone else have the same assignment? Or are they pressed for time on their own studies this quarter? I don't think any of you've ever studied so late at the library before," Giles remarked.

Is he annoyed or jealous about us working late at the library together? Loren wondered. *Or is it an honest question?* She decided to play it cool by answering without emotion, "They were all helping me on my project. I told them it was bigger than me, and they all pitched in and looked things up for me faster than I could've done on my own. We got a ton of stuff done and everyone was so into it, we lost track of time. Weird, huh?"

She tried thinking of something else to discuss.

"Collin and Drew too? They hate studying and doing research. What could be so riveting to them that they couldn't pull themselves away?" Giles was annoyed. This was the start of

The Library Room

a typical Giles-pout session, and he didn't even know the topic of the project yet.

Still avoiding the project topic, Loren decided to deal with one issue at a time. She was too exhausted to argue with Giles. "Can we talk about this in the morning? I'm exhausted. I need to sleep. I've an eight o'clock Camtasia class, and I don't want to miss any part of it by dozing off. I'm glad my friends found it in their hearts to help me on this project. It's very selfless of them. I'm proud of the company I keep, so if you're insinuating one way or another there may be ulterior motives, you're wrong." She stormed off to take a shower while thinking, *Lord, make Giles go back to bed and be asleep by the time I crawl in.*

"Okay, Okay! Stop getting so defensive about things all the time!" Giles walked to the bedroom to go back to bed.

The morning alarm on the cell phone under Loren's pillow was felt as soon as she fell asleep. Giles remained snoring.

Loren dressed in the living room. She looked at the clock on the microwave after removing a cup of hot oatmeal. It was 7:46 a.m. *How can it be? I just heard my alarm clock go off about two minutes ago,* she thought.

She burned the roof of her mouth as she gulped her oatmeal, while carrying her books, laptop, and purse out the door. The walk to class took eight minutes. Her burnt tongue played with the roof of her mouth all the way to class.

Camtasia was her favorite class. Her professor asked them to perform different techniques using a movie clip on a thumb drive. While doing this somewhat mindless operation, she thought. *Wouldn't it be cool if I were to do a video documentary on all the information we gathered? Wait! Stay focused on splitting the current video file and moving the sound.*

After class, she walked to Samson Marketing to work a few hours. While walking, she wondered, *Who is God? Is there really a*

God? Why'd people take the time to record all those names and lineage we pieced together last night? If there's a God, why doesn't he still perform miracles like turning water into wine? I like wine. What did Mom mean about my purpose in life? Why does God love me? Why do I care if God loves me? Will God ever prove himself to me to make sure I know he's there for me? Is it blasphemy to expect God to prove himself to me? Is there really a devil? Why is there a devil? There's no doubt evil. I see and read about evil things every day. Is God only there to make rules for us to keep? I've too many rules already. I don't want more rules in my life. Are the fortunetellers I go see once in a while when my life gets out of control the same as the prophets in the Bible?

Drew and Collin each took a shower on different floors in the big house they'd rented with Adam and Ray.

Their roommates were already in classes; they were constantly in classes. Adam and Ray loved cramming as many credit hours into a semester as they could, so when they were home, they studied. There were more pros than cons in sharing a house with the brainiest geeks on campus. Besides the obvious, being able to pick their brains with their homework and studies, they were neat freaks and rarely home in the mornings due to classes. Another great benefit to having two other roommates was Collin and Drew could afford a nicer place since rent was being split four ways.

As they walked to the gym together, the light drizzle beaded on Collin's shaved head while it formed dew like beads on Drew's stiff hair. The overcast sky didn't help their lack of energy.

Being on the football team required dedication. Even though neither felt they'd be a draft pick, they loved being committed to the football team.

Both were lost in their own thoughts of last night's research as they proceeded to the treadmills in silence. They worked out side by side. It motivated them to push harder in order to outdo the other. This was always a friendly competition as well as a good balance of encouragement between the two of them. The treadmill provided their best conversations on how to solve the world's problems, or it'd become a heated race against each other for miles. Today, the treadmill pace was a conversational stride.

Both were handsome. They knew that together, young ladies couldn't resist taking a look at them. And as much as the ladies loved looking at them, they loved looking at the ladies.

Collin initiated conversation. "So what do you think about Loren's project? Do you think we can figure it out for real? Or do you think it'll always be the age-old question taunting Hebrews and Gentiles?"

Drew responded, "Well, just because we were able to figure out that crazy bloodline last night still doesn't prove Yeshua's the Mashiach. There are still too many reasons why he can't be that we haven't checked into yet, so don't get all excited, thinking you've won the prize. I'm not convinced and probably never be. Besides, my parents would kill me if I even considered it."

Collin replied, "Okay, fair. I can't stop thinking about it though. I've a lot of questions floating around in my mind, like if Christ isn't the Messiah, why aren't we still making blood sacrifices to God at a temple? I mean, wasn't the purpose of sacrificing a lamb to God a way of finding favor with him so he'd forgive our sins? And what if we figure out that he's indeed the Messiah, Drew, and all this information is right there for anyone to figure out? What do we do with it? And why isn't it easy to find? And I'm saying *if* here again, Drew, don't get all defensive it makes your hair spike out more…*if* it's the truth, and it's been here all along why are the Hebrews so dead set against the truth?"

Drew argued, "Well, I, for one, and don't take this the wrong way, Collin, it's nothing personal, however, I'm not too keen on joining an organization so eager on wiping out Hebrews. I mean, take a look at all the genocides and holocausts against us in the name of Christianity, Islam, atheism, or paganism. And while this occurred, were the Christians standing up for us? Were they being Christians in watching it all take place day after day?"

Collin defended, "I can understand your reservations. I can also tell you every religion has had corrupt and evil players, even in Judaism. I do know in my heart that my family and I wouldn't have stood by watching you, or Rachel, or your families, be tortured in any way in the name of religion or anything else. History books mention there were millions of Christians who gave up their lives in saving Jewish people. And don't forget a lot of innocent Christians were clueless as to what was being done. They were fed lies. Drew, I cannot change the past and all the evil that's been aimed at your people. I can tell you I consider you a good friend, and it'd never happen today on my watch as a Christian."

Neither had noticed their pace on the treadmill had increased during their discussion of Jewish persecutions. Both were getting winded from the pace. Since they'd attracted an audience of three beauties, they stopped talking and amplified the pace to show-off mode.

Amy was scheduled for first shift at the nursing home every Friday, which, most often, turned into a double shift. She liked the extra money on payday; therefore, she often volunteered to help the short staffing situation.

She loved her job of caring for people, even helping them to the toilet or cleaning them after they've used it. She couldn't imagine any other type of job for herself.

She was smart enough to become a doctor; however, to her, it felt like the profession had become too impersonal for her liking. Doctors distanced themselves more and more from their patients by over-scheduling, pushing drugs for pharmaceutical company perks, and egos. Not all doctors were like this, of course, some do take the time to get to know their patients.

She wasn't a morning person, so she'd arrived early to chitchat with Mrs. Rosenberg.

The day she started working at Grace Tree Elder Care Villages, she knew she loved this woman. You're not supposed to have favorite patients, yet everyone knew Mrs. Rosenberg was Amy's special-special. Sometimes, after work Amy would talk with the woman or nap in a chair while she slept. Mrs. Rosenberg understood Amy's heart needed to heal from losing her mother to cancer. Mrs. Rosenberg's family all lived far away and weren't able to see her often, so having Amy around filled a void in her life too. They were adopted family to each other.

Amy was excited to tell Ms. Roses Are My Favorite Flowers, Amy's pet name for Mrs. Rosenberg, about helping Loren with her project. It was all she could think about after their victory in piecing together the bloodline from Adam to Joseph last night.

Mrs. Rosenberg was in her room, combing her white hair into a bun. She perked up and welcomed Amy to sit while she finished.

Amy accepted the seat next to her dressing table and smiled at the old woman. The old woman smiled back and asked, "What's on that precious brain of yours today? It must be exciting news. You're bubbling with enthusiasm, and it's not even what you'd call noon-thirty yet."

"Yes, I am. I mean, I'm happy to see your face."

"And?" Mrs. Rosenberg pressed.

"And my girlfriend, Loren, was assigned a project yesterday. The gang decided it needed to be done by our group instead of Loren doing it all on her own."

"Are you allowed to do that in college? I thought all of your work had to be done by you and authored by you alone," Mrs. Rosenberg asked.

"Her professor encouraged her to ask for help, interview, and do whatever she can to figure out the legitimacy. Only thing is, she isn't allowed to ask a former student who's already had the project for a copy of their work or solicit their help."

"Well, what's the project, child? Tell me! You have my curiosity now."

"We must prove Jesus is the Messiah or not."

"Whoa! That's quite the undertaking. How's it coming along?"

"Quite fine, and I feel it won't be biased one way or the other since the whole gang's in on it. We're quite a diverse group as I learned last night: two Hebrews, two Catholics, an I-don't-know-what-to-call-myself new-ager, a Baptist, and me, a Methodist. Everyone dug right in and found clues. We've the bloodline from Adam to Joseph. That feat took all night with everyone helping because questions kept coming up and it's not all in one spot."

"That'd be exciting. What did your two Jewish friends think about the bloodline part of the project?"

"At first, they were excited to prove it couldn't be done. Then, in the end, I think they were as happy as the rest of us when we pieced a couple quirky areas together."

"So, you found it all through the male line and through King David as it says it needs to be in our Tanakh? May I see a copy of this bloodline you've found?"

"Yes," Amy answered. "Ms. Roses Are My Favorite Flowers, I didn't know you knew the Tanakh. I thought I've seen a Holy Bible here in your room. I learned the Tanakh and The Old Testament of the Bible are the same."

"Oh yes, I've a Holy Bible in my room. It came with the room. They're exact in content, but it takes me a while to find things since the books are all mixed up. My rabbi once told us Christians changed the books around to be deceitful in helping them convince Hebrews about Yeshua being Messiah."

"How'd that play into it?" Amy asked. "Don't all the books say the same thing?"

"Yes, but our book's order is done according to book types: Torah, the first five books of the Bible, then Nevi'im, the Prophets, and lastly, Ketuvim, the writings. That's why it's called

The Library Room

the Tanakh. Christians changed the books around. 2 Chronicles isn't the last book or verse. Instead, it's a prophet telling about the upcoming Mashiach. Here, get my book from inside my bed stand and I'll show you what I mean."

The drawer was arranged with pictures, knick-knacks, a pair of earrings, and a Bible. Without disturbing Mrs. Rosenberg's piles in the drawer, Amy brought it to her.

"Let's see if I can get this right." Mrs. Rosenberg leafed through the thick book. "Here we go." She pointed to the topics on the last page in the book of Malachi: "The Day of Judgment," "Temple Tithes," "The Faithful Few," and "The Day of the Lord." Mrs. Rosenberg read a passage starting from Malachi 3:1–5 KJV, "'Behold, I will send my messenger, and he shall prepare the way before me: and the LORD, whom ye seek, shall suddenly come to his temple, even the messenger of the covenant, whom ye delight in: behold, he shall come, saith the LORD of hosts. But who may abide the day of his coming? And who shall stand when he appeareth? for he is like a refiner's fire, and like fullers' soap: And he shall sit as a refiner and purifier of silver: and he shall purify the sons of Levi, and purge them as gold and silver, that they may offer unto the LORD an offering in righteousness. Then shall the offering of Judah and Jerusalem be pleasant unto the Lord, as in the days of old, and as in former years. And I will come near to you to judgment; and I will be a swift witness against the sorcerers, and against the adulterers, and against false swearers, and against those that oppress the hireling in his wages, the widow, and the fatherless, and that turn aside the stranger from his right, and fear not me, saith the LORD of hosts.'"

"Well, that's an interesting passage. I don't recall ever reading that passage before." Amy pondered over the words like a clue she'd show everyone later. "I feel it's a clue or a reminder to us that God himself will be coming as the Mashiach…'So *I'll* come near to you for judgment…the offerings of *Judah* and *Jerusalem* will be acceptable.' Thank you, Ms. Roses Are My Favorite Flowers."

Mrs. Rosenberg rolled her eyes as she thumbed through the books flipping back and forth until she found 1 Chronicles. She smiled since she knew she was close and then leaped a few pages at a time until at last she found the last page in the book of 2 Chronicles.

"Now see, the Tanakh has this verse being the last. 2 Chronicles 36:23 KJV: "Thus saith Cyrus king of Persia, All the kingdoms of the earth hath the Lord God of heaven given me; and he hath charged me to build him a house in Jerusalem, which is in Judah. Who is there among you of all his people? The Lord his God be with him, and let him go up."

Mrs. Rosenberg shut the book and placed it upon the dressing table, saying, "I understand why they'd do it. However, do you think it's right to change things around, so it'll lead the reader into wanting to read your new books, we call Brit Chadashah?" She finished the last sentence pointing to New Testament, so Amy understood.

Amy answered, "I suppose I'll have to think about it. Perhaps it'll make more sense once our project's complete. It may be as you feel, a motivating push towards reading the New Testament or to ease the reader into accepting the first book, which is Matthew describing the bloodline and birth of Jesus. Have you read any of the books in the New Testament?"

"No, sweetie, I haven't. We've always been instructed not to do so as it's a waste of time since we're Jewish and don't accept Yeshua as the Messiah. We're still waiting for Mashiach to come. I don't think he'll come in my time because the twelve tribes haven't returned to Israel yet."

"What do you mean?" Amy's curiosity was piqued as she hadn't heard of this part of prophecies needing to be fulfilled.

"I wish I could recall all the details. The way I understood it, Jacob, whom God changed his name to Israel, had children representing each of the 12 tribes. At one point their tribes scattered in different directions; they're to return to Israel. When this happens the Messiah will come and there'll be an end to death and suffering with worldwide peace."

"Wow! What happened? Why did they all scatter in different directions? Why do you suppose they haven't returned for such a long time?" Amy asked.

"That, my child, I leave to your young minds to figure out. This old one doesn't remember the details as sharp as it did when I was your age. I do, however, feel it may be something you'll need to address in this quest of truth with your friends. Don't you? You'll keep me informed on how well the progress is coming one way or the other? I think it's important for me to know before I go off to meet my maker in Olam Ha-Ba."

Mrs. Rosenberg looked up to a picture fastened to the upper right corner of her mirror. "If I've learned one thing in life it's this: If God wants something, he'll get it done in his time and in his way. Still, he leaves it up to each individual to look to him for the truths. Many times I've chosen to listen to God and not my peers. Especially, when I've asked God to show me what I've needed to see. You can't be afraid of the truth if it's coming from God. It may not be the answer you want, but it won't be wrong coming from God. I'm grateful he showed me my fiancé drank too much and wouldn't make a good husband despite what my friends and family told me. I was married to the love of my life for sixty-four years. It wasn't the man I was engaged to marry. Henry saw me crying in the park over my family's anger in calling off the wedding." She stood and stroked the face of the man in the picture.

Amy glanced at her watch. She'd lost track of time and was now late clocking in for her shift. She gave Mrs. Rosenberg a peck on the cheek and promised to check in later during her rounds.

Mrs. Rosenberg picked up the Bible on her dressing table and headed in the direction of her bed to put it back in its place.

Rachel looked out her bedroom window and saw it was raining. She then selected her outfit for working at the art gallery, her soft orange cashmere sweater with her wool camel-colored slacks. She also decided to wear a tan-colored headband to keep her curls under control with the humidity.

She contemplated going home for the weekend. She hadn't been home for over a month, and it wasn't like her to be away for so long. Her mother would want to go shopping for an outfit to wear on her anniversary date—always, a fun adventure. And yet she didn't want to leave the Judaic research up to Drew and Jessica. She knew more about Judaism, and they'd need her input before giving information over to Loren. However, she craved mother-daughter time too.

Then, a thought crossed her mind. *Let's see how Mom feels. Maybe she'll want alone time with Dad this anniversary or maybe she'll want me to stay to help on the project once she understands the topic.*

As she walked to the art gallery, she called to see if her mother expected her to come home. Her mother answered on the first ring.

"Hello?"

"Hi, Mom! Happy anniversary week!" Rachel yelled.

"Hello? Who's this?" Rachel's mother inquired.

"Mom, it's me, Rachel, your favorite daughter!" she replied in alarm. How could her mother not recognize her voice?

"I'm sorry. Rachel? She's not here. I'm Rachel's mother."

"No! Mom, it's me, Rachel, your daughter calling you! Can you hear me now?"

"Ha-ha, I got'cha, I knew it was you. I was trying to play a joke on you to prove to your father I've a sense of humor every once in a while." Rachel could hear giddiness in her mother's voice and her father in the background mumbling something in reply to what her mother had said.

"Mom! You're sounding playful around Dad?" Rachel laughed. "So how many years have you two made each other miserable?"

"The number's now thirty-eight, darling."

"Wow! I'm so impressed the two of you've stayed together for so long. Thank you for that, by the way. Most of my friends' parents are divorced, and they've the extended-family issues. I'm grateful we don't have those issues."

"Well, there were years where the jury was hung on whether or not we'd stick it out. Or was it they wanted me to hang him? Hung jury. Jury says hang. I get confused on that one."

"Mother! You're terrible to that sweet man! Oh, the things he's had to endure over the years!" Both laughed over that comment.

"So what are your plans for your anniversary?"

"Your father surprised me this morning with tickets for the two of us. We leave first thing tomorrow morning for Israel!"

"Mom! That's awesome! That's always been my dream trip! Wow! I guess I'm glad I called before packing up my things and coming home for the weekend."

"Oh, sweetie, I was grabbing the phone to call you to let you know when the phone rang, and it was you!"

"Well, that'd explain why you answered the phone on the first ring for a change."

"Yep, but I can't stay on too long because I need to head to the store to grab a few things for our trip and start packing. I could almost kill your father for not giving me much notice on something so big."

"He probably wanted to make sure he'd have money left to spend once he got there instead of you spending it all on travel attire."

"Oh, come on now. I'm not that bad," she whined out in defense. Unfortunately, both knew she wasn't kidding anyone. Rachel had been right about her father not telling her mother sooner.

"So how long are you going to be gone on this wonderful trip?" Rachel asked.

"We'll be gone three weeks. It's the longest vacation we've ever taken. I don't know what's gotten into your father. He 'feels called' to visit the places of his forefathers. Several of his friends at the firm have gone over the past couple of years. Two of them moved there. There are so many places we're going to see, Rachel!"

"Mom, send me a copy of your itinerary with the hotel numbers in case I need to talk to you, and I can look at the calendar each day to see where you're at and let my imagination travel with you. I'm so happy for you both! Dad works so hard. He deserves this time away from the firm. Be extra nice to him, Mom."

"I'm always nice to him!"

"I know, but be extra nice. He's not used to spending that much time with you, and you're not used to spending that much time with him. Patience will be crucial, Mom," Rachel said with a nervous giggle at the thought of them together for so long.

"Mom, take as many notes as you can and send them to my phone whenever you get a chance. I want to experience it with you, and you'll want to reminisce over those notes when you get home. Oh, I'm so jealous! All the art, artifacts, history, architect, and lessons, you'll be learning without me, the daughter who loves and appreciates those kinds of things."

"Oh, don't be jealous, honey. Someday, you'll have a husband who'll hear about how great your father was in doing this surprise after thirty some years, and he'll do the same. Remember what I always say, your generation doesn't need to have everything to keep up with their parents. You need to know what it's like to struggle, work for what you get, and not be equal to all of the Finkelsteins."

"Spoken like a true Jewish mom." Rachel laughs every time her mother delivers that speech she'd made up ten years ago.

"I love you, Mom. Tell Dad happy anniversary and that I love him very much too. Have a safe trip and don't forget to send your itinerary to me!"

"We adore you too, sweetie."

Rachel was staying to help with the project. The decision was made for her as she thought, *All for Loren and Loren for all.*

She'd arrived at the gallery while she'd been on the phone with her mother. Without thinking, she set her purse behind the counter and picked up the dusting wand to go over the numerous pictures in frames made by talented students on consignment.

A secured room at the far end of the gallery displays artwork borrowed from different galleries across the world. She looked past the stationed security guard. She'd been admiring the painting for a couple of weeks, but today, she absorbed the picture. It was a loaner from the Cleveland Museum of Art, oil on canvas painting of *Laban Searching for his Stolen Household Gods* by Bartolomé Esteban Murillo, c. 1665–70. It depicts the story her namesake, Rachel, told in the Tanakh, Torah, Genesis 29–35.

Five

Jessica and Sarah didn't speak after meeting in the lobby except for the customary "good morning" greetings. It was different than their typical Friday mornings when they were excited about weekend activities. Today, they were quiet, each respecting the other's meditative silence.

Once they were inside the coffee shop, the bustle brought them out of their reveries. They sat at a small table near the window with their coffees.

"That was quite an interesting night last night," Jessica initiated.

"Yep, not sure what happened or how I got conned into helping, but it was fun nonetheless," Sarah added.

"Really? You felt like you'd been conned into participating with us? I thought you were into it too, like the rest of us," Jessica said.

Sarah explained, "I don't hate it. I could think of a hundred different things I'd rather be doing than revisiting Sunday school lessons. But who can say no to y'all? It always turns out fun. I love hanging with everyone. I just never saw this religious thing coming along and me being a part of it. Y'all think differently about God and Jesus."

"What do you mean?" Jessica asked.

Sarah answered, "I grew up in a church where it seemed like fun equaled sin: no drinking, no dancing, no movies, no card playing, no slacks or jeans for females, and rarely laughter. It was all shame and guilt. If we fell on hard times, we were taught we were being punished for sins. I ended up being the only teen left in the church. Everyone reported everything I did to Momma, from looking at magazines in stores to changing into jeans at friend's house before attending the forbidden school dance."

"Um, wow! Sarah, I'd never have guessed you were brought up that way! Your mom didn't come across that way when you took me to your house for a weekend last year."

"She changed churches after she and Dad divorced. I told them how I'd felt about their church when they'd asked if I'd found a similar church. I told them I'd prayed I wouldn't."

"So what kind of church do they attend now?"

"Mom still attends a Baptist, but it's more uplifting. I'm not sure about Dad. We don't talk too often. I taught Mom how to play rummy with playing cards a couple years ago while home on Christmas break. She told me she understood what I was saying when I'd said it. It caused her to look to God's word as opposed to what some man was feeling convicted of and putting on an entire congregation. She concluded, if the pastor or his members feel it's sinful to dance, then it's God convicting them of their naughty thoughts when they see others gyrate while dancing. *But that doesn't mean you or I do the same. God doesn't make us feel like it's a sin, and it's not for us. Unless, we do start thinking that way, and we'll know because God speaks to our hearts real fast if we're doing something he doesn't like.*"

"Yes, I kind of know what you mean," Jessica added. "When I was younger, some of the girls in my class were drinking and dirty dancing at parties throughout the year. I went a few times. It didn't feel right. It was fun to a point, but it didn't feel *right*, for lack of a better expression. In my gut, I knew it wasn't right. So I skipped a few parties to the point they stopped inviting me."

"Yeah. However, I grew rebellious from being denied all that fun. Remember my sophomore year here? I was a wild girl! I'm still amazed I passed all my classes!"

Jessica nodded her head. "Oh yeah, I remember."

The Library Room

"If it weren't for y'all calling me out, I'd be in bad shape with no scholarship. I'm grateful for y'all being blunt with me. I'm sure if my parents knew what I'd been doing they'd be grateful too."

"You're our favorite wild child, Sarah. For the life of me, I don't know what got into us either. That wasn't like us to gang up and call a person out like we did with you." Jessica's mind flashed to their sophomore year.

Sarah slouched on a couch in a local pub ranting. She drank with imaginary friends who owed her drinks. With no one to stop her, she ordered another Long Island iced tea from her former lover bartender who no longer cared about his latest conquest.

If someone tried striking up a conversation with the cool, smart, flirty girl sitting with books and papers scattered across the couch, they'd think she was there type until she'd try to speak, and then they'd realize she was inebriated. Luckily, no one wanted to cross the forbidden line of taking advantage of her.

Collin received a text, saying a "drunk friend is ripe for the picking tonight." He understood it to be Sarah. Without showing anyone the text, he suggested they find Sarah. He insisted she needed to hang out with them. "She's been out of touch for a couple of weeks, and I don't want her to feel like we've given up on her friendship." Each agreed they should find out what she's been up to even though they already knew.

Drew and Jessica found her at the Volkswagen Pub, sprawled out on the couch with her books and notepads. They knew she was in trouble and needed help. Jessica texted the others. Collin, Rachel, and Loren were there within minutes.

Drew was furious and seemed ready to fight anyone about the condition of his friend. He shot death stares in the direction of the bartender, Matt. It was irresponsible on his part to over serve and both knew it, especially an underage girl.

Rachel kept a safe distance as she voiced out her prediction, "She's going to blow chunks soon."

Collin grabbed her by the arms and tried to get her to stand. He gave up and hoisted her over his shoulder.

Drew questioned Matt about her tab. He was told it was fifty dollars and some change. Drew threw a wadded twenty at him while informing Matt, "The rest is on the house." Meaning, Drew was stiffing Matt for the balance. Matt understood what Drew meant. If Matt wanted to pursue the issue, Drew was more than willing to press it with legal action and risk having the establishment lose their license. It's a strict county when it comes to over serving and even more severe when it comes to serving under-aged drinkers.

In the fresh air, everyone assessed the situation. Collin couldn't carry Sarah across campus to her apartment and risk having her tagged with public intoxication. They called Amy at work and asked her if they could "crash" at her place to sober her up. At first, Amy was hesitant; however, she trusted these friends. She even liked Sarah's quirky Southern expressions she'd say. She agreed on the condition they cleaned up after Sarah if she made a mess. They found the key hidden where Amy told them it'd be and entered her tidy apartment.

Amy had lucked out in finding this apartment on campus. It was a small one-bedroom flat. Amy always kept it neat and clean. The furnishings were eclectic ranging from antique to ultra modern. She pulled it off with her natural staging talents. A two-year lease helped secure the great price. Most college students want to rent during the school season. However, she knew once she'd start working at the nursing home she'd be there year round.

Sarah's color grayed as she claimed a need for air. Collin set her on a hard wooden chair next to the window and opened it.

Rachel placed a waste basket next to her for the inevitable.

Sarah sat with one arm over the back of the chair and her other arm draped between her parted legs. Her head was too heavy to hold up. Her eyes weren't able to focus on anything, so she closed them.

Coffee was found in the cupboard, and a strong pot was made for everyone. They knew it'd be a long night for everyone.

Eventually, Sarah emptied the contents of her stomach a few times and fell asleep on the couch. No one left the responsibility of taking care of Sarah to the others. They all pitched in and took turns helping her, but the girls were in charge of helping her in and out the bathroom.

"We've all been there." They'd smirk and try to make light of the situation as her body heaved against the poisons in her system.

Around one in the morning, everyone found a sleeping spot on the floor while Sarah was passed out on the comfortable couch.

Amy came home at three in the morning after working two shifts. She was amazed everyone was still there for Sarah. She went to her closet and grabbed blankets, crocheted throws her patients had made, throw pillows, and sheets to offer her guests. The boys mumbled, and the girls woke enough to thank her before falling back to sleep.

Morning brought a new attitude from everyone as they stretched stiff muscles. "I don't know how she does it. Amy can work twenty hours without complaining." Rachel yawned.

"Sh. Don't tell her it's work," Jessica explained. "She loves what she does. The paycheck's a bonus."

"Did I hear my name?" Amy appeared with her hair tussled like the rest of them. "What time is it, anyway?"

"Yes, I was bragging about how you love what you do regardless of the hours. It's eleven-thirty. Do you have plans?" Jessica asked.

"Don't give me so much credit about enjoying the hours after working twenty straight. I'd hate to disappoint you."

The boys grabbed a cup of coffee, and Loren prepared another pot.

"What are we going to do with her?" Collin pointed at Sarah.

Everyone stared into their coffee mugs while Sarah snored.

Drew started, "The way I see it, here are our choices. We either confront her with her behavior, pray she listens to us, and cleans up her act, or we pretend it's normal college crap everyone goes through, or we tell her mother and let her deal with Sarah. I feel she needs help. We saw that last night. She's going to get hurt if it isn't addressed."

They all agreed with Drew's assessment and options.

"I vote we talk to her first. If she listens great, if she tells us to all go to hell, well, then we call her mom," Jessica pitched.

"I'd have a hard time snitching a friend out to their parents," Rachel admitted, and Collin agreed with her.

Loren spoke, "Look, I understand the concern with telling her mom. It may not be an issue if she stops this behavior. However, we can threaten to do that. What I saw last night scared me. If I were partying like I've been hearing about her, I'd hope you'd all kick my butt back to reality and not to the curb. Why do you think she's partying? She's smart and pretty. We must do something, playing it off as normal behavior isn't an option. She'll end up dead or raped." Loren became emotional.

Jessica voiced everyone's fears. Jessica mumbled, "She's going to hate us. She's going to be hung over in an apartment she won't remember being taken to while she was in a blackout. She won't remember trying to drink herself to death. When she figures out we didn't party with her, she'll become embarrassed and want to leave. When she leaves, she'll hate us for meddling."

Loren said, "Perhaps, but a friend should take the risk. I haven't in the past. Now, I cannot. They're gone. I'm not making that mistake again and living with another person's life on my shoulders. I'd rather lose her friendship than not say anything."

"They're gone. You mean, like moved off to college before you could say something and you'll never be able to or want to track them down? Right?" Collin clarified.

"No, Collin," Loren answered. "I mean she died. She was a high school friend. Everyone thought it was fun to party to the point of blackouts and then compared our pictures and text messages the next day. I feared the game after a dude tried raping me in a bathroom. I barely yelled for help. I don't know how someone heard me. A friend forced his way in and pulled the bad dude off me with a couple punches. We hid in the tub with the curtain pulled until I sobered enough to find Mindy. Mindy thought it was hysterical when I told her what had happened. I laughed too because I didn't want her to stop liking me. I should've told her we were being stupid and where it was leading. I should've told her what I felt."

Loren's face became more somber. "One night, she was passed out in her front yard. She choked on her vomit. The toxicology report indicated she'd consumed Rohypnol also known as roofies. Someone slipped it into her drink. There were also signs of intercourse. They had a few suspects, but no one was charged. Her parents asked me not to attend her funeral. I wasn't even with her that night, but they blamed me. And I blame myself too." Tears slid down her cheeks as she still mourned a friend and harbored guilt.

Rachel too wiped her eyes, imagining it to be Sarah.

"So how do we pull off an intervention with her?" Drew asked.

Jessica surprised everyone with her answer. "We had to do this with my close cousin who felt more like a sister. Only, we had a week to think about what to say. Everyone wrote a note so we wouldn't forget anything when it got emotional."

"Should I get paper and pencils for everyone?" Amy asked.

Jessica answered, "Yes, not a bad idea. But I wouldn't write a long woeful letter. It sort of loses its effect after the second or third one. Just write a word or two to keep you on track."

Everyone liked Jessica's idea.

Amy tiptoed to her bedroom and returned with supplies.

Jessica noticed Sarah's sleeping had become lighter. "We need to write fast. I think she's going to be up soon," Jessica said.

It took ten minutes for everyone to write their notes. They stood waiting for a sign to begin. Sarah still dozed.

Drew signaled everyone to stand around her. Collin shook her shoulder. She flew up like a caged animal. She didn't understand what was going on. She felt she was in danger. Collin and Drew caught her and sat her back down.

"What's going on?" Sarah asked.

"Well, that's what we'd like to know," Jessica answered.

"What do ya mean? What time is it? Why y'all staring at me? Am I in trouble?" Sarah asked.

Collin blurted, "*You* smell like a drunk. Do you know why?"

"Well, duh! Everyone partied last night," Sarah explained. "Sorry for the offensive odor. I'll be better after I go home, take a shower, and brush my teeth. Thank you very little for the compliment." She laughed, trying to lighten the mood. "Do I smell coffee? I'd kill for a cup right now." Sarah looked at Amy. "Hey, why y'all standing, and why are we at Amy's?"

"Sarah, first off," Rachel began, "we didn't party with you last night. We went looking for our friend whom we haven't seen for a couple of weeks because she got bored with us and decided drinking herself to death could be more fun. However, we like you, and we missed you. Secondly, when we found you, it wasn't pretty! You couldn't talk, you couldn't walk, and your former boyfriend-lover-schmuck had you so drunk, I thought Drew and Collin would kill him!"

Never in Sarah's wildest dreams would she believe Rachel could be so mean. She sat thinking, *Rachel's accusing me of what? Getting tipsy? I've seen Rachel drunk. Why is she over reacting to having one too many Long Island iced teas?*

Amy handed Sarah a cup of coffee. "Drink this."

Sarah cradled the cup in her hands as if protecting herself from the chill she was feeling from her friends.

Loren took her turn next. "Sarah, I know we haven't known you long, but we're here *for* you, not *against* you. Proof is that we didn't abandon you when we saw how vulnerable you'd become last night. Proof is that Collin carried you to Amy's place instead risking you getting nailed with public intoxication and underage consumption charges and then being expelled! Proof is that everyone took turns holding you while you threw up in Amy's bathroom."

Amy's face showed panic. She wanted to run to the bathroom to check on the mess.

Loren continued, "And Jessica thoroughly cleaned it, so Amy wouldn't freak out after working two shifts. Proof is that we *stayed* with you and slept on the floor while you slept on the couch. It's what friends do. We feel you're a friend. *However*, let me tell you this. I won't watch a friend drink herself to death again. I can't allow your dangerous behavior to continue without pointing out your destructive path. Clean your act up girl. I won't be here the next time."

Sarah's head pounded as she pouted. *Must they do this right now? Can't they tell me not to do it again and be done with it? If I tell them it won't happen again, will they let me go? What are they talking about me dying? I only had one or two Long Islands, I think. How'd I get here? What'd she mean Collin carried me?*

Amy came around with a carafe of coffee to refill cups.

Drew began his turn. "Sarah, you're a smart girl, gifted actually. The fact that you're passing your classes while drinking every night's a testament to your genius. My concern is you're jeopardizing your full scholarship, which, I'll admit to being envious. It'd be ironic for someone of your intelligence to lose it out of stupidity. If you'd been seen by the authorities last night, you'd have been expelled and forfeited your entire scholarship! How'd that affect your future? Your family? Your ability to get into Yale? You did mention you wanted to attend Yale to get your masters degree in chemistry, right? What were you thinking? What am I missing? Are you trying to sabotage your future? I don't get it! Help me understand what's going through that brain of yours. Are you running away from something? Were you abused by someone? Why are you acting like a drunken sailor? Don't you know you're getting a bad reputation for being a party girl? Is that what you want? Attention from men? Are you capable of having a single drink anymore without wanting to get drunk? Are you even capable of going a whole week without getting drunk? I'm scared for you, your future, physical, and mental health."

Sarah didn't answer. She fought the hangover crying urges. She tired of the lectures from her so called friends. *Really? They barely know me! Why is it different for me? I've seen everyone drunk before!*

Drew continued, "Sarah, are you with us?"

"Yes, Drew, I'm here taking it *all* in," Sarah spat.

Hearing the tone from Sarah, the future attorney Drew sprung into action. "You're taking it *all* in. That's nice. Does that mean you don't give a crap about how much we love and care about you?"

She was silent for a while. "I didn't mean it like that. Don't twist my words."

"Fair enough, I'll try not to twist your words. Let's take it slow," Drew continued. "Does it bother you that your *true friends*, not your *partying friends* who *weren't* there to help you last night, are taking time to address your behavior?"

"It's my life. I've seen y'all drunk at times," she argued.

"Yes," Drew addressed. "We've all been drunk at times, but not every night, not even every weekend, not by ourselves, and not to the point of not being able to hold our heads up. There's the difference. Do you understand? It's important you understand the differences."

"I *haven't* been drinking every night," Sarah argued.

"Oh, did you miss a night this past month?" Drew retorted. "Because I'm pretty sure you've hit the daily campus gossip for at least a month now, so yes, you *have*. Remember how we'd make fun of serial drunks last year? Guess what? You're it this year. How do you feel about that, Sarah?"

"How do you know it's me they're talking about? There are a lot of serial drunks on this campus," Sarah spat.

"Are they all named Sarah?" Drew wasn't holding back. He saw the light in her head flickering as he fed her the truth. "No, they aren't. Now, be honest with yourself and your friends. Tell us what's going on."

Sarah cried from embarrassment. She asked herself, *Have I really become a talked about serial drunk?* She still didn't believe it.

Drew persisted. "Sarah, what happens to students who get that reputation on this campus, and it reaches the professor level? Do you think your straight A's will be so easy to obtain? Or do you think they'll start scrutinizing everything you do? What happens to girls when certain guys learn about their reputation? Do you find a better quality of dates or quantity of dates that want to get you drunk and have sex?"

Sarah's mind shouted, *I'm a good Christian girl. How dare he insinuate such a thing! Guys want to go out with me because I'm pretty, fun, smart, etc. Not because I'm easy when I get drunk!*

"*Drew!* I don't think I attract that kind of guy!" Sarah objected.

Collin stood up from beside her on the couch. "You're wrong there, Sarah. Here. Read this." Collin handed her his phone with the text message indicating she was ripe for the picking. "I haven't shown it to anyone. It's why I suggested we find you before someone else did. It's about you since the rest of my friends were already with me. Sorry but some dudes think this way. They aren't always interested in conversation, beauty, or a lasting relationship."

Sarah's face turned scarlet. She cried as she saw what everyone else saw about her recent activities.

Amy sat next to her. "Sarah, do you need help? Is this something you cannot control? Or do you even know if it's something you can control? Do you trust us?"

Sarah nodded. "I'm not an alcoholic if that's what you're asking. I don't crave being drunk. I wanted to have fun. Does that make sense? I wanted to see what I'm missing. Don't you ever feel like you've missed out on something?"

"Not really," Amy admitted. "But I believe you."

"Sarah," Jessica said as she kneeled down in front of her. "You've been my best friend since we've landed here. God put us together as dorm mates last year. I've watched you change since coming back and having separate apartments. Can you forgive me for not saying something sooner? Can you promise to let us know if can't stop drinking? My cousin's active in AA. I could put you two in touch. We'd never think less of you if you needed it. We'd all support you. Do you believe me?"

"Yes, I believe you, and I promise to be honest with myself and you, if I feel like I *must* drink."

"Thanks," Jessica said. "You won't get annoyed if we watch you now? We've our concerns, and we love you that much."

"Watch all you want. It won't happen again," Sarah assured.

From that day forward, Sarah didn't have an issue with being a party girl. She became self-conscience of her actions to the point of being a health nut. Pharmaceutical chemistry's been her dream. Once she became aware of the poisons in alcohol, she didn't mind sharing her findings.

Six

Collin grabbed Sarah and Jessica's food trays and followed them to where Drew was waiting to pull out chairs for them. The manners of both men were always appreciated.

"Thank you, gentlemen," Jessica complimented their chivalry.

"Yes, thank you both," Sarah added.

Both men beamed from the positive acknowledgments.

They waited for Sarah to pray over her meal. Even though she'd complain about growing up ultra-Christian conservative, she'd still take time to thank God.

Jessica was already thinking about the research. "My goodness, it felt good to get that much done last night. I think we're making good time, thanks to everyone helping," Jessica said trying to read Drew. *How far will we go before Drew, our favorite Hebrew, says something derogatory? It must be hard for him to see where this is going.*

Drew watched Jessica too. He knew her thoughts. He'd never rub it in their faces when they disproved the Christian theories. He thought, *How can they be so naive? Can't they see it's all manipulated? When will they get it? Yeshua was born to Mary. Yeshua wasn't Joseph's child! I thought we proved that. They'll be depressed when they discover their beloved Yeshua isn't Mashiach.*

"What's our plan for tonight?" Sarah asked, easing the tension. "Anyone find anything exciting for us?"

Collin piped up, "Drew and I discussed that before you gals came along. There are two parties tomorrow night with free drinks and food. Unfortunately, the campus will be quiet tonight. We thought about doing the library thing to get as much of it out of the way so Loren can breathe. Did you see how panicked she looked last night?"

"Oh, I saw her," Jessica agreed. "She's a basket case. She's not comfortable with this project. I don't know if it's from not wanting to face God on a few issues or if it's from fear of what her tyrant-jerk of a boyfriend Giles will say when he finds out what she's researching. He'll have an opinion as he 'feels passionately' about everything."

"Oh!" Both men chimed at Jessica's description.

Jessica smirked. "What! Like you two don't feel the same?"

They shook their heads and finished eating.

"Hey, Drew!" Collin called, shifting the subject. "Did you notice the camera bubble in the middle of the room?"

"I sure did. I heard they installed cameras over the summer in every room as a result of bombings and shootings at other schools. I guess this way, they'll be able to see where the bad guys or gals are when the crap hits the fan."

"Drew!" Sarah yelled. "That's a serious problem all schools, colleges, work places, and such are facing today."

"Oh, I know, Sarah, but it's pretty much what it'd be used for if it ever happens. I mean, you don't think they installed them to monitor professors hitting on students to prevent lawsuits? Or eavesdropping on conversations of the latest conspiracy theorists? I mean, that might be too much big brother prying into our privacy. Right?" Drew said, glaring at the camera.

"Drew, are your parents as cynical as you?" Sarah asked.

"No, my parents are optimists to a fault. I, on the other hand, am a happy soul with honest perceptions of humans," Drew answered.

"What do you think? Should we head to the library and start working?" Collin suggested while grabbing everyone's empty trays.

As they walked across campus, Jessica asked, "Remember when everyone decided to take a humanities English class together? What was it called...the period of Enlightenment?"

Collin responded, "Our sophomore year, Dr. Gregory Harmonty, a pompous idiot! Whose idea was it to all take that class together anyway? That was the most boring and painful three-hour credit I've ever had to endure! Thank you Jessica, by the way, for helping me with my project on that...even though you scored an eight-seven, and I only scored an eighty-three."

"Ever since that class, I've had questions. Working on this project brought back those questions and the déjà vu of working with everyone each night on our reports. Everyone passed, which was a miracle, since none of us were serious about the material," Jessica announced.

"Hey, speak for yourself. That class was a great!" Drew added.

"You sucked up to the professor to earn a ninety-eight! Didn't he tell us it was the highest score he'd ever given?" Sarah accused.

Drew puffed his chest and smiled. "Yes, he did. I can't help it if a professor recognized genius and wanted to reward it."

"Drew, you wrote a bunch of stuff you yourself wouldn't believe, but you knew the professor would love the argumentative side of it!" Jessica argued.

"All true. Who received the highest grade?" Drew taunted.

"But it was a lie, Drew, and you knew it," Jessica persisted.

"But, it was a grade Jessica, and I didn't care," Drew rested his argument.

"Okay, smarty-pants, you've got a point," Jessica accepted defeat. "Tell me this. Have you ever wondered why we're here on earth? What's it all for? Why should I behave? Why are we friends? Was it part of God's plan? And if it's part of God's big plan how do I fit in it?"

"Do you *feel* there's a big plan?" Sarah added.

"Right! What's the plan?" Jessica pondered. "What if the famous philosopher, David Hume, we learned about was right in thinking,

> there's a God. He created the universe. Then, He got bored with it, and went off to create other universes. For us to believe He wants anything to do with us lowly creatures He put on this earth as more than a part of His creation is our egos talking. He's too big to consider having an individual relationship with humans.

That was him who said that wasn't it? I can't remember which one, although for some reason his name comes to mind on that philosophy."

As they entered the doors of the library, Amida, the librarian, rushed toward them. "Hello, Collin, Drew, Jessica, and Sarah. Will the others be joining you?" she greeted.

"Good afternoon, Amida." Sarah surprised everyone by knowing her name. "I'm sure they'll all end up here."

"Wonderful. I'm taking you to a private study room for Loren's project." Amida signaled them to follow.

Collin was curious. "Amida, I take it Loren called to let you know our plans for the evening and made the arrangements? We're grateful."

"Oh no, sweetie, I knew Professor Finkel would be assigning this project. He likes things private. Sometimes opinions can become, shall we say…*heated*. So it's best to keep everyone in a private room."

She handed them security badges then swiped one in front of a fake book to the right of a hidden door. It allowed the door to open. "This room is for your use for the rest of the year. You may keep your reference books here on the table," she pointed to the oak conference table, "opened to the page you want without fear

The Library Room

of losing your place." She placed the remaining three badges on the table.

They stood near the door, staring at the conference table, soft leather swivel chairs, royal purple carpeting, oversized bean bag chairs in the corners with a reading table next to each and their reference books. The books they set aside for the night sat in a neat pile on the conference table.

Collin walked to the left side of the door. A SMARTboard was mounted on the shimmering cream-colored wall. To the left of it was a gold leaf Star of David, and to the right was a gold leaf cross.

Drew walked to the right side of the door to read the gold name plates under each painting done throughout the years by students of the college. He couldn't wait to watch Rachel's face when she sees them.

Jessica found a letter in an envelope addressed to Loren.

Amida programmed Collin's laptop to the SMARTboard and showed them how to use it. She then went to the far side of the room, pressed a button, and a gold leaf painted menorah cracked in the middle as it exposed a flatscreen TV computer monitor. Again, she configured Collin's laptop. Everyone thanked Amida for her help as she left the room with the four of them inside.

"Wow! The college went all out on this, didn't they?" Drew proclaimed as he walked around exploring every nook and cranny.

The plaque on the door says the following:

> *In this room, we discovered the meaning of our lives, the truth regarding eternity, and deeper friendships than any of us could've imagined.*
> *Glory to God in the Highest!*
> *Private Room Built by Project Team 2000*
> *Exterior Room Entrance Designed by Project Team 2001*
> *Security System by Project Team 2002*
> *Corner Closet and Refrigerator by Project Team 2003*
> *Gold Leaf Ceiling Constellation by Project Team 2004*

Wool Plush Carpeting by Project Team 2005
Italian Leather Executive Chairs by Project Team 2006
Gold Leaf Antique Picture Frames by Project Team 2007
Solid Oak Conference Table by Project Team 2008
Suede Beanbags and Reading Desks by Project Team 2009
SMARTboard and Flatscreen by Project Team 2010
Sky Dome by the Project Team 2011

"Gee!" Sarah exclaimed. "What will they expect us to come up with next?" Her question went unnoticed.

As soon as Drew had read the last line out loud, everyone looked up to see a perfect constellation on the ceiling with nearly invisible lines going through it. Sarah and Jessica raced to the far wall where Amida showed them the button to expose the flat screen. They pushed the button and the flat screen eased back into its protective cubby as the panels slid back into place. They pressed the button again, and the panels parted while the flat screen popped back out.

"Well, that's not it!" Sarah discouraged.

"Try pressing it twice!" Drew almost shouted with excitement.

Sarah did. The panels shut and then reopened.

Sarah smiled. "It sounded good in theory, Drew."

Jessica and Collin searched for a hidden knob, discrete button, pull string, and even patted the rough textured walls with their hands.

They investigated a corner closet. Inside were reams of paper, pens, dry-erase markers, a wireless printer/scanner/copy machine sitting atop a refrigerator with bottled waters.

"We should get started so they won't think we've been slacking while they've been working." Collin grabbed the Holy Bible off the pile of books and handed Drew the Tanakh.

"What time did they say they'd be here?" Jessica asked to no one in particular.

Drew volunteered. "Not sure they did. I'll text them."

The Library Room

Amy responded first with, "I B there 1 hour. Seeing Roses B4 leaving. Lost tribes of Israel? Said we need 2 know 4 Mashiach."

Drew replied, "On it. Surprise here. Text me and I'll get U."

Rachel's text came in next. "Locking up. Meeting at library?"

Drew replied, "Yes. We're here. Text me. Not at our table."

Loren replied, "Meet at library? We going out?"

Drew replied, "Staying in. Not at table. Text me. I'll get you."

Sarah used the printer to make a copy of the Messianic Prophesies spreadsheet for everyone.

Everyone tried figuring it out. There was no chronological order to it nor was it grouped by pre, during, or post Jesus.

Collin displayed it on the flat screen. He added, "PRE Jesus, DURING Jesus, and POST Jesus" columns, dividing each prophecy as the coming of the Messiah or what the Messiah would do while here or what happens after the Messiah ascends to heaven.

Rachel texted Drew saying she was at the library. He made a bet with Sarah. "Fifty bucks says Rachel walks over to the paintings before noticing your outfit." He laughed as he left.

Sarah texted Rachel. "Before looking at anything, comment on my outfit. Split $50! Bet with Drew." She smiled. As soon as the door rattled, she jumped in front of it. Rachel was in front of Drew as he held the door for her. Sarah twirled showing off her newest outfit.

Rachel held her hand out to Drew. "It's going to cost you sixty bucks to not say a thing."

Collin and Jessica roared over Drew's dilemma.

Drew handed her four tens and a twenty. He'd been played.

Rachel took the money, walked to the paintings, and gave half to Sarah. "The way I see it, I negotiated a raise."

"You rock," Sarah said, taking her half from Rachel.

"I've got chutzpah," Rachel declared. "These paintings are breathtaking!" Rachel proclaimed. "Did you notice they're not only in order of Torah timeline? They're also done by a different student each year. Cleverly done, quite clever. See the first one at the top right? You read right to left in Hebrew. The creation of the heavens, earth, water, land was painted in 1999. Next one, to the left, is Adam and Eve leaving a gate guarded by an angel with a twirling sword of fire. It looks like it moves as your eyes try to focus on it. Amazing!"

Loren texted Drew she was steps away from the library. "All bets are off. You've bled me dry for two weeks! I'm getting Loren. I can't wait to see her face when she figures out it's a result of her assignment," he announced before leaving.

Loren struggled carrying her laptop, purse, and bags of snacks. Drew relieved her from the heavy bags and laptop. She followed him to the door disguised as bookshelves. He ushered her in.

"Surprise!" everyone shouted.

"What in the world did you guys do to get this room for us? I didn't even know it existed! This is so cool!"

Everyone waited.

Collin counted backward, waiting for the images to register. *Four, three, two—wait for it.*

"No way!" She looked again at the Star of David, the Crucifix, and paintings. "This room's for our project!" she whispered.

"Yes," Collin whispered back. "It's all about you and your project…our project. Read the door. We're not the first team."

"Here." Jessica pointed to the head chair. "This is yours. There's an envelope with your name on it."

Loren sat and stared at the flat screen with scriptures and different columns for notes.

"Why me?" she whispered. "This isn't where I'd planned to be. God's demanding I walk with him instead of walking along trees and gardens thinking of a higher power. I wasn't looking for anything more from God. Now this…it overwhelms me. I couldn't keep my mind focused during class or work. I couldn't stop thinking about the project." She dabbed her eyes with her sleeve.

Jessica grabbed boxes of tissues from the supply closet. She handed one to Loren and one to Rachel.

"You're like one of those people we read about in the Tanakh that God calls on to do something big," Rachel sniffled.

"Oh goodness, Loren! Look at what you've done! You've gone off being a girl and got poor Ms. Rachel all verklempt!" Drew declared.

The mood lightened. Everyone sat while Loren opened the envelope and then stopped. "Is Amy coming tonight?"

Drew said, "She'll be here in fifteen minutes."

Loren put the envelope down, "I'll read it when we're *all* together. I feel like this journey isn't about me alone. Drew, where'd you put the snacks?" Loren asked.

Drew walked to the cabinet, grabbed cookies, and slid them down the table. "I know you didn't buy those for me and Collin. Are you trying to ruin our beefy figures?"

"Loren, have I ever told you how much I love you as a friend?" Collin stared at the box of gingersnaps.

"Yes, cookies for my *beefy* boys." Loren winked at both.

Jessica feigned a bass voice, "And *beefy* girls?"

Everyone laughed. They opened the cookies and dove into working. They looked up verses in the Tanakh, verified it said the same thing in the Holy Bible, determined what was going on at the time, and decided if the verse or adjoining verses could be justified as a Messianic Prophecy that could be interpreted by an average person

Amy texted Drew. Drew excused himself again. He met her at the entrance. She tried hiding her red swollen eyes from him, but he noticed. Out of courtesy, he didn't say anything. He took her heavy bags to carry for her.

A tear trickled down Amy's cheek. "Ms. Roses Are My Favorite Flowers is not doing well. She's uncomfortable. She's refusing any lifesaving efforts now. It's spread. She knows the odds. I support her decision. I hate watching her die like my mother. I love her."

Drew hugged her as she wept. He held her up when her knees gave out due to a hard tummy tug as her lungs fought for the air she exhaled during a long winded cry out. He didn't move, didn't look around to see who was watching and let her get it out.

When she finished, she said, "Wow! That came over me like a ton of bricks."

"You okay? Do you want to go talk?" Drew offered.

"No, thanks. I'll be okay. I need to focus on something else. That's why I'm here. She told me to come, learn, and bring her everything we discover. She wants to know." Amy's eyes watered.

"Okay, it's your call, but don't feel bad if you need to leave or if you get tired," Drew coached as he walked toward the room.

Amy blinked when she realized the bookshelf was a three dimensional wall painting with a door barely visible. Drew opened the door and allowed her to walk in as everyone shouted, "Surprise!"

"Aw, gee! You shouldn't have!" She smiled and her eyes widened in awe. "Way cool," she said, looking from the left to the right. She knew she'd needed to be here.

Loren opened the letter and read it aloud.

"Dear Team,
You're embarking on a journey so powerful it'll either divide or bind your group as friends forever.

Each must answer the following questions: How much do I love my friends, God, and myself? Do I love my friends enough to endure hours of them challenging my beliefs? Do I love myself enough to keep an open mind in learning truths even if it goes against what I've been taught? Do I trust God enough to ask him to show me what I need to learn and accept it? Am I brave enough to pray in my mind, and out loud?"

The Library Room

If you don't think you can, no one will think less of you if you excuse yourself from this project.

Loren, give them time to think about the questions I wrote before continuing with the rest of my letter."

She put the letter down and gave everyone a few moments to digest what was written and then asked, "Everyone in?" Everyone nodded their head.

Loren continued reading.

"If anyone left, judge them not. They leave knowing they've been honest and are fearful.

It's no accident you were born. It's no accident you're here and God had me choose Loren for this project this year. It's no accident you're friends. Nothing's ever an accident. God planned it all. Life's a test, and I pray everyone passes.

Loren, when you're strangling the table sides, look up to God, and ask him for directions instead of trying to guess his wants.

Each time you work on this project, whether alone or in a group, please bow your head and pray this prayer:

Lord, I come to you in your special place to seek your wisdom, to learn your word, your works, and your future plans for me. Guide my lips as I speak what you need me to say, guard my mind as I discover disturbing things in your word I wasn't prepared to read. Encourage my heart to seek you fully. Thank you for calling me to know you better. Thank you for wanting to know me. Amen.

My prayers are with you as your journey progresses. God bless and may you pass the test by proving the truth.

Yours Truly,
Professor Jeffery Finkel"

Everyone stared at the table.

"Think it's too early to strangle the table?" Loren squeezed the table edge in jest.

The ceiling folded like an accordion from the center until the sky appeared with all the stars shining down.

"Whoa!" whispered Collin.

Seven

Collin turned off the lights so the stars would be clearer. Then he used his phone as a flashlight to navigate to a bean bag chair before slipping it into his pocket.

Loren fished her phone out of her purse and used its light to read the prayer. "Lord, we come to you in your special place to seek your wisdom, to learn your word, your works, and your future plans for us. Guide our lips as we speak what you need us to say, guard our minds as we discover disturbing things in your word we weren't prepared to read. Encourage our hearts to seek you fully. Thank you for calling us to know you better. Thank you for wanting to know us. Amen."

They all said "amen" together.

Drew felt naked, praying without his yarmulke. He decided he'd bring one tomorrow since he assumed group prayers would be ongoing.

Collin turned the lights back on in the room. Everyone felt comforted, peaceful, and hungry.

Rachel ordered two large pizzas for delivery. She and Sarah would use the money they'd finagled out of Drew.

The group evolved from two teams competing into one team scrubbing the verses on the cell sheet. If anyone didn't understand the prophetic scripture, they'd write the verse down and leave the note column blank.

Occasionally, everyone argued over the relevance of a verse. However, in the end, everyone agreed to keep it or discard it.

Very few scriptures seemed to be obvious. Most scriptures required reading a few chapters to gain a better sense of what was going on at the time or who was speaking to whom and why. Seven minds pieced information together like a puzzle.

Rachel's phone jingled, letting her know the pizza arrived. She and Sarah excused themselves to retrieve it.

When Sarah bowed her head, Collin asked if she'd mind sharing her prayer with everyone. In most cases, it was all she could do to muster up the courage to close her eyes and concentrate on thanking God in public. This was even scarier to her, praying *out loud* with her peers.

"Certainly, if it's all right with everyone," she said. She bowed her head and prayed, "Thank you, Father, for this meal we're about to receive. Help it to nourish our bodies and minds. Thank you for the friends you've placed in my life. Amen." They all raised their heads and smiled at each other. It felt like being at home with family.

Hours passed as each got up, stretched, and digested what they'd just eaten or read. It stayed quiet unless a verse required a group discussion.

Loren's phone startled everyone. She saw it was Giles, and it was already *eleven* o'clock! They'd worked for hours without noticing the time again.

She called him back from the main library area. She didn't want to talk to him while she was in the room.

Giles answered on the first ring. "There you are!" He sounded excited to hear her voice.

"Hey there! Are you still working?" Loren was hopeful and did her best not to sound that way.

"No, I'm at the apartment. I thought I'd surprise you by swinging by the library to help work on the project you and your friends seemed obsessed about last night. Not so much tonight though, right? Where are you? Did you find a fun party? I'll meet you if you're not ready to come home yet." He was prying and spying. She felt it.

"Actually, we're in a private room working on the project." Loren said, hoping he didn't want to come.

"Really? I've never heard of such a place in that library. I thought I knew it pretty well since I've taken about every different type of course to keep my student status. Where's this room, and how did you find out about it?" He sounded irritated. Loren sensed a pouting fit about to erupt.

Loren clarified, "There's a special room hidden in the library that's been designed for this project with—"

Giles cut her off. "Wait a minute! They've built a hidden room exclusively for this project? You make it sound like you're a secret agent! Why can't the research be done in the open? There are men and women in the room together for hours?"

"Are you accusing *me* of doing something wrong or the school?" Loren tried sidestepping the issue. He was now in pout mode.

"Loren, what *are* you up to? You haven't invited me to see your private room. You didn't answer your phone when I called you. Therefore, you must've stepped out and called me back so no one would know it was me calling!" he shouted.

"Oh no! They all know it's you. Yes, I did step out of the room before returning your call. No, I haven't invited you to help. I don't want you to feel uncomfortable and you make everyone else miserable when the topic's mentioned." Then she thought, *There I said it! Where'd that come from?*

She continued while he was still silent, "We're working hard on this project, and I'm grateful for the privacy of the room. Sometimes, the research brings us to conversations that may offend people around us. God forbid, we offend one of your types who think nothing of offending everyone else!"

"Whoa! Slow down there! What in the Sam Hill are you talking about!?" he shouted.

"I'm talking about God! Okay? It's a project concerning God, his people, Jesus, Jewish people!" She shouted it almost as loud as he'd shouted. Then she thought, *Wait for it. It's coming. The explosion's about to happen...Nothing? Not a word from him?*

She could hear him breathing. He was mad beyond speech.

"Listen," Loren said, calmly this time. "I shouldn't have yelled at you. I felt like I was being attacked for doing nothing wrong. I need to get back. I'm not sure how much longer we'll be working. I didn't realize the time until you called."

"Yes, you should go back and work all through the night. It's a twenty-four-hour library with a special room. I'm going to bed. Don't call back to apologize. I'm turning my phone off. Call me when you're ready to come home in the morning, and we'll discuss where that might be." He'd hung up on her.

She replayed everything in her mind. *Could I've presented it better? Should he feel hurt over being left out?*

She was irate at him telling her not to come home. *What am I supposed to do for clothes? And who does he think he is claiming the apartment!*

The more she thought about his reaction, the madder she became. *I won't go home tonight. Tonight it'll be me and God under his heavens.* She pictured herself on the beanbag chairs sleeping beneath the sky dome.

They all turned to see her walk in and resumed their note taking. She hurried over to her chair without making eye contact.

"Did you tell him?" Sarah asked for everyone.

"Yep," Loren replied, letting out a deep breath.

"He didn't take it too well?" Sarah persisted.

"It may have been the delivery on my part. But no, he didn't take it well," Loren admitted.

"Is he on his way?" Collin asked. He wasn't sure he wanted to know the answer except he wanted to be prepared.

"No, I pretty much told him he wasn't invited. Part of that delivery thing I messed up." Loren saw everyone's face relax.

"He's cool with you staying to work on the project?" Rachel added her question too.

"Um...Well, the way the call ended," Loren felt her face redden. She wasn't sure if it was from anger or from embarrassment. "He's acceptable with me spending the night here working on my project." She'd hoped everyone would drop it.

"Acceptable?" Amy repeated. "Does he expect you to sleep here if everyone goes home for the night?"

"Yes." Loren exhaled. "He's crossed the line, and I...I can't remember a time when I've been madder. I need time to digest it all." *There, that should shut them up.*

"We'll help him move out," Collin offered, and everyone shot him the don't-go-there look. "Just saying—"

"Thanks, Collin. I think all relationships go through rough patches. I'm sure we'll work it out. I explained why I didn't want to tell him. I hurt his feelings by making him feel left out, my bad. He must overcome his rudeness when anyone mentions God or Jesus."

"Why do you think he hates God?" Sarah wondered out loud. "I wonder what church offended him?"

"Actually, no church. His parents never took him to church," Loren explained. "They told him he could make his own decisions about God. My theory is since he's never attended church he's never felt God. Can you imagine growing up in a world listening to people talk about God and how God was there to help them? He'd never been taught about God or how to talk to God. And yet, he didn't turn into a psycho killer, he does well in school, he's smart, he's a gourmet chef, and he can be charming." Loren defended him.

"I think there's more to the story," Drew argued. "You can't go through life without learning about God. No matter how hard they try to keep it out of schools, people talk. As long as people talk, they're going to converse about God or religion. I'll bet his parents fought his school about having rights not to believe in God. By doing so, they programmed him into not believing in God. Based on the protests he's demonstrated, I pictured him being raised that way. It's all about them. To hell with everyone else's beliefs or rights to discuss or pray. Self-absorbed people hate God because they can't stand the idea that there may be a better opinion than their own."

"Drew has a point," Rachel agreed. "Giles always has to be right, and everything's about Giles. I feel it's time to address your relationship, which, I feel, isn't healthy. As a friend, I'm telling you he frightens me with the way he manipulates and bullies you. Like this project, Loren, for the past year, you've been anti-religion and nearly anti-God. Yet when you walked into this room, we saw a believer in God and not only God but your religion too."

"So what are we doing tonight?" Sarah asked. "Work on the project without stopping? Do you want us to stay with you? Do you want to be alone? You're welcome to spend the night at my place. Do you want us to stay and work on the project some more until we get tired and go as we please? Give us directions and nothing you say will be wrong."

"I'm not sure. I'll say stay until you're tired," Loren said. "Rachel, you're right. I don't know me anymore or what I believe." Loren then changed the subject. "Where are we with the research?"

Collin answered from his laptop. "Right now, I think we've all the relevant prophesies telling about the coming of the Messiah—where he'll be born, when he'll be born, and to what family line. That's the Tanakh side of it. Now, we'll see if it matches up to the New Testament or, as I've learned tonight through research, it should be called the New Covenant."

Drew interjected, "I can tell you right now it won't. There's no way he can be of the line of David if he isn't Joseph's son; and he's not. Mary was pregnant before she married him."

"Drew," Collin explained, "I understand what you're saying. However, it also says he must be born from a virgin. How could any Messiah fit both? And Luke proves Mary's from the line of David too."

"And I told you," Drew said, displaying his future lawyer skills, "we Jewish people don't count that since it's not the paternal line. All bloodlines are from the men, not the women. So it needs to be Joseph's if you're arguing with me being Hebrew."

Collin wasn't giving up. It was the truth to him, and he couldn't see why Drew didn't want to admit it. "Then you *must* admit if you only count the father's bloodline, the Messiah needs to be *adopted* into the father's bloodline since the Messiah will be God's seed since the mother's a virgin, right?"

"Collin, I'm not convinced," Drew argued. "There are more qualifications according to prophecy we've unearthed today. Don't dance the victory dance. I don't need to be right all the time. However, I feel I am on this one. So let's agree to disagree for now."

"You're right. I may be biased based on my upbringing like you may be biased based upon yours," Collin said, relenting.

"Sorry, Collin," Drew offered. "I get defensive. I mean, I feel for Giles on this one. You're taught one thing at home and then hear Christmas carols from November to January. It makes me grumpy every year to the point where I can barely enjoy Hanukah."

Loren sympathized. "I never quite thought about it. I'm sick of the same songs every year and the commercialism. When you add your perspective it changes the way I see it even more."

"And when was the last time you were able to enjoy a Hanukah Special at the White House?" Rachel added.

This was the perfect room to talk about such topics—no criticizing, just this-is-how-it's-affected-me-over-the-years discussion.

Amy added, "So many religions and so many different beliefs as to what's right or wrong, it's confusing seeing some things are tolerable for one religion but forbidden in others."

"True, Amy," Rachel agreed. "However, one thing you'll find consistent in every religion is a woman will never have more than one husband at a time. Do you know why?"

"Good point." Amy pondered awhile. "There are religions allowing men multiple wives but none that I'm aware of allowing women multiple husbands. I've never thought about it before. Why?"

"Because, no woman could pick up after, clean up after, and cater to so many egos at the same time!" Rachel laughed.

The girls laughed. Collin and Drew scowled since both were neat and kept their egos in check.

"Nice, that's an old one by the way," Drew commented.

"Apparently, it's not old enough if Amy's never heard it." Rachel's father would be proud.

The boys left first. They had football practice in the morning. The girls stayed behind in case Loren needed girl talk; however, after a half hour, they sensed she needed alone time with God.

Loren sat alone with her God as she understood him. He was different than the one she'd toyed with over the past year.

She arranged the beanbag chairs next to each other to form a bed. She was exhausted mentally, spiritually, and physically. She flipped the light switch and made the room black except for her lit phone, then blackness and sparkling stars.

"Good night, Lord. Help me." She fell fast asleep.

Eight

Loren's Notes Part II—Birth of Yeshua

While investigating verses on the spreadsheet, we divided them into sections. The verses in this section concern the birth of the Messiah.

The first verse we investigated was Tanakh, Nevi'im, Isaiah 7:13–14 NIV: Then Isaiah said, "Hear now, you house of David! It's not enough to try the patience of men? You'll try the patience of God also? Therefore the Lord Himself will give you a sign: The virgin will be with child and will give birth to a son, and will call him Immanuel."

Amy explained the background of the prophecy. "Ahaz was King David's eleventh great-grandson. God through Isaiah told Ahaz not to worry about the plans of Aram, Ephraim, and Remaliah's son, devising plans to invade Judah and dividing it. It won't take place '*unless*, you don't stand firm in your faith.' Then God, used Isaiah to test Ahaz's faith, by instructing Ahaz to 'ask the Lord for a sign.'"

God was checking Ahaz's faith and wanted to assure him with a message. But Ahaz wouldn't ask! Why? He didn't want to risk losing Assyria's protection by offending them with his beliefs. He said, "I don't want to put the Lord to the test."

So much for "stand firm in your faith." Epic fail!

Drew feels this was prophesied seven hundred years before Yeshua showed up on the scene; it wasn't about him.

Sarah argued that the prophecy doesn't specify when the child would be born only that it'll happen and no other child had been born a virgin so it wasn't a "recycled prophecy" as you'd consider it.

Jessica pointed out two things: the child will be born of a virgin, almah, and will be called Immanuel, God with us.

Amy: New Testament, Matthew 1:18 KJV: Now the birth of Jesus Christ was on this wise: When as his mother Mary was espoused to Joseph, before they came together, she was found with child of the Holy Ghost.

Sara read New Testament, Matthew 1:20–25 NIV: Joseph saw an angel of the Lord in a dream saying, "Joseph, son of David, don't be afraid to take Mary as your wife. What's conceived in her is from the Holy Spirit. She'll give birth to a Son. You're to name Him Jesus. He'll save His people from their sins." All this took place to fulfill what the Lord had said through Isaiah: "The virgin [parthenos] will be with child and will give birth to a son, and they'll call Him Immanuel," meaning "God with us." Joseph took Mary home as his wife. But he had no union with her until she gave birth to a son whom he named Jesus.

Rachel questions if Isaiah means a virgin or a young woman who's never been married? she'd heard speakers criticize the virgin conception and birth Isaiah prophesied. They said it's not only impossible, but it's not what Isaiah meant.

Amy said, "Not possible? God's capable of anything! He granted Abraham at age one hundred and his wife, Sarah, in her nineties with their first child. He opened Rachel's closed womb after being barren for over thirty years. There are many miracle births in the Tanakh!"

In questioning the word *maiden* or *almah* [singular] or *almot* [plural] in the Tanakh/Old Testament and how we use the word *almah* we found it's only been used to describe young ladies who are virgins and have never been married, although the specific term for virgin is *bethulah*. There are seven occurrences in the Bible using the word maiden or almah, per Strong's coding, H5959: Genesis 24:43; Exodus 2:8; Psalms 68:25; Proverbs 30:19; Song of Solomn 1:3; Song of Solomn 6.8; Isaiah 7:14.

The first example indicated above: Tanakh, Torah, Chayei Sarah, Genesis 24:43 JPS: Behold, I stand by the fountain of water; and let it come to pass, that the maiden [almah] that cometh forth to draw, to whom I shall say, "Give me, I pray thee, a little water from thy pitcher to drink."

Abraham sent his servant out to find a wife for his son Isaac. Rebecca was a virgin, a bethulah. Almah perfectly described her.

The next example as indicated above: Tanakh, Torah, Shemot, Exodus 2:8 JPS: And Pharaoh's daughter said to her, "Go." And the *maiden* [almah] went and called the child's mother.

Baby Moses's mother placed him in a basket to float near Pharaoh's daughter and her maidens. One the Pharaoh's daughter's maidens [almah], Moses's sister, brought him to the Pharaoh's daughter. Moses's sister was a young lady who was a virgin and once again vindicates the use of the word throughout the Tanakh or Bible.

Collin read through the rest of the listed verses and we determined nowhere in the Tanakh or Bible does it use the word *almah*, maiden, or the young lady, as anything different; always a young unmarried virgin. Therefore, the New Testament describing Mary as being a maiden carrying Yeshua was to reinforce she was indeed a virgin. Besides, she declared her virginity to the angel as described and written by the apostle Luke. New Testament, Luke 1:34–35 NIV: "How'll this be," Mary asked the angel, "since I'm a virgin?" Other translations interpret "since I know no man."

Rachel argued some scholars feel the translation of the word *almah* was erroneously translated from Hebrew to English and could mean young woman regardless of virginity or not."

After heated discussions over a virgin giving birth without the use of artificial insemination, which, they didn't do back then, we finally concluded: There are several instances where God opened closed wombs. God's all-powerful. There's nothing God cannot do if he wants it done, even opening wombs of ninety year old women, women who proved to be barren, or impregnating a virgin. Therefore, *impossible* used as an argument of Jesus being born of a virgin holds no ground.

Look at where Messiah will be born. Tanakh, Nevi'im, Micah 5:1 JPS: And you, O Bethlehem of Ephrath, least among the clans of Judah, from you One shall come forth to rule Israel for Me— One whose origin is from of old, from ancient times.

The Mashiach will be born in Bethlehem.

Amy found verses supporting the timing and what'll happen at the Messiah's birth. Tanakh, Nevi'im, Isaiah 60:1–3 JPS: "Arise, shine, for Your light's dawned; The Presence of the Lord has shown upon You! Behold! Darkness shall cover the earth and thick clouds the peoples; but, upon You the Lord will shine and His Presence be seen over You. And nations shall walk by Your light, Kings by Your shining radiance." And Tanakh, Ketuvim, Psalms 72:10 JPS: "Let kings of Tarshish and the islands pay tribute, king of Sheba and Seba offer gifts. Let all kings bow to Him, and all nations serve Him."

Drew asked how she figures those two verses support anything?

Amy answered, "The first tells about the kings and wise men bringing gifts to Jesus. The Second tells how they'll find him by following the Star in the sky."

Collin read Tanakh, Nevi'im, Jeremiah 23: 5–6 ESV: "Behold, the days are coming," declares the Lord, "when I will raise up for David a righteous Branch, and he shall reign as king and deal wisely, and shall execute justice and righteousness in the land. In his days Judah will be saved, and Israel will dwell securely. And this is the name by which he will be called: 'The Lord is our righteousness.'"

Rachel asked, "And how do you explain this one?"

Collin's answer was, "Have you ever read or listened to the events concerning Jesus's birth? It'll make more sense once you do."

Collin then summarized New Testament, Luke 2:1–7 KJV: Caesar Augustus issued a decree that a census [the first census that took place while Quirinius was governor of Syria] should be taken of the entire Roman world. Everyone was mandated to his own town to register.

Joseph, from Nazareth, in Galilee went to Judea, to Bethlehem the town of David, because he belonged to the house and line of David. He went there to register with Mary, who was pledged to be married to him and was expecting a child. While they were there, she gave birth to her firstborn, a son. She wrapped him in cloths and placed Him in a manger, because there was no room for them in the inn.

Sarah summarized New Testament, Matthew 2:1–8 KJV: After Jesus was born in Bethlehem, Magi from the east came to Jerusalem and asked King Herod, "Where's the one who's been born King of the Jews? We saw His star in the east and come to worship him."

King Herod and all of Jerusalem were disturbed when they'd heard. He gathered all the people's chief priests and rabbis. He asked them where the Christ was to be born. "In Bethlehem, in Judea," they'd replied. That's what Micah 5:2 says, "But you, Bethlehem, in the land of Judah, are by no means least among the rulers of Judah; for out of you will come a ruler who'll be the shepherd of my people Israel."

Then Herod called the Magi and found out from them the exact time the star had appeared. He sent them to Bethlehem and said, "Go and make a careful search for the child. As soon as you find Him, report to me, so that I too may go and worship Him.'"

Collin summarized New Testament, Luke 2:8–39 KJV: Shepherds were watching over their flocks in a field when an angel of the Lord appeared to them. It terrified them. But the angel said, "Don't be afraid. I bring you good news for all the people. Today, in the town of David, a Savior has been born to you. He's Christ the Lord. Here's your sign: You'll find a baby wrapped in cloths and lying in a manger."

The shepherds said to one another, "Let's go to Bethlehem and see this thing that's happened."

They found Mary, and Joseph, with a baby lying in a manger. After seeing him, they went out sharing what had been told them about this child, and all who heard it were amazed.

On the eighth day, they circumcised him and named him Jesus [Yeshua], the name the angel declared before he'd been conceived.

Joseph and Mary then took him to Jerusalem to present him to the Lord [as it's written in the Law of the Lord, "Every firstborn male's to be consecrated to the Lord"] and to offer a sacrifice."

Simeon had been waiting for the consolation of Israel, and the Holy Spirit was upon him. It'd been revealed to him by the Holy Spirit that he wouldn't die before seeing the Lord's Christ. Moved by the Spirit, he went into the temple courts. When the parents brought in Jesus, Simeon took him in his arms and praised God saying, "Sovereign Lord, as You've promised, You now dismiss Your servant in peace. For my eyes have seen Your salvation, which You've prepared in the sight of all people, a light for revelation to the Gentiles and for glory to Your people Israel." Then Simeon blessed them and said to Mary, "This child's destined to cause the falling and rising of many in Israel, and to be a sign that'll be spoken against, so the thoughts of many hearts will be revealed. And a sword will pierce your own soul too."

There was also a prophetess, Anna. She was eighty-four and never left the temple. She worshiped night and day, fasting and praying. She came to them giving thanks to God and spoke about the child to all who were looking forward to the redemption of Jerusalem.

Then they returned to their town of Nazareth. And the child grew and became strong; He was filled with wisdom, and the grace of God was upon Him.

Sarah summarized New Testament, Matthew 2:9-12 KJV: After the Magi who King Herod had spoken to had heard about the king, they went on their way, and the star they'd seen in the east went ahead of them until it stopped over Jesus's home. They were overjoyed. Inside, they saw the child with His mother Mary, and they bowed down and worshiped Him. Then they opened their treasures and presented Him with gifts of gold and of incense and of myrrh. And having been warned in a dream not to go back to Herod, they returned to their country by another route.

Rachel still doesn't get it. "He's technically not from Joseph's seed so how can this fulfill prophecy?"

Amy explained it this way, "If he were from Joseph's seed how could he be born of a virgin *and* be called Immanuel. God with us? Look, Tanakh, Nevi'im, Isaiah 4:2 NJB: 'That day, Yahweh's [God's] seedling will turn to beauty and glory. What the earth brings forth will turn to the pride and ornament of Israel's survivors.' Human thinking has gotten us into trouble! We doubt God's abilities or second guess what He says."

Jessica added, "Tanakh, Nevi'im, Isaiah 4:2 KJV: —Yahweh's seedling. Along with Tanakh, Nevi'im, Isaiah 7:14 KJV: — the virgin will give birth to a child called Immanuel. And Tanakh, Nevi'im, Jeremiah 23:5-6 KJV: The Lord will raise "the Vindicator" from the true branch of David. Those three verses tell us, yes, a virgin will give birth to the Mashiach, and he'll be adopted by a direct descendant of David, that's Joseph, and he'll be God's own seed as well as God with us.

Sarah told us Malachi wrote about four hundred years earlier the Messiah would indeed be God, himself, born in human form, meaning incarnate. And, he tells us there'll be a messenger announcing Mashiach's existence right before He's to publicly proclaim Himself as the Messiah. Then she recapped Tanakh,

Nevi'im, Malachi 3:1–5 NIV: "I'll send my messenger, who'll prepare the way before. Then suddenly the Lord you're seeking will come." I'll come near to you for judgment. I'll be quick to testify against sorcerers, adulterers, and perjurers, against those who defraud laborers of their wages, who oppress the widows and the fatherless, and deprive the aliens of justice, and those who don't fear me,' says the Lord Almighty.

So we should include John the Baptizer [Yochanan ben Zechariah] in the report and how he too was prophesied as being an important role to the Messiah?"

Collin feels it's important in substantiating what happened and how it happened according to prophecies.

Not the answer I really wanted to hear.

Sarah jumped in with Tanakh, Nevi'im, Malachi 4:5 NJB: "Look, I shall send you the prophet Elijah before the great and awesome Day of Yahweh comes."

Jessica: Here's another one. Tanakh, Nevi'im, Isaiah 40:3 KJV: The voice of him that crieth in the wilderness, Prepare ye the way of the Lord, make straight in the desert a highway for our God.

Collin shared the story of John the Baptizer [Yochanan ben Zechariah]. He was prophesied prior to his birth; as well as, Yeshua's birth. Zechariah was a priest married to Elizabeth. Both were old and Elizabeth was barren. An angel of the Lord appeared to Zechariah and told him Elizabeth would bear him a son called John. New Testament, Luke 1:14-25 NIV:…he'll be great in the sight of the Lord; he must drink no wine, no strong drink. Even from his mother's womb he'll be filled with the Holy Spirit, and he'll bring back many Israelites to the Lord their God. With the spirit and power of Elijah, he'll go before Him to reconcile fathers to their children and the disobedient to the good sense of the upright, preparing for the Lord a people fit for Him. Zechariah asked the angel, "How can this be? My wife and I are very old." The angel replied, "I'm Gabriel, who stands in God's presence, and I've been sent to speak to you and bring you this good news. Look! Since you didn't believe my words, which will come true at their appointed time, you'll be silenced and unable to speak until this has happened." Meanwhile, the people waiting for Zechariah were surprised that he'd stayed in the sanctuary so long. When he came out he couldn't speak to them, and they realized that he'd seen a vision in the sanctuary. But he could only make signs to them and remained silent. When his time of service came to an end he returned home. Later his wife, Elizabeth, conceived and for five months kept to herself, saying, "The Lord has done this for me, now that it's pleased him to take away the humiliation I suffered in public."

Jessica summarized New Testament, Luke 1:36–45 NJB: "Then Gabriel, the angel, told Mary she'll be with child from the Holy Spirit and her cousin, Elizabeth, whom the people called barren was already six months pregnant for nothing's impossible to God."

Mary said, "You see before you the Lord's servant, let it happen to me as you've said." And the angel left her. Mary went as fast as she could to a town in Judah. She went into Zechariah's house and greeted Elizabeth. As soon as Elizabeth heard Mary's greeting, the child leapt in her womb and Elizabeth was filled with the Holy Spirit. She gave a loud cry and said, "Of all women you're the most blessed, and blessed is the fruit of your womb. Why should I be honored with a visit from the mother of our Lord? Look, the moment your greeting reached my ears, the child in my womb leapt for joy. Yes, blessed is she who believed that the promise made her by the Lord would be fulfilled."

Elizabeth gave birth to a son, and all the neighbors and relatives came to celebrate. On the eighth day they circumcised him. Since Zechariah couldn't speak, they asked Elizabeth to name the child. She'd announced, "John." Everyone questioned that name since no one in her family had ever been called John [Yochanan]. They asked Zechariah. He wrote, "His name is John [Yochanan]."

Then Zechariah regained his speech and prophesied. New Testament, Luke 1:76–79 NIV: "And you, little child, you'll be called Prophet of the Most High, for you'll go before the Lord to prepare a way for Him, to give His people knowledge of salvation through the forgiveness of their sins, because of the faithful love of our God in which the rising Sun has come from on high to visit us, to give light to those who live in darkness and the shadow dark as death, and to guide our feet into the way of peace."

Nine

Collin and Drew were too tired for conversation as they walked home across campus. Their minds were digesting the information everyone'd puzzled together as well as information they'd stumbled upon doing Internet searches. Once home, they continued their silence by giving each other a fist bump to say good night.

Without turning on the light, Drew found his bed, climbed in, and groped the night stand for his yarmulke. He placed it on his head and recited his bedtime prayer of protection, "In the name of Adonai, the God of Israel, may the angel Michael be at my right, and the angel Gabriel be at my left; and in front of me the angel Uriel, and behind me the angel Raphael and…above…my…head…[1]"

Before he finished the prayer he fell asleep.

He woke up leaning on the counter in a candle shop. There were no customers. Drew wondered, *How long did I nap? I need to see father!* He walked out the door.

He noticed a crowd in the street looking at a stage. He paid little attention to it as he walked to his father's shop.

The tan-colored trousers showed off his athletic legs and were complemented by plain white knee stockings. A linen shirt with a high collar skimming his sideburns was worn under his maroon colored overcoat. It was cutaway in the front with a long tail in the back, a common French style for 1794. The overcoat was plain without décor for fear of appearing to look like the hated French aristocrats.

The crowd grew louder. It made him walk faster. He needed to find his father. Something was urgent.

Inside a shop, he found his nervous father with a rag stick wiping the floor. His gray linen trousers were tailored to fit to mid-calf while his high boots brushed the bottoms of his knee. His black overcoat and white shirt underneath indicated a recent weight loss. Beads of sweat formed on his temples running into his tight ponytail. The mid-July temperature was taking a toll on everyone's fashion today.

The shop was larger than Drew's candle shop. Bolts of fabrics were stacked on tables according to colors. A long cutting counter was in front of the more expensive materials kept in a cedar wall unit.

As soon as Drew's father saw him, he rushed over and whispered, "They did it. They convicted and guillotined Jassé Carcassonne as a federalist! We must leave. We'll be next. They're suspecting everyone now."

"Who? What?" Drew whispered back.

"We must leave Orange now!" his father insisted.

"Who was killed? Why?" Drew questioned.

"Come, child, we must go! Your mother waits! We leave now while they're preoccupied with the nuns!"

"Father! Wait!" Drew yelled while following him.

Drew entered the street. He looked at the nuns standing on the stage singing with smiles. He thought people were watching a musical. On the end of the stage was a tall guillotine. The sun's reflection off of the blade brought his attention to a nun lying at the bottom. But it wasn't any nun. It was his friend, Jessica!

He was torn. Help his parents or save Jessica?

Then he felt everyone questioning his loyalties.

He had to save all three! His heart raced. Perspiration gathered beneath the overcoat. His collar tightened around his neck. He couldn't breathe. The alarm in the background annoyed him. He had to think fast about what to do next. The alarm kept sounding. He had to get his panic attack under control so he could move. He was frozen in place.

His father was calling him to get up.

"Dude, wake up!" someone shouted at the back of his mind. He sat up in bed and looked at the posters and clock on his bedroom wall. Adam stood in the doorway telling him the alarm had been sounding for over fifteen minutes. Drew gasped and was covered in sweat.

"Dude, you okay? You look like you're about to hurl everything you drank last night. Rough night, huh?"

"No, I didn't go out drinking last night. It's Saturday, right?" Drew asked to no one there recovering from his nightmare. *Whew! It was a nightmare. Just a bad dream.*

When he couldn't find his yarmulke on the nightstand, he touched the top of his head and felt the moist fabric. He realized he'd fallen asleep in the middle of praying last night.

"I give thanks before you, living and eternal king. You've returned within me my soul with compassion. Abundant is your faithfulness![1]" Drew recited his prayer with extra enthusiasm while in the back of his mind giving thanks for what he'd dreamt wasn't real.

As he climbed out of bed he grumbled at God, "And what was that all about? Are you trying to give me a heart attack in my sleep?"

<hr />

Collin was relieved Ray and Adam were in bed for the night. He wasn't in the mood to explain where they'd been all night and why.

Once Collin heard Drew's bedroom floor creak, he knew it was safe to raid the refrigerator in peace. He needed alone time with God—all to himself while feeding his appetite.

The light from the refrigerator glared brighter than he wanted so he quickly grabbed bologna, milk, and mustard. Once the door to the refrigerator was closed, the room went black. He felt for the bread next to the microwave. Using his phone as a light, he made himself a sandwich.

When he'd finished his sandwich and milk, he set his alarm on his phone so he wouldn't be late for morning football practice. He placed a twenty-dollar bill on the counter to cover the costs of the bologna, bread, milk, and gas to buy more.

Man, that snack hit the spot, God. Thank You for that by the way, he prayed as an afterthought.

As he walked to his bedroom, he stretched his shoulders to relax the stiff muscles from studying all day. "Thank you, God, for a great day with my friends," he whispered.

How does the ending of that prayer go? Thank you for calling me to know you better. Thank you for wanting to know me. Amen.

Drew stood over Collin, shaking him awake. He looked different somehow. *Does he have a swollen lip and a black eye? What did he do, fall down the steps?*

Collin sat up in his cot and took in his surroundings. There was no furniture in the cool dark room, and the wooden shutters in his window had been drawn closed. His feet grew cold as soon as they touched the concrete floor. There was a smell of beer in the air...hops and malts.

Drew wore a dirtied knee-length tunic synched at the waist by a leather belt. It showed bloody skin beneath the tears in the sleeves from a struggle. His long hair spilled out over the hooded shoulder cape. The knees of his tights and his leather shoes were stained with mud.

"They killed her. They burned Rachel. Now, they want to kill me. They think we poisoned the water. I tried to save her. I tried, but I couldn't get to her in time. They told me if I confessed they'd let her live, but they lied. They *killed* her. They killed my Rachel." Drew was crying and talking in circles. "I escaped. I

The Library Room

don't know how, but I broke free. I ran so fast I couldn't see where I was going. I knew I had to make it to your monastery. Please tell them I'm innocent. I've lost my whole family from burnings or the Great Pestilence. Rachel was all I had left. Make them stop, please help me. I didn't do it. They made me say it. They told me they wouldn't hurt her, but they did. Make them stop." Tears formed grey streaks on his face as they mixed with the grime.

Collin heard yelling outside. He cracked the shutters enough to look outside and caught a breath of chilled Munich air. He saw men carrying torches in the forest and heard them yelling back and forth to each other. They were getting closer. They were looking for Drew.

Drew slumped in the corner and shook. His left arm was being held by his right hand. No mistaking. It'd been snapped between the elbow and wrist. Collin had to get him to the secret room in the brewery.

"Are you affected?" Collin tried, standing him up.

"I don't have the Great Mortality. Rachel's clean too," Drew answered before passing out.

Collin's chest tightened watching his friend suffer, and he envisioned flames engulfing Rachel while Drew watched. It was as if he'd watched them suffer from above, the squirming, the cries, the stillness, and then the flames. The Bull from Pope Clement VI was re-read daily in the public squares where people gathered for the latest news; but, the burnings continued.

Collin lifted his friend onto his shoulder. Drew deliriously fought him, thinking he was being taken by the mob. The thrashing caused Collin to stumble. He lost his grip and tried again while coaxing Drew to trust him.

Collin whispered "You must get to the secret room. If they find you, they'll burn down the monastery after accusing me, a monk, of being a coconspirator in the poisonings! They'll burn us both at the stake. I must get you to the room!"

Collin had heard some of Drew's family had died from the black lumps and coughing up blood. His healthy relatives were questioned and beaten until one member confessed to contaminating the wells and water streams with poisons. One by one, Drew had lost loved ones. *How's he escaped persecution?* Collin wondered as Drew moaned.

The noise from the vigilantes grew louder. Collin couldn't control Drew's delirious thrashings. They were coming to kill him. The noise from the vigilantes kept growing louder and louder.

Collin's phone alarm woke him. He was back in his room, breathing hard from trying to lift...what...the balled up bed linens and blankets?

The dream left him feeling vulnerable. His chest ached from the emotions of seeing a friend burned at the stake while the other cried.

Jessica and Sarah decided to walk Rachel home first and then go to Amy's. They said they didn't mind since they'd been sitting all day and needed the exercise. Besides, it was safest for everyone this way.

The night air was crisp and the sound of their heels echoed through the streets as they walked two by two to Rachel's house.

"Rachel, I thought you were going home for your parents' anniversary?" Amy asked.

"Oh! I forgot to tell everyone! My parents are on their way to Israel," Rachel informed them.

"Wow!" Amy said. "That's awesome! Good for them! And good for us since you're able to spend time working on the project. You're good, by the way. You know your Tanakh. We'd learned the stories in Sunday school growing up. Unfortunately, it seems once you hit a certain age they focus on the New Testament. I needed a reminder of how it started and how it's the foundation of our beliefs."

The Library Room

"Well, if you come to my synagogue, it'd be all you'll need to know as it covers the past, the present, and future," Rachel said while grabbing Amy's arm in an affectionate hug.

"Ah, but there's more to the future as predicted by the prophets; you'll see." Amy rested her head on Rachel's shoulder returning a plug as they reached Rachel's walkway.

"Good night, everyone. I love you very much as friends. You know that don't you?" Rachel asked.

"Yes, of course we do, Rachel. We love you very much too," Jessica answered as they all exchanged hugs.

"Same place tomorrow morning when we get there?" Rachel confirmed. "I'm going to try to get there early. I'm worried about Loren. I don't trust Giles. I doubt he'd do anything to her. However, I don't have a good feeling about him. I try not to talk about people behind their backs, but you're *mishpocheh*. We must keep an eye out for Ms. Loren." When she saw their blank looks, she added. "*Mishpocheh* means family. Oy vey! I need to Yiddish you goyim up!"

"Yep," Sarah agreed. "I agree with y'all on this one about Giles. I'll get there early too. I think I'm the same size as her and she'll need fresh clothes."

"Sarah, that's very thoughtful," Jessica said.

Everyone grew quiet again as Rachel walked to her door. Once she was inside, the smaller group continued onward.

Ah, home at last, Rachel thought as she slid her shoes off at the door. *And time for bed.*

Within minutes she climbed in between the sheets and snuggled into the luxury of a down mattress cover and comforter. She recited the Hashkivenu she prayed every night.

"Lay us down, Adonai our God, in peace, and raise us up again, our ruler, in life. Spread over us your Sukkah of peace, direct us with your good counsel, and save us for your own namesake. Shield us. Remove from us every enemy, pestilence, sword, famine, and sorrow. Remove all adversaries from before us and from behind us, and shelter us in the shadow of your wings. For you're our guarding and saving God, yes, a gracious and compassionate God and King. Guard our going out and our coming in for life and peace, now and always…[1]"

Rachel's mother woke her up with taps on her arm and hurried words she didn't comprehend. The quilts on the bed as well as the multi-layers in her night gown prevented the coldness from chilling her skin. She cast her mother a pleading look. Her mother shot her the eyin harah as she left the room to let her know it was time to get up!

A hand cupped her mouth closed keeping her from screaming. Sitting on top of Rachel was a young boy.

"Sh," the boy whispered. "It's me, Amy. Please don't scream. They'll kill me." Amy removed her hand once Rachel recognized her.

"What are you doing here? You and your family went to the better land," Rachel stated.

"It wasn't better, Rachel. They lied to everyone, to you, your mother, your father, and me. We were told we were going to meet up with father in the new land for the Armenian Christians. It was a lie. Mother's dead. She killed the baby before they tortured him like Adwa's toddler. I think father's dead too. We learned they'd been sent to a death camp."

"What are you talking about? I saw everyone get in the wagons with your belongings for your new homes. We were told you Christians were being offered an opportunity to build up a new area for the Ottoman Empire." Rachel argued, not wanting to believe what she'd just heard.

"That's what we were told too. We were tricked! They killed the old men, old women, and boys, once we were secluded. They forced us to walk naked after they'd confiscated our belongings. I don't know where we were going or how long we'd been walking, but Mother couldn't keep up. They killed her on the road." Amy wept. "I must hide. I don't know where to go. I'm so hungry I can't think."

The Library Room

"How'd you get here and why are you wearing men's clothing? Amy! What happened to your long braids?" Rachel struggled with what she'd learned.

Amy jumped down and readied herself to hide under the bed again in case the footsteps she'd heard were coming to Rachel's room.

Rachel said, "I'll get Father. He'll know what to do." She grabbed her cape. "It's early. He'll still be here."

"Don't do that!" Amy warned and grabbed Rachel's ankle to stop her. "They killed the last family. They didn't even know me. They'd leave food out for me. I watched from the small cave I'd discovered. They hung the whole family." She then said with deep remorse. "I'm sorry. I shouldn't have come. I need food so I can go hide in the woods until I can figure out a better plan. Please, can you get me some food?" Amy cried, knowing she was jeopardizing another family for food.

"Why are they trying to kill you?" Rachel was still confused on the whole issue.

"They're killing all the Christians: men, children, and women. The beautiful girls are being used to satisfy men. They aren't killed if they convert to Islam. I can't do it. I'm not pretty, and I refuse to be Muslim. I'm a Christian. I'll die a martyred Christian if I must. However, I'm not going down without a fight. I must survive for my mom, my dad, my younger brothers, and my sisters. I don't know where they've taken my sisters yet…" Her voice trailed off.

Rachel put her finger to her lips, pointed to the bed, and within seconds, Amy was under the unmade bed with the quilts draped over the side to keep her from view.

Rachel slipped to the kitchen to grab bread, milk, and cheese. She'll be punished later. There were food rationings during the famine.

Amy ate and drank as fast as she could chew and swallow. Then she heaved against having food in her stomach.

That was when Rachel noticed how anorexic Amy had become; her arms, shins, neck, and face were skeletal. Her hair was missing in spots as well as being cut in a boy's style.

"When'd you eat last?" Rachel asked.

"Last week, I think," Amy answered as she tried forcing another swallow down but ended up spitting it into her hand and putting the uneaten bite into a pocket.

"Where are your clothes?" Rachel asked as she observed the horrible scene.

"They took them. The soldiers took all of our clothes and said we wouldn't need them. They fought over mine. I think they're going to their wives or family," Amy said matter-of-factly.

"Whose clothes are you wearing?" Rachel asked.

"They belonged to the soldier who told me he had orders to kill all Christians. He…raped me. He…left his knife near…" She looked to the ground with shame. "I buried him to buy me time. God gave me the strength and wisdom to do it. I believe that. I was a crazy woman. I wanted to hurt him as much as he hurt me. I witnessed other soldiers do it to other girls before they picked me, even toddler girls." Amy took the knife out of her pocket and showed it to Rachel. Then, she explained how she bound her breast to make herself appear masculine. She whispered, "No man will ever defile me again unless he kills me first."

Rachel inhaled, visualizing what her friend had endured. The knife didn't frighten Rachel as much as the madness in Amy's eyes. She'd become a tormented soul. Rachel didn't want to learn anymore.

"I must leave," Amy told her. "They can't know I was here, do you understand? They'll kill you. You can't tell anyone. They'll kill you if they think you're hiding something."

In a second Amy was gone. She'd slipped out the window in her young soldier attire. The bread and cheese tucked into her silk waist wrap. Her innocence lost forever.

The Library Room

Rachel stared out the window. She shook from cold and fear. Angered at being deceived by the Ottoman Empire and no one to tell anyone what she'd learned. Depression overwhelmed her. She needed the comfort of her mother. She needed to shut the window to keep the coldness out. She couldn't move. She needed to sweep the bread crumbs. She was frozen in place.

She closed her eyes and wept.

Rachel's crying woke her up. She stood in front of the living room window. She hadn't walked in her sleep since being a child.

She looked at her bed and noted she'd started there; but, the sheets felt cold to the touch indicating she'd been out of bed for a while.

She grabbed the prayer shawl her mother had given to her for Hanukah last year. It was a white soft cotton wrap with intricate embroidery work done in pastel pinks, salmons, and whites. She fondled the four tassels in her hand before praying a prayer over it.

"Blessed art thou, O Lord our God, king of the universe, who hast hallowed us by thy commandments, and hast commanded us to enwrap ourselves in the fringed garment.[1]"

With it wrapped around her shoulders, she recited her morning prayers in earnest. With the nightmare still fresh in her mind she asked God to enlighten her as to why she needed to see those images and know those disturbing thoughts.

While Sarah, Jessica, and Amy, continued on to Amy's house, Sarah asked. "What'd y'all think Rachel meant by telling us that she loved us? I mean, of course, we all love each other. Y'all are like my sisters. Did she just realize that tonight? Or does she want to make sure we know she loves us in case their side wins the contest on this project?"

"Sarah," Amy corrected, "this isn't a contest of Christians versus Jewish people. It's not a game. It's a real examination for us to determine. I'm doing my best to keep an open mind. I'm human. I question what I've been taught. I feel God wants us to check things out. In the end, we'll know for sure, and he'll know we know."

Jessica added, "I doubt Rachel looks at this as a contest either. I believe she's looking at this as an investigation too. Drew, on the other hand, he's competitive-minded. That's his personality—the competitor, arguing angles, playing devil's advocate. No pun intended there. I love him for it. I think Drew has a thing for Ms. Rachel too."

"Where'd that come from?" Sarah asked.

"Really?" Amy continued. "How'd I miss that?"

"I missed it too!" Sarah said in astonishment.

"I doubt he knows yet." Jessica said. "But, he can't keep his eyes off her. Watch how he treats her compared to the rest of us. He adores her. I see it."

"They've never gone out together," Sarah said. "How long do you think it'll take before he realizes it? Oh smack! What if he asks her out and she shoots him down?"

Jessica smiled. "I've a feeling that won't happen."

"Huh?" Amy sucked in air. "She has a thing for him too?"

"Yep," Jessica answered and changed the subject. "Oh, back to Rachel wanting us to know she loves us. You should do that once in a while. It's a good thing. Never assume your friends or loved ones know how you feel. You never know when you're going to go, so make sure no one has to wonder at your funeral if you loved them as much as they loved you."

"Oh, that makes me feel good. Thanks," Sarah said, "And just so y'all know, I love ya both very much too. I mean I love y'all and the others...I love all y'all."

Amy smiled. "No, we know you love us more."

Sarah laughed. "Yah, that's it. Just don't tell."

When Amy walked into her house, she removed her shoes, locked the deadbolt, dropped her purse, and let her hair down, all in one motion. Ten minutes later, she was kneeling next to her bed. Head bowed, she began her chat with God.

"Hi, God. You've given me an interesting day. Help me, Lord, to keep my eyes, ears, heart, and mind, open to you and you only. Please keep Ms. Roses Are My Favorite Flowers comfortable. May the information I'm showing her be what you need her to see—one way or the other. Keep my friends safe and bless them with contentment. Use me as your servant. I love you with all of my heart. Hallelujah! Amen.

---

1. Eisenberg, Ronald L. *The JPS Guide to Jewish Traditions*. PA: Jewish Publication Society, 2004; "Prayer Kriat Sh'ma", http://www.jewishvirtuallibrary.org/jsource/Judaism/bedtime.html

Ten

The sun flirted with Loren's eyelids through the sky window. She awoke feeling refreshed. Her phone showed seven thirty. She decided to go home, shower, change clothes, and deal with Giles.

She walked home soaking in God's beautiful day. As she took out her key, the door opened.

Giles stood there and glared at her.

"Glad to see you too," she shot.

"Where've you been?" Giles demanded.

"I've *been* where I said I'd be, the library," she defended.

"Stop lying. I've been there three times, and no one's heard about a hidden room," he said in a very accusing tone.

"I'm sure there aren't a lot of people who know about it. I just learned of it yesterday. I was there. I slept on bean bag chairs… alone," she added the last word clarifying her status to Giles.

"Look, if you're having an affair, I understand with all the hours I've been working. However, if you continue, then I'll ask you to pack your clothes and live elsewhere," Giles commanded.

"Well, first off, Giles, I take offense to your accusation. Second, it's my apartment with my furniture. If any of us need to find another place to live, it'd be you." She stood taller.

"We shopped for the furniture together," Giles countered.

"Yes, we did for a few items. However, most of the furniture I inherited from my grandmother's estate. The few items we shopped for together we did so with *my* money. Your money's spent on…Where *do* you spend your money? It's not food. It's not rent. It's not drinks or entertainment when we go out."

"My mo-money?" he stammered. "I, my dear, wasn't blessed to be born into wealth. My money pays for my college classes. So when we're married, we won't have that hanging over our heads."

We're getting married? Her head spun. *He's never mentioned that word in a positive light.*

She didn't respond. He clarified, "I'd planned on asking you once you graduated this spring. I thought we loved each other. You know, settle down and produce a couple brats."

Her head spun more. *A family?* She'd dreamed of having a family. However, it wasn't what she thought of when she looked at Giles.

Giles read her body language. He opened his arms, "Come, baby, let's not fight. We love each other, and that's more important than these silly issues."

She fell into his arms. Loren tilted her head up for a kiss. "I agree. I'm glad you're not upset anymore."

He kissed her back.

Loren tested the waters. "You know I'm not having an affair."

"Yes, but where'd you stay last night?" He was still unconvinced.

"I'll show you," Loren said. "Let me shower and change. I'll take you to the room so your imagination will stop running wild."

"Can't, gotta go prep for lunch and dinner," Giles whined.

"I need to get this project done as fast as possible," Loren said. "We've made a lot of headway. I don't want it to lose its momentum. Right now, it's fun. I don't want it to become a chore, or I'll lose my help. It's important I have help."

"Whatever," he said, feeling discouraged. "You know how I feel about God stuff. What a waste of time, Loren. You shouldn't do it for the mere principle of it."

"Yes, everyone knows how *you* feel. However, that's a conversation we'll need to address later. I don't agree. Regardless,

I'm not a quitter-for-the-mere-principle-of-it type of person. If I were, I wouldn't be in your arms right now." She smiled.

Once she left the room, Giles thought, *Why didn't she bring the laptop home? There isn't a room. She's lying. I'm calling her bluff!*

When she walked back into the living room, she saw her purse had been moved to the door. Giles was waiting to walk her to the library.

"Oh, you'll have time to see the library room?" She rushed. She was happy he was interested, annoyed he didn't trust her, and sad knowing he was going to mock the holy room.

They arrived at the library the same time as Jessica. She hugged Loren and whispered, "Are you okay?"

"All good. I'll explain later," Loren whispered back.

Giles knew they'd conversed. He stretched his arms out. Jessica obliged with a whisper, "Don't rain on her parade."

He smiled back. "I gave her the parade. No rain in the forecast."

"Okay, you two, claws down. This is a happy day. Giles still doesn't believe the room exists." Loren felt suffocated from the tension.

"I'd never have found this room," Giles said. "They glued book spines to the painted images. They look like real books sitting on a shelf which is wood trim. But why disguise a room?"

Loren swiped open the door.

"And what's with the security system?" Giles looked from the sky dome, to the furnishings and technology equipment. "I see why they don't let just anyone know about it. It'd be fought over by others who also deserve to use it since it's part of a public library. It's not fair to keep it for just this project. There are more important assignments being researched without the amenities you're offered to do your fantasy project." He excused himself to go to work where it wasn't as luxurious.

Sarah broke the silence. "A storm warning's been issued. Seek shelter." Sarah had been in a bean bag during Giles' review, grateful for the lack of acknowledgment. "I never weighed the importance of a secured room until now."

"Now he knows I'm not cheating and where I'd stayed last night," Loren announced.

"By the way," Sarah said, "I brought ya' clothes in case ya' didn't want to go home."

"Thanks, that was thoughtful!" Loren appreciated.

"Is he okay now?" Jessica asked.

Amy startled everyone as she entered the room. "What's up? It looks like you were expecting a monster."

"Close enough," Sarah commented. "Giles just left."

Amy shot Sarah a glance. "How'd everyone sleep?" Amy wondered if God had given them a dream.

"I actually slept the best I've slept in months, right here, under the stars in the beanbags," Loren declared.

"I slept like a log. I closed my eyes, and then my alarm went off!" Jessica answered.

"Same here," Sarah said. "I felt refreshed when I woke up. How about you, Amy?"

Amy closed her eyes. "I had a nightmare. Rachel's family was under investigation during the Spanish Inquisition. Her family needed help out of a jam. We were running to thwart the inevitable by telling the horsemen her family were coming to my house for Easter dinner."

"Did you make it?" Loren asked.

"I don't know. I'm tired from sprinting in my heavy quilts last night." Amy tried to make light of it. "I feel like God was trying to share something important. I know if I wait upon the Lord, he'll show me. So that's what I'm doing, waiting for him to reveal whatever we need to learn." Amy plopped into a beanbag.

"Maybe God wants you to research the Spanish Inquisition to find out how it's affected Christianity or Judaism," Loren said.

Rachel arrived a couple hours later. "Morning, everyone. Oh, I didn't mean to interrupt. Carry on." She unpacked a bag of groceries to restock the refrigerator. "I brought some bagels and lox. I saw the toaster yesterday, and it inspired me," Rachel admitted.

"I love it when you're inspired." Loren smiled.

"Me too!" Jessica replied.

"Did I miss the special prayer?" Rachel asked.

Everyone looked downward while Loren confessed. "Nope, we got sidetracked and forgot."

Sarah added, "Giles checked out the room. It unnerved us. He didn't explode like I'd predicted. But he made it clear the rest of the world should be allowed to use this room too." Sarah looked to see how Loren handled her bluntness.

"I see." Rachel imagined Giles's hateful attitude.

Loren handed the prayer to Rachel. "Would you do us the honors today?"

Once they sat down after praying, Rachel felt compelled to discuss her nightmare. "Have you ever felt like God was trying to send you a message through a dream?" Rachel started.

They all stared at her.

Amy answered, "Yes. He gave me one last night too. I told them before you arrived. Was it the same? What was yours about?"

Rachel processed Amy's words. "Everybody had the same nightmare last night?"

"No, just you and Amy," Loren answered. "What's your dream about?"

"I'm not sure; but, Amy was in it," Rachel said.

"And you were in mine!" Amy exclaimed and then waited for Rachel to continue.

"I remember praying. Then, my mother tried waking me up. When she left the room, a young man covered my mouth to keep me from screaming, but it wasn't a man. It was Amy disguised as a soldier and begging for food. She'd killed a man with his knife that'd stolen her clothes and virginity. They killed her family. She told me they'd kill my family if they discovered her there. She said something about being Armenian or Christian. She ate and ran out the window into the woods. I woke up crying in front of my living room window." She cried as the details of the dream haunted her.

"You were so skinny and crazy from it." Rachel closed her eyes against the flashbacks. "I felt powerless. I couldn't do anything to stop what was happening. Why did God give me such a horrible dream? What's he trying to tell me? What good can come from that?"

"Wow, mine was disturbing, but it seemed light compared to what you went through last night. I dreamed you and your family were about to be subjected to the Spanish Inquisition," Amy said.

Rachel eyes widened. "The Spanish Inquisition? We've grown up learning about the coerced confessions and forced conversions. They'd use various tortures on Hebrews to break their wills."

The guys arrived from football practice. When they saw the girls gathered around, Rachel they remained quiet.

Loren saw Drew focused on Rachel's face. "Rachel and Amy had nightmares last night," she informed them.

"I had one too!" Collin and Drew exclaimed at the same time.

"I feel left out," Jessica said. "And I'm not complaining."

"You first, Collin," Loren instructed.

"I was a monk in a monastery. Drew was beaten up by villagers who'd thought he'd poisoned the waters. I tried hiding him." Collin kept it short avoiding the scary details. He'd kept out the part about Rachel being burned at the stake since she'd appeared upset already, and he wasn't sure how Drew would like being told he's in love with Ms. Rachel either.

"The Black Plague," Drew offered insight. "Jewish people were persecuted by Christians for a plague that nearly wiped out Europe. Ignorant people!"

"Drew, your turn," Loren directed.

"I was caught between helping my family and saving Jessica's neck. She was a nun being guillotined." Drew kept his short as well and watched Jessica's hand go to her throat.

"I liked being left *out* of the dream club better," Jessica said.

"What do they mean? Why did they have to be real to us?" Drew remembered his panic attack.

"God's trying to tell us something," Loren reasoned. "Perhaps we should research the dreams?"

"And the missing tribes of Israel," Amy blurted out.

"Oh, I forgot to mention that!" Drew admitted. "She's right. It's another sign. When the tribes start returning to Jerusalem, we'll know the Mashiach's coming."

"I'll take that one!" Jessica volunteered.

"Wait!" Rachel interrupted. "The prayer!"

"Thanks for the reminder." Loren handed Drew the prayer, and he read it aloud.

At two o'clock, they were hungry. Lunch meat, bread, cheese, and condiments were spread across the table. Everyone made a sandwich after praying and thanked Rachel for dealing with her nightmare by using retail therapy.

They sorted myth from fact. The Internet provided strong evidences in some cases and embellishments in others. Discerning between truth and folklore took time, research, and prayer.

Loren noted the distraught faces of Collin, Drew, Amy, and Rachel. "Hey, what's going on?" Loren asked

"It's evil," Collin said.

Amy summed up, "I'm finding much our religious beliefs have been influenced by sin, power, money, politics, and zeal. Our forefathers were a scary group of untrustworthy people."

Drew added his findings, "Fear, ignorance, power-happy people, all races, religions, and nationalities are to blame at one point. Every race and every religion's had a dark era due to power."

Rachel shrunk in her chair. "I can't read much more of what the Turks did to the Christians in Armenia. And get this, it became *the* recipe for Hitler to use on the Jews! We weren't taught about the Armenian genocide in school. It's still not acknowledged by all nations as genocide. Turkey's never been held accountable for their lack of humanity! I almost threw up when I read what they'd done to women and children. They're claiming it was war. Those acts are never excusable, but they're being excused. And they'd encouraged the extreme cruelty. How can they claim it was war when it was never declared? The Christians had no weapons! They served in the same armed forces, were demoted, and stripped of everything before being executed. They weren't torturing for information; but, torturing to be meaner than anything a mind could imagine. Each soldier was trying to outdo the other. It's gross!"

"I've never heard about this, Rachel," Loren said, exasperated.

"That's what has me so upset!" Rachel continued. "Being Jewish, we were brought up learning about Nazi's and Hitler from our grandparents, rabbis, and school. We were told the bad things that were done to our people in prison and death camps. We've memorials in every city with advocates ensuring this never happens again. But who's singing their anguish? Too few."

She pounded the conference table. "The Armenians were peaceful Christians. Know why I said it became Hitler's recipe? Because he gave this speech a week before invading Poland." She read verbatim the last few sentences of his speech. "Accordingly, I have placed my death-head formation in readiness—for the present only in the East with orders to them to send to death mercilessly and without compassion, men, women, and children, of Polish derivation and language. Only thus shall we gain the living space which we need. Who, after all, speaks today of the annihilation of the Armenians?"

"Turkey won't admit their wrongdoings. They're justifying it as a part of war, like Hitler. Only the world made Germany accountable. I guess we had enough survivors and spokesmen to make sure that happened. No one understood or knew the full extent of what was going on since Turkey was better at covering their tracks."

Rachel's face was red with anger. "The Armenians were nearly exterminated. They lost their loudest voices as well as everything they owned or loved. One and a half million Armenians were murdered, and we don't learn about *this* in school? Where's their justice? Where are their memorials? A hundred years later, Turkey's still not making restitution to those families!"

"Yes," Collin said. "However, I doubt they ever will without international pressures. We need more media coverage on the topic. Perhaps, when this project's done we should become a louder voice. Everyone, Hebrews and Christians."

"The media?" Jessica scoffed. "They're pushed by an agenda. They're used by the puppet masters to distract us from the truths. For example, my great-grandparents were killed at a death camp in Poland because they were Catholic! No offense, Drew and Rachel, but, there were a lot of Christians killed by Nazis too. They didn't kill Jews only. They killed anyone rebelling against their beliefs, trying to protect others, or refusing their new religion."

After more thought and conversation over the atrocities of Armenia, everyone agreed to become activists in exposing the history of Turkey against Armenian Christians.

Collin told everyone about his dream. "People persecuted Jews for The Black Plague disease. Were they persecuted by Christians? Some called themselves Christians, but they weren't acting like it. Pope Clement VI demanded they stop persecuting Jewish people for the disease pointing out they too were affected by it. So then, Catholics were accused of spreading the virus too. Some men and women flogged each other for thirty one days for each year Christ walked the earth, believing the world was coming to an end. The church didn't condone that even though it sounded righteous. Some people performed lewd sexual acts and held orgies trying to rid the disease supernaturally or through witchcraft. Where do people get these notions?"

"Satan," Sarah said. "He's more powerful than people give him credit. He'll take over thoughts when people invite. He wiggles in through pride, desperation, ego, and looking for answers not of God. Like, tarot cards, fortunetellers, even white witchcraft as it's called to invite. They're all sources of inviting Satan into your mind. It's dangerous stuff."

"Having my cards read is inviting Satan into my mind?" Loren argued.

"I'm not judging. I've done it. I got caught up once, but I won't do it again. Something bad came true after a reading. I'm convinced it wasn't a good thing, and it wasn't coming from God. In my gut, I knew I'd done something wrong," Sarah admitted.

"I just felt curious, not good or bad getting my cards read," Jessica stated. "I don't remember what was said. It's a hoax anyway."

"Think about it," Sarah challenged. "The information's coming from somewhere. God condemns it in the scriptures. Where does the information come from if it's not God?"

"Let's get back on track." Drew steered. "My dream about the French Reign of Terror and anti-religion was probably punishment for writing that paper on Deism. Christians, mostly Catholics, were killed in the name of politics. It boggles the mind what people will follow.

Amy added to his comment, "*Or* what they'll do if they feel it'll benefit their pockets. People worship money. They don't realize they're idolizing gold and silver. They desire wealth more than God. They'll slave for that idol before worshiping God in His house."

"True, but," Drew bickered, "not all of the genocides were about money. Most were about power and enforcing what they felt was the right way to be or the right God in their minds to worship."

The Library Room

Amy pushed her theory. "The power part's right, Drew. But, if you dig deeper you'll see it came down to control *and* banking."

"My dream, the Spanish Inquisition" Amy continued, "has been exaggerated in terms of death tolls, counts, and tortures. I'm not saying it wasn't bad. I'm saying it wasn't Armenia or Nazi Germany. A lot of the bad things were done by the state, not by the church. Yet the church took the blame for a lot of folklore. William Shakespeare didn't help matters with his imaginative writings either. Anyway, I'm in no way trying to downplay the evilness of the agenda; it was evil. But I've repeatedly read whenever the Hebrews or Christians become financially ahead of 'authorities who aren't of the same beliefs' they've been persecuted. Most of the time, it's the Hebrews. Shame on you Hebrews for being gifted." Amy joked at Drew and Rachel.

"Did God give us those dreams," Loren asked, "to scare us away from money?"

Jessica concluded, "I think there were many things God pointed out in those dreams, like helping us foreseeing future problems with our country worshiping wealth, but I feel his lessons go even deeper."

Loren supplied, "Like, placing principals above personalities? Jewish people fear Christianity because Christians people have wronged them. And Christians fear Hebrews because Jewish people have wronged them. All religions whether it's Jewish, Catholic, Lutheran, etc., at some point have had bad people in charge."

Collin asked, "Do you think Hebrews or Christians would hesitate changing their religion if the evidence is clear?"

"Ha!" Rachel half laughed. "We're taught in synagogue to never consider becoming Christians because they've persecuted Hebrews, or they hate Jews." Be careful who your friends are because Christians will try to convert you, they always say. Yes, the Holocaust is brought up often so we don't forget. "So yes,

Collin, I think some people are incapable of making their own decisions. Yes, stereotyping plays a role in religions."

"My grandmother always said," Sarah included, "the church is perfect. Unfortunately, the people aren't, which is why they need to go to church. Principals above personalities, like Loren said."

Drew interjected. "But not every church or synagogue *is* perfect, Sarah. My father changed synagogues when the rabbi was getting too farfetched in his own interpretations."

"Amen!" Sarah agreed. "There are many churches out there teaching what they want to teach and not what the scriptures teach. It's like they've their own agendas!"

Rachel challenged Drew and Sarah. "How do you know the difference between a good or bad church or synagogue?"

"I think we'll know what to look for once we're done with this project." Loren stated. "I'm still up in the air about the whole Messiah for Hebrews, or just for Gentiles."

Sarah pointed to the Tanakh. "Pray for direction while reading the word of God. It's all right there in that book—wrong or right, if it makes sense or not."

Loren regained control, "Okay, so Hebrews and Christians have been persecuted by Hebrews and Christians. Both have been guilty of having sinful people in power during a certain era in history. We're who we are today; a more mature and intelligent human being. We *must* move on from the depressing wrongdoers of history and work on the Messianic Cell sheet again.

Eleven

Jessica continued researching the missing tribes. She'd found encouraging information; conversely, there are fewer missing tribes in Israel than most realize.

Around five o'clock, Collin asked, "Drew, are we still doing the parties tonight? Or staying until we're exhausted again?"

"Cool! Let's start at Tommy's," Drew suggested.

"Yes!" Sarah closed her laptop for emphasis.

Loren's phone rang. "Yep, gimme five minutes to take this call." She hustled out of the room before answering. "Hey, what's up?" Loren asked Giles.

"Could you be talked into a date?" Giles inquired. "I'll take the night off."

"Awesome! Crash a couple of parties with everyone? Or just you and I?" she asked.

"I'd hoped just us. We haven't had alone time forever," Giles replied. "I'll see you in an hour with the best guy in the world."

"And the most humble too." She giggled.

"I'm your humble servant." Giles said in his sexy voice. "Try not to miss me too much."

Loren returned to a somber room. "Hey, what's up?"

"Mrs. Rosenberg isn't well and is asking for Amy," Jessica spoke for Amy. "She's printing the work we've done so far."

Amy added, "She's denying dialysis. She doesn't want to prolong her life. It's her choice. I didn't know she'd been in so much pain." Amy cried as she gathered papers. "She's been my mom since I lost mine to cancer, and now I'm losing her too."

Everyone huddled around Amy. Collin prayed out loud, "Lord, please send your Spirit down to bless Mrs. Rosenberg and Amy during this time. Thank you for bringing them together. Help each to hold tight to the love you've blessed them with today. This we pray. Amen."

"Amen," everyone echoed.

Amy thanked everyone. The prayer calmed her.

"Well, it looks like it's just us," Drew announced.

"Actually, Giles is taking me on a date." Loren waited for backlash.

"Ah, go, Giles!" Collin laughed. "There's nothing greater than a woman's guilt-trip on a misbehaved man. You could ask him for gold and get it tonight."

Rachel perked up. "That's how we get jewelry? Thanks for the tip. I'll try that on my future husband. Wait for him to do something stupid and then guilt him into paying for his penitence. I like it!"

Drew stepped in for Collin. "It's only one way. There are more."

"Really! Are you two going to let us ladies in on these, so we'll know when to expect treasures?" Rachel asked.

"Never!" Drew ushered everyone out. "If we tell all of our secrets, then it won't be fun when you get them nor will it be fun walking on eggshells when we can't afford it. Whomever you marry, Ms. Rachel, had better be a perfect man or have deep pockets."

"You're right, Drew." Rachel flirted back.

Jessica, Sarah, and Collin, observed the flirting between Drew and Rachel. It appeared the only people not knowing the two were crazy about each other were the two who were crazy for each other.

Giles knocked on the hidden door. He kissed Loren when she opened it. "Are you ready to have fun?"

"I sure am." She smiled. "Where are we going tonight?"

"I picked up subs, sodas, and chips for a canoe trip down the river. We'll be at the lake by sunset," Giles said, proud of himself for thinking of such an idea.

She planted a kiss on his lips.

"Wow! I'd have come up with this sooner if I'd known I'd get that response! Shall we, my love?" He led her out the door. "I brought a sweater from your closet."

"Nice touch, Mr. Smooth!" she cooed.

"Anything for you, my love," he cooed back.

A taxi drove them to the canoe livery where they were greeted by Lenny, the owner. He handed each a life jacket, paddle, and paperwork. They walked to the river and boarded a tethered canoe where Loren smelled apple cider being pressed at a nearby orchard.

"What's on your mind? What would you like to talk about tonight?" Giles inquired.

"Hmm…What do people talk about on dates?" Loren was absorbing all the nature she could while paddling.

"How was your day of research? Almost done with the project?" Giles sounded interested.

"We've accomplished a lot, and oh my goodness, I must tell you about the dreams!" Loren gushed.

"Dreams?" Giles echoed.

"Yes! Drew, Collin, Amy, and Rachel had different dreams last night about historical events against Christians or Jewish people!" Loren couldn't contain her excitement. She told him about each dream. When she finished, she realized she'd dominated the conversation. "So what do you think? Pretty weird, huh? Enough about my project and friends. Tell me how work's going."

"Yes, very weird. I don't think God, if there's one, would put nightmares into someone's mind to get a point across. Do you hear how absurd that sounds?" He didn't want to be critical, "You believe what you want. We're all entitled to our own beliefs."

Change the subject! Loren's mind screamed "True. And you didn't answer my question."

"We hired a sous-chef. She obeys without question, which is what I've been asking for in a sous-chef. For once, I don't feel like someone's trying to outdo me when it's their job to help." Giles continued talking about the restaurant, servers dating bartenders, and a former manager asking him to switch to his new restaurant.

At the halfway marker, they stopped for dinner.

Mrs. Rosenberg's children, Amelia and Alec, welcomed Amy with hugs. She tried concealing the tears in her eyes.

Ms. Roses Are My Favorite Flowers lifted her arm to signal Amy to her side. They hugged and when they were done Mrs. Rosenberg held Amy's hand.

"We're all here now," Mrs. Rosenberg addressed the three.

"Yes, Mamma, we're all here." Amelia confirmed. Amelia wore a loose fitting scarf to disguise her thick neck and double chin. She made most of the staff nervous with her frank demeanor; yet, she was gentle around her mother.

"Good, you remember Ms. Amy here?" Mrs. Rosenberg reintroduced. "Ms. Amy lost her mother not long ago. We've been important to each other. She takes care of me, but I feel I've had a hand in taking care of her as well. I've asked her to share with me what she and her friends discover during their assignment concerning Yeshua being the Mashiach or not."

Amelia and Alec rolled their eyes. Amy and Mrs. Rosenberg saw it but ignored it.

"I'm not seeking your opinions. However, I want you to respect my curiosity. Amy informed me there's no bias one way or the other since two Jewish friends are working on this project. I feel I need to know the truth and not what some politician or paid preacher wants me to hear before meeting my maker."

Her two children glared at Amy.

"Don't mind those two and their eyin' harah." Mrs. Rosenberg pointed to her squinting eyes, "I taught them the *evil eye* look." Calling them out caused her children to smile.

"You two may listen without objecting everything she presents. If the later becomes an issue, I'll ask you to leave until I can digest it myself. Versteh?" she said using the okay sign.

"Versteh," both echoed.

"Amy, is the report complete yet?" Ms. Roses Are My Favorite Flowers inquired.

"I brought what we've accomplished so far. We needed a break. We'll begin again tomorrow." Amy felt bad for not having it finished.

"Let's see what you've got." Ms. Roses Are My Favorite Flowers leaned toward Amy's paperwork.

Amy navigated the lineage and then explained the virgin birth.

"What do you think, Ms. Roses Are My Favorite Flower? Do you understand how the Mashiach needs to be from the seed of God and *placed* into the lineage no matter the Mashiach's time?" Amy asked.

"I can see how it'd perplex a well laid arrangement. Only God could provide the seed if Mashiach is born of a virgin. To me, it's a no-brainer, as you young folks say. He's certainly capable. He's God and can do anything." Mrs. Rosenberg concluded. "What's next?"

Amy quoted prophecies. Mrs. Rosenberg wanted Amy to show her in her own Bible where the information could be found. The long process fatigued Mrs. Rosenberg as they read the verses and then commented. The two of them became lost in each other's company as they enjoyed the discoveries through an older point of view.

There were too many drunks by the time they'd arrived at the second party, so Collin, Jessica, Sarah, Drew, and Rachel decided to go to their favorite piano bar instead.

They weren't able to push the last two available tables together since they were bolted to the floor as were the stools. Collin, Jessica, and Sarah took one table leaving Drew and Rachel across the aisle. Drew and Rachel didn't mind the seating arrangement.

After a round of sodas for Jessica and Sarah and a beer for Collin, they were ready to go home.

Drew and Rachel stayed nursing their glasses of wine while enjoying the music. The pianist was a friend of Drew's from high school. This also gave Drew another reason to stay longer.

When the pianist played "New York State of Mind," Rachel informed Drew it was her favorite song. Drew took it as a request to dance. He led her to the floor as she smiled.

"Hey, you're a great dancer!" Rachel acknowledged.

"Thank my mother. Much to my brothers and me bellyaching, she forced us to take ballroom dance classes. She'll be happy her money didn't go to waste," Drew said.

"Your mother *forced* dance classes on you?" Rachel questioned.

"Yes," Drew nodded, "and we obeyed. My father said she was famous for her *hak meir ein chainik* talents."

"Ah! I've heard my grandfather use that expression about my grandmother! What does it mean?" Rachel asked.

"I think in Yiddish it literally means 'to bang on a tea kettle until one's worn down,' a nagging person," Drew interpreted and laughed.

"Well, I pray I'm never accused of such talents." Rachel saw him smiling down on her. It warmed her and she realized how intimate they were dancing, not ballroom protocol. *Drew?* This wasn't something she'd ever considered. *He's attractive, smart, kind, Jewish...and a friend. Drew...Is he feeling the same?*

Is she blushing? He'd realized they were dancing closer than his instructor would've allowed but made no attempt to correct the postures. He enjoyed her closeness. It didn't feel sexual. It felt *natural.* Then he thought, *Warning! This is Rachel, your friend, not a girlfriend. Don't go there! You'll screw it up! You like her friendship too much to botch it up by being romantic. Stop! You'll lose her as a friend if it fails.*

Rachel felt him withdraw. She responded likewise. The song ended and he led her back to the table.

When she smiled over the rim of her glass while sipping her wine, it was all he could do to keep from leaning over the table to taste her lips. *When did she become so beautiful? When did she become more special than the others?* He watched her as he swished the wine around his tongue before swallowing. *She must go home before I end up doing or saying something stupid.*

"Wow! What a day. Are you almost ready to hit the road, princess?" Drew said. *That's what Dad calls Mom! Why did I call her that?! Stop it! Take her home now!*

"Sure, are you okay? You seem to be drifting off." She sensed something was wrong and didn't know if it was something she'd done.

"It's all good. I thought about something I need to do tomorrow before heading to the library. How are your classes this year?" *Liar, liar, pants on fire. What if she doesn't feel the same?*

"Classes this year are pretty mild. On the home stretch now. I did all the hard stuff at the beginning to get it out of the way knowing I'd be interning my last year," Rachel explained.

"Oh yeah, and how's that going?" he asked. "Do you love working in an art museum slash gallery?"

Rachel glowed. "I love it! I can't wait to start a shop of my own. I've met some great artists across the country over the years and I'm sure I'll be able to fill it with quality limited pieces."

"So you're moving back to the city after graduation?" Drew considered how he'd fit into her plans.

She saw it flash across his face. *He does feel the same! Okay, girl, don't panic. Don't blow it either! What was the question? Moving back to the city? Well, until two seconds ago it was the plan...Wait! I can't change my life on the slim chance of being with a man!*

"Sorry, Drew, my mind drifted. Must be the wine. I'm not sure where I'll set up my gallery. I've looked around but haven't committed to any of them." *What do you mean you don't know where? You've had it pinpointed to a precise block for over a year now! Don't lead him on.*

As she walked from the table, he grabbed the sweater she'd forgotten and placed it around her shoulders. A soft fragrance of perfume hit his nostrils. He bent closer to smell it again. She felt his nearness and didn't step away.

"Ms. Rachel, I need to get you home," Drew confessed. "For some reason, I find you attractive tonight and your perfume could drive any man crazy. I try conducting myself as a gentleman around you and the girls. I'd hate to ruin a relationship by doing something inappropriate. I love what I have with all of you. I mean, especially you. I mean...I don't know what I mean. Can we pretend like I didn't say a thing?" His embarrassment caused her to laugh with him.

Rachel's mother's words came to mind: *Never let a man feel embarrassed for acting weird when he develops a crush. It's a gift, not an annoyance. If you're not interested, let them down gently. A man's ego's fragile. That's what ladies do.*

"I'm flattered more than you could ever know. There are hundreds of girls on this campus wishing they were me right now," Rachel said. "Shall we get me home, my friend?" Then, she wrapped her arm around his and let him lead like a gentleman.

⚜

Mrs. Rosenberg absorbed as much information as she could. They were near the end of Yeshua's birth when Amy suggested they stop. At first, Mrs. Rosenberg argued; however, once her children saw signs of exhaustion, they sided with Amy. They promised to let her start from wherever she remembered in the morning. She couldn't read her notes written in the margins of the papers. She finally gave into their pleas as Alec, assured her he'd walk Amy home.

Alec was a divorced mid-fifties successful attorney. He trusted no one. He intimidated Amy. She dreaded his lecturing her over the report.

As Amy readied to leave, Amelia embraced her. She'd never feared Amelia like the other aids; nonetheless, she'd never felt affection from her either. It was an unexpected friendliness she'd needed.

Walking home, Alec initiated the conversation. "She loves and trusts you. You've been kind to her over the past few years. My sister and I tried coaxing her to move closer to where one of us lived so she wouldn't be lonely; however, she's stubborn. She demanded to stay where she'd met Father."

"She's sentimental," Amy confirmed.

"You're in her will. Did she tell you?" Alec stated.

"No. She's never mentioned that. I don't need payment for her friendship," Amy objected.

"Don't worry," Alec assured. "Amelia and I aren't upset. Your schooling will be paid for and there are a few trinkets she'd like you to have. She loves you and we've seen it's reciprocated."

"Yes, it is," Amy agreed. "She's been kind to me since my mother passed. I had my friends, but she was an older person who nurtured me through my grieving. I feel blessed knowing God put her in my life at the right time."

"Yes, God has a way of giving some people a perfect friend when they need one. Unfortunately, he let me down. I still resent him," Alec confessed. "Weren't you angry at God when he took your mother away?"

Amy answered. "At first, yes. I begged him to change his mind, and then it evolved to helping her graduate. That's what she'd taught me during her year of sickness."

"What do you mean?" he questioned.

"At first, she'd cry knowing it'd be the last time she'd do this or that." Amy paused. "As she grew stronger in her faith, she realized she was graduating to her next stage with God and wanted me to be happy for her. We prepared for her graduation, not her death. It helped, but I still grieved. I was sickened by her pain as well as what I was losing." A tear hit her cheek before she wiped it away.

"I didn't mean to make you cry," Alec offered his handkerchief.

"It still gets me. Watching your mom brings it back again. I'm sure you'll be seeing me do it again." Amy smiled.

"Then I'll stock up on handkerchiefs." He smiled. "How do you ask God to help you when you're mad at him? That's the problem I'm facing. I'm mad at him for my failed marriage and yet I need Him to help mother. See my dilemma?"

"Was the failed marriage your fault?" Amy asked.

"No, I was a faithful husband who gave my wife a comfortable lifestyle."

"Was it her fault?" Amy summed.

"No, she tried. She says it's my fault since I worked so much. I had to keep food on the table and a roof over our heads. A roof, by the way, she wanted, loved, and received in the divorce."

"So you're not to blame and you can't blame her, so you're blaming God? Why can't I think these thoughts instead of saying them out loud?" she reprimanded herself.

Alec laughed. "Well, there might be my problem or at least some of it. Cheating is destructive. I'll mull over your youthful wisdom." He smiled and frowned at the same time.

"Pray for her," Amy offered as a solution.

"I can't. Some people aren't worth prayers," Alec spat.

The Library Room

"Not true. We are to love everyone. That doesn't mean we must like them or condone their actions. Pray for her. It'll have a metamorphic effect. I know this first hand," Amy offered.

"I sense a story. Tell me how this worked for you. And then, I'll tell you how it can't work for everyone," Alec argued.

"You sound like my friend, Drew; always challenging. I'll tell you, but we may need to sit down for a bite to eat. Have you eaten anything today?" Amy warmed to the unapproachable Alec.

Their pace picked up as they made their way to the diner. They chose a booth away from the rowdiest crowd.

"Start," Alec demanded after they ordered.

"Jeez Louise!" Amy half complained. "Once upon a time, there was a person who didn't like me. I thought she was mean. Of course, she was popular, and everyone liked her."

"Good start. Continue," Alec encouraged.

"One day, I'd read her name on the church prayer list. What went through my mind when a lifelong grudge hits the please-pray-for-healing list?" Amy asked.

"Please tell me. This story's getting longer," Alec teased.

Amy ignored his comment. "I didn't want my mind to go there, but it went there. Well, look at that! Karma baby! What goes around comes around. I almost felt guilty."

Alec finished for her, "So you prayed a quick prayer for her. 'God take care of her' and then all was well?"

Amy sighed. "No, I saw her name the following week and prayed again. The third week, I knew it was serious and prayed harder. The following week—"

Alec interrupted, "Week number what? How many weeks does it take to get to the center of a tootsie roll pop? Sorry, that's before your time."

"Alec, you expected immediate results after a few selfish prayers? And you call *us* the instant gratification generation?" Amy pointed her finger. "Week four, I met her parents. They'd explained she's better, but she has Lupus. Whenever they take her name off the list, she has episodes. Therefore, they keep her on the list."

Alec was amused. "Hold it! Weeks of praying for someone who isn't doing as bad as you think had been helpful?"

Amy was in a defensive mode. "Did I revert back to not liking her because she's better? It's an incurable disease. Or should I stop praying? Or did I pray for her because I liked her parents and hoped she'd grown up to be like them? My mind overrode the thoughts of being tricked into praying. Because I knew she wasn't all right."

Alec challenged, "So my wife having affairs throughout our marriage wasn't all right? I should still pray for her even though she's no longer my problem?"

Amy said a silent prayer for his bitterness. "Even when you put it that way, the answer is yes. The most important thing to do is pray. Grudges aside, pray for her." Amy challenged back at him. "At least, I did. 'God, she's sick and her parents are worried about her condition. Comfort her family, comfort her, ease her pain, and keep her in good condition,' I prayed. Week five, she became a person to me instead of a memory. God was transforming my heart. 'Hi, God, I need you to comfort her and her family. I'd like to see her smile,' I kept praying."

Alec sighed. "Amy, I'm trying to relate to this, but she wasn't an elementary grudge. She'd betrayed me as my wife. I've already spent too much time and energy trying to forgive and forget. However, continue with your story. I'm interested in the ending. There *is* an ending, isn't there?"

Amy continued, "The bright side to *my* character, Alec, is I kept praying. And then, week seven, she came to church. I knew I loved a human being who was put on this earth to teach me to pray, Alec. I'm telling you to pray for her, that's all. One week at a time until it transforms into what God wants it to be in your heart."

The Library Room

Alec sat back and clapped his hands. "Bravo, kiddo! That was a great story! Thanks for entertaining me this evening. I'm glad it worked."

Amy realized he's still hurting and hasn't done anything to help himself heal. "Thanks for being a great listener. I pray you're not set on staying bitter the rest of your life. If you do get tired of feeling resentful every time you think about her or see something that reminds you of her. Give it a try."

He smiled. "I don't know what got into me. It was rude. Please forgive me," Alec said as he paid the check and left a tip. "Let's call it a night, shall we?"

"Yes, I'm sorry too. I didn't mean to snap. I'm tired from the research and Ms. Roses Are My Favorite Flowers." Amy held out her hand as a peace offering.

Alec ignored her hand and hugged her instead.

Loren and Giles started down the river again after eating and a couple of kisses. She felt relaxed, but tired. She'd needed the time in nature to unwind; however, she looked forward to the end.

Once they reached the lake, they sat on top of the picnic table waiting for the equipment pick up, and Giles' security deposit.

"You're not talking. Why?" Giles questioned.

"Sorry, I'm exhausted from researching over the last few days," Loren apologized.

"I hope I'm not going to hear about this report much more. It's already monopolized all of our topics this evening," Giles spat.

"Giles, why do you hate God? What do you think he's done to you to deserve such hatred from you?" Loren expected a sob story.

"Nothing. First of all, one has to believe in God in order to hate God," he answered.

"Such a typical response from an atheist," Loren said under her breath and then covered it by saying louder. "But when you throw tantrums like a five-year-old over any topic about God, it leads me to believe you know there's a God and you're angry at him."

"Why must you ruin a great date?" Giles defended. "Are you trying to tick me off?"

"No, that's the last thing I want. I'm trying to develop a relationship where we can be honest with each other." Loren was upset.

"Good, but we've just had fun. That topic gets me worked up and you know it," Giles said, pouting.

Loren sighed. "Giles, you must chill out on God talk. I find the topic stimulating. I like hearing different views."

Giles argued, "When we met, you didn't believe in God. You were my hippy princess. You were into trees, sun, earth, and things you can see, touch, and know. I told you I was an atheist and we fell in love. We had that in common."

"I never said I'm an atheist!" Loren objected. "I like the earth, stars, and trees, but I never thought they'd *replace* God. The hippy thing was a phase, but I've matured and know life isn't life without a higher power that created life. I know we're not here by accident. I don't believe in coincidences. *I believe* in God."

Giles snarled, "Everything I believed about you was a lie."

"No. You refused to listen because you're convinced you're always right." She wasn't backing down this time.

"Fine. Then figure out how *you're* going to work this out because I'm not changing. I don't change for anyone. I can't change what *I believe* to suit your latest phase." Giles jumped off the table.

Loren asserted, "Maybe we should rethink our relationship. It'll become an issue on what to teach our children."

"It *won't* be an issue!" Giles said, his voice rising. "We'll do what my parents did. Let *them* figure it out. I wasn't brainwashed into believing there's a God. I'm against organized religion. All churches are full of hypocrites. I don't want to be a part of their fantasy world."

"Thank God for those churches where hypocrites can go learn how not to be one! At least they're recognizing their need for God to change them! I hate it when people use that excuse to circumvent going to church, when the real reason is they're lazy or egocentric. God forbid non-church goers own up to *their* character defects!" Loren shouted.

"Nice! Because screaming at me will change the way I feel about church?" Giles yelled back.

Loren took a deep breath and brought her voice down. "Giles, it's hard for me to fathom how you've arrived at your initiatives of what church could be like since you've never attended any." Loren was beyond frustrated by this conversation.

"Stay here and wait for my security deposit! I'll see you when you get home. This'll give us time to reflect on what's happening between us. I sense it may be more than a religious thing. I think you're being selfish." Giles left her alone at the lake.

Twelve

Loren sat in the dark on the table. It was obvious the owner had forgotten his equipment and Giles's security deposit.

Questions plagued her mind. *Where's the cool sweet guy I met a year and a half ago? What happened? How did it get this far out of control?*

She phoned her parent's home.

"Hello?" Her father, Mitch, answered.

"Hey, Dad. Mom around?" Loren's voice cracked.

"No, honey, she's at the movies with the girls. The ones who dress up in purple and red and act like six-year-olds." Mitch chuckled.

"They're an interesting group, Dad," Loren said. "Mom doesn't miss a meeting."

"No, she doesn't," he agreed. "How's my angel doing?"

"I'm tired. Mom tell you about my assignment?" Loren enjoyed talking with her father although they didn't talk often.

"Yep. How's it coming?" Mitch asked.

"It's getting there," Loren said. "It comes with a secret room in the library. You should see it, Dad! It has everything we need. And oh! The dreams. I can't get over the dreams, Dad. God gave four people four different but same types of dreams in the same night! I'll tell you about them the next time I'm home. I'm still digesting it." Her voice fluctuated from sad to excited and then tired with each sentence. Her father heard it.

"It sounds like a lot of work. I'm excited for all of you." Loren could tell Mitch was smiling. Then, his tone became serious. "So what's upsetting ya? You okay? Need money?"

"Um…No, I don't need money. I'm good there. I called because I…love." Her eyes watered as she realized why she'd called. "I needed to hear how you two adore each other. I love you, Dad."

Mitch, sensing more, asked, "How are you and Giles doing? How's he treating you?" He heard her sniffling.

Loren steadied her voice. "We're addressing some issues."

Mitch spoke, "Your mother and I've had issues over the years too. We do adore each other although it takes work on your mother's part. I'm a guy. We think differently." He chuckled at himself. "Loren, if you can't agree on important issues, or if you find you're always giving in to the other person even on unimportant things, it may not be a good match for you."

Loren thought out loud. "Giles and I don't seem agreeable anymore. It's evolved into being Giles's way or no way."

Mitch stressed, "Love adores. That means it builds the other up. It's never about being the winner, and it's never feeling like the loser either. It's a balance of give and take. Your mother and I don't argue because if it's important to her, I'll back down. Likewise, if it's important to me, she'll back down. When we encounter an issue, we say, 'This is important to me' so the other knows. Helpful hint: Don't make *everything* important. Over the years I've learned I don't always have to be right even when I am, and I don't always have to win even if I can. Life's peaceful when both hold that attitude." He heard her crying.

Mitch had witnessed how Giles treated Loren. It led him to assert another point. "Loren, another important component to a relationship is cherishing the other person. I had to learn how to celebrate your mother. I remind her how much I love her. I make sure she believes me by doing special things. My efforts changed the way she treated me. Cherishing each other is vital. Loren, if he's incapable of cherishing you, you'll end up feeling

The Library Room

unloved, unattractive, and develop a low self-worth. Eventually, it'll lead to breaking up or finding someone who makes you feel worthy, sexy, and loved. Cherishing is giving without expecting something in return. However, if it isn't reciprocated after a while it's not fun and takes too much energy.

"I don't think I've ever heard you two say a cross word to each other the whole time I was growing up," Loren said, thinking back in her life.

"Because we promised we wouldn't. If we get mad at each other and it happens, we aren't perfect...or at least I'm not." He chuckled at himself again. "If we get mad, we keep it private. No one needs to know our business. Oh, I'm sure she's called a friend for advice or back in the day her mother, but never a foul word to each other or about each other in public or in front of you. Drama kills relationships."

"Yep, I can see that. The drama queens on campus burn through many relationships." Loren said. "Thanks for sharing tonight. I'm lucky to have such a wise father. I love you."

"I love you too, sweetheart. Oh, hey! Your mother just walked in. Did you want to talk to her?" Mitch offered.

"Actually, no. I'm going to go home to bed. Let her know I love her and thanks again, Dad. Good night," Loren said walking home.

"Okay, your mother and I love you. Good night." Mitch ended the call.

Rachel enjoyed being the center of Drew's attention while walking home. She hoped everyone saw them walking together. *Why? We're not boyfriend and girlfriend...yet.*

Drew enjoyed their relaxed pace. Her hand rested in the crook of his right arm. It was all he could to do to keep from flexing an extra firm bicep for her to feel. He enjoyed her attention.

They reached her walkway gate. Instead of waiting at the gate for her to enter her house, he walked her to the door.

She searched her purse for her key. She became nervous with him standing near. She couldn't stop thinking about his eyes, those same eyes watching her every move. *Finally!* she thought finding the key and then dropping it back into the purse. It didn't take long to find it again. She was embarrassed and gripped it while unlocking the door.

Drew spoke, "I've had a great day with you. Are you going to the library tomorrow?"

"Yes. And you?" Rachel squirmed.

"Yes, I'll be there tomorrow." Drew sensed her nervousness. He hated leaving her but knew if he didn't it'd become complicated.

"I enjoyed having fun together with you too," Rachel commented. She didn't know if he'd intended to kiss good night or not. It wasn't unusual to hug; so, she opened her arms.

Drew accepted the invitation. He bent his head, smelling more of her perfume. He didn't let go. She didn't push away. Time stopped as they embraced in the moonlight acknowledging the other's attraction. After a few minutes, Drew said, "Good night, Ms. Rachel. I look forward to seeing you tomorrow. Text me to let me know what time to meet you, and I'll walk with you."

"Good night, Mr. Drew. I'll do that. I look forward to seeing you tomorrow as well." She blushed as she waved good night.

Once Drew turned the corner, he lifted his shirt to where her head had rested on it to see if her perfume was still there. It was, so he'd lift the area to his nose on his way home.

Loren arrived home to a locked door. She clutched her key with irritation. Then she justified Giles locking it out of habit, thus giving Giles the benefit of the doubt.

The house was dark with nothing welcoming Loren home.

The Library Room

Giles strolled down the hall, pretending to be shocked by her arrival. "What are you doing home? I thought you'd spend the night at your library room again."

"No, I'm spending the night in my own bed. I'll be researching in the library all day tomorrow and don't want to wear out my welcome." She was annoyed at his attitude.

"I was already asleep," he said, heading back to bed.

"I'm glad to see you aren't now, so I won't have to wake you up to tell you to sleep on the couch." Her fists were clenched. "This is important to me. You're moving out tomorrow."

"Look, baby, I understand you're upset over this evening, but I think..."

"*I'm* upset over the fact that I sat waiting for *your* security deposit because *you* weren't man enough to wait for it. *I'm* upset they forgot about us and never brought it. *I'm* upset because you accused *me* of being selfish when *I'm* the one always giving into *you*! *I'm* upset I've been there for over two hours without you checking on my safety. *I'm* upset because if I'd been with my friends, you'd have used the excuse of making sure I was safe to check up on me. I'm *furious* over a *lot* of things. *I'm* going to sleep alone in *my* bed, and *you're* moving out in the morning! Do *you* understand, *baby*?" Loren stomped to the bedroom closet, grabbed a pillow and a blanket, threw them into the hallway, slammed the bedroom door, locked it, leapt onto the bed, and cried into her pillows.

"Dad was right on so many issues," she whispered to the picture of her parents on her dresser. *Thanks, God, for giving me a good dad. Help me, God, to stay strong. Amen.*

Giles collected the pillow and blanket. He listened to her weeping. He'd never seen her so upset. It'll take a lot to undo what he'd done this time. He wasn't about to give up. She'd see it his way once he apologizes and gives her a ring.

In the morning, Giles rushed to the store. His panicked thoughts bounced, *Okay, I'll admit I'm an idiot. She's changed.*

Where'd my soft-spoken angel go? She's tiring of me like the others. I can't lose this one. We need each other. We'll need help from her family and friends with the start up costs and marketing of our new restaurant. They'll do anything for her. They'll help us open it, make sure it looks nice, and runs smoothly. Then we'll be comfortable, and she can play while giving her parent's lots of grandchildren. It's all about the money. Give the woman enough money, so she's not working while raising the kids, and she'll be happy. We're not there yet. That's why she's tired of my moodiness.

Giles felt confident about their future plans together. He'd make sure she didn't give up and miss out on the plans for their future.

He smiled as the cashier chatted about him being in another world. He pretended like he was still in another world and didn't respond to her. He wasn't in the mood to be chatty in return. He was on a mission and needed to stay focused.

Collin awoke to the landlord mowing the grass.

What time is it? he wondered, grabbing his phone. *Seven-thirty!*

He'd planned to meet Jessica and Sarah for the eight o'clock mass.

Jessica and Sarah were in their lobby of their building when they spotted him. They stood as he rushed to meet them.

"You look like you've run a marathon. You okay?" Sarah asked.

"You two look like angels from heaven. I overslept and I apologize. How are we doing on time?" Collin said, panting.

"We're okay," Jessica said. "But we should be on our way."

The three walked toward the church. "So which of you were going to fill me in on the Rachel and Drew thing?" Collin looked to each with an accusing grin. "Am I the last to know?"

They laughed. "I think we're the first to know," Jessica said.

"Yeah, I'm not even sure they know, yet." Sarah agreed.

"Then we'll have to make sure they do soon," Collin conspired. "They're perfect for each other. Don't you think?"

Both girls concurred.

Loren woke up to a quiet house. She tiptoed her way to the kitchen verifying Giles was not in the house and let out an audible sigh of relief.

She loved him but, knew it'd never work. He'd make a good husband someday, just not hers.

She made a mental list of Giles's belongings and started boxing them up for him, so he'd have no excuses to keep coming back to woo her. She then had an epiphany of his manipulative style. "Clothes, toiletries, and his bike…that's it?" she said to herself.

It occurred to her she may end up with more money each month by not living together. *I'm paying rent, utilities, garbage pickup, cable, Internet, food, my phone bill, and sometimes, his phone bill too. Where are his paychecks going? Surely, he's getting paid for working as a gourmet chef? I'll let him take the laundry basket to transport his clothes. Where'll he go? He's no family living around here; dad lives in Minnesota and mother in St. Louis? Not that his cold and strange family would help him in anyway. Does he have friends?*

Loren was showering when Giles returned and began cooking breakfast. He wondered how long she'd been in there. He tiptoed, but, he figured the smells would alert her.

And that's what happened. Loren smelled the bacon. She saw through the manipulation. She sent a group text. "Meet at my house? Asked Giles to move out. May need support."

Rachel wondered if Drew was up yet and when they should go to the library. While the phone battery charged, she sent a message letting him know she could be ready to go within the hour. She loved mornings like this—mellow and unrushed.

Rachel heard the phone indicating a new text had arrived. She was excited to read Drew's message, only it was Loren's text instead. Her phone then rang with the caller ID showing Amy. "Good morning, Ms. Amy," Rachel answered. "Are you calling about a text I just received?"

Drew suffered another restless night. He'd heard Collin run out the door before finding out the plans for the day. He wanted to talk to someone about last night.

I can't believe I almost kissed her last night when I walked her home.

He was in the kitchen drinking the last of the coffee when Adam, one of his roommates, walked in and made a fresh pot.

"You look horrible. Fun night out?" Adam prompted for a story.

"Hate to disappoint you, buddy, but no. It was a relaxing night. A few of us went to a party, ate food, had a beer, and then moved to a second party. We didn't stay. It was a drunken fest that reeked of being raided by police. So we went to the piano bar for a glass of wine before retiring home." Drew replayed the events out loud, trying to figure out why he felt so tired.

"Maybe you should see a doctor? Yesterday morning, you looked sick, and today, you look like you have a hangover. You're telling me you look this bad without alcohol binges? I'm so disappointed in you," Adam teased. "Seriously, I hope nothing's wrong."

"I'm sure I'm fine," Drew tried to assure him. "I haven't slept well the past couple of nights. Weird dream the night before and then I had something on my mind last night that kept me up."

"Ah." Adam smirked, realizing his friend's predicament. "Women problems."

Drew mocked back. "Ah, what would *you* know about women problems?"

Adam laughed. "I may not be the cat's meow, but believe it or not, I've a gal waiting back home for me. We Skype every night before bed and before morning classes. I've lost sleep over that woman."

"Dude! I had no idea! No wonder you don't go trolling." Drew shook his hand.

"I keep a low profile," Adam explained. "Before when everyone knew I was committed, I'd be hit on by other girls. I think some like the challenge of stealing a man away from another woman. Anyway, I don't want to mess this up. I love her."

"Yah, some girls are weird like that," Drew agreed as his phone indicated a new text. He beamed at Rachel's message. Adam noticed.

Adam smiled. "Did the girl problem just text you?"

"Um…yeah. I mean no, we're just friends." Drew's face reddened. "But we're supposed to just be friends. I may like her more than a friend and same with her. I don't know what to do. I don't want to lose her friendship over doing something stupid like dating her."

Adam poured his coffee and said, "If it's a true friendship it'll withstand anything. And if it's true love, it'll always be there after graduation, serving in a war, or traveling on a long business trip. I'd considered dropping out, getting a job, and marrying her before someone else swept her off of her feet. Dad convinced me to finish college, get a *great* job, and *then* pamper her like a princess. I shared his advice and she agreed. She told me to stop worrying since she'd been worried about me being swept away."

"Hmm. Never thought about it like that before," Drew said. "So take it slow?"

"Yes, but give her a clue of your intensions. Don't delay in telling her." Adam laughed.

Drew swallowed hard. "I haven't told her how I feel yet."

Adam smirked. "Based upon the way you look this morning, if you were with her last night, she knows."

"Yeah, you're right." Drew recalled the long hug.

He picked up his phone to text Ms. Rachel back. *Or better yet, call her, so I can hear her voice.* His phone indicated a new text. He was excited to read something from his Rachel, but Loren's words appeared instead.

Amy brewed coffee while reading the newspaper. She loved Sunday mornings. She relaxed in the lounge chair before getting ready for church.

She picked up her phone to check her messages. *None! Yippee! No one needs me and Ms. Roses Are My Favorite Flowers's in good shape for the time being.* She sank deeper into her chair.

She planned her day. *First church, then Ms. Roses Are My Favorite Flowers, go over the material from the last point of her memory, then library, then back to Mrs. Rosenberg this evening. One more minute of doing nothing before starting the day. Sip and smell my coffee.*

"Mmmm," she said out loud as she smiled.

Her phone signaled a new text had arrived. She picked it up expecting news about Ms. Roses Are My Favorite Flowers. She read Loren's text and felt alarmed.

Jessica, Collin, and Sarah stood in line, waiting to exit the church. The bishop who was visiting the church stood by the door shaking everyone's hand with the priest who'd conducted the mass.

When the priest took Sarah's hand, he asked her name because he hadn't seen her before. "You're friends with Collin and Jessica?"

The Library Room

"Yes, we've been friends since we were freshmen," Sarah proclaimed.

"You haven't attended mass here before?" He smiled. "It's good to see you today."

"I usually go to my church on the other side of campus. I didn't feel like going to church by myself today, so I tagged along with Collin and Jessica. It was a lovely service," Sarah explained.

The priest's and bishop's facial expressions changed from welcoming to alarm. Sarah sensing their mannerisms had changed looked at Jessica and Collin who'd also made note of the change.

"Didn't I see you taking communion this morning as a Catholic?" the priest whispered to avoid a scene.

Sarah seemed confused by the question. "Yes, I take communion at my church too."

"You're not Catholic. You're not allowed to partake. It's not the same," the bishop scolded.

"What do you mean I can't take communion?" Sarah challenged. "I've been baptized, my heart's good with God, and I ask for forgiveness before partaking. I understand communion."

"No, child, transubstantiation," the priest advised in a softer tone acting as liaison between Sarah and the offended Bishop. "You do yours in remembrance, and we commune with God. I'd love for you to come to classes to learn more about our faith. If you accept the Catholic teachings, then you'll have your first communion." After finishing his invitation, he smiled.

Sarah lifted her reddened face and said, "I appreciate the invitation. However, I'm still adjusting to the idea of y'all denying another Christian communion based on a religious sect. We're talking about the same Christ, the same God, and the same Holy Spirit. It doesn't seem right to me. Thank you. Enjoy your afternoon." She left Jessica and Collin with the priest and bishop.

"Collin and Jessica," the priest called after them. "I hope this doesn't happen again. You must encourage your friends to become Catholic in order to commune with Christ."

"I'm not sure what to say right now, Father," Collin said, leading Jessica out the door before she told them what's on her mind.

"Oh, the nerve!" Jessica said, fuming, and scurried to catch Sarah. "Sarah, we're sorry." Jessica caught up with Sarah and hugged her right arm, trying to slow her down. "Collin and I didn't know, and we'd never have let you go through what you went through if we'd known."

"How'd y'all've stopped me from taking communion without embarrassing me? And who gives y'all the right to determine whose good enough to take your communion?" Sarah asked with tears in her eyes. "I love y'all, but I'll never join a church turning people away from celebrating communion with God!"

"I understand why you're upset, Sarah. I'm upset too," Collin said. "Like Jessica said, we didn't know. I've never had a friend who wasn't a Catholic attend church with me. I'll get clarification. It doesn't seem fair." He put his arm around Sarah's shoulders to slow her down too.

Sarah asked with her head tilted skyward to God. "I'm offended. How do you expect your churches to grow if you embarrass Christians by denying them communion with you, God? It's a head scratcher to me!"

Just then, all of their phones buzzed with a new text.

Loren stomped into the kitchen. "Giles, I asked you to leave."

"Good morning, beautiful," Giles responded.

"I mean it, Giles," Loren reinforced her wishes. "You should be packing your clothes instead of trying to make breakfast to butter me up. It won't work this time. I need peace in my life. I need you to find another place to live."

"Honey, we'll talk this out over breakfast." Giles insisted.

"I'd rather not. There's nothing to discuss." Loren stood firm. "I've emptied my clothes out of the laundry basket so you can use it to transport your belongings easier."

Giles's face turned red and the vein in his neck throbbed as he stared at the stove.

She'd seen those signs before. She needed to think fast. "Giles, I'll pack your things for you and deliver them to any address you text me. I'm sure packing will be hard for you. I'll do it to make it easier for you," she offered.

Giles swung around with a whisk in his hand and glared at her. "I'll leave when I'm ready to leave. We're going to sit down and eat breakfast to discuss this matter. I'm not leaving today, so you might as well get that in your head. Also I'm not sleeping on the uncomfortable couch again. Get over it."

"No!" was the only word she managed while running to the bedroom and locking the door.

He tried opening the door. It infuriated him to be shut out. He needed her to see how passionate he felt about staying with her. She'd agree if she'd eat breakfast with him. He tapped on the door.

"Loren, please don't lock me out. I'm not going to hurt you. I'd never hurt you. I love you. I want to marry you. We don't have to wait for you to graduate. We can elope this week if that's what you want. Please, Loren, don't give up on me. I've changed. See, I'm not even mad. Loren, honey, please let's talk this over like adults."

"Giles, we can talk on the phone after you leave the house. I've told you before you scare me when you get like this," Loren pleaded. He needed to leave before his calmness disappeared. She'd seen it too often over the past year. She'd done well hiding that part of his personality from her friends.

He'd promised if he's ever this angry he'd go work out his frustrations at the gym, she thought. "Let's talk later, Giles. Go work out. I'll talk to you after you've had time to cool down."

"Loren, stop bringing up that incident. I'm not breaking things or punching walls. Did I touch you while we were in the kitchen? No, I didn't. Please look into my eyes. You'll see I'm calm. Besides, how am I going to get my clothes? I need to work later."

"Loren, I'm going to go check on breakfast." He walked down the hallway, tossed his whisk into the kitchen, and tiptoed back past the door standing plush against the wall.

"I think she's asking us to help with Giles without coming out and asking," Rachel spoke over the phone. Amy had created a conference call to connect everyone.

"Has he ever hurt her?" Drew asked.

Jessica recalled what Loren had once hinted. "I think he's done something in the past to make her afraid. Last spring."

"If he puts a hand her—" Collin was interrupted by Rachel.

"Calm down, Nitro! We're all probably reading way too much into this text. Let's meet over there and assess the situation?" Rachel instructed.

"We're headed there now," Collin agreed.

"I'll meet you at your house, Rachel, since I'm already on your street," Drew informed her.

"Then I'd better get moving." Rachel dashed in a panic. "Amy, wait for us at the coffee shop on the corner. I don't think you should go over there by yourself. It might get him more excited."

Amy's gut agreed with Rachel's insight.

Loren looked down the hallway to see if Giles was near. She didn't know he was standing against the wall behind the door. She tiptoed out into the hallway to go to the bathroom.

Giles slammed the door stopping her in her tracks. He pulled her close. "Settle down, Loren. I don't want to hurt you. I want to sit and eat breakfast with you! Can you do this? You *never* do what I ask, but you're allowed to order *me* around?" Giles eyed her.

"Let me go, or I'll scream!" Loren threatened.

Giles held her arms. "I'll let you go if you eat breakfast and listen to me."

She stopped struggling. "Fine, eat. And then you must leave."

He let one arm go free but continued squeezing her other wrist while walking her to the kitchen table.

She needed to send a 911 message to her friends but realized she'd left her phone in the bedroom. She shook inside from fright. She knew she'd never get down the hall without Giles catching her.

He turned the burners back on to reheat the hollandaise sauce. He set the table without making eye contact.

She needed to distract him. "May I get my phone? I'm expecting to hear about the plans for the day."

"They can wait," he said in a cool tone. "I'm not sharing the attention. It's important you understand how much I care for you. Here, eat this." He'd prepared her plate. "They're such a pain to make but well worth the effort. Don't you agree?" He was trying to start small talk.

She shook from fear.

"So, my love, how are your eggs benedicts?" Giles asked and then noticed her plate hadn't been touched.

"I told you, I'm not hungry." Loren inhaled shallow breathes to combat the nausea.

"You must eat," Giles demanded. "I insist. I didn't go through all of this effort and money for you to snub your nose to it."

A knock on the door interrupted them. Giles sprang to the door and saw Collin, Jessica, and Sarah. He cracked the door opened, so they couldn't see Loren.

"Loren's not feeling well. I'll have her call you when she's better. Perhaps, tomorrow." All three noticed Giles was acting odd.

Sarah inquired, "Can I get her anything? A soda will calm her tummy if it's that, or I have aspirin I can bring inside to give her."

"No, it won't be necessary. We've all that here. She'll call you when she's better," Giles insisted.

Loren slid off of her seat, hoping the motion wouldn't be noticed in his peripheral vision. She'd hoped while they were distracting him she could make it to her phone.

"Okay, tell her we're sorry we didn't get a chance to meet up, and if she's feeling better, we'll be at the library. Don't you work tonight? I can stop in to check on her later." Jessica was fishing for information.

"I've taken the day off." Giles slammed the door and watched them through the peephole walk down the sidewalk without speaking to each other.

He turned to see Loren was no longer sitting at the table. "Loren, please come out!" Giles pounded on the bedroom door.

Loren sent texts to everyone. "Giles is coo-coo. Locked in bedroom. Get police. No big scene. It'll make him worse."

"Giles, I don't feel well." Loren shook.

Drew called 911. Collin asked the girls to stay at the coffee shop. They weren't happy. Nonetheless, they stood at the corner windows watching Loren's house.

The police met Drew and Collin in front of the house next door. Each showed an officer the messages from Loren. Both were instructed to stay behind the police car.

Officer Jones knocked on the door. Officer Gordon ran to the back, looking into windows to see if weapons were involved or if he could see Loren. No one answered, so he knocked again after ensuring they had the right house.

"Loren, this is the police. We need you to come to the door." Officer Jones drew his pistol as Giles walked to the door.

Giles opened the door. "Is something wrong, Officers?"

The Library Room

"We believe a lady named Loren's being holed up in her bedroom and needs our assistance," Officer Gordon said. "Could you ask her to come to the door, please?"

"She's not here. She's at the library," Giles lied. "If you'll excuse me, Officers, I need to get ready for work. Thanks for checking on her. I'm sure her friends have found her in the secret library room by now."

"How about we come in to make sure she isn't here. You can get ready while we take a look around," Officer Jones challenged.

"Unless you've a warrant, I don't think so," Giles argued.

"We don't need a warrant if we feel someone's in danger, and by the way you're behaving, I'm going to insist you let us inside." Officer Jones pushed the door open as Giles tried slamming it.

Giles shoved Officer Gordon who spun him around and handcuffed him.

"Loren, it's safe now. We need to see you're all right," Officer Jones yelled while walking down the hall.

Loren emerged, shaking from fear, and was led to the kitchen.

Giles sat handcuffed on the sofa, glaring at her.

"Do you know this person?" Officer Gordon asked.

"Yes, his name is Giles," she answered.

"Is his name on the lease?" Officer Gordon asked as if he were reciting a script.

"No," she answered. She'd learned from friend if both names were on a deed or lease, they'd only receive a warning and could stay until a judge decides which one has to leave.

"Was he confining you to the bedroom? Did you feel threatened or did he threaten you?" Officer Jones questioned.

"He insisted I eat breakfast, so he could talk me into letting him stay. I'd asked him to leave. I didn't want to eat. I didn't want to hide in the bedroom, but I had to get away from him. He was scaring me." Loren shook harder.

He pointed to the untouched plate of food. "Is this one yours?"

"Yes," she answered. "He was acting crazy. He promised he'd never hit me again, and I believed him, but I saw the same look in his eyes. I lost my appetite."

"Loren, I'd never hit you!" Giles shouted from the sofa. "I made a promise! Why are you telling them about that? It was an accident and you know it! I swear! I don't hit women!"

Officer Gordon escorted Giles to the police car while Officer Jones asked, "What'd you like us to do with him?"

"What do you mean?" Loren was confused.

"We're taking him to jail. However, you need to file kidnapping charges since he wouldn't let you leave." Officer Jones was assessing if she was being dramatic or if she was sincere.

"I'm sure he'd have let me leave eventually, especially after you showed up," Loren defended Giles. Kidnapping seemed excessive.

"Loren, he claimed you were at the library!" Officer Jones watched her fear return. "Are you familiar with domestic abuse?"

"He has a temper, but he doesn't hit." Loren didn't like the turn the conversation had taken. "It *was* an accident the last time. I zigged when he zagged."

Officer Jones was used to hearing abused partners defend the other. It's humbling to admit they've entered into an abusive relationship.

"Loren, domestic abuse is about control. It doesn't mean you're being beaten. If one person controls the other, it's abuse," Officer Jones said. "What I'm going to ask are abuses I see every day. Does he control the money? Or make you spend yours so you can't do things with friends?" he asked.

Loren blinked back tears. "We've our own money. I pay rent and utilities because they're in my name."

"Does he help with those expenses?" Officer Jones raised his eyebrows. "What about food and other expenses?"

"I don't know what he spends his money on. I usually buy that stuff. I think he has high tuition payments he's paying off," Loren said.

The Library Room

"Are there topics you can't discuss because it causes him to explode or people he won't let you see or places you can't go that aren't bad places?" He watched each phrase wrinkle her forehead.

"Yes, all of those," Loren admitted.

"Does he blame you for his bad behavior?" Officer Jones asked.

"No, he takes responsibility for being a jerk once I point it out to him." She laughed to lighten the mood.

Officer Jones remained serious. "Does he make you feel bad about your accomplishments or ignores your opinions or yells at you?" He needed her to realize her problem's serious. Her eyes were tearing up. He asserted, "Do you ever feel like *you're* the crazy one? Or suspect he's unbalanced?"

She nodded.

"Does he check on where or who you're with out of jealousy?"

She nodded and hid her face with her hands while sobbing.

"Has he ever threatened to kill you or hurt you or loved ones? Has he ever forced you to have sex with him?"

Her head snapped up and looked at him. "No!"

"Good, and now you know the next level," Officer Jones promised. "I see this all the time, Loren. It's serious. It's not something you hear about in the news, but I'm telling you, it's everywhere, and you're not alone."

"What happens if I don't press charges?" Loren inquired.

"We've enough to keep him overnight from pushing Officer Gordon. I want you to press charges on the kidnapping. It'll hold up in court along with our testimony," Officer Jones explained.

"So he goes to jail for the night?" Loren asked. "What happens when he gets out? He'll blame me! He'll make my life a living hell!"

"We'll file a restraining order. He'll see a judge sometime tomorrow, and we'll get that in place. We'll make sure he understands his boundaries," he assured.

"What should I do with his belongings?" She'd thought about changing the locks to keep him from entering the house again.

Office Jones asked, "Does he work somewhere? Does he have family nearby? Take them to his work or where he'll be staying."

"No, his family lives out of state," she thought out loud. "I'll have to take them to his work. I don't know where he'll go. I don't think he has friends. I hate making him homeless. I don't think he has money."

"Loren, he's not paying for rent, utilities, or food. He has money somewhere. I can't give you legal advice. I can tell you I've seen this trend end fatally. You're in an abusive relationship whether you want to admit it or not," Officer Jones said.

Loren believed his eyes. "Okay, what do I need to do next?"

As the police drove off, Drew and Collin entered the house. Both asked Loren if she's okay.

"I will be," Loren said. "I didn't realize how bad the relationship had gotten until I'd spoken to Dad last night and then Officer Jones today. I think there's something wrong with him, more than anger issues. He's charming one minute and then a horrible person the next."

The girls walked in and each took their turn, hugging Loren.

"So what happens next?" Sarah asked.

"I'm not sure, I mean. I'm sure he told me, but it's not registering yet. I hope they sentence him to some sort of counseling or check his chemical levels.

"Does he do drugs?" Drew asked Loren.

"No, I don't think so. He rarely drinks. You've seen him. Maybe weed every once in a while, but even then, it's every great once in a while. It's not a habit, and it mellows his butt out," Loren surmised.

"What can we do to help?" Rachel asked.

"I need to ask God for direction." Loren paused. "I think we should go to the library and work. Tonight, I'll pack and take his

The Library Room

things to the restaurant. He won't be allowed to come near the house or me. He'll be released tomorrow sometime."

"You should go to your parents' for a while," Collin suggested.

Loren dismissed the idea with, "I need to freshen up before going to the library. I'll meet everybody there."

"Should we go to lunch first? We'll wait up if you want," Jessica suggested, and then everyone noticed the plates on the table.

"Eggs benedicts for breakfast," Rachel noted. "How ironic."

Loren giggled.

Thirteen

Loren's Notes Part III—Messiah's Life on Earth

Tanakh, Nevi'im, Hosea 11:1-4 NIV: "When Israel was a child I loved Him, and out of Egypt I called my son. But the more they were called, the more they went away from me. They sacrificed to the Baals and they burned incense to images. I, Myself, taught Ephraim to walk. I, Myself, took them by the arm, but they didn't realize it was I who healed them, I led them with cords of human kindness, with leading-strings of love. To them, I was like someone lifting an infant to His cheek, and I bent down to feed them."

Collin explained the verse above by summarizing New Testament, Matthew 2:10–18 KJV. Yeshua was born in Bethlehem. After he was circumcised, he was taken to his home in Nazareth where the wise men following the star found him. This is where commercialism messes it up. They went into the house and saw the child with Mary. They fell to their knees, and did him homage. Then, they offered Him gifts of gold, frankincense, and myrrh. They'd been warned in a dream not to tell Herod; instead, return to their own country by a different route.

"After they left, the Angel of the Lord appeared to Joseph in a dream saying, 'Get up, take the child and His mother, and escape into Egypt. Stay there until I say, because Herod's searching for the child to kill Him.' So Joseph left that night with Jesus and

Mary for Egypt, where they stayed until Herod died. This was to fulfill what the Lord had spoken through the prophet: 'I called My son out of Egypt.'

"Herod was furious at being fooled by the wise men. In Bethlehem and its surrounding district, he ordered all males two years old or younger killed. That fulfilled the words spoken through the prophet Jeremiah: 'A voice is heard in Ramah, lamenting and weeping bitterly: it's Rachel weeping for her children, refusing to be comforted because they're no more." Matthew had quoted Tanakh, Nevi'im, Jeremiah 31:15.

Sarah points out this prophecy's twofold. It describes how Yeshua and family will flee to Egypt and it reiterates Yeshua will be God incarnate.

Drew didn't know about them fleeing to Egypt or the infanticide either.

Amy showed us where God reiterated the "out of Egypt" prophecy through Balaam too. In the book of Numbers, Balaam was a diviner who predicted the future and could also perform rituals to change it, a rare gift. Balak, the king of Moab, worried about being attacked by the Israelites. He hired Balaam to curse Israel. When Balaam tried, God told Balaam to bless Israel instead of cursing it. After several attempts to override God's desire Balaam went to Balak explaining his problem. Tanakh, Torah, Chukat-Balak, Numbers 23:21 NJB: "I have perceived to guilt in Jacob, have seen no perversity in Israel. Yahweh, his God, is with him, and a royal acclamation to greet him. God's brought him out of Egypt; like the wild ox's horns to him."

So five prophecies were fulfilled by the birth of Yeshua alone. First, Jesus was born in Bethlehem. Second, he had to flee and be called out of Egypt. Third, God's seed became Yeshua, God incarnate. Fourth, Yeshua had to be placed into the David's bloodline. And fifth, Rachel wept over the death of children.

Drew argues the Tanakh, Nevi'im, Jeremiah 23:5–6 JPS: "See, a time's coming," declares the Lord, "when I'll raise up a true branch of David's line. He'll reign as king and will prosper, and He'll do what's just and right in the land. In His days Judah shall be delivered and Israel shall dwell secure. And He'll be called: 'The Lord is our Vindicator.'" This prophecy was reiterated in Jeremiah 33:14–16.

Collin explained in this prophecy, we learn the Mashiach must not only be from the line of David, which we've explored, but he needs to be righteous, without sin, and blameless.

Amy claims only God is *incapable* of sinning. Humans sin. Anyone not the Messiah is a normal human and sins. There are several verses in the New Testament stating Yeshua was sinless despite being tempted. Yeshua was able to overcome. We would've failed.

Sarah read New Testament, Hebrews 4:14–15 NJB: "Since in Jesus, the Son of God, we've the supreme high priest who's gone through to the highest heaven, we must hold firm to our profession of faith. For the high priest we have isn't incapable of feeling our weaknesses with us, but has been put to the test in exactly the same way as ourselves, apart from sin."

Sarah then read New Testament, Hebrews 7:26–28 NJB: "Such is the High Priest that met our need, Holy, innocent and uncontaminated, set apart from sinners, and raised up above the heavens; He's no need to offer sacrifices every day, as the high priests do, first for their own sins and only then for those of the people; this He did once and for all by offering Himself. The Law appoints high priests who're men subject to weakness; but the promise on oath, which came after the Law, appointed the Son who is made perfect for ever."

In other words, Jesus was on earth and tempted like a human. He felt the feelings we feel when it comes to temptation. However, unlike us, he overcame all temptations.

Amy: Here are more verses supporting his innocence. New Testament 1 John 3:5 KJV: "...in Him there's no sin."

New Testament, 2 Corinthians 5:21 KJV: "For our sake He made the 'Sinless One' a victim for sin, so in Him we might become the uprightness of God."

Collin reminded us of a scene you may be more familiar with seeing depicted in movies or plays. In the New Testament book of John, John writes about Yeshua challenging the crowd about his sinless life to which no one could accuse Jesus of sin. New Testament, John 8:46 NJB: "Can any of you convict Me of sin? If I speak the truth, why do you not believe me?"

Tanakh, Nevi'im, Isaiah 53:2–12 speaks about Mashiach's character, what he'll endure and why. We should tackle it as a group one verse at a time.

Tanakh, Torah, Nevi'im, Isaiah 53:2 NJB: "Like a sapling He grew up before Him, like a root in arid ground. He had no form or charm to attract us, no beauty to win our hearts."

Jessica interprets that to mean the Messiah will be humble, not handsome, nor charming, like everyone expected. It's the opposite of what the world would follow.

Sarah agreed pointing out Yeshua was born a son of a carpenter, not royalty like the Hebrews were anticipating. He was humble with an attitude of servitude, not a flamboyant king.

Collin told us there isn't a lot of information on Yeshua's childhood once they returned to Nazareth. And then he summarized New Testament, Luke 2:40-49 NJB: Jesus grew to maturity, He was filled with wisdom; and God's favor was with Him. Once he became an adult, He shared the wisdom God. He was twelve years old, they went up for the feast [of Passover] as usual. When the days of the feast were over and they set off home, the boy Jesus stayed behind in Jerusalem, without his parents knowing it. They assumed He was somewhere in the party, and it was after a day's journey that they went to look for Him among their relations and acquaintances. When they failed to find Him they went back to Jerusalem looking for Him everywhere.

"Three days later, they found Him in the Temple, sitting among the teachers, listening to them, and asking them questions; and all those who heard Him were astounded at His intelligence and His replies. They were overcome when they saw Him, and His mother said to Him, 'My child, why've you done this to us? See how worried Your father and I've been looking for you?' He replied, 'Why were you looking for me? Didn't you know I'd be in my Father's house?" But they didn't understand what He'd meant."

Can you imagine Mary and Joseph's panic when discovering Jesus was missing? What you discover later by reading other books in the New Testament is that he had other half-brothers and half-sisters. They'd have to be half because God was Jesus's biological father and Joseph was the biological father to the other children. How many we don't know but we know there were more than six for sure according to Matthew 13:54. That's a lot of kids to keep track of on a long hike with hundreds of friends and relatives from the town of Nazareth.

Rachel believes it could happen. At Passover, the entire town of believers traveled together. Adolescents walk and talk from one friend to another.

Sarah further explains that Yeshua had been a perfect child. He'd never sinned. This part of his story is to lay evidence not that he'd do something to make them worry as a child, but to show us how much they took for granted at how well behaved Yeshua had been as a child *and* how he longed to be in the presence of his heavenly Father by being in his Father's house, that wasn't a sin, for it was pleasing to God.

Next verse, Tanakh, Torah, Neviim, Isaiah 53:3 NJB: "He was despised, the lowest of men, a man of sorrows, familiar with suffering, one from whom, as it were, we averted our gaze, despised, for whom we had no regard." I think this speaks for itself knowing what happened to him.

Amy pitched, "You're only thinking about his end days. I read this and think about his emotional side. Like in New Testament, John 11.35 KJV: "Jesus wept." His reaction to seeing Mary and Martha crying over Lazarus's death. Or in New Testament, Luke 19:41–44 NJB: where He cried prophesying the destruction of Jerusalem and the temple."

Collin visualizes these things when he reads it. New Testament, John 1:11 KJV: He came unto his own, and his own received him not. And New Testament, John 7:5 KJV: For neither did his brethren believe in him.

For Jessica it's different too. She thinks of New Testament, Luke 22:63–65 NJB: "Meanwhile the men who guarded Jesus were mocking and beating Him. They blindfolded him and questioned Him saying, 'Prophesy! Who hit You then?' And then heaped many other insults on Him." And then this scene, New Testament, Matthew 27:15–26 ESV: Now at the feast the governor was accustomed to release for the crowd any one prisoner whom they wanted. And they had then a notorious prisoner called Barabbas. So when they had gathered, Pilate said to them, "Whom do you want me to release for you: Barabbas, or Jesus who is called Christ?" For he knew that it was out of envy that they had delivered him up. Besides, while he was sitting on the judgment seat, his wife sent word to him, "Have nothing to do with that righteous man, for I have suffered much because of him today in a dream." Now the chief priests and the elders persuaded the crowd to ask for Barabbas and destroy Jesus. The governor again said to them, "Which of the two do you want me to release for you?" And they said, "Barabbas." Pilate said to them, "Then what shall I do with Jesus who is called Christ?" They all said, "Let him be crucified!" And he said, "Why, what evil has he done?" But they shouted all the more, "Let him be crucified!"

So when Pilate saw that he was gaining nothing, but rather that a riot was beginning, he took water and washed his hands before the crowd, saying, "I am innocent of this man's blood; see to it yourselves." And all the people answered, "His blood be on us and on our children!" Then he released for them Barabbas, and having scourged Jesus, delivered him to be crucified.

The next two verses need to stay together. Tanakh, Nevi'im, Isaiah 53:4–5 njb: "Yet ours were the sufferings He was bearing, ours the sorrows He was carrying, while we thought of Him as someone being punished and struck with the affliction by God; whereas He was being wounded for our rebellions, crushed because of our guilt; the punishment reconciling us fell on Him, and we've been healed by His bruises."

Sarah thinks of New Testament, 1 Peter 2:24 njb: "He was bearing our sins in His own body on the cross, so that we might die to our sins and live for uprightness; through his bruises you've been healed."

Amy agrees and then displays New Testament, Matthew 8:16–17 njb: That evening they brought Him many who were possessed by devils. He drove out the spirits with a command and cured all who were sick. This was to fulfill what was spoken by the prophet Isaiah: He Himself bore our sicknesses away and carried our diseases."

Collin suggests New Testament, 1 Peter 3:18–19 njb: "Christ, Himself, died once and for all for sins, the upright for the sake of the guilty, to lead us to God. In the body He was put to death, in the spirit He was raised to life, and, in the spirit, He went to preach to the spirits in prison."

Rachel questions how God could allow a human sacrifice? "Murder's a sin and human sacrificing is forbidden. However, God okayed us to sacrifice Yeshua for our sins? Doesn't that seem wrong or excessive?"

Amy explained, "Yes, it's wrong to raise a child for the purpose of sacrificing it to God. God detests human sacrifice as indicated in Tanakh Torah Re'eh Deuteronomy 12:31 NIV: 'You must not worship the Lord your God in their way, because in worshiping their gods, they do all kinds of detestable things the Lord hates. They even burn their sons and daughters in the fire as sacrifices to their gods.' However, God 'volunteered' Himself as a perfect sacrifice as a righteous adult. Children being sacrificed don't volunteer for such an act. We, as humans, could never raise another to be sinless or perfect. It'd need to be raised from God, Himself, as Himself. Only God with the help of His Holy Spirit could be perfect in human form; the Father, the Holy Spirit, and Son, are One."

Collin reiterated, "Yeshua was a gift from God to us. God sacrificed his son for everyone. Yeshua told us and prepared us for his ultimate solution to our constant sin. Yes, humans were and are sinful. No, we didn't and don't deserve that kind of a sacrifice. Yes, Yahweh loves us that much."

Next verse. Tanakh, Torah, Nevi'im, Isaiah 53:6 NJB: "We had all gone astray like sheep, each taking his own way, and Yahweh brought the acts of rebellion of all of us to bear on Him."

I know from living on a farm sheep will wonder when left on their own. It's what sheep do. And we do too. It's why sheep need to be hedged by a shepherd. Does God condone going astray? No, straying is sinful. However, if it's our nature and yet going astray is a sin, what's the solution? God provided a way to save us from sin through Yeshua the Mashiach our sinless Shepherd.

Sarah read New Testament, John 10:11–18 NIV: "I'm the good shepherd. The good shepherd lays down his life for the sheep. The hired hand isn't the shepherd who owns the sheep. So when he sees the wolf coming, he abandons the sheep and runs away. Then the wolf attacks the flock and scatters it. The man runs away because he's a hired hand and cares nothing for the sheep.

The Library Room

I'm the good shepherd. I know my sheep and my sheep know me—just as the Father knows me and I know the Father—and I lay down my life for the sheep. I've other sheep that aren't of this sheep pen. I must bring them also. They'll also listen to my voice, and there'll be one flock and one shepherd. The reason my Father loves me is that I lay down my life—only to take it up again. No one takes it from me, but I lay it down of my own accord. I've authority to lay it down and authority to take it up again. This command I received from my Father."

Next one. I cringe reading this one. Tanakh, Torah, Nevi'im, Isaiah 53:7, NJB: "Ill-treated and afflicted, He never opened His mouth, like a lamb led to the slaughter-house, like a sheep dumb before its shearers He never opened His mouth."

Drew asked, "you're trying to say Yeshua allowed it all to happen even though He could've stopped it with a word?"

Collin answered, "Yes, New Testament, Luke 22:8–11 NIV: "Herod was delighted to see Jesus. He'd heard about Him and had wanted for a long time to set eyes on Him; moreover, he was hoping to see some miracle worked on Him. So he questioned Him at length with no reply. Meanwhile, the chief priests and the scribes pressed their accusations. Then Herod and his guards treated him with contempt and made fun of Him; he put a rich cloak on Him and sent Him back to Pilate."

Amy added, "New Testament 1 Peter 2:21–23 NJB: "This, in fact, is what you were called to do, because Christ suffered for you and left an example for you to follow in his steps. He had done nothing wrong, and had spoken no deceit. He was insulted and didn't retaliate with insults; when he was suffering he made no threats but put his trust in the upright judge."

And it leads to the next verse Tanakh, Torah, Nevi'im, Isaiah 53:8 NJB: "Forcibly after sentence, He was taken. Which of His contemporaries was concerned at His having been cut off from the land of the living, at His having been struck dead for His people's rebellion?"

Collin summarized New Testament, Matthew 26:48–56 NJB: "Yeshua's disciple, Judas, had arranged a sign with the high priest's servants by saying, 'The one I kiss is the man to arrest.' So Judas went up to Jesus at once and said, 'Greetings, Rabbi,' and kissed Him. Jesus said to him, 'My friend, do what you're here for.' Then they came forward, seized Jesus, and arrested Him. One of the followers of Jesus grasped his sword and drew it; he struck the high priest's servant and cut off his ear." with "A follower of Jesus's drew his sword and cut the ear off of the high priest's servant. Jesus then said, 'Put your sword back, for all who draw the sword will die by the sword. Or do you think that I cannot appeal to my Father, who'd send more than twelve legions of angels to my defense? But then, how would the scriptures be fulfilled that say it must be this way?' Then Jesus addressed the crowds, 'Am I a bandit that you'd to set out to capture me with swords and clubs? I sat teaching in the Temple day after day and you never laid a hand on me.' All this happened to fulfill the prophecies in the scripture. Then all the disciples deserted him and ran away."

Sarah read New Testament, Mark 14:50–52 NJB: "And they all deserted Him and ran away. A young man followed with nothing on but a linen cloth. They caught hold of him, but he left the cloth in their hands and ran away naked."

Amy read New Testament, Romans 5:6–8 NJB: "When we were still helpless, at the appointed time, Christ died for the godless. You could hardly find anyone ready to die even for someone upright; though it's just possible that, for a good person, someone might undertake to die. So it's proof of God's own love for us that Christ died for us while we were still sinners."

This next piece is powerful to me. Tanakh, Torah, Nevi'im, Isaiah 53:9 NJB: "He was given a grave with the wicked, and

His tomb is with the rich, although He'd done no violence, had spoken no deceit."

Amy agreed, "Yes, It's well documented. New Testament, Mark 15: 20–27 NJB: "When they'd finished making fun of Him, they took off the purple robe and dressed Him in His own clothes. They led Him out to crucify Him. They enlisted a passer-by Simon of Cyrene, father of Alexander and Rufus, who was coming in from the country to carry His cross. They brought Jesus to the place called Golgotha, which means 'the place of the skull.' And they crucified two bandits with him, one on his right and one on his left."

New Testament, Luke 23:32–34 NJB: "Now, they were also leading out two others, criminals, to be executed with Him. When they reached the place called 'The Skull,' they crucified Him and the two criminals, one on His right, the other on His left. Jesus said, 'Father, forgive them; they don't know what they're doing.' Then they cast lots to share out His clothing."

Amy summarized New Testament, Mark 15:42–46 NJB: "It was now evening, and since it was Preparation Day—that's, the day before the Sabbath—there came Joseph of Arimathaea, a prominent member of the Council, who himself lived in the hope of seeing the kingdom of God, and he boldly went to Pilate and asked for the body of Jesus. Pilate, astonished that he'd died so soon, summoned the centurion and enquired if he'd been dead for some time. Having been assured of this by the centurion [soldier] he granted the corpse to Joseph who bought a shroud, took Jesus down from the cross, wrapped Him in the shroud and laid Him in a tomb which had been hewn out of rock. He then rolled a stone against the entrance to the tomb. Joseph of Arimathaea was a wealthy man and he'd given up his own tomb for Jesus. It was where the elite were buried and had cost him a lot of money having it carved out."

Here are the last three verses of the Isaiah 53 prophecies. Tanakh, Torah, Nevi'im, Isaiah 53:10–12 NJB: "It was Yahweh's good pleasure to crush Him with pain; if He gives His life as a sin offering, He'll see His offspring and prolong His life, and through Him Yahweh's good pleasure will be done. After the ordeal He's endured, He'll see the light and be content. By His knowledge, the upright One, My Servant will justify many by taking their guilt on Himself. Hence I'll give Him a portion with the many, and He'll share the booty with the Mighty, for having exposed Himself to death and for being counted as one of the rebellious, whereas He was bearing the sin of many and interceding for the rebellious."

Sarah said, "It tells us the Messiah will be a sacrifice here, Rachel, addressing your earlier question about it being necessary. It wasn't something spontaneous. God told us it'd happen long before it happened and why."

Collin reminded us to keep John the Baptizer's story in with the Messianic notes because he was prophesied having an important role with the Mashiach.

The last piece in the notes was from New Testament, Luke 1:80 NIV: "And the child grew and became strong in spirit; and he lived in the desert until he appeared to Israel."

Next should be New Testament Matthew 3:3–4, NJB: "This was the man spoken of by the prophet Isaiah when he said, 'A voice of one that cries in the desert, "Prepare a way for the Lord, Make his paths straight."' This man John [Yochanan ben Zechariah] wore a garment made of camel-hair with a leather loin-cloth round his waist, and his food was locusts and wild honey."

Amy summarized New Testament Luke 3:2–18 NJB: "While the high-priesthood was held by Annas and Caiaphas, the word of God came to John the son of Zechariah, in the desert. He went throughout Jordan proclaiming a baptism of repentance for the forgiveness of sins, as it's written in the book of Isaiah, 'A voice of one that cries in the desert: Prepare a way for the Lord,

The Library Room

make his paths straight...roads made smooth, and all humanity will see the salvation of God.'

"He said to the crowds who came to be baptized, 'Brood of vipers, who warned you to flee from the coming retribution? Produce fruit in keeping with repentance, and don't start telling yourselves, "We've Abraham as our father," because I tell you, God can raise children for Abraham from these stones. Yes, even now the axe is being laid to the root of the trees, so that any tree failing to produce good fruit will be cut down and thrown on the fire.'

"A feeling of expectancy had grown among the people, who were beginning to wonder whether John might be the Christ, so John declared before everyone, 'I baptize you with water, but Someone's coming more powerful than I, and I'm not fit to undo the strap on His sandals; He'll baptize you with the Holy Spirit and fire. His winnowing-fan is in His hand, to clear His threshing-floor and to gather the wheat into His barn; but the chaff He'll burn in a fire that'll never go out.' And he proclaimed the good news."

Then Yeshua comes to his cousin John the Baptizer.

Drew asked if John the Baptizer was one of Yeshua's twelve disciples?

No, John the Baptizer [Yochanan ben Zechariah] and the disciple John who wrote the books of John aren't the same person—two different Johns.

Jessica will cover Matthew's view. She started by summarizing New Testament, Matthew 3:13–17 NIV: "Jesus came to be baptized by John [Yochanan ben Zechariah]. John argued saying, 'It's I who need baptism from You, and yet You come to me!' Jesus replied, 'Leave it like this for the time being; it's fitting that we should, in this way, do all that uprightness demands.' Then John gave in to Him.

"And when Jesus had been baptized He came up from the water, and the heavens opened and He saw the Spirit of God descending like a dove and coming down on Him and a voice sounded from heaven, 'This is My Son, the Beloved; My favour rests on Him.'"

Amy will take Mark's view. She summarized. New Testament, Mark 1:9–11 NJB: "Yeshua came from Nazareth and was baptized in the Jordan by John [Yochanan ben Zechariah]. And as He was coming up out of the water, he saw the heavens torn apart and the Spirit, like a dove, descended upon Him. And a voice came from heaven, 'You are My Son, the Beloved; My favor rests on You.'"

Sarah will take John's view. She summarized New Testament, John 1:19–34 NIV: "The Jews sent priests and Levites to ask John the Baptist [Yochanan ben Zechariah] 'Who are you?' He declared, 'I'm not the Christ.' So they asked, 'Then, are you Elijah?' He replied, 'I'm not.' 'Are you the prophet?' John answered, 'No.' So, they asked, 'Who are you? We must take back an answer to those who sent us. What have you to say about yourself?' So John said, 'I'm, as Isaiah prophesied: "A voice of one that cries in the desert: Prepare a way for the Lord. Make His paths straight!"'

"The Pharisees asked, 'Why are you baptizing if you're not the Christ, or Elijah, or the Prophet?' John answered them, 'I baptize with water: but standing among you—unknown to you—is The One who is coming after me; and I'm not fit to undo the strap of His sandal.'

"The next day, John saw Jesus coming towards him and said, 'Look, there's the Lamb of God that takes away the sins of the world. It was of Him that I said, "Behind me comes One who's passed ahead of me because He existed before me." I didn't know Him myself; but, He who sent me to baptize with water told me, "The Man on whom you see the Spirit come down and rest is The One who is to baptize with the Holy Spirit." I've seen and I testify that He's the Chosen One of God.'"

Sarah summarized New Testament, John 3:22–36 NIV: Jesus and his disciples went into the Judaean and baptized followers.

The Library Room

John [Yochanan ben Zechariah] was also baptizing at Aenon near Salim.

Some of John's disciples went to John saying, "Rabbi, the man to whom you bore witness, is baptizing now, and everyone's going to Him."

John replied, "No one can have anything except what's given him from heaven. You, yourselves, can bear me out. I said, 'I'm not the Christ; I'm the one who has been sent to go in front of Him.' He must grow greater, I must grow less. He who comes from above is above all others; he who is of the earth…speaks in an earthly way. He who God has sent speaks God's own words, for God gives Him the Spirit without reserve. The Father loves the Son and has entrusted everything to His hands. Anyone who believes in the Son has eternal life, but anyone who refuses to believe in the Son will never see life: God's retribution hangs over Him."

Jessica explained New Testament Matthew 14:3–5 NIV: Herod arrested John, chained him up, and put him in prison; because, of Herodias, his brother, Philip's wife. John told him, 'It's against the Law for you having her.' Herod had wanted to kill John but was afraid of the people who regarded John as a prophet.

Amy summarized New Testament Mark 6:19–28 NJB: Herodias was furious and wanted to kill John. But couldn't, because Herod was in awe of John and gave him his protection. When he'd heard him speak he was perplexed, and yet he liked listening to him.

When Herodias's daughter, Salome, danced at Herod's birthday she delighted Herod and his guests. Herod told Salome to ask him for anything he'd give it to her, even half of his kingdom. She asked her mother, "What shall I ask for?" Herodias replied, "The head of John the Baptizer [Yochanan ben Zechariah]." Salome rushed back to Herod and told him she wanted John's head on a dish. Herod was distressed; he was reluctant to break his word. Herod ordered a bodyguard to bring

John's head. The guard beheaded him, and then gave John's head on a dish to Salome who gave it to Herodias.

Jessica read New Testament Matthew 14:12 NJB: "John's [Yochanan ben Zechariah] disciples came and took the body and buried it: then they went off to tell Jesus."

Collin told us about Sir Robert Anderson's book called, *The Coming Prince*. This next verse makes sense if using a prophetic calendar which was configured a hundred plus years ago by him.[1]

Tanakh, Ketuvim, Daniel 9:25 JPS: "You must know and understand: From the issuance of the word to restore the rebuild Jerusalem until the [time of the] anointed leader is seven weeks; and for sixty-two weeks it'll be rebuilt, square and moat, but in a time of distress. And after those sixty-two weeks, the anointed one will disappear and vanish."

In the sixth chapter of Sir Robert Anderson's book, he explains how English interprets a week to mean seven days. The Hebrew language, interprets a week to mean seven. Therefore, week could also mean seven years.

The year of issuance to restore Jerusalem was decreed of Artaxerxes in 445 BC according to Tanakh, Ketuvim, Nehemiah 2:1–8 KJV.

Collin walked everyone through the calculations on the SMARTboard. With a year being three hundred sixty days as it was calculated in the ancient calendars of that time period. If you add 483 years (seven years of seven plus sixty-two years of seven equals 483 years) taking into consideration the leap years, errors in calendar, the change from BC to AD, Sir Robert's theory puts the end, the day of Jesus's triumphal entry into Jerusalem, five days before his death on the cross!

---

1. You may download and/or read this entire book by going to http://philologos.org/__eb-tcp/

Fourteen

Loren looked in the mirror and promised to never again allow anyone so much control over her conversations, beliefs, and thoughts. Her eyes were red and her face was blotchy from crying.

My real friends love me for being me, not for my looks. Then she added a quick silent prayer. *Thank you, God, for helping me through that scary situation. I pray Giles seeks the help he needs in order to become a person of faith. Keep my friends and me safe as we continue on the journey you've placed in our laps. And one more thing, God, thank you for loving me throughout my doubts of you. Thank you for not giving up on me and listening to the prayers of my parents. Amen.*

She pulled out a plastic grocery bag out from under the sink and placed his toiletries she'd packed earlier for him inside. There were no tears, no fears, no regrets, and no anger. She knew he needed more than what she could give.

Everyone lunched in the cafeteria. As much as they didn't like leaving her alone, they respected her request for alone time.

They reached the library room the same time as Loren. "Hey, perfect timing," Loren said to everyone as she swiped her card and opened the door.

Drew withdrew two yarmulkes from his back pocket. He placed one on his head and offered the other to Collin.

"Is this for me?" Collin asked.

"Yes, I brought it as a gift for you. In our faith, we wear these during prayer, while studying or reading the Tanakh or in the synagogue. It's a symbol of faith in believing God's greater than us and we should be humble," Drew instructed.

"Isn't it for Jewish people only? I'd hate to be offensive," Collin asked.

"I'm not offended, or I wouldn't have given it to you. I feel closer to God having it on when I pray. It reminds me of God's power. That's why I cover my head," Drew continued.

"Thanks, my friend." Collin placed the gift on his head.

Loren read the prayer aloud as each person closed their eyes to concentrate on the words in the prayer. "Lord, I come to you in your special place to seek your wisdom, to learn your word, your works, and your future plans for me. Guide my lips as I speak what you need me to say, guard my mind as I discover disturbing things in your word I wasn't prepared to read. Encourage my heart to seek you. Thank you for calling me to know you better. Thank you for wanting to know me. Amen."

"Amen" was echoed by everyone.

"Is it just me, or does this prayer seem to gain more meaning each time we read it?" Jessica asked.

"It touches me deeper every time I say it," Rachel agreed as the rest nodded.

"Where were we?" Amy questioned. "Doesn't it seem like we were here a week ago instead of just yesterday evening?"

"It seems like a lot's happened since yesterday evening," Loren wondered aloud. "Do you think it's a supernatural resistance? Like maybe Satan wants to keep us distracted from finding out the truth by placing obstacles in our way?"

Drew made a *pfft* sound and said, "I don't believe in all the hocus-pocus parts of religions. Besides, we're making swift headway given the topic."

The Library Room

Jessica plugged her laptop into the flatscreen showing them the information she'd found regarding the missing tribes. They all discussed and added notes to her findings.

Everyone appreciated Jessica's information and its importance. "Thanks everyone. I've learned a lot. It's amazing how God directed me. I became discouraged here and there, but as soon as I thought I'd hit a dead end, God guided me to important information."

"Jessica, this is awesome stuff! May I print off a copy to take to Mrs. Rosenberg later? I think she'd find it fascinating! It's because of her we looked into this part of the prophecies."

Collin interjected, "I'd like to research why Catholic churches feel they're only allowed to celebrate Communion. Sarah, I again apologize for their rudeness. I want to get to the bottom of it and see what makes our communion so special they feel they can be a bigot about it."

Sarah's cheeks reddened again as Rachel looked to Sarah for an explanation. "Apparently, Protestants aren't allowed to partake in Catholic communions. I was called out."

Drew joined in the conversation. "See! And this is what I don't get about all these different Christian religions. Everyone has different ideas on what or how to believe," Drew griped. "Jewish people are Jewish. We read the Tanakh and believe in the same God. No baptisms, no communions, nothing denying each other from joining."

"Not so true, Drew," Rachel argued. "We've several Jewish denominations: Orthodox, Reform, Conservative, Reconstructionist, Secular Humanistic, and what's that other one,"—she turned looking to Drew for the answer—"oh, Jewish Renewal! And lest we forget, Messianic, although most Jewish people will tell you they're no longer Jewish if they become Messianic Jew. On top of that, there are several different denominations inside those different types like Ashkenazi, Haredi, Masorti, Hasidic, and Sephardic. These are confusing to even us Jewish people."

"Yes, I guess you're right," Drew agreed. "I never gave it much thought before."

"What? What did you say Mr. Drew?" Rachel teased. "Did I hear you say I was right? You're giving up an argument?"

"Hey, I'm matured enough to admit when I'm wrong. I also agree Messianic Jews are no longer Jewish. They're Christians playing Jewish dress up. Or Jewish people who've converted to Christianity. They're not Jewish anymore. It angers me when they try tricking Jewish people into thinking it's acceptable," Drew griped.

Jessica questioned, "I thought being Jewish was a nationality not a religious statement, Drew. Don't you need to be born Jewish to be Jewish? If you're born Jewish, Mexican, or Asian, aren't you Jewish, Mexican, or Asian, regardless of your religious beliefs?"

"Some feel that way," Drew said in a derogatory tone. "The Messianic Jews do and perhaps Jewish people who've married non-Jewish people and don't claim any denomination but still claim to be Jewish."

Jessica claimed, "I don't mean to get your hairs all ruffled up. However, what if, for argument purposes, Jewish people who've converted to Christianity wanted a church similar to their synagogue and created the Messianic Jewish church? Instead of thinking of it like Christians are trying to trick Jewish people into becoming Christians, why not think of it as Jewish converts trying to bring Christians back towards Judaism? I see it as a way to bridge them together. Besides, weren't you the one claiming a couple years ago, 'New Shabbat, new ways of being forgiven, new Tanakh, New books added to the Tanakh. Why does everyone try to wipe out Judaism? Why can't we keep our faith? It works for us. Why do Christians always shove the Jesus thing down our throats as well as force us to change to their ways?' Weren't those a few reasons you gave us as to why Jewish people won't accept Christianity?"

The Library Room

"Yes, those were reasons, and another is kids making fun of kids by tossing our yarmulkes around. They'd call them beanies for weenies. Just bigotry growing up," Drew told them.

"Sorry, Drew. Kids can be mean no matter what religion they've been taught," Amy said. "Some are just born bullies."

Drew smirked. "Once I hit adolescence and outgrew them, I took my resentments out on them during football practices. I loved being flagged for 'unnecessary roughness.' They stopped. Then I asked a girl to the spring dance, and she said 'No, my mom won't let me because Jews killed Jesus.' Now I ask you, why should I want to give up everything Jewish to judge *my* relatives that way? I didn't judge her blond hair and her last name ending in *man* as being a German who'd murdered my great-grandfather!"

"Good for you for not stooping to her level," Jessica complimented him. "But keep in mind the dreams God sent. As you pointed out, all religions have had bad spots in the past and some not nice people thinking ignorantly. You can't judge an entire religion based upon an ignorant girl."

"We're getting sidetracked," Loren called the two back to order. "We need to stay focused so we can find out if Christ is the Messiah or not with an open mind and heart. We must eliminate past teachings and prejudices to stay unbiased in our mission. Right?" Everyone agreed. "Good. Now someone find me cookies from the goody stash."

The room fell silent as everyone returned to the research mode.

At five o'clock, the boys feigned hunger sounds to each other.

"Growl!" Drew conspired with Collin.

"Grumble. Rawr. Grumble. Gurgle." Collin smiled while keeping his nose in his book.

"Wow! Was that a hunger sound, Collin?" Drew asked, keeping his nose to his book too.

"Umm, growl. By George, I think you may be—rawrl—on to something, Drew. Do you think we'll work through this starvation drive the women are forcing upon us or should we be men and go hunt in the wilderness for meals?" Collin suggested.

"Okay, I get it." Loren smiled. "Let's grab a bite to eat. Sound good to everyone?" Everyone was ready to leave before she finished her sentence.

As they walked out the door, Collin suggested the Italian bistro or the school cafeteria, which was serving creamed chicken over rice. Everyone voted for the bistro.

The wait for a table was eight minutes. Collin and Drew growled to receive love taps from whichever girl was standing near. It became their newest game, and they loved the attention.

Rachel and Drew sat next to each other. The linen tablecloth added an extra touch of ambiance to the relaxed dinner amongst friends. A large carafe of wine was shared with everyone at the table. They'd learned it was cheaper than buying it by the glass. Collin dispersed the wine.

Drew lifted his glass. "I'm blessed calling you friends. You're family to me. This past week I've reflected upon how important you all are to me. I've never appreciated Professor Finkel's teachings. However, I feel like we're being blessed from this assignment because of him. Therefore, I've a new fondness for the old guy. Loren, thanks for including us in your project. We're all learning more than we ever thought we'd want to about ancient Israel *and* each other. This may be the most important class I've never paid for nor received credit hours for taking. Let's lift our glasses to Professor Finkel!"

"To Professor Finkel."

Everyone laughed as glasses clinked.

They became quiet, thinking about Drew's toast. They were learning about history, religions, and about each other. It was drawing them closer as friends. It was also drawing them closer to God. And, they craved more of him as they edged closer to the truth.

A small group sat in the corner greeting each other as each arrived. They obviously don't see each other often but are close friends.

"Look," Sarah said, "that'll be us in twenty years."

"Absolutely!" Loren agreed with her glass in the center of the table for everyone to clink, which they did.

"You know what? You're right, Sarah!" Jessica sipped her wine. "We should make a pact today. We should promise to get together every five years. Even, if we're married, have a kids, and have busy careers. We'll set aside a weekend to get together."

"Absolutely!" Loren agreed with her glass in the center of the table for everyone to clink, which they did.

"And if we continue clinking our glasses, we'll be ordering another carafe, and drunk before our meals arrive." Amy laughed in merriment.

"Absolutely!" Loren agreed with her glass in the center of the table for everyone to clink again; which, they did and laughed knowing they'd be holding off on more group cheers.

"On one hand, I'll be glad when it's done and I can hand Professor Finkel his report. On the other hand, I don't want to stop researching," Loren admitted. "I'm enjoying time with all of you. I couldn't have picked better friends to journey this with me."

"I know what you mean," Sarah said. "I never thought I'd see the day where I'd enjoy discovering things about Judaism and Ancient Christian cultures. And it's weird when you're looking for one thing, then end up looking up something else for clarification, which leads you to something relevant in some ways but not relevant to what you're looking for at the time but becomes relevant down the road."

"Yah, I get that!" Collin spoke. "I don't know how it happened exactly, but I learned two thousand years ago the Tanakh was hand printed by scribes. It makes sense because they didn't have printing presses back then. There were so many rules. They had to be certified. They weren't allowed to write any of God's names down without first bathing their body and cleaning their writing utensil. Can you imagine how often they bathed in order to complete a page? And the pages had to contain so many columns and no more than so many lines; with no mistakes. If there was a mistake it couldn't be used and had to be fixed within thirty days or buried. They weren't allowed to write by memory. They had to keep a copy beside them and write word for word saying each word out loud as they wrote it. I found it fascinating."

"That's true, Collin," Rachel said. "Did you also know if any two letters touched each other it invalidated the document? And no two words could be so close that they looked like one word and no one word could be spaced looking like two words. They were meticulous in detail. They still are when it comes to hand writing the Shema for the scroll inside a mezuzah. God's Word is meaningful to us. It's of God."

"Wait," Jessica interrupted, "What's a shee-ma-mezoo-zoo?"

"Mezuzah," Rachel corrected, "is a case on the right side of a doorpost on Jewish homes, or at least most Jewish homes in my neighborhood. Unfortunately, not all Hebrew adhere to the mitzvah…our laws. Inside the mezuzah, is a scroll with the words of the Shema. They're a couple of passages from Deuteronomy 6, written on one side and God's name written on the other. It's to remind us to keep God's words in our hearts and minds."

"Wow, very cool," Jessica said. "What do they look like?"

"Mezuzot, plural for mezuzah, vary," Rachel answered. "If you'd like we'll look them up online when we get back to the library. Some are elaborate. The scroll inside, however, is the most expensive part. I think my father paid around forty bucks a piece for them."

"How many do you need?" Amy seemed confused.

"My father has them on every doorpost in the condo as well as the entrance. We don't put them on the bathroom doorposts." Rachel wrinkled up her nose. "Or closet doorposts since a closet isn't big enough to qualify as a room. Some only put it on their entrance door."

"So is it a reminder of the Passover? Like when blood needed to be placed on the doorposts?" Collin asked.

"No, not at all," Drew answered for Rachel. "Nor is it a good-luck charm. It's as Rachel mentioned, a reminder to keep God's words in your mind and heart."

"Sorry, dude, I meant no disrespect. It's all new to me...to us. No one teaches these things to Christians. I find it fascinating," Collin said. "And I get what you mean about it being misconstrued as a form of charm or to ward off evil. I see that happening with the cross all the time. It's supposed to be a reminder of the free gift God sent to us through his Son. It was never meant to become a protective shield against vampires, or a gaudy sacrilegious piece of jewelry worn by someone who has no idea of its meaning, nor is it something we pray to or worship to gain special powers. It's a reminder of Jesus' sacrifice for sinners."

Rachel and Drew's chairs inched closer to each other's as the meal passed. No one said a word for fear of breaking the attraction.

Amy finished eating first and was preoccupied with checking her phone. Jessica placed a hand on her arm as she picked her phone up for the hundredth time, "Amy, go. Go be with your friend. It's important and we understand."

Amy hugged Jessica. "I want to...I don't know if I'm ready to see her go like I did my mom. I need to go over more information with her if she's up to it. I hate watching her body fail more and more."

"I'm not sure what to say other than I'm sure it's breaking your heart again, and my heart breaks for you knowing you're in pain. I keep you in my prayers for God to send you comfort," Jessica comforted her.

Amy asked everyone to excuse her for the rest of the night. Everyone gave her a parting hug.

No one noticed Rachel and Drew holding hands under the table.

After divvying up the bill, they called it a night. They were satisfied with their efforts and the facts they'd uncovered for the day.

Jessica and Sarah offered to help Loren with Giles' things. Loren welcomed the company, help, and support.

Drew offered to walk Rachel home. She smiled when she realized they were still holding hands.

Collin was excited about watching the Sunday night football game at his house.

Rachel and Drew walked off, holding hands. No one mentioned a word to cause embarrassment.

That was hard for Collin. Sarah persuaded him by pinching his lower bicep area. He understood her hint and smile.

Collin hoped Adam and Ray wanted to watch the game, so he wouldn't feel uncomfortable yelling at the TV while they were studying. It was fun to vent and cheer with other dudes in the house even if they didn't understand the stakes.

Loren, Jessica, and Sarah walked together. While Jessica and Sarah were excited about packing Giles's stuff, Loren was sad. She wasn't walking as fast as her two friends. They'd slow down every few steps for her to catch up.

Meanwhile, Amy left the library with two new folders of information: Missing Tribes and the Prophecies of the Messiah's Life. Her pace switched between urgent to hesitant. She was eager to see Mrs. Rosenberg's children as a result of last night's bonding time with Alec and the affectionate hug from Amelia.

When Amy arrived she was informed before going to Ms. Roses Are My Favorite Flower's room that she'd retained water due to her kidneys not functioning. Still, it hadn't prepared Amy for the sight of her friend's swollen legs, arms, and hands.

The Library Room

Mrs. Rosenberg was sleeping when Amy entered the room. Amelia and Alec were sitting on the small couch with Amelia's head resting on Alec's shoulder. Amy noted Amelia's taunt facial expression.

"Hey," Amy whispered. "I thought I'd drop by with new information and check on her."

Amelia answered, "She's had a rough day. She's refusing her dialysis treatment, so she's retaining water."

Amy felt her eyes swell up with tears.

"She's slept most of the day and wouldn't eat," Amelia continued. "The aides have done their best to entice her to eat something—anything—just a bite, but she's stubborn and won't. She says she's fasting for her Lord."

"Sometimes, older people get ideas in their heads about such things and you can't change their minds no matter how much you try," Amy explained while tears streamed down Amelia's face.

"What are you two hens clucking about over there?" asked a raspy voice from the bed.

Amy gave Ms. Roses Are My Favorite Flowers a hug.

"We're clucking about a hen not cooperating with everyone. What do you think about that?" Amy smiled to the words to the eyes of an adoring friend.

"I think peeps should respect the mother hen and not place demands upon them." Ms. Roses Are My Favorite Flowers answered.

"And, I think a mother hen shouldn't make their peeps worry," Amelia argued, kissing her mother's forehead.

"I'm so glad to see you, Amy. I'd wondered if you'd be able to bring more information this evening with it being a Sunday," Mrs. Rosenberg inquired.

"We've uncovered prophecies concerning the life of the Mashiach," Amy answered and went to her book bag.

"Alec reread me the information you left," Mrs. Rosenberg informed. "We've had delightful conversations about our faith and the information you've provided. Alec's strong in his faith. He's not convinced we need a Mashiach in our Jewish faith. He feels our covenant with God at Mount Sinai is irrevocable. He isn't saying it's not needed for the Gentiles. However, it's not needed for our Jewish faith since it's complete. God forgives our sins when we pray. I've been taught that too. However, you can't fault me for wanting to know for sure. What do you think, Amy?"

Amy felt tension in the room. On one hand, she felt she needed to 'share this good news to all of your family and friends that Jesus is here to save them!' On the other hand, she feared Alec may be right; after all, God gave it to the people of faith at Mount Sinai. *He certainly wouldn't recant his offer, would he? Could he? Should he?*

"Ms. Roses Are My Favorite Flowers, I'm not comfortable answering that question without completing the research needed to do so. I'm giving you information as we're finding it. I don't want to get into a debate as to which religion trumps which one if/and when…I know what I've been taught. I also know as a result of this report I've some questions regarding Christianity as well as Judaism. Both can't be wrong, and both can't be right. I'll let God speak the truth to my heart. This way, I'll know in *my* heart where I need to be with him. I think before counseling someone over an eternal decision I'd better know for sure. Right?" Amy answered. "I don't know."

"My sweet child." Ms. Roses Are My Favorite Flowers admired Amy. "You're becoming wiser as a result of this project aren't you? God's directing your group! I knew God's project was special for it to include you." Mrs. Rosenberg looked at the faces of her two children. "I trust God will speak the truth to *our* hearts too even if, they interpret it differently. Now, where does this start?" Suddenly, Ms. Roses Are My Favorite Flowers showed enthusiasm and sat up in her bed.

"In this file, we've information on the missing tribes I feel you'll find interesting. I see them as coming into play later. We're

The Library Room

getting close to all of them being in Jerusalem." Amy then picked up the other folder. "In this file folder, we've pieced together prophecies regarding the Mashiach's life on earth. We've begun the Moses comparison since the prophecy says God will send a prophet like Moses. We'd built a comparison chart between Yeshua and Moses when we called it quits for the night."

Alec startled everyone in the room when he said, "I'd like to see the Moses part of the project when you're done."

"Sure, Alec," Amy said. "I'll bring an extra copy for you once it's completed. May I ask why that part of the research captures your attention and the prophetic parts haven't interested to you?"

"Because," Alec declared, "using or twisting the Tanakh's words by prophets hundreds or thousands of years before a happening isn't relevant. I mean, yes, they were prophesying. However, it was prophecy for their own time not for an upcoming Mashiach we Hebrews don't need once God made his covenant with us on Mount Sinai. And to use scriptures as *typology* is a farce. It's like me declaring I'm the long-awaited Messiah, and now I'll dig through scriptures to prove my point. I'm sure I can scrounge up verses to secure my rightful placement since Psalms has scriptures dealing with everything from life to death to sorrow to happiness. See what I'm saying?"

"Yes, I see how your skeptical mind works," Amy said. "Interesting."

"I don't think you can call an entire religious community skeptic. It's what we believe," Alec corrected her.

"So you're telling me *all* Jewish people don't believe in the Messianic Prophecies? Then why'd God leave so many obvious pointers? Why were these prophecies given to the Hebrews regarding a Mashiach *after* God gave you the Covenant at Mount Sinai? Don't you think that's strange?" Amy challenged.

"Yes, *most* Hebrews, and we don't see them as clues. It was useful prophecy for the time at hand." Alec corrected.

"Okay, you two, I'm still curious about them anyway. I guess I'm not a *most* type of Hebrew. I want to know the information and decide if it's true, or coincidence, or if it's as you feel, Alec, cleverly selected verses." Mrs. Rosenberg scowled.

Amy began going over the new information pertaining to the life of Yeshua while Alec and Amelia again pretended not to listen.

Fifteen

Loren turned on the lights to all of her furniture missing and the kitchen cupboards opened and emptied. Loren stopped breathing and listened. *Where's my stuff? Who took it? Are they gone? How'd they get it all out so fast?*

Loren spun in circles where her kitchen table had been. She saw a note stuck to the refrigerator. She grabbed it and recognized the writing from Giles. Her heart pumped in her ears while every scary movie she'd ever seen rushed into her mind.

She read the note to Jessica and Sarah.

> Dear Loren,
>
> I'm writing this from the jail cell you had me placed in this evening. I can't believe you thought I'd ever hurt you, but it proves our relationship has run its course. I tried to love you. I even considered marrying you and bought a ring.
>
> Since I'm not there to help Mellissa, I don't know when you'll get this. I can't call you, and they tell me I won't be able to go within a hundred yards of you once I'm released from jail.
>
> Wow! It appears you're holding all the power now! You're wrong. I hold my own power. I'm my own person.
>
> Mellissa loves me and wants to be with me. She accepts my beliefs. I don't love her yet, but she understands I didn't love you at first either.
>
> I told Mellissa to take the apartment key to the restaurant for you to pick up tonight if you're not out

late partying with your friends or tomorrow before I post bond. She's there covering for me so I don't lose my job.

    I gave Mellissa a list of items I felt were mine since I was the only one who ever used them—like, all the kitchen items, cleaning supplies, and furniture I picked out for our home. You at least owe me these things since you kicked me out with nothing but the clothes on my back before they dressed me in orange here in jail. She'll give you a list of the items she wasn't able to fit into the moving truck. Make arrangements with her to get them to her apartment since I'm not allowed to come near our home.

    I can't wait to see you in court tomorrow. I hope you go to jail for falsely accusing me of kidnapping and domestic abuse. How or when did I ever abuse you? I've done everything for you. I stayed in this two bit rotten college town working in a restaurant so you could finish your lame career in marketing. You've ruined my life!

    I don't know how you'll be able to sleep. I hope your shame keeps you up all night. Yes, I took the bed. I'm not letting you make love to anyone else in it.

    If I were you, I'd move in with a friend. You'll never be able to live by yourself. You need someone to take care of you. That's what I did. You're a full-time job. You'll never survive on your own.

    Too bad I'll be outside one hundred yards from you and won't be watching when karma gets a hold of you.

    Don't ever call me again!

Giles

"Why do mean people always think karma's going to get someone else?" Sarah asked.

"Loren, are you all right?" Jessica asked.

"I'm just livid right now." Loren was seething from anger. "What'd they take?"

"By the looks of it, I'd say she helped herself to as much as she could fit into a moving truck." Sarah headed to the bedroom.

The Library Room

"What used to be here?" Sarah pointed to a dusty two-foot square snuggled in the corner of the hallway next to the bathroom.

"My linen tower." Loren wanted to sit and cry, but she'd nowhere to sit. "He took it all. Everything I've earned while working and everything passed down to me from grandmother's estate. I paid for everything—rent, food, utilities, furniture, linens, and toiletries. Where'd *his* money go? What was he using his money for all this time?"

"Um, if I were you, I'd make a police report to see if you can get any of it back," Jessica suggested. "They still have your key, and I'd think about changing all of the locks tonight too." Jessica stood back, giving Loren time to think. It was eight o'clock.

Loren agreed. Sarah called the police. The dispatch said she'd send someone over right away.

Within a couple of minutes, Officer Jones and Officer Gordon from this morning arrived at her apartment again.

They walked into the house and saw everything was missing.

Officer Jones stayed at the house filling out the report while Officer Gordon drove to the restaurant to locate the stolen property.

Loren called her landlord to see if there were spare locks on the property. He told her he'd be over to do the change himself.

A few minutes later, Officer Gordon radioed saying he was going inside to discuss the moving truck parked behind the restaurant.

Jessica sent a text to Drew, Collin, and Rachel.

***

Drew and Rachel found themselves facing each other again at the door while she looked for the key. Like the night before, she struggled staying focused with him so near.

He placed his hand on her elbow and said, "Hey, it's me. Don't be so nervous. We're friends. Take your time."

She lifted her head and looked into his eyes. She felt the key with the tip of her finger and pulled it out.

"Don't look at me like that, or I'll kiss those lips," Drew confessed. "It isn't where I want to go at this point in our relationship."

Drew watched disappointment shadow her face. He realized how it sounded. "Wait, I don't think you understand my intensions, Ms. Rachel. I have intensions. I intend to sweep you off of your feet and make you fall in love with one of your best friends."

Rachel beamed. "Oh, well, that cleared things up."

Drew watched elation replace the upset look.

She turned her body keeping her eyes on his face and felt for the doorknob. She unlocked and opened the door. It was a time of invite or good night. She watched his face.

Her face felt warm, and her throat became dry as she recognized not only was she in love with him but he was in love with her as well.

Rachel said, "Drew, would you like to watch the game with me? I don't have beer. I don't keep anything on hand except diet pop."

"If you promise not to molest me." Drew followed her.

"I think I can handle that. I've been able to contain my ravenous urges towards you for years." Rachel opened the refrigerator. "Okay, I have Diet Cola, Diet Root Beer, Diet Ginger Ale, and—"

"Let me guess Diet." Drew rolled his eyes. "You know, that stuff will kill you."

Rachel snickered. "Yep, but I won't die of obesity."

He gave her an up and down look and smiled. "Rachel, you could wear a burlap sack and it'd become the trend here on campus." Drew knew a lot of girls on campus looked to Rachel's style as an example of the latest fashion.

Rachel smirked. "Ha, I'd need to cinch it with bling!"

"I'll have whatever you're having." Drew decided.

While pouring the colas, she asked him to find the game.

The Library Room

He turned the game on and sat all the way over to the right side of the loveseat so she'd sit next to him.

❈

Collin's roommates were engrossed in the show *Computer Intelligence*. He prayed their show ended soon, he'd looked forward to watching football. He read the note in his room, "Drew phoned you were coming home. We found geeky show. Welcome to football night! Blame Drew, his idea. Beers are in the fridge."

"Nice!" Collin fell into his recliner. "I owe you three a prank."

The living room was large but felt small since there were four recliners side by side in front of an old projector television the boys called The Dinosaur.

Collin sent a text to Drew. "R U coming home for football or kissy-face with Ms. Rachel? Bout time U 2 figured it out!'

"Watching game at Rachel's. Sorry I missed the fun I caused. Got U big time?" was Drew's returned text.

A few minutes later, his cell phone indicated a new text. Collin reread the message from Jessica a couple of times and responded back.

❈

Drew's phone signaled Collin's text. He laughed and shared the message with Rachel since she'd been with him when he'd called Ray.

"He expects you to kiss and tell?" Rachel laughed.

"No, no," Drew assured her. "It's his way of letting us know to expect jabs here or there about us seeing each other."

Rachel didn't miss a beat. "We're seeing each other?"

Drew rolled his eyes. "If it's acceptable to you, I'd like to date exclusively."

Rachel bounced in her seat as she answered, "Yes!"

"Here's the thing," Drew began.

"Oh? A thing?" Rachel repeated.

"I've dated girls without commitment," Drew said.

There it is, Rachel thought. *He wants to tie up my life without any commitment on his part; typical.* She distanced herself.

"I don't want that with you," Drew confessed.

"You don't want a commitment? You want to date exclusively without a commitment. You expect *me* to commit." Rachel tried sounding like she wasn't getting angry at his proposal.

"Oh, Rachel!" Drew laughed. "That's not what I meant. What I'm trying to say is you mean more to me than the physical attraction I feel, which is a lot. We've been friends for years."

"Okay." Rachel was confused "So, what's the catch?"

"The catch is—and this is where my relationships in the past have fallen short." Drew hesitated. "Look, I want to kiss you. But I don't want to kiss you. And it's not because I don't know how. Yes, I know how to kiss, or so I've been told. Nor do I think you're not sexy because, you certainly are."

"Let me get this straight." Rachel raised her brows in concern. "We're dating, but we're not going to kiss?"

"When we kiss, it'll be for one of two reasons. I'm either telling you good-bye as *you're* breaking up with *me*, or after we've said I do as man and wife." Drew waited for the response he'd received in the past—the kiss good-bye with the Yiddish word *meshuggener*.

"Oh, wow, that's a first." Rachel appreciated the respect, felt disappointed over not kissing him for a while, and battled the "run, he's a meshuggener" thought. "I'd wondered why your relationships never lasted. They didn't trust God? Or they wanted instant gratification?"

"Probably both," Drew answered.

"It's sweet. I'm worried about your expectations." Rachel needed to confess what may become the deal breaker.

"How so?" he asked.

The Library Room

"I'm not as pure as most think." Rachel waited.

"I'm not either," Drew confessed, knowing what she'd implied.

Rachel explained for Drew to judge. "I dated a guy for three years in high school. We'd been intimate." She'd never felt embarrassed over her actions until this moment.

Unfortunately, she'd learned a hard lesson. Your relationship changes if that line is crossed before marriage. With most young people, it fails.

"I've heard you speak about him. You trusted him, and he failed," Drew acknowledged her honesty and heart.

"Drew, I've only been in that long-term relationship. Since then, my relationships haven't lasted more than two or three weeks. I've been called high-maintenance, a Jewish American princess and spoiled. I like you a lot and don't want our dating to ruin our friendship. I thought about that last night while trying to sleep." Rachel squirmed while sharing.

"Let me guess." Drew caressed her hand. "You refused to put out after the first few dates."

"In some cases, but not all." Rachel sorted through the files in her mind. "I ended a few when they didn't want to do anything more than play video games or get stoned. I got bored with partying. It's the same drunk drama every week."

Their phones indicated a new text. He thought it'd be Collin conducting a hand-check text, so he laughed while picking it up. He stopped laughing when he read Jessica's text. He sent a returned text, "How can we help?"

Jessica returned a text saying, "Stay tuned. We may need you."

"So what'll happen to Giles and Mellissa in regards to the robbery?" Sarah asked Officer Jones.

"Loren has the right to press charges," Officer Jones said. "However, in this case where the truck may still be loaded with

Loren's belongings, and the person who loaded them didn't realize she was trespassing and stealing from Loren, I feel, if she cooperates by returning the items, it may be punishment enough. It may wake her up as to whom she's taken on as a partner."

"I agree," Loren said. "I wish someone had warned me. I've never known this side of him. Just that one incident I mentioned before where I zigged and he zagged. There haven't been any other issues since. This project I'm working on sent him over the top, and I knew it would. I mean, I don't know how I knew, but I knew. He's always been anti-God and anti-religion, so I knew it'd be a sore subject. However, this coo-coo side show scares me."

"Well, let me tell you," Jessica said, "that man's like Dr. Jekyll and Mr. Hyde. Once you leave his sight, he's mean. Remember Cali's wedding? You went to the ladies room, and he jumped into the seat next to me. I didn't think anything about it. He leaned over and said, 'If you ever do anything to sabotage my relationship with Loren, you'll pay. I'm marrying her, and I'll be damned if her friends muck it up.' I almost told you, but then, I thought maybe I misunderstood him. When you returned, he was his happy, tipsy self again."

"Loren," Officer Jones alerted, "I'm hearing, and seeing, signs that aren't healthy. Are you sure he's never hurt you?"

"No, never," Loren assured everyone. "Do you think he'll hurt me or my friends once he gets out?"

"It's a concern," Officer Jones answered. "People like him have done serious harm to loved ones they could no longer control. I'm going to request they keep him incarcerated until a psychologist can analyze him. My gut's telling me he's a danger to himself and others."

"Really? I think the more he's in *jail*,"—Loren exaggerated the word like his letter—"the more he'll blame *me* like he says in his letter."

"You have a letter?" Office Jones asked.

The Library Room

"Yes," Loren pulled the letter from her pocket. "It was on my refrigerator when I got home. He feels I won't survive without him, and he deserves all of my belongings because I've ruined his life."

"More proof he's psychotic," Sarah spatted.

Jessica sent a text to Drew, Rachel, and Collin. "May need help unloading truck."

Officer Gordon radioed, "I've spoken to Mellissa. She's willing to cooperate by returning the stolen goods this evening. I recognized the furniture from this afternoon. Over."

"Ten-four. Over," Officer Jones replied.

Officer Gordon radioed back, "I'll stay with the truck until Mellissa's able to lock up the kitchen. All orders have been cooked and served. Over."

"Ten-four. Over," Officer Jones replied again and then turned to the girls. "It's a good thing it's a small town. Otherwise, we wouldn't be able to spend so much time on this case making sure it's taken care of the right way for you."

"Thanks," Sarah said. "We're grateful."

"Is she bringing someone to help her unload and put my stuff back where it belongs?" Loren asked as she answered the door and saw her landlord, Mr. O'Mallee.

Then it hit her. Her mind swirled, *He's changing the locks to keep Giles and Mellissa out. I was held against my will by a man I thought was my best friend. I was robbed while studying about God. Everyone's sitting on my floor with a policeman. Giles is in jail waiting to meet a judge on kidnapping and assaulting an officer. My whole life's been turned upside down in the past twenty-four hours.* She felt nauseated and dizzy.

Officer Jones saw the sway of the head. He leapt in front of her. Placing her hand on his chest, he took deep breaths. "Loren, look at me. Breathe with me. Slow deep breaths."

It wasn't working. Her breathing quickened as her face paled.

"What'da'ya tryin' to do? Cast ya'self in ya own Hollywood film?" Mr. O'Mallee barked as he grabbed Loren and helped her down to the floor. "Now, listen up, youngsta. I need ya ta get on ya hands and knees and put ya head ta the floorah."

Loren barely understood her landlord's New England accent with a clear head. Now, all she heard were ahs and irritation in his voice.

She understood his instructions from the shoving actions he demanded with his hands. She was on her knees with her butt in the air and her head on the floor. Her breathing slowed to normal, and her head stopped spinning. When she felt better she lifted her head and sat on her heels. She looked around seeing everyone standing in a circle around her; the panic returned, and once again, she swayed.

The landlord lifted her middle section with one arm, pushed her head down with the other, and said, "Get ya arse back up and ya head lowered again."

After a few minutes, she was herself again.

Officer Jones's radio squawked, "Does she have anyone to unload? Mellissa's driving, but she no longer has hired hands. Over."

Sarah nodded.

"Ten-four, she does. Do we have an ETA? Over."

"Ah, I'd say another twenty-five minutes or so. Over," Officer Gordon replied.

Within minutes Drew, Rachel, and Collin with Adam and Ray arrived at Loren's house.

Sixteen

Loren's Notes Part IV—
The Twelve Tribes of Israel

Tanakh, Nevi'im, Ezekiel 11: 17–21 KJV: Therefore say, Thus saith the Lord God; I will even gather you from the people, and assemble you out of the countries where ye have been scattered, and I will give you the land of Israel. And they shall come thither, and they shall take away all the detestable things thereof and all the abominations thereof from thence. And I will give them one heart, and I will put a new spirit within you; and I will take the stony heart out of their flesh, and will give them an heart of flesh: That they may walk in my statutes, and keep mine ordinances, and do them: and they shall be my people, and I will be their God. But as for them whose heart walketh after the heart of their detestable things and their abominations, I will recompense their way upon their own heads, saith the Lord God.

Jessica taught us the original tribes were the sons of Jacob whom God renamed to Israel.

Tanakh Torah Va-Yishlah Genesis 32:24-29 NIV (Summarized): Jacob was left alone. A Man wrestled with him until the break of dawn. When He saw that He hadn't prevailed against him, He wretched Jacob's hip at its socket. Then the Man said, "Let me go, for dawn is breaking." But Jacob answered, "I'll not let You go, unless You bless me." The Man asked, "What's your name?" Jacob replied, "Jacob." The Man said, "Your name shall no longer be Jacob, but Israel, for you've striven with beings divine and human, and have prevailed." Jacob asked, "Pray tell me Your name." But He said, "You must not ask My name!" and He took leave of him there.

Drew clarified Jacob was wrestling with God all night. It's unclear why God chose to attack Jacob. It's also unclear at first the true identity of the man until the end. He's read several different commentaries on the matter and the Man has been viewed as the Angel of Jehovah, the Lord Himself, God in human form, and the patron angel of Esau.

Amy claimed that in the Tanakh and New Testament, God can appear in human form or in angelic form.

Rachel added that at the end of this constant struggle, God wants Jacob to admit his name is Jacob which means, deceiver, con-man, conniver, and he'd lived up to the name over the years—like with his brother Esau's birth right and then tricking his father into receiving Esau's blessing. God then named him Israel which has various translations: "Struggles with God" is the most common interpretation, "Perseveres," "God Persists," and "Let El [God] Persist."

In Tanakh, Torah, Vayishlach, Genesis 35:10 God reiterates Jacob is to be renamed Israel.

The Twelve Tribes of Israel are listed in a few places. Here's Tanakh, Torah, Vayishlach, Genesis 35:23–26 KJV: The sons of Leah: Reuben, Simeon, Levi, Judah, Issachar, and Zebulun. The sons of Rachel: Joseph and Benjamin. The Sons of Bilhah, Rachel's maid: Dan and Naphtali. And the sons of Zilpah, Leah's maid: Gad and Asher.

Other places include the following :Tanakh, Torah, Shemot, Exodus 1:1–5, Tanakh, Torah, Bamidbar, Numbers 1:20-43, and Tanakh, Ketuvim, I Chronicles 2:1–2.

As I skim over these lists, I'm seeing some are different. Look at Numbers. What happened to Levi? Why are there thirteen tribes?

Jessica explained the twelve sons of Israel were Reuben, Simeon, Levi, Judah, Issachar, Zebulun, Benjamin, Dan, Naphtali, Gad, Asher, and Joseph. These were the original twelve tribes. Then an event caused Israel to reassign the names of the tribal leaders. Reuben lost his rights as firstborn by sleeping with Bilhah. Yep, a modern-day trashy television talk show episode! Reuben slept with his half-brothers, Dan and Naphtali's mom."

Yep, he did. Ew. Tanakh, Torah, Vayishlach, Genesis 35:22 KJV:…Reuben went and lay with Bilhah, his father's concubine, and Israel heard of it…

Tanakh, Torah, Vayechi, Genesis 49:3-4 NIV "Reuben…you went up onto your father's bed, and defiled it."

Jessica then showed us in Reuben's place, Israel gave Joseph's two sons, Ephraim and Manasseh status of being a tribe of Israel. Tanakh, Torah, Vayechi, Genesis 48:5-6 NIV Now Ephraim and Manasseh will be mine. Israel adopted his two grandsons as his own.

Keeping track, Joseph now had two portions of assigned land which were given to each of his sons. Israel actually claimed Joseph's two sons as equals to his own sons and told Joseph if he bears any more sons they'll count as grandchild status, not child status as he gave to Ephraim and Manasseh. As a result, the twelve tribes were modified to Simeon, Levi, Judah, Issachar, Zebulun, Benjamin, Dan, Naphtali, Gad, Asher, Ephraim, and Manasseh.

Collin showed another list, Levi isn't mentioned. It's stated in Numbers that because the Levites were assigned to serve at the tabernacle they weren't apportioned tribal land of their own in Israel. This is further clarified Tanakh, Nevi'im, Joshua 14:3-4 NIV: "Moses had granted the two half-tribes their inheritance east of the Jordan but hadn't granted the Levites an inheritance among the rest, for the sons of Joseph had become two tribes—Manasseh and Ephraim."

Drew points to another reason. Israel was disgusted with Levi and Simeon's behavior as mentioned in Tanakh, Torah, Vayechi, Genesis 49:5–7 NIV: "Simeon and Levi use their weapons as tools of lawlessness…When they're angry they slay men, and when they're happy they maim oxen. Cursed be their violent anger, and their wrath so relentless. I'll divide them in Jacob, scatter them in Israel."

Simeonites ended up being absorbed into the tribe of Judah. Jessica summarized Tanakh, Nevi'im, Joshua 19:1–9 NIV: "The second lot came out for the tribe of Simeon, clan by clan. Their inheritance lay within the territory of Judah.…The inheritance of the Simeonites was taken from the share of Judah, because Judah's portion was more than they needed. So the Simeonites received their inheritance within the territory of Judah."

Rachel enlightened us how the Levites were divided amongst forty-eight cities throughout the land but were given no land. They became God's servants, including the hereditary priesthood, and that cursed behavior went away. So if you notice above, you'll see that Israel cursed their behaviors but not the people for people can and do change over time.

I now understand who the tribes were. But where'd they go and why?

Jessica answered, "The Levites went on to become a heart for the Lord. The landowning tribes paid tithe to the Levites — Maaser Rishon or Levite Tithe. They were the Torah readers, maintainers, and builders, of the tabernacle and temples, sang Psalms during the Temple services, ministered to Kohanim—priests—translated and interpreted Torah when it was read publicly, and many other missions and services to glorify God. They were still thriving in the time of Jesus. A few well known Levites include: Moses, his brother Aaron, John the Baptizer, two of Jesus' disciples Matthew and Mark, Samuel, Isaiah, Jeremiah,

The Library Room

Ezekiel, Ezra, Miriam, Malachi, and also Barnabas in the book of Acts. Of all the tribes they kept their faith in God.

But remember Rueben the naughty son? Even though Israel didn't grant him land he still had a following, a tribe, because of his children, wives, and slaves. It's important to know this because in doing research some researchers have been sloppy in keeping Rueben as one of Israel's twelve entitled tribes.

Because they see his name and tribes listed later in different areas, such as in Numbers 1:5-15 when all the tribes were in the days of exile. Joseph was with the two tribes of Ephraim and Manasseh and not counted as a tribe.

The Israelites grew as God promised. God told Moses and his brother Aaron to conduct a census of all males over the age of twenty from each tribe. They don't include wives and children—male and female—under twenty. Tanakh, Torah, Bamidbar, Numbers 1:20. Rueben: 46,500. Simeon: 59,300. Gad: 45,650. Judah:74,600. Issachar: 54,400. Zebulun: 57,400. Ephraim: 40,500. Manasseh: 32,200. Benjamin: 35,400. Dan: 62,700. Asher: 41,500. Naphtali: 53,400. The Levites weren't counted as Moses was instructed not to count them.

Once in Canaan, the tribes partitioned off and settled their assigned regions on either side of the Jordan River.

Over time, King Solomon established a monarchy amongst all the tribes. However, once he died the tribes split up due to politics and apostasy. Judah—Simeon was by then absorbed by Judah—and Benjamin stayed loyal to the House of David. The rest of the tribes were ruled by different monarchies over the years. The tribes of Judah and Benjamin were in the southern region and were the forefathers to most of the Jewish people we know today. The Levites also remained steady in the regions and cities throughout all.

So that leaves us with eight missing tribes. Not ten like everyone concludes.

Jessica agreed and point out that Rueben's tribe is still forever in time out for being naughty. In Tanakh, Torah, Matot Masei, Numbers 32:1–5 niv: the Reubenites and the Gadites owned cattle in very great numbers. Noticing the lands of Jazer and Gilead were a region suitable for livestock, the Gadites and the Reubenites approached Moses, Eleazar the priest, and the chieftains of the community, and said, "The land the Lord's conquered for the community of Israel is cattle country, and your servants have cattle. It'd be a favor to us." They continued, "If this land were given to us as a holding. Don't move us across the Jordan." With this text, we can assume the two tribes blended together and became one.

At first, Moses was like, "What's the deal here? You're not going to help your other fellow tribesmen fight the heathens for the Promised Land after we've spent forty years bonding and learning that everyone needs to help take what God's telling us to take? You're going to tick off God like your forefathers and then God's going to make us walk around the wilderness for years!" He may have actually said that more eloquently than I interpreted.

The two tribes Gad and Rueben assured Moses three different times of their intentions to be team players and help the other tribes win back the land. However, once that mission's done, they'd like come back to this land instead of staying over there. Moses agreed to the arrangement as long as they upheld their end of the deal.

To add to that, the Half-tribe known as Manasseh was also a part of that melding together.

After a few years, the tribes conquered most of Canaan and took back their lands. Because the tribes of Gad, Manasseh, and Reuben, upheld their end of the bargain, Moses not only let them come back to the land they wanted; but, gave them even more. Tanakh, Nevi'im, Joshua 13:15–23 describes what Moses had given to the tribe of Reuben, clan by clan. Tanakh, Nevi'im, Joshua 13:24–28 describes what Moses had given to the tribe of Gad, clan by clan. And Tanakh, Nevi'im, Joshua 13:29–31 describes what Moses had given to the half-tribe of Manasseh, clan by clan.

The Josephites complained about getting one portion—instead of two—inside Canaan and they were a large people. I think I see what happened here. Manasseh, which was a half-tribe, received a portion; but, with the tribes of Gad and Rueben. It'd been counted as one portion which left out the other half-tribe of Ephraim. It was written Joseph would get two portions in the Promised Land and Ephraim had one so where's the other one? Not counting the one outside the Promised Land. Joshua understood and assigned them the forest covered hill country.

Where's all of this located?

Jessica displayed a map and showed us it is basically all of what constitutes the territory of modern day Israel. The other three mentioned tribes were in a small central western territory which was gobbled up by Jordan.

Everyone was settled. Everyone was always on guard decade after decade, generation after generation. They constantly fought to defend their established territories. Sometimes you win and sometimes you lose.

Amy wants noted, when the Israelites turn their eyes off God, they'll lose because God becomes annoyed. He'll allow enemies to win when people become lazy and self-satisfied in their own walk instead of looking to him to be satisfied. That's why the New Age "do what feels good" doesn't work. Sometimes, God needs us to be uncomfortable, so we're humbled enough to seek him.

Rachel agreed and asked, "Have you ever felt like God was testing you, or you were learning a hard lesson in life? You're right! We're put on this earth for a reason, pleasing and having a relationship with God. That's the first and foremost purpose of our lives. And then, God blesses us with talents. If a student isn't doing well, a caring teacher figures ways to encourage the student to do better. With God, we're often a strong-willed student thinking we can slide by with no effort. After a few failures due to stubbornness, God, our teacher, places us in detention or expels us for our behavior."

Amy said, "Yes, but not forever. *Grace* and *mercy* are the two strongest words in the English language. When you're fully humbled and ask for forgiveness, it's given to you. And guess what happens next? You restart those lessons. You're back in school learning again. God wants us to learn those lessons and develop talents."

Collin feels the tribes of Israel often behaved like stubborn students. That isn't saying every person within a tribe fell away or out of touch with God. And some tribes endured better for the reason that their continual lineage kept God in their hearts.

There are several theories about what happened to each tribe individually. Some speculate certain tribes were expelled to other regions of Europe, Asia, South America, North America, India, and other parts of the Middle East. Some claim Incas and Aztec Indians are missing tribes. We've found no proof or disproof in those theories.

Regarding the four centuries of apostasy in the Northern Kingdom after Solomon, that kingdom was diluted by the Assyrians in a genocidal inbreeding campaign that resulted in the Samaritans being a tiny remnant of the Northern Kingdom. Today, they're nearly extinct.

Jessica informed us the term *Zionism* was coined in 1890 by Nathan Birnbaum. It refers to the national movement of Jews of all persuasions and religions returning to their homeland, Israel. She also pointed out several faces of Senators and Congressmen with dual citizenship to both the US and Israel.

Drew wants us to note that on November 30, 1947 through July 20, 1949, the Israelis claimed victory in re-establishing their land. They defeated Palestinian Arabs. They won despite the odds being against them. When Israel declared its independence in May 1948, the army didn't own cannons or tanks. The Jews were forced to secretly bring in weapons from other countries—mostly Czechoslovakia. Its air force had nine out-of-date planes. The Arabs, on the other hand, had no problems getting arms and support from Brittan. Bew RAF planes, plenty of arms from the Arabs, Iraq, and Transjordan. The United States didn't want to supply weapons to Israel for fear the Arabs would use those weapons on the Israelis and the Israelis would use them on the Arabs. They wanted to stay neutral and kept pushing for the proposed partition plan. Less than 1 percent of the six hundred fifty thousand Jewish people were killed in that war. They endured. They overcame the odds.

Rachel claims today, most of the people of Israel are from Judah, Simeon, and Benjamin, along with parts of Levi. *Jew* is actually an abbreviation of The Kingdom of Judah. All Jews are Israelites, but in today's world, not all Israelites are Jews. Some Levites and all Benjaminites are Jewish.

How does that happen?

It's like Paul from the New Testament. When the soldiers were about to take Paul to the barracks he asked to speak to the crowd. The commander condoned it and Paul spoke to them in Aramaic. New Testament, Acts 22:3 NIV: Paul says, "I'm a Jew, born in Tarsus of Cilicia, but brought up in this city. Under Gamaliel I was thoroughly trained in the law of our fathers and was just as zealous for God as any of you are today." Then again in the New Testament, Romans 11:1 NIV: Paul says,—"I ask then, 'Did God reject his people? By no means! I'm an Israelite myself, a descendant of Abraham, from the tribe of Benjamin.'"

How can Paul be a Benjaminite and claim to be a Jew?

It's easy once you understand. The Kingdom of Judah is the religious side. The Tribe of Judah, Tribe of Benjamin, and Tribe of Levi is the lineage side. These three tribes all practiced Judaism. That's why they're all Jewish.

Therefore, it's safe to assume most people in today's Israel are from the tribes of Judah, Benjamin, Simeon, and Levi.

Remember, Simeon was absorbed into the tribe of Judah since their territory was encircled by Judah and they got along.

Jessica displayed a website and informed us there are a few hundred or so *Samaritans*, which is a Hebrew term derived from the word *Shamerim* meaning keepers of the law in Israel as well. The Samaritans are descendants of the Northern Israelite tribes of Ephraim and Manasseh and a few Levi. On January 1, 2012, the Community numbered 751 persons [353 in Kiryat Luza-Mount Gerizim, Samaria; 398 in the State of Israel: 396 males [190:206] and 355 females [170: 185].[1]

Jessica displayed a news article for us to read. On October 25, 2011, David Lev of the Israeli National News reported Druze in Israel were one of the missing tribes [2]—probably the Zebulons—based upon DNA evidence. Druze MK Ayoub Kara [Likud] says, "members of the Druze communities believe in many of the same things that Jews do. And that's not surprising," he adds, "since the Druze are actually descended from the Jewish people—and he says he can bring genetic evidence to prove it." David Lev continues quoting Ayoub Kara, "And then there's the genetic study, which shows Druze display genetic attributes quite similar to those of Jews. See the study for the technical details.[3] A major genetic test from last year, the first extensive test done of the Druze, proves my contention clearly," says Kara."

We're up to seeing seven in Israel at this point which means only five are missing. Right? As Jessica read the article about David Lev writing about the Druze descendants, I wonder how many more are already there in Israel and not saying anything due to persecution to family in other countries? Maybe all the tribes are there? Maybe all the tribes have been migrating there since Israel became a nation again and has proven itself for over sixty years. However, The Druze hesitated because it'd only been a little more than sixty years.

Why is it important that Messiah bring back the missing tribes to Israel?

Jessica explained it this way. It starts with the twelve tribes and King Solomon, the third king of Israel. The tribes were settled, King Solomon ruled over all the tribes, and everyone was happy and should've lived happily ever after. Unfortunately Solomon messed up...in a big way. In his later years, he worshipped idols. What was he thinking? All those years of God giving Solomon wisdom and power, appearing to him not once but twice instructing him bluntly not to follow other gods, and he chose to worship idols. For a king famous for being wise that was incredibly dumb. We must reach inside and remind ourselves to be like Jacob/Israel in cursing the actions, not the person.

God was ticked off. Wouldn't you be ticked off too if you were God? Tanakh, Torah, Nevi'im, 1 Kings 11:11–13 NIV: "The Lord said to Solomon, 'Because you're guilty of not keeping My covenant and the laws which I enjoined upon you, I'm tearing the kingdom away from you and giving it to one of your servants. But, for the sake of your father David, I'll not do it in your lifetime; I'll tear it away from your son. However, I'll not tear away my whole kingdom; I'll give your son one tribe, for the sake of My servant David and for the sake of Jerusalem which I've chosen.'"

Jessica continued describing how this caused the great divide between the tribes. Ten of them were given to Jeroboam. One tribe was to remain with King Solomon's son, Rehoboam. Yeah, just try to keep those two names separate at night when you're trying to piece all this stuff together...Anyway, Rehoboam will get one of the tribes so that a light will forever shine as a lamp in remembering his grandfather, King David's, service to God. And the tribe will be in Jerusalem, the city God chose to establish His name. Jeroboam was grateful and if you can imagine being in his shoes pretty excited about this huge promotion from God. Tanakh, Torah, Nevi'im, 1 Kings 11:37 NIV: "You've been chosen by Me. Reign wherever you wish, and you'll be king over Israel. If you heed all that I command you, and walk in My ways, and do what's right in My sight, keeping My laws and commandments as My servant David did, then I'll be with you and I'll build for you a lasting dynasty as I did for David. I hereby give Israel to you; and I'll chastise David's descendants for sinning; though, not forever."

I don't get it. These men of old actually saw God, talked to God, and God blesses them beyond what you or any of us could ever imagine in our life time. And what do they do? They do something insanely stupid, like worship idols…Yep, that's what Jeroboam did with all that power, all that territory. He messed it up big time just like King Solomon. You think he'd have at least learned from his immediate predecessor on what not to do.

Jessica continued explaining. Jeroboam wanted to make sure the Northern tribes which were now his wouldn't intermingle or reunite with the southern tribe in Jerusalem while he mandated idolatry. Although there was initially fighting between the two kingdoms it eventually faded out since both were facing common enemies. Nonetheless, Jeroboam felt he should create his own worship system and holidays to prevent the men from going to Jerusalem for Passover, Pentecost, and Sukkot each year. He feared a reunification of the tribes. This led to the Northern tribes not only worshipping idols, but not going to Jerusalem to repent. God was infuriated. He allowed the tribes to be captured and scattered throughout the nations just as Jacob had prophesied.

Jessica feels this verse gives us hope and a reason why the tribes need to return to Israel. Tanakh, Torah, Nitzavim-Vayelech, Deuteronomy 30:1–5 NIV : "When you realize the blessing and curse I've set before you, and you take them to heart while residing in the various nations I've banished you, and you return to Me, the Lord your God, and you and your children heed My commands with all your heart and soul, just as I instruct you this day, then I, the Lord your God, will restore your fortunes and take you back in love. I'll bring you together again from all the peoples where I've scattered you. Even if your outcasts are at the ends of the world I'll gather you from there I'll fetch you.

The Library Room

And I, the Lord your God, will bring you to the land that your fathers possessed, and you shall possess it; and I'll make you more prosperous and more numerous than your fathers."

After Yeshua was hung on the cross, died, and then rose from the grave, he appeared to them over a period of forty days and spoke about the kingdom of God. New Testament, Acts 1:6 NIV: "So when they met together, they asked him, 'Lord, are you at this time going to restore the kingdom of Israel?' He said to them, 'It isn't for you to know the times or dates the Father's set by His own authority. But you'll receive power when the Holy Spirit comes on you; and you'll be My witness in Jerusalem, and in all Judea and Samaria, and to the ends of the earth.' After He said this He was taken up before their very eyes, and a cloud hid Him from their sight."

From a Christian's stand point, there are a lot of reasons why they want all the tribes to return to Israel. Here's a clue why. It isn't in Satan's interest to have that happen which is why so many obstacles have been put in the way. Satan uses the tools God blesses us with to keep a division of tribes; it's that important to Satan that it never happens…But it'll happen. It was prophesied.

Jessica says a vast amount of information can be found on the Internet concerning DNA tracking and the Y chromosome found in Moses's ancestors. As tracking and identifying the different DNA of Israelites, regardless of what nation they're currently residing in today, everyone'll see how many of the missing tribes are currently no longer missing; but, may be living outside of Israel. It's exciting to follow the DNA studies. The missing are perhaps all there already.

---

1. This can be found at http://www.thesamaritanupdate.com/
2. This article can be found online at: http://www.israelnationalnews.com/News/News.aspx/140251#.T5In9NXfz6g or by writing and requesting a copy of the article.
3. The study can be found at: http://www.hayadan.org.il/a-yidishe-genetica-0111101/

Seventeen

Loren stood outside the door as Mr. O'Mallee changed the lock.

"What do you think she looks like?" Mr. O'Mallee asked Loren.

Loren didn't seem to hear and continued to stare at the stars.

"Outside or inside?" Mr. O'Mallee asked.

Loren snapped from her daydreaming trance. "What?"

"I'm asking if you think she'll be a monstah for what she's done. Is she evil? Is she prettiah to be able to seduce ya lovah away so fast? Will you hate or sympathize?" Mr. O'Mallee pressed. "Will I be watching an immaturah cat fight? Or will a classy lady show empathy towards someone duped by Giles?"

"Gotcha." Loren understood. "I can attack by calling her a slut, and thief, *or* I can show compassion to Giles's latest victim."

"Ah, yep." Mr. O'Mallee tightened the last screw and gathered his tools to take to the back door. "In life, you'ah doing God's will or being Satan's pawn."

Loren challenged. "I've known mean gossipy churchy people. Are you saying they're Satan's pawns?"

"Ah, yep. They doing God's will by gossiping? Bearing false witness kills a church. There's a reason God put that law in the Ten Commandments. They'ah just as important to God in his view as not worshiping idols. Sin is sin no mattah the degree of it in man's eyes. That othah commandment to love ya neighbah instructs us to overlook the faults. Love the human, not the sin."

"Well, I'm not going to start a cat fight. I hope she doesn't start one either," Loren assured Mr. O'Mallee.

Rachel stood with Loren after the landlord moved to the back door. "How are you doing?"

"Good so far," Loren said with a false smile.

"Officer Jones told us you don't need to go to his arraignment tomorrow. The restraining order's in place. He's not allowed to contact you. Nor, is he allowed to contact friends and parents." Rachel hoped to make her feel safer.

"We need to be kind to Mellissa tonight." Loren regarded Rachel's information as trivial compared to the upcoming undertaking. "She'll be embarrassed. She needs to know we're not judging her especially since she's returning my stuff."

"Yes, but she's helped Giles rob you. I don't think you'd want her as your new best friend," Rachel cautioned.

"Giles is cunning. Look how he's controlled me. It's easier to go along than to disagree," Loren defended.

"All right, we'll be nice," Rachel huffed. "Shall I bake cookies to send home with her?"

"No." Loren chuckled. "Just be nice…And here's our test." Loren watched Mellissa park in front of the curb.

Ms. Roses Are My Favorite Flowers repeated everything she'd hear. She'd become a woman desperate to know God's truths. It hurt Amy seeing her fight her physical condition.

When Amy suggested stopping for the night, Mrs. Rosenberg scowled. "If I can handle it, then you should too." Amy looked to her children for support, but they encouraged her to continue.

"Amy, do you think it's all coincidental as Alec says? Or do you believe Yeshua was born in Bethlehem, by a virgin, spoke Torah in the temple at twelve as if he'd written it, performed miracles, became wrongfully accused, crucified with criminals, and then buried in a tomb of the rich?" Mrs. Rosenberg's eyes showed she feared the conclusion she'd arrived at based upon what she'd learned. "I don't feel someone could control their life in such a manner, nor find scriptures of prophecy to fit around such a life. I don't think it's a coincidence. Will you be here tomorrow with the Moses information? And what happens after he dies? How does that play into the prophecies we've gone over?"

"You ask a lot of questions, Ms. Roses Are My Favorite Flowers." Amy smiled. "I'm trying to be nonbiased. I know I'm falling short of that by displaying enthusiasm. I don't see how someone could fulfill so many prophecies, even if the prophecies were for another scenario. Why couldn't they be so prophetic they withstood time to help us determine the Mashiach when he arrived? Yes, there was more prophecy fulfillment after he was resurrected. And yes, I'll bring more information tomorrow."

"If I can't speak tomorrow, you know I love you, right?" Mrs. Rosenberg asked.

"Yes, of course, I know you love me." Amy felt panic rising in her chest. "You know I love you very much too, right?"

"Yes, I do." Mrs. Rosenberg smiled. "Now, there comes a time when you have to let a person know they've the go-ahead to seek God's face. I've appreciated the encouragements to 'fight it'; but, it's time to give me permission to say, 'adieu.'"

"Yes." Amy was disheartened now. "I know. I don't want you to suffer, but I don't want to say good-bye yet." Amy saw Amelia cover her face in Alec's chest while they wept together.

It was apparent to Amy that Ms. Roses Are My Favorite Flowers had used her speech to convey the message to her children too.

"Before you leave, I have something I'd like to share with you tonight," Mrs. Rosenberg sang, pointing to her bed stand. "There's a poem I wrote to my Henry. I miss him and look forward to being together again. He was my best friend."

Amy opened the drawer and touched the thin parchment paper.

"Yes, that's it," Mrs. Rosenberg said. "Read it for me, would you?"

Amy unfolded the paper. "Yes, I'll read it for you.

I Dreamed of You Last Night

I dreamed of you last night
Your hair was tussled in a careless manner
Your voice was smooth and low
Your movements were slow and deliberate
And you smiled that impish grin

I dreamed of you last night
Mounted high upon a black bicycle
Riding off into the sunset
Your clothing rippling in the wind
Your expressions beckoning me to follow

I dreamed of you last night
Soft music playing in the background
You were listening so intently
Holding me as we danced
I remember the clouds around our feet

I dreamed of you last night
The colored leaves complimented your eyes
You play in the pile with kids
Your arms stretched out to me
Your playfulness too much to resist

I dreamed of you last night
Your shoulders tense with anger
Determination in your stride
We knew we were both right
We held hands and compromised

I dreamed of you last night
A mischievous grin as you stole another bite

The Library Room

The children were coming for dinner
The table wasn't quite set
You were humming a happy tune

I dreamed of you last night
We were sitting on the porch swing together
You held my hand with affection
I felt deep admiration for you my friend
And you looked at me with love

I dreamed of you last night
Your hair silver and your head bent in prayer
You waited patiently in the lobby
As our son-in-law came to deliver the news
Joy of a new grandchild

I dreamed of you last night
In your favorite chair with a newspaper
Tears were in your eyes
Another friend gone from this world
It is so hard to say good-bye

I dreamed of you last night
A bright light shining all around your being
We both have new bodies
We dance on a golden road
As the angels continually sing

So as I go to sleep this night
Rest assured I'll be dreaming of you.

"That's a lovely poem, Ms. Roses Are My Favorite Flowers. Thanks for sharing this." Amy refolded the paper.

"I want you to read it at my Shiva, please," Mrs. Rosenberg instructed. "Amelia can't without becoming *verklempt*. Will you do it?

Amelia smiled fondly. Amy nodded in acceptance.

Mrs. Rosenberg closed her eyes. When Amy thought she was asleep, she moved away from the bed. Mrs. Rosenberg suddenly moved. "Wait," she whispered. "I need to ask something."

"Sure, I won't leave until you say." Amy held her hand.

"Hypothetically, if someone were convinced Yeshua's the Mashiach, what would a person have to do to become right with God?" Mrs. Rosenberg whispered.

"You admit to God you're a sinner and ask God to remove all of your sins using the blood of Yeshua," Amy instructed. "Once a person does this, they're free to talk to God as a friend for all eternity. It's what God desires, our friendship, trust, attention, and praise. It's his reason for the Mashiach."

"Okay, I'd still like to see more, but it's good to know. Thank you for sharing tonight. I look forward to seeing you tomorrow." Mrs. Rosenberg released Amy's hand.

Alec stood, and Amy assumed he'd intended to walk her home.

"Alec, if you don't mind, I'd like to walk home alone tonight. I haven't had alone time to solve the world's problems so everything seems better," Amy told him.

Alec hugged her. "I understand. I too need a lot of Alec time in order to function. You'll be safe this late?"

"This is the safest college campus in the world!" Amy hugged Amelia good night. "I'll promise not to mug anyone." She left them watching their mother.

Once she was home, she cried again over the loss of her mother and for the upcoming loss of her Ms. Roses Are My Favorite Flowers. She slipped her shoes off, crumpled into a ball on the floor, and cried into her lap. To an outsider, she'd have appeared to be alone. Conversely, she felt comforted by God and allowed him to hold her while she mourned.

⁂

Loren sorted boxes as they were taken off the truck. There were items she repacked for Giles since they weren't from her grandmother's estate, gifts from relatives, or she'd bought herself.

Everyone "thanked" Mellissa. She'd stayed in the truck showing signs of remorse. Her meek nature left everyone feeling sorry for her. She'll never be herself until she breaks free of Giles.

It was after midnight when the guys left. The girls finished putting things away while Officer Jones assured Loren she wasn't needed at the arraignment, and Giles will likely post bail.

"So he'll be out tomorrow?" Loren trembled.

"If he posts bail. The restraining order won't allow him to come here, contact you, or anyone on the list. If he does, he'll forfeit his money and wait in jail until his trial. I doubt he'll risk it," Officer Jones assured.

"What about Mellissa?" Loren asked.

"Loren, I doubt she'll harass you. If she does, call my cell." Officer Jones was patient with her asking the same questions over and over. Trauma has a strange effect on a victim's mind.

"Thanks for your help. This has been a long day for you and Officer Gordon." Loren calculated the time since their first encounter.

"Yes, but it's how we handle things here in Miranda County," Officer Jones explained. "Officer Gordon and I like working in this county because they allow us flexible hours for cases like this."

"I hate to interrupt," Rachel said, "but, Loren, your bed's made for you. Jessica and Sarah are walking me home. We'll meet tomorrow at the library?"

"Whoa! Tomorrow's Monday!" Loren realized. "Everybody has class tomorrow morning! Yes! Everyone go home and sleep! If anyone needs to nap before coming to the library tomorrow feel free to do so."

Everyone left. She hated being alone. She was frightened. Every noise startled her. Once in bed, she pulled the covers around her like a cocoon and cried. Loneliness, anxiety, and fear came out in a terrified prayer. "I'm sorry, God. Please forgive me for downplaying your existence. Please help me understand you better. Please keep me, my friends, and my family safe. Help me, God, not to feel so alone. Help me, Lord. Thanks for not giving up on me. Thank you for loving and protecting me. Thank you, Father. Amen."

Rachel awoke to Drew's text: "Good morning, beautiful." She reread it while the coffee machine dripped her wakeup potion. She sent Drew a text. "Good morning, handsome. I can't W8 2 C U L8R 2day." She thought about the conversation they'd started yesterday and never finished discussing due to Loren's crisis.

She wished her mother were in town so she could talk to her about Drew. She looked at the itinerary on the refrigerator. "Cairo. Six hours ahead. Noon. She's eating lunch." A glance at the clock told her she didn't have time to chat. She needed to get ready for her first class.

Loren selected the snooze on her phone. *Five more minutes*, she thought while drifting back to sleep.

Bahhmp, bahhmp, bahhmp, bahhmp.

"Okay, I'm up," she whined. She looked at the time and realized she must have selected the snooze more than once. She threw back the covers and noticed with further irritation it was chilly.

She didn't have time to eat or make coffee. She struggled with the feel of the new lock as she rushed out the door. *Don't think about it. Think about anything but that today. Don't think about him*, She lectured herself. *Today's a new beginning.*

The Library Room

Mr. Finkel's classroom was full of students waiting their turn to go over their notes with him. She waited her turn.

She was tired and her pity party refreshed itself as she pouted over the impossible assignment, being manipulated into using her friends, and the project becoming the end of her relationship with Giles. Then something divine happened. She acknowledged the blessings instead: the secret library room, the quality time spent with her friends, and bringing her back to knowing God is real. He's not just a spiritual being found in nature. He's a God who longs for personal relationships. She became grateful.

"Loren," Professor Finkel called her out of her reverie, "let's see how your project's coming along. You understand why I'm speaking to you last? The other projects don't have the special amenities offered to them. I've been watching you this morning. Is everything okay?"

"Yes," Loren said. "Rough day yesterday, held against my will, then later, my house was broken into, even later my belongings were returned, and upcoming court hearings as a result. You know, the worst day you could ever imagine."

"Interesting," Professor said. "It never ceases to amaze me what Satan does when my students become engaged in this project. However, I think this one might take the cake."

He thumbed through Loren's notes. "Let's see what you've discovered so far. Lineage, good...Prophecies up to the birth of Jesus, good...Prophecies about the life of Jesus to the tomb, good...What's this? Twelve tribes information...Interesting but not convinced it's relevant and you're still working on the Messianic prophecies after the resurrection and Moses comparisons, good. What else?" Professor asked. "Loren, this project's biased. How does your team feel about this project? What have *you* discovered as someone who didn't believe in religions? Don't you have Jewish friends helping you?"

"Yes," Loren answered. "How'd you know that?"

"It's my business to know whose helping," he said, straight-faced and then cracked a chuckled admission. "Amida, the librarian, told me when I asked how everyone liked the room. I get excited every year when the room's shown to a new group of students."

Loren didn't respond.

"By the way," he added, "other professors are in on the challenge, we place bets each year on the outcome. They need to know whose helping so they can make sure their student gets a quality education in their class, but they're lenient on overdue assignments. In other words, you and your friends won't be passed through, but you'll pass your courses even if it takes longer or more effort from the professors to pass and without having to pay a tutor."

"We're *lab rats*?" Loren exclaimed before she realized what she'd said. "I'm sorry, that sounded like I'm ungrateful. I'm not…I mean, you caught me off guard by telling me everyone places bets on our outcome."

"Oh no, it's not for money." Professor Finkel downplayed what he'd mentioned. "We just discuss the outcome over dinner. Based upon your notes, I'll need to see more soul-searching material in which everyone agrees or disagrees."

"What we've been doing isn't enough?" Loren asked.

"No, it's not," Professor Finkel advised. "Any junior high or high school student can find what you've discovered using text books and the Internet. I need more. Give me something to applaud."

"Ouch! We've already spent a lot of time and energy on this. You know, it's not in one easy location. It takes a lot of digging for good information and sifting out stretched truths!" Loren defended. "And if kids can find this stuff, why aren't they?"

"Sh." Professor Finkel put his finger to his lips. "I didn't say it's bad information. I just need more. Yes, what you've produced

The Library Room

is the beginning of what you should be discerning...But God has more to show you, tell you, and share with all of you. When you find the truth, you'll be astounded, and no one will be the same."

With that explanation of elucidating nothing, he left the room.

What a peculiar man, she thought as she gathered her belongings and headed to Samson Marketing.

Amy considered skipping class; however, after a cup of coffee and texts from Jessica and Sarah, she reconsidered.

Jessica's text: "You're my hero. I know your heart's hurting. My prayers are with you."

Sarah's text: "You're one of my best friends. What you're going through stinks. I'd take on the pain for you if I could since I can't I'll offer my shoulder. No need to explain how you're feeling. Just a good cry partner when you need it. Love you like a sis."

Amy texted both: "I love you too!" Their words inspired her. She dressed in bright scrubs since she was scheduled to work after classes.

Jessica and Sarah sat in the coffee shop next to the window watching students hurry to class. Their class didn't start until eight thirty. They sipped their coffees and nibbled on scones.

It was a typical morning conversation between the two. Sarah's full of energy, while Jessica answers with as few words as possible until her second or third cup of coffee.

Sarah asked, "So Rachel and Drew are seeing each other now?"

"Yep," Jessica confirmed.

"Do you think they'll get married?" Sarah continued.

"Yes." Jessica stared off into space.

"Do you think we'll be invited to the wedding or even be in the wedding?" Sarah sat up.

"Probably." Jessica played with the coffee cup lid.

"Have you ever been to a Jewish wedding?" Sarah tried pulling Jessica into her conversation.

"Nope." Jessica yawned.

"Do you think they're different than Christian weddings?" Sarah persisted.

"Don't know," Jessica muttered.

"Do you think Giles will bother Loren once he posts bail?" Sarah switched topics.

"If he's got half a brain, he won't," Jessica answered with more than one word and little regard for grammar.

"What if he does?" Sarah encouraged Jessica to speak.

"Back to jail and loses his bond money from what I understand." Jessica took a bite of her scone.

"Think Mellissa will stay with him?" Sarah asked with concern.

"I hope not considering the embarrassment she's already endured being his minion," Jessica answered.

"How do you think Loren's project's coming along?" Sarah changed topics again, which happens when she's tired.

"I'm sensing stumbling blocks ahead. We don't have a definitive answer. I get the feeling Drew and Rachel have been so absorbed in looking at each other they've lost their focus. We need better arguments, or we'll lose the purpose of the research. Don't you feel the same?" Jessica finished her second cup.

"It looked to be a clear cut case. However, I see what you're saying," Sarah said. "I've been too caught up to offer objections I've come across when talking to Jewish friends back home. It's not as straightforward as we think…I mean, as far as Jews are concerned."

"That's why we need more from them," Jessica said.

They resumed their mindless people watching until it was time to head to their classes.

The Library Room

Amy arrived earlier than usual at the nursing home. She saw strangers standing outside Mrs. Rosenberg's room dabbing their eyes. It was a common scene to Amy.

They've called the family in to say their good-byes. It was a sucker punch to Amy's raw emotions.

She saw Amelia hugging someone she assumed to be her daughter based upon looks. She was a replica of Amelia only twenty-five years younger. Amelia finished her hug and introduced her niece, Emily, Alec's daughter.

Emily cast an air of importance through attitude and a fingertip handshake. Amy shook the tips and smiled without being intimidated.

"How's Ms. Roses Are My Favorite Flowers today?" Amy asked Amelia and Alec.

"Not looking so well. Her water retention's wreaking havoc on her internal organs," Amelia answered. "As you can see, our relatives have come to see her. We'll introduce you to everyone."

She guessed ten to twelve new faces were in the room. They exceeded the visitor limit; however, when she saw the happy face on the larger Mrs. Rosenberg she overlooked the rule.

Mrs. Rosenberg had gained so much water her breathing was labored. She didn't try sitting up on her own.

Amy approached. "You've drawn an attractive crowd."

"I certainly have." Mrs. Rosenberg smiled. "It's good to see them although I've scolded them for wasting so much time and money."

"They want you to know they love you. Don't scold them," Amy instructed. "I don't blame them. I'd be doing the same if I were them. I just stopped in before my shift to check on you." Then, Amy bent and whispered, "If you need to rest, I want you to blink twice like you're going to sneeze so Amelia, Alec, or

I will know you need quiet time. We'll take everyone into the lobby for a while. Do you understand?"

Mrs. Rosenberg squeezed Amy's hand. "I'm fine for now though." She did not want to miss any time with her loved ones.

"I know." Amy knew from past patients it's hard for them to stop and rest. "I need to go check in. I'll see you in a bit." Amy kissed her forehead noting the temperature against her lips.

Cool as a cucumber. Good.

Amy instructed Amelia and Alec to watch for fatigue. Both agreed to watch for her blinking and the other signs Amy listed.

Loren arrived at the library and climbed into a beanbag chair holding the notes she'd shown Professor Finkel. Six minutes later, the notes hit the floor as she slept.

Jessica and Sarah arrived to Loren snoring. They put their fingers to their lips and sat at the table. Within minutes, all were napping. Forty minutes later, they awoke to the laughter of Drew, Rachel, and Collin.

"Well, it looks as though we've stumbled upon three sleeping beauties," Collin said to Rachel and Drew.

"We *were* sleeping beauties *and* beautifully sleeping until y'alls ruckus woke us," Sarah replied.

Loren stretched and yawned. "Hey, everyone…Sorry, I fell asleep. When did all of you arrive?"

"Just walked in." Rachel replied.

Doing a quick calculation, Jessica said, "Sarah and I arrived forty-five minutes ago. We didn't want to wake you."

"Wow!" Loren said. "You should've woke me up. I need to work harder and get this off of my plate."

"We *have* been working hard on it," Sarah objected.

"I know," Loren whined, "but we're too biased. Professor Finkel feels I've slanted it in favor of Christianity with little fight from the Judaic side."

Sarah looked at Jessica recalling their earlier conversation. Rachel looked at Drew realizing their lackadaisical stand in arguments.

Collin looked around in disbelief. "What's he mean it's biased?"

"He means it doesn't mean much as far as our Jewish faith is concerned," Drew countered.

"What do you mean?" Collin argued. "We've proven Jesus fulfilled prophecies no human could ever fulfill. How can you doubt after you've gone through this with us?"

"Are you serious? Think about it Collin," Drew said. "Do you think our people were stupid back then? You don't think they would've picked up on a true Mashiach? Yes, Yeshua was well learned in the Mitzvot. He was a prophet and a rabbi. He *wasn't* a priest or a royal king. He didn't fulfill *all* of the prophecies especially the ones of bringing world peace and making Israel the nation amongst all nations. He didn't prevent the Jewish people from becoming captives after He died. What part of 'we just don't buy into it' don't *you* understand?"

Collin watched Drew's face redden and sat down. "I guess we should address those things; and, I'll say it's time for you two to speak up. I see your points."

Rachel also sat down. "Collin, I've been taught Yeshua's the Mashiach for the *Gentiles*. Not all synagogues teach this, of course. Jewish people don't need a Mashiach in the way of having our sins forgiven like Gentiles. We were given a covenant at Mount Sinai when Moses gave us the Mitzvot. He doesn't go back on his word. He's God. We just need to live by his laws and when we make a mistake we ask for forgiveness and he says, 'Okay, try again harder,' and we do."

"Hey, hey, hey!" Sarah interjected. "So if I'm hearing correctly, there are *two* different ways to get to heaven? One is if we keep the commandments, also known as Mitzvot, and the other is if you can't or aren't Jewish, then you've Yeshua as a backup?"

Drew answered, "*If* you're a Gentile, according to Rachel. I, however, was taught by my rabbi there's only one option for Judaism—keeping God's Mitzvot, period. It's all we need."

"I think our project's taken a new turn." Loren sighed, knowing it'll require much more research to find the answers—if there are answers. "I'll bet this is what Professor Finkel was alluding to this morning. So what do we do? Continue researching prophecies and the Moses comparison? What else should we do to find those answers?"

Rachel gazed up into the sky dome. "God, help us to find your truth, not what some rabbi or minister or priest wants to promote for their own agenda. Seriously God, we need your help."

"Amen," Loren said. "So tonight we'll work on the Moses comparisons."

Amy entered the room as Collin displayed the prayer on the smart board and placed his yarmulke on his head like Drew. They all prayed out loud holding hands.

Eighteen

Loren noticed a glow in the room even though it was dark outside. In her mesmerized trance, she conversed with God.

Has it always been like this with us humans—a desire to find your truth when challenged instead of on our own? Why do we stray from your love once we feel Your love? Yes, I know I did that; but, why? Why don't we want to do whatever we can for you? Why don't some believe even after researching the truth? What are they hoping for in the end?

Then God placed a thought in Loren's mind. *The flesh wants self-gratifying, instant results. Life's short. Love me, your God, and don't settle for worldly pleasures. I promise the walk with me, your Father, is more satisfying, especially in the end.*

Drew and Rachel listed different areas of Moses's personality, talents, spirituality, and accomplishments. As each thoughtful point was listed Jesus was shown to not only be like Moses but exceeded Moses's accomplishments.

"How do you know your stories weren't just made up?" Drew asked Amy while she researched Yeshua's miracles.

"Because in most cases, they were witnessed by hundreds or thousands of people," Amy offered. "Like Moses, when God wanted people to know who he was he'd make himself evident by displaying his miracles in front of many. That way, it'd be told to others faster and last for generations. He'd publically create credibility."

"But not all of Yeshua's miracles as we read were in front of hundreds. He even asked some not to tell anyone. Moses never downplayed God's miracles. So in those cases, he's *not* like Moses," Rachel argued. "And why are the only writings done by his disciples? Why didn't other ordinary people write about them? Like a newsletter or crier? Why weren't those writings ever discovered?"

"There *are* Pagan and Jewish records of Jesus's life, crucifixion, resurrection, and ascension: Josephus, Tacitus, Thallus, Mara Bar-Serapion, to name a few. They aren't pro-Christian, so they're not in the Bible. Are you having a hard time believing all the miracles Yeshua did to prove he was the Son of God?" Amy asked.

"Yes," Drew answered and Rachel nodded her head.

"Why?" Amy continued. "They were witnessed. If they hadn't been, then people wouldn't have followed and Christianity would've disappeared. As it stands there were *millions of Hebrews* as well as Gentiles converted because of Yeshua's miracles, more so than the High Priests wanted to admit. And more than government officials were comfortable with too."

"I think there were more Gentiles converted than Hebrews," Rachel argued. "I believe the Hebrews who converted weren't strong in their faith. Think about it. If it were so evident, why didn't *all* Jewish people jump on board? There's something amiss that I'm not catching, but I know I should know it. I know I've been taught it. I just need to speak to my rabbi to figure it out." Rachel sounded exhausted.

"All right, everyone, I hereby call it quits for the night. Thanks for being more aggressive in standing up for your beliefs. I've documented the arguments. It's added meat to the report," Loren announced. "However, none of us are up to our normal capabilities so let's go home and rest."

"Sounds good to me!" Collin stood and stretched.

When Drew touched Rachel's hand, she latched on to his. "Would you mind if I walked you home?"

"I'd love for you to do that," Rachel replied.

Collin decided to walk Amy to the nursing home. He'd been watching her hide her emotions all night. He didn't ask permission. He just walked beside her.

Jessica and Sarah walked Loren home. They didn't ask permission either. Although no one broached the topic, the three were concerned about Giles being out on bail.

As Loren opened her door, she sighed. She hugged them and said, "Good night." They listened for the door lock before leaving her.

"I think he's finally gone," Jessica declared.

"I don't trust him. He's got a screw loose and he's obsessive," Sarah disagreed.

"True," Jessica settled. "But he won't risk the bail money. You've seen how he's tight with money. And we're not even sure he posted bail. We're just assuming he did."

"True point," Sarah agreed.

Alone in her apartment, Loren reflected. *Hi, God, I thought the work on the project was supposed to be a slam dunk in you showing us who you are and what you are to us. I was buying into it. Now, I've more research on top of dealing with personal stresses. What do you want from me? Why can't it be black and white? Why are there so many rebuttals over our findings?*

She left the questions hanging in the air. She went into the kitchen to find something to eat.

"Faith?" Loren said out loud. "Okay, why did you put that word into my head? What are you trying to tell me? Have 'faith' you'll show us the answers? Have 'faith' you exist? Have 'faith' that what we've discovered isn't a coincidence in events?" Each time she said the word *faith*, she'd use her fingers to put quotation marks around the word. "To whom am I talking to? Who spoke to me earlier in the library? Am I going crazy? Did I really hear you whisper those words to me earlier and the word 'faith' just now in my head? Or is my mind grasping for answers in an attempt to keep my 'faith' from falling apart?"

She scrambled a couple of eggs while toasting bread in the toaster.

"Well, how about I put a word into your head tonight. Okay, ready? Fear! Try that word out. I have 'fear' in my heart. I 'fear' you might not be all I'm believing you to be for me. I 'fear' the scriptures are made by those who needed to write something down to make sense of their life. I 'fear' if I discover you aren't as almighty as I've been told, my world will crumble, and I'll lose my 'faith' in you. I 'fear' I'm losing my mind. I 'fear' there's no heaven or hell, and if that's the case, then what's it all for? I 'fear' putting these fears into my report for 'fear' of being criticized by my family, friends, or professor."

She stirred the eggs so fast, droplets splashed onto the stove and smoked until she wiped them off. The toast popped up and the pieces broke in half from pressing too hard with the butter knife.

Then she breathed in and slowly let it out. *Be still and know that I am God.*

Loren looked upward. "Wow. Thanks, God."

She placed the scrambled eggs on a plate and dabbed them with ketchup before praying over her meal.

Collin waited in the lobby while Amy continued to Mrs. Rosenberg's room with the Moses comparison file.

Mrs. Rosenberg's room was dark. Amy peeked in and saw Amelia and Alec sitting on the loveseat. They saw her and stood. Amy put a finger to her lips and patted the air signaling them to "sit." Both nodded and signaled her over to them.

The Library Room

"They've given her a sedative," Alec informed. "She seemed uncomfortable. We asked everyone to wait outside until she's rested."

Mrs. Rosenberg acquired a pronounced gurgling in her breathing. It was a noise Amy recognized as fluids forming in her lungs. Amy's face saddened hearing the noise. She also noted tummy rises instead of her working her lungs with her chest.

"We finished the Moses comparison. I thought I'd drop it off." Amy offered the file to Alec.

"Thanks, sweetie," Amelia said. "I'm sure if she's up to it in the morning, she'll be keyed up to get one of us to read it to her. She'd asked a few times this evening if you'd come back yet."

Amy smiled with tears in her eyes. "I'm sorry I couldn't get it to her sooner. Everybody worked to get it done faster. I think you'll find it interesting. I did."

Alec smiled and then looked serious. "You look rough."

"I'm feeling a bit rough," Amy admitted. "I have a friend in the lobby waiting for me."

"Do I hear my Amy?" Ms. Roses Are My Favorite Flowers' voice was raspy.

Amy rushed to the bed. "Yes, Ms. Roses Are My Favorite Flowers," she whispered. "I'm here. I love you, and you need to go back to sleep. I brought your information on the Moses comparison, but I insist you sleep until morning."

"Was Yeshua was like Moses?" Mrs. Rosenberg persisted.

"Very much," Amy answered without hesitation.

"Good," Mrs. Rosenberg took a deep belly breath. "I want to hear it in the morning." She held her breath for what seemed like a lifetime before taking another belly breath. "I've been talking with God. He knows my heart and I know him. He understands my decision." With that last statement, she fell back asleep with more pronounced gurgling.

Collin thought about what they'd learned so far. What became obvious to him was there has to be a God. Little did anyone know, and Collin barely admitted it only to himself. He'd developed a slight skepticism toward God's existence or even Jesus. His faith dwindled from doubts being placed in his mind through acquaintances, the media, college social classes, and human nature. Although he attended church, he didn't feel the closeness he'd felt as a child. He thought, *It should've grown with me, right? Why don't I feel closer to God after all this time of being a Christian?*

He called his mother for Father Tim's number without thought of time. He glanced around the room at the sad faces. Some were zoning out watching TV, some rested with their eyes closed sleeping or in prayer, and others chitchatted with each other, and all waited for news concerning Mrs. Rosenberg.

The connection ring from his phone brought him back from his surroundings. He then realized how quiet the room was and hoped no one answered the phone until he made it outside. Outside in the night air, their recorded message began.

At the beep, Collin recorded, "Hi, Mom and Dad. I've been working on a project, and I need Father Tim's number to ask him a few questions. I love you both and miss you. You can call me tomorrow since I just realized the time. I hope I didn't wake you up. It's not the first time we've lost track of time while working on this project. Okay, I'm rambling now. Love you." Collin smiled, knowing his dad would hear it first, shake his head at the long message, and then tell his mom to call him back to make sure everything's all right.

Before he could get that thought processed his cell phone rang with the caller ID showing Mom/Dad Home.

"Hi, Mom," Collin answered the phone.

"Try Dad," Andy corrected him.

The Library Room

"Oh, hey, Dad, how are you? I hope I didn't wake you up." Collin did his best at sounding apologetic and guilty.

"Nope, we just walked in to hear your rambling message. We went to our dancing lessons tonight. I'm humoring your mother by attempting this even though I'd warned her about being born with two left feet." Andy sounded happy. "So what's this project of yours?"

"Actually, this project's my friend's, Loren's, but she's allowed to use friends to help with the research," Collin explained. "It's too biased on the side of Jewish people needing Jesus as their Messiah, and now, my two Jewish friends told us a few things in their defense."

"Okay, but you lost me somewhere. You're helping Loren with a project. Right?" Andy asked.

"Yes, and so are my other friends." Collin then explained details and what they've researched.

"Oh," Andy said. "That seems pretty deep. Didn't any of your friends attend church growing up?"

"Yes, I think everyone did except Rachel and Drew went to synagogues. They're the two Jewish friends working on this with us. They've brought different angles to the interpretations. I've learned a lot from everyone."

"So when do you think it'll be done?" Andy asked.

"I'm not sure. We're still researching, and we've discovered some people don't feel prophecies can be used over again for something different," Collin said in exasperated tone. "And there's the issue of the Old Covenant. Would God go back on his word? Do they even need a messiah? Is Christ a messiah for the Gentiles only since they've a covenant with God?"

"Wow, I guess I never thought about it since *we're* taught *we* need Jesus. I've never thought about the Jewish side of it. Never needed to either. Very interesting information, Collin. Let me know what you discover. Let's see." Andy became distracted. "I know we've a mass missal from last Sunday with Father Tim's number...Ah, here's Faaather Tim...Father Timothy Woleski, 546-897-4568. Did you attend church Sunday?"

"Thanks, Dad, and yes, I attended mass here on campus. We had an embarrassing situation though. The priest called Sarah out for taking communion since she's Protestant. Apparently, that's a no-no." Collin growled.

"Ah yes, transubstantiation. The turning of the wine and bread into Christ's blood and flesh for Eucharist. Your mother had a hard time with that," Andy related. "Prior to taking the adult catechism classes, she'd attempted to take communion. She'd partake in her own church. When she was denied in front of everyone during mass, she felt humiliated. It almost caused us not to be married. She didn't want to become Catholic and I wasn't becoming Protestant. I was the man of the house. After months of her regarding my church as a bunch of snobs, I calmed her down enough to talk to a priest."

Collin was stunned. "I didn't know Mom had been a Protestant."

"We wanted to raise our family in one faith when we married," Andy explained. "We learned about transubstantiation. That's the part your mom had an issue with when it was explained. When the bread and wine are consecrated by an ordained priest, it's turned into the flesh and blood of Jesus Christ."

"What? I thought it was a symbolic thing! I'm not sure *I* buy into that even as a Catholic, Dad!" Collin objected. "I mean, your tongue and eyes tell you it's not flesh or blood. They're not changing it."

"Yes, we Catholics believe it's changed. And our faith overrides the taste and sight. The *accidents*. That's what it's called when it's changed by a priest, takes place once it's consecrated. The looks and taste in a scientific form remain, but the transformation of it in our faith is Christ's flesh and blood. It's a divine mystery of faith Christ gave us at his last supper. Don't you remember this lesson in Catechism?" Andy tried helping Collin recall the lesson.

"I remember going to Catechism. Not all the kids in my school attended. I think it was the second grade." Collin searched his memory.

"Right, second grade," Andy confirmed. "I feel it's too young to grasp the transubstantiation concept."

"I just don't remember anyone telling me I was eating real flesh and blood." Collin glowered. "That's gross. Don't you think? Isn't that cannibalistic? I like thinking of it as a remembrance thing rather than I'm eating Jesus. Ew."

"It's not quite like that. However, I can appreciate what you're saying. I had to hear it from your mother for a long time before it sunk in as to the meaning and how much we're blessed by what Jesus gave to us," Andy countered. "Think of it this way. W*e* have the divine mysteries also known as the Holy Gifts. God sent his Son, Jesus, who taught us to have communion with him to remember him, to take him into our bodies. For someone to partake without believing defiles the sacrament. You have to believe in order to receive the gifted host.

"Okay." Collin tried making sense of it. Still, it wasn't clear to him. "I think I get it. However, why can't or don't all churches teach and believe in this? Why is it so confusing to be a Christian, Dad? Don't all these rules and special mysteries dissuade a nonbeliever from believing?"

"For me, it's simple," Andy answered. "I believe because it makes sense to me. My heart tells me it's what I need to believe."

"I know what I believe too, or at least, I thought I did. Now, I've questioning thoughts discouraging my beliefs," Collin confessed.

"You're young. We tend to question things when we're young. As you get older, you become more comfortable in your faith," Andy stated. "Just be careful of what you believe and pray for wisdom to know the truth from the latest hype. Talk to Father Tim. He's much better at explaining our faith than I've been tonight."

"Thanks, Dad. I have to go. Amy's ready to go home now," Collin said. "I love you. Thanks for talking tonight."

"Love you too, son," Andy said before hanging up.

Collin reentered the building and made it to the lobby just as Amy arrived. He hugged her. "How'd it go?"

"Fine," Amy said. "She's out of it. They have her sedated. She stirred awake, but I told her to go back to sleep, and we'll go over the information in the morning. She said, 'He knows my heart and understands my decision.' I don't know her decision. However, it sounds like she's made up her mind."

"Should I call the priest in for a baptismal?" Collin offered.

Amy pondered aloud, "Why does she need to be baptized? I don't think it's necessary at this point. If her decision is to accept Christ into her heart, she's saved."

"Yes, but our church teaches you need to be baptized too. My parents baptized me as child. Haven't you been baptized?" Collin asked.

"Yes, at a Christian summer camp when I was a teenager," Amy answered. "Our church does it as an outward sign of showing your faith to your peers and declaring openly Jesus Christ is your Savior. It doesn't have anything to do with sins or being accepted into heaven."

"I think it does. I'm pretty sure it's an important step, or at least, our church places a huge importance on it," Collin said less assured. "Looks like that's one more thing I'll ask Father Tim."

Rachel talked about the new painting that arrived at the art studio as they walked hand in hand down the street. The new arrival was ahead of schedule, and Rachel seemed sad to see the other piece returned. Drew hung on her every word.

Drew spoke about football. Although he and Collin are above average in size, they're still no match for the condition, strength,

The Library Room

and size, of their fellow players. Nonetheless, they love being a part of the team experience. Rachel hung on his every word.

They reached Rachel's place and continued talking by her door stoop. Both had avoided the conversation they needed to finish.

Drew said, "Rachel, let's talk. I can tell it's on your mind." He glanced at her white-knuckled grip on his hand.

When she realized, she was crushing his hand she released her hold and opened the front door. "Yes, perhaps we should."

They entered. Drew slipped his shoes off and offered his hand while she unbuckled hers. He then led her to the couch.

"Okay, I'll start." Drew breathed. "As I mentioned, I want to be *Shomer Negiah* with you, observant of the laws of touching."

"Yes, I understand Shomer Negiah," Rachel said. "Many people, not just Jewish people are becoming more observant of the laws before marriage. I'm just surprised you want to observe them. I've seen girls you've dated pawing all over you. And doesn't that mean we can't touch or dance too?"

"Well, for some they feel dancing, hand holding, and touching in any way especially kissing, and sex, is forbidden," Drew offered. "My past relationships aside, I want to do this the right way with *you*. I guess I'm selective in what I consider intimate touching. I don't feel we should kiss, make out, engage in oral sex, nor go all the way before we get married. However, if you can't control your urges to touch my handsome body until I've asked for your hand, before becoming man and wife, I'll run to the nearest jeweler, buy a ring tonight, and arrange for a rabbi to be here in the morning. We can get married as fast as your heart wants to commit under a Chuppah."

Drew's flirtatious look was daring. She squirmed imagining being touched in passionate ways. Her heart pounded in her ears. She didn't take her eyes off his as he awaited her answer.

She whispered, "I can wait for Dad to come home." She paused. "So you intend to marry me? You don't want to date while we're in school and then go our separate ways?"

"I have no intentions,"—Drew swallowed—"of letting us go in separate directions. We'll decide where we want to live, and I'll study for the bar in whatever state we decide. I'll become the hardest working attorney to support you in the lifestyle your father's spoiled you and your mother. You may not see me for a few years unless you bring me food at the office, but I'll provide well for us. I love you, Rachel. And I'm in love with you."

"We can still hold hands and dance together during this time?" Rachel was letting everything sink in.

"Yes," Drew answered. "Do you want to marry me? I mean, do I have your blessing to ask your father for your hand before I ask *you* to marry me?"

"Yes! Yes! Yes!" she yelled and reached around his neck to hug him and stopped in midair before touching him.

Drew read her mind and closed her arms around his neck. Then, he enclosed her tiny frame in his arms. "Hugging is okay as long as it doesn't lead to petting or grinding." As they hugged, he smelled her perfume and almost lost all resolve as the intoxicating fragrance hit him.

She loves me and she's mine to love!

"One more thing." He waited until she could look into his eyes.

"What's that?" *What new rule could he come up with now?*

"I don't want you to drop any weight for the wedding. You're skinny enough. You're perfect to me."

"What happens if I gain weight? When I get nervous, I eat, not a great gene in our family."

"I want you to be happy. I don't care what your weight is as long as you're happy and not anorexic. If you intend to get that way, I'll force feed you while you sleep at night. Men love curves. Designers don't like curves, but most are gay men who think girls need figures like boys."

"Drew! That's a horrible thing to say! I have many designer friends in New York City! Most of them are women I'll have you know!" Rachel laughed.

The Library Room

"Good! Then tell them to start designing clothes accentuating a woman's beautiful waist, show off and pad every chest, put ruffles on the rump to make a large one look bigger, and emphasize fuller hips. Oh, man, put full hips on a woman and I can barely breathe."

"Drew!" Rachel looked horrified as she thought of her skinny long legs and nearly there chest.

"Darling, you're body's gorgeous. It's youthful looking. You've kept it well maintained. I'm super fine if it stays this way forever. However, as you age and have children, it's bound to change. Let it be natural, don't kill yourself keeping it this perfect. I'm giving you permission to be a woman."

Rachel envisioned herself with the tummy bump she'd seen on her friends who've had children. She smiled at the thought of their husbands giving them the same lecture.

"Well, I'd better be off. I have to outdo Collin in practice tomorrow. I love you, Ms. Rachel." Drew pulled himself from Rachel's embrace and stood. "You should talk to your landlord about replacing the lighting in here. It seems dark."

"I love you too, Drew." Rachel laughed. They'd conversed in the dark on the couch without it leading to promiscuity. However, she'll turn the lights on in the future.

Jessica left Sarah in the lobby after they checked their mailboxes. Jessica's shoulders drooped in exhaustion. She debated if she wanted to eat or just take a bath and go to bed. A tour through the cupboards helped her decide. She hadn't gone grocery shopping, and there were no leftover containers in the refrigerator. Exhaustion was winning the battle.

When the water in the tub was drawn, she slid in, reclined, and closed her eyes.

Hi, God, it's me again. She conversed in her mind. *I'm tired and feeling discouraged tonight. I'm not sure why, but I have a list. I feel sad for Amy, mad about Giles, discouraged over the project obstacles, jealous of Rachel and Drew, homesick for Mom and Stewie, broke all the time, ticked off at a priest, and don't feel like I fit in anywhere. What's wrong with my life, Lord? Why can't I be content? I'm tired of putting on a good show.*

She sighed and dunked her head under the water for a few seconds. *I know. Fake it until you make it. Well, boo-hoo, listen to my pity party! I'm sorry, God. I don't mean to sound ungrateful. I know you're going to take care of everything. I know my needs will be supplied and your timing's perfect even if it feels like it's three days late. I also know you know me more than I know myself and trying to hide my feelings from you is useless. So please calm my heart and make me happy, so I stop pretending.*

Her phone rang inside her jean pocket. She reached over the tub wall, fished the phone out, and looked at the caller ID. *That'll teach me for complaining about being homesick.*

"Hi, Mom," Jessica answered. "What keeps you up this late?"

"Hi, precious. I just called to check in. You've been on my mind and I miss you," Karen replied.

"Aw, thanks, Mom. I'm doing okay. How're you and Stewie?" Jessica eased back into the tub to soak.

"We're doing well. How's your first week back to school? Do you need anything? Did all of your friends come back? What're they all up to these days?" Karen questioned.

Jessica updated her about Loren and Giles, Rachel and Drew, Amy and Mrs. Rosenberg, Sarah and the priest, and Collin. She talked nonstop while her mother focused on keeping up.

"Jessica, are you okay? I mean, you sound different. Are you sleeping enough? Are you happy, honey?" Karen sounded concerned.

"Yes, I'm okay." Jessica's eyes reddened. "Why do you ask?"

"You don't seem your chipper self, that's all," Karen answered.

"I'm tired from all the drama and research. Why does everyone expect me to always be chipper? Can't I have a pity party every once in a while?" Jessica whined.

"Hey, it's all right, honey," Karen comforted.

"Sorry, Mom." Jessica let a tear rolled down her cheek. "I feel stressed. I'm not sure if it's from Loren's project, the romances, the dramas, I can't find a guy I'd date again after a first date, the college loans starting this spring, or that the coffee shop hasn't scheduled me for any shifts since I've returned."

"Ahhh," said Karen. "When you put it in that perspective it does seem overwhelming. What are you going to do about it? Are you going to let it fester and continue building? Have you prayed?"

"Of *course* I prayed about it!" Jessica shouted more than she'd intended, indicating a nerve had been hit. "Isn't that what Catholic girls have been taught to do since elementary? I was doing that when you called. As a matter of fact, my bathwater's cold from praying and then talking with you. I just need to sleep, and I'll be okay because I prayed and God knows my needs." Jessica hoped she hadn't come across as sarcastic as she'd felt. How can her mom make her show her true feelings when she doesn't even know her true feelings until she talks to her mom?

"Jessica," Karen said, "drain the tub, dry off, and call me back. I love you, and if you don't call back in ten minutes, I'll keep calling you until your voice mail's full."

Jessica did as her mother instructed. Besides, if she tried the I-won't-call-Mom-back-and-I'll-ignore-her-calls approach, she'd hear banging on her apartment door in three hours.

"How long has this been going on?" Karen asked.

"How long has what been going on?" Jessica responded.

"How long have you been depressed?" Karen pressed.

"I'm not sure I'd call it depression. I think it's more like I feel overwhelmed with everything because I'm tired," said Jessica.

"Have you eaten today?" Karen asked.

"I had breakfast and lunch. I thought about ordering Chinese, but now it's too late," Jessica said.

"Earlier, I asked if you'd prayed. I didn't mean to upset you by asking that question nor did I insinuate you don't pray enough either," Karen stated.

"I know." Jessica sighed. "I'm just your typical twenty-something instant gratification student. The only difference is I know it has to be God's timing and not mine, and it irritates me. Why can't he do it on my time once in a while?" Jessica laughed.

"Perhaps His lesson is simply for you to learn his place in your life. You know, he's in control and not you?" Karen jested knowing there was a lot of truth to the statement. "You, life, and timing don't have to be perfect. It's okay if they're not because eventually it all works out when you let God be God."

"But it's different today. Women have to work harder to compete. Our GPAs have to be higher. If I'm competing against a man, I have to be more ambitious and compelling. If I'm competing against another woman, I have to not only be more ambitious and compelling, but I have to watch my back and be absolutely perfect so I don't get pushed aside as she's doing her best to show she too can be ambitious and compelling against me and the male." Jessica felt this was a legitimate argument to justify not letting God be in control. "I can't be lazy in the things I'm in control of. I need to survive once the bills begin."

"Oh, Jessie. No!" Karen's heart broke for Jessica. "I mean, I understand competition in the workforce. You'll always need to work hard and do your best. Nevertheless, killing yourself to the point of not having a life defeats our purpose."

Jessica said with a tearful voice, "What's my purpose? What's it all for? Am I to go to school, teach, earn money, retire, and then die?"

"Jess," Karen said in a soothing voice, "I know you don't see it right now because you're in the thick of things, but trust me, life's beautiful. There's life after school. Life's not about being the best of the best. Life's more enjoyable if you learn to live with purpose, not what corporations pound into our brains."

"Ugh." Jessica wiped her eyes. "More God stuff. It seems everywhere I turn I'm learning about God."

"That's interesting, and there's a reason God has you working on this project with Loren and your friends." Karen assured. "It's no accident she was selected for this project."

"So what's my purpose? To help on this project and then what?" Loren challenged.

"Everyone's main purpose is the same," Karen said, "to please God. How you please God is key to finding your purpose."

Jessica replied, "So if I'm pleasing God and I figure out how to please God, then I don't have to worry about anything else? I don't have to worry about my grades, finding a decent-paying job, paying bills, finding Mr. Right, and raising the kids?"

"In a nutshell," Karen said, "yes."

"It sounds ridiculous." Jessica yawned. "I don't get it."

"Let's talk tomorrow." Karen knew explaining how letting go of things that don't matter wasn't computing. "Go to bed and don't dilly-dally like you did when you were a kid."

"Thanks for calling, Mom." Jessica closed her eyes. "Love you."

"I love you too," Karen said. "You're important to me."

"Give Stewie a big hug and kiss from me." Jessica smiled as they hung up.

Nineteen

Loren's Notes Part V—The Moses Comparison

Rachel and Drew both feel they don't the need our Messiah since Moses delivered God's Covenant to his chosen people.

Collin questions the reason(s) God would give Moses this prophecy after the Convenant was given on Mt Sinai. Tanakh, Torah, Shoftim, Deuteronomy 18:15 NIV: The Lord, your God, will raise up for you a prophet like me from among you from your fellow Israelites. You must listen to him. So, we should do a comparison between the two.

The verses provide a good start as to the likeness of Moses. However, I feel we'll find more similarities.

Below is a list of comparisons Jessica wrote on the SMARTboard.

- Both survived a King demanding male infanticide
- Egypt as an infant
- Jewish; of their people, an Israelite, a Hebrew
- Both were prophets
- Brothers and Sisters misunderstood them
- Humble
- They trusted God and God trusted them

- Chosen by God to lead people
- Lawgiver
- God spoke to Him mouth to mouth plainly
- Both beheld the likeness of the Lord
- Chose twelve special leaders
- Founded a religion
- Chose a life of hardship
- Taught others how to pray
- Performed great miracles
- Provided bread for a multitude
- Not liked by the Governing officials
- Interceded for people
- Brought people out of bondage
- Provided a way to the Promised Land

Let's document each one.

- Both survived a king demanding male infanticide
  We've already documented Yeshua's situation.
  Rachel loves the story of Moses's birth and his miraculous survival. She summarized Tanakh, Torah, Shemot, Exodus 1:15–2:10 JPS. The king of Egypt instructed the Hebrew midwives attending Hebrew women in childbirth to kill the boys and let the girls live. But the midwives were God-fearing women and allowed the boys to live. When the king asked, "Why are you allowing the boys to live?" The midwives answered, "Hebrew women are hardier than Egyptian women and give birth before a midwife can arrive." For this, God was good to the midwives by giving them families of their own. And the people increased

and grew more powerful. Pharaoh then instructed all his people: "Throw every newborn boy into the river, but let all the girls live."

Moses's mother hid him for three months after giving birth. When she couldn't hide him any longer, she made a waterproof basket and laid Moses in it among the reeds where the Pharaoh's daughter bathed in the river.

Pharaoh's daughter sent Moses's sister, Miriam, one of her maids, to fetch the crying basket. Pharaoh's daughter felt sorry for the baby.

Miriam volunteered to find a wet nurse. Pharaoh's daughter agreed. Miriam introduced her mother. Pharaoh's daughter instructed the mother, "I'll pay you myself to nurse this child for me." Moses's biological mother nursed him until he was old enough to live with the Pharaoh's daughter who then raised him like a son. She named him Moses because as she said, "I drew him out of the water."

- Egypt as an infant
  Moses grew up in Egypt with the Pharaoh's daughter treating him as her own son.

  Yeshua with his family lived in Egypt until King Herod died.

- He'll be a Hebrew
  Moses and Yeshua were Hebrew.

- Brothers and Sisters misunderstood them
  Rachel told us for Moses, it was Miriam and Aaron, his sister and brother. They became jealous and didn't like that he'd married a Cushite woman. She'd summarized Tanakh, Torah, Beha'alotecha, Numbers 12:1–9 JPS.

  Collin told us with Yeshua, as the Jewish feast of Shelters drew near, his brothers told him to "go to Judaea, so Your disciples can see the works You're doing. Anyone

who wants to be publicly known doesn't act in secret. If this is what You're doing, You should reveal Yourself to the world." His brothers lacked faith in Him. Jesus replied, "For Me the right time hasn't come yet, but for you any time's right. The world cannot hate you, but it does hate Me, because I give evidence that its ways are evil. Go to the festival yourselves. I'm not going to this festival, because for Me the time isn't ripe yet." Having said that, he stayed behind in Galilee. He'd summarized New Testament, John 7:2–9 NIV.

They're close. But I'm not putting a lot of weight into it as a similarity. I feel there may be more supportive things on this list."

- Humble

The dictionary's meaning for *humble* is "not proud or arrogant." Being humble is living a life of self-denial and total dependence upon God. I feel both were extremely humble.

Drew told us Moses was raised as the son of Pharaoh's daughter, a king's grandson. However, once he'd learned he was Hebrew, he denounced ties with Pharaoh. He forfeited those luxuries to become God's servant for his chosen people.

Tanakh Torah Beha'alotecha Numbers 12:3 NJB, "Now, Moses was a very humble man, more so than any other man on earth."

Jessica feels you can't get more humble than being born in a manger like Jesus. Also, Jesus consistently gave credit and honor to the Father.

Rachel argued that where you're born or how you're born doesn't make you humble. We have babies born in dirty taxis all the time. Humble is a choice. Moses chose to be humble.

New Testament, John 5:30 NJB: "By Myself I can do nothing; I can judge only as I'm told to judge, and My judging is just, because I seek to do not My own will but the will of Him who sent me."

Sarah pointed out He talked to and touched those who were considered untouchable: lepers and demon possessed. He had dinner with hypocrites, Pharisees, and sinners.

Jessica found New Testament, Philippians 2:7–8 NJB: "He emptied Himself, taking on the form of a slave, becoming as human beings are; and being in every way like a human being, He was humbler yet, even to accepting death, death on a cross. I don't know if I could be that humble to accept death without a fight knowing I've done nothing wrong to save those who do wrong all the time."

They were both undeniably humble.

- He trusts God and God trusts him

    God trusted Moses to negotiate with the Pharaoh the release of his people by proving God's all powerful.

    God trusted Moses to lead his people.

    God trusted Moses to deliver his words and laws.

    Moses trusted God's seemingly impossible will.

    Moses trusted God to supply all of their needs while they wandered the desert.

    God trusted Yeshua to remain sinless, to be the perfect sacrifice for all humanity.

    God trusted Yeshua to teach all the new laws of God.

    God trusted Yeshua to show all how to ask God for forgiveness.

    Yeshua trusted God to supply his needs as well as the multitudes who'd gathered wherever he taught.

    Yeshua trusted God to forgive as a result of the cross.

    Yeshua trusted God would raise him from the grave.

We could go on forever listing trust to and from God for both. I think it's understood and undeniable.

- Chosen by God to lead people

   God chose Moses to lead his people through the desert to the Promised Land while instructing God's laws to his people.

   God gave Moses instructions on how to lead his people. He constructed the laws, told him where to go, gave him wisdom to judge, and kept him motivated.

   Moses kept a strong team who followed and believed in God. He did this by consistently showing the Israelites God's miracles while God supplied their needs. He also consistently mediated and prayed to God for wisdom, guidance, direction, and offered praises.

   As a leader, Yeshua understood his mission, his purpose, and he maintained a strong level of motivation. He too managed a team which grew into a multitude of followers. He taught his disciples how to trust God, ask for miracles in his name, and to teach and train, future leaders to do the same.

   God created and chose Yeshua to lead and teach God's love and grace, to lead all of humanity to God by becoming a sacrifice for all of our sins.

- Lawgivers

   Moses taught God's laws. Moses delivered the Ten Commandments Tanakh, Torah, Ki Tissa, Exodus 31:18 KJV: And he gave unto Moses, when he had made an end of communing with him upon mount Sinai, two tables of testimony, tables of stone, written with the finger of God.

   Moses under God's instruction clarified and developed the 613 Mitzvot in the Torah, although many cannot be observed since the destruction of the Second Temple.

Yeshua taught laws of love, grace, and forgiveness. Yeshua became the Law of the Holy Spirit. The New Covenant. Paul wrote in New Testament, Romans 8:1–4: "Condemnation will never come to those who are in Christ Jesus, because the law of the Spirit which gives life in Christ Jesus has set you free from the law of sin and death. What the Law couldn't do because of the weakness of human nature, God did, sending His own Son in the same human nature as any sinner to be a sacrifice for sin, and condemning sin in that human nature. This was so that the Law's requirements might be fully satisfied in us as we direct our lives not by our natural inclination but by the Spirit."

Yeshua gave us a new commandment: New Testament, John 13:34, NJB: "I give you a new commandment: love one another; you must love one another just as I have loved you."

- God will speak to him mouth to mouth

    Rachel pointed back to God reprimanding Moses's brother and sister by saying, "With you two, I make Myself known in a vision or dream. With Moses, I speak mouth to mouth, plainly and not in riddles…" She was referring to Tanakh, Torah, Beha'alotecha, Numbers 12:1–9 JPS.

    Tanakh, Torah, Ki Tissa, Exodus 33:11 KJV: And the Lord spake unto Moses face to face, as a man speaketh unto his friend.

    New Testament, Matthew 3:16–17 NJB: "And when Yeshua had been baptized He at once came up from the water and saw the Spirit of God descending like a dove and coming down on Him. And suddenly there was a voice from heaven, 'This is My Son, the Beloved; My favor rests on Him.'"

Amy points out that The Holy Trinity was witnessed! God the Son was baptized, God in the form of the Holy Spirit descended like a dove and came down upon the Son, and the voice of God the Father was heard. Also recorded and witnessed by his disciples in Mark 1:9–11, John 1:29–34, and Luke 3:21–22. This event was seen by hundreds of people!

New Testament, Matthew 17:5-7 NIV: "Peter was speaking to Jesus when a bright cloud covered them a voice said, 'This is My Son, The Beloved; He enjoys My favor. Listen to Him.' When Peter, James, and John, heard this they fell on their faces, overcome with fear. But Jesus said, 'Stand up, don't be afraid.'" This too was witnessed by hundreds.

New Testament, John 12:27–30 ESV: "My soul's troubled. What shall I say? 'Father, save Me from this hour? But it's for this very reason I've come to this hour. Father, glorify Your name!' A voice came from heaven, 'I have glorified it, and I'll again glorify it.' Some of the crowd who'd heard this said it was a clap of thunder. Others claimed it was an angel speaking to Him. Jesus answered, 'It wasn't for My sake this voice came, but for yours.'"

- He'll behold the likeness of the Lord

    Both were like God in how they cared about others, they cared about right and wrong, they mandated righteousness from those who followed, they were upright, performed miracles, were rescuers of an entire people, and delivered God's covenants.

- Chose twelve special leaders

    Rachel: After forty years wandering in the dessert, Moses and his people came upon the Promised Land. The land was apportioned under twelve tribal leaders

Tanakh, Torah, Numbers 1:5–15, NJB

- Simeon
- Asher
- Benjamin
- Levi
- Gad (with Reuben's tribe)
- Dan
- Judah
- Zebulun
- Manasseh (with 1st half of his father, Joseph's tribe)
- Ephraim (with 2nd half of his father, Joseph's tribe)
- Issachar
- Naphtali

Yeshua's "Twelve Disciples" can be found in Matthew 10:2-4, Mark 3:16-19, Luke 6:14-16, and Acts 1:13

- Simon bar-Jona who was also known as Simon Peter
- James who was also know as James ben Zebedee
- John ben Zebedee
- Andrew
- Philip
- Bartholomew
- Matthew
- Thomas
- James son of Alphaeus
- Thaddeus
- Simon the Cananean also known as Simon the Zealot

- Jude of James (whom replaced Judas Iscariot after Judas killed himself, or to replace Thaddeus at a later point. It's unclear in the four different areas of scriptures)

- Chose a life of hardship

  Moses, with God's people, roughed it in the desert until reaching the Promise Land, instead of staying in a palace as the Pharaoh's daughter's adopted son.

  Yeshua traveled to several cities, towns, and villages, with extremely modest means instead of marketing his miraculous abilities to gain earthly wealth.

  Sarah found New Testament, Philippians 2:6–8 NJB: Who being in the form of God, didn't count equality with God something to be grasped. But He emptied Himself, taking the form of a slave, becoming as human beings are, and being in every way like a human being, He was humbler yet, even to accepting death, death on a cross.

- Taught others how to pray

  We learned from Moses, to be humble, to seek more knowledge from God in how to better please Him, pray for others, and to converse with God like a friend.

  Moses prayed for others more than himself. At the beginning of Numbers 14 God even offered to disown his disobedient people and make a great nation out of Moses. Moses could have jumped for joy to be rid of the whiners and at the honorable position God offered. However, Moses was so humble he didn't even consider it. Instead he pleaded with God to forgive the people; those same people who were ready to stone him! He cared more about the agenda of a nation than about himself or his own agenda.

  Moses prayed for God's will and glory. In all of Moses's prayers, Moses asked for God's will and ensured all glory was credited to God. Moses cared about what people thought about or how they viewed his living God.

Moses prayed from a clean heart. Was Moses sinless? No. However, Moses tried living according to God's laws. He wasn't the kind who deliberately misbehaved and then asked God to forgive his sins.

Drew pointed out when prayer was vital Moses fell prostrate and fasted. Tanakh, Torah, Ekev, Deuteronomy 9:18 NJB: "Then I fell prostrate before Yahweh; as before, I spent forty days and forty nights with nothing to eat or drink, on account of all the sins which you'd committed, by doing what was displeasing to Yahweh and thus arousing His anger."

Imagine fasting and praying for forty days and forty nights. Praying the same thing over and over, but using different arguments. Moses did this! You'll read he did it several times in Deuteronomy.

Moses would go off to be alone with God and pray too. A mountain, in the Meeting Tent or anywhere he'd have privacy and no distractions.

Yeshua will always be remembered for The Lord's Prayer, which became a training session on how and what to pray when a disciple asked him how to pray. New Testament, Matthew 6:5–13 NIV: "Jesus instructed, 'And when you pray, don't be like the hypocrites, for they love to pray standing in the synagogues and on the street corners to be seen by men. I tell you the truth; they've received their reward in full. But when you pray, go into your room, close the door and pray to your Father, who is unseen. Then God, who sees what's done in secret will reward you. And when you pray, don't babble like pagans, for they think they'll be heard because of their many words. Don't be like them, for your Father knows what you need before you ask Him. This, then, is how you should pray, "Our Father in heaven, Holy is Your name, Your kingdom come, Your will be done on earth as it is in heaven. Give us today our daily bread. Forgive us our sins, as we also have forgiven those who have sinned against us. And lead us not into temptation, but deliver us from the evil.'"

Some people only pray in front of others. They're assumed righteous since they're always seen praying. There's a time and place for public prayer; however, God also wants us to pray to Him in private. God likes personal communication.

It's acceptable to pray for things over and over as Moses did. However, the pagans chanted words in magical incantations. God encourages persistent prayer but hates incantations offered without sincerity.

Yeshua kept private prayer time, just one-on-one time. He prayed in gardens, up on a mountain, at night or early in the morning avoiding distractions. He enjoyed his alone time with the Father. New Testament, Matthew 14:23 NJB: "After sending the crowds away He went up into the hills by Himself to pray. When evening came, He was there alone." And in New Testament, Mark 1:35 NJB: "In the morning long before dawn, He got up and left the house and went off to a lonely place and prayed there."

- Performed great miracles

Both, through God, performed great miracles. The miracles of Moses are detailed under the topic of "Both Were Prophets" to keep from reiterating.

Turned staff into a snake—Tanakh, Torah, Va'ayrah, Exodus 7:8–13

Water turned to blood—Tanakh, Torah, Va'ayrah, Exodus 7:14–25

Frogs—Tanakh, Torah, Va'ayrah, Exodus 7:26–8:11

Mosquitoes—Tanakh, Torah, Va'ayrah, Exodus 8:12–15

Horseflies—Tanakh, Torah, Va'ayrah, Exodus 8:16–28

Egyptian livestock—Tanakh, Torah, Va'ayrah, Exodus 9:1–12

Hail—Tanakh, Torah, Va'ayrah, Exodus 9:13–35

Locusts—Tanakh, Torah, Bo, Exodus 10:1–20

Darkness—Tanakh, Torah, Bo, Exodus 10:21–29

Death of the first-born—Tanakh, Torah, Bo, Exodus 11:1–12:34

The Red Sea parting—Tanakh, Torah, Beshalach, Exodus 14:15–31

Bitter water to sweet—Tanakh, Torah, Beshalach, Exodus 15:22–25

Manna—Tanakh, Torah, Beshalach, Exodus 16:4–36

Quails—Tanakh, Torah, Beshalach, Exodus 16:8–13

Water from a Rock—Tanakh, Torah, Beshalach, Exodus 17:1–7

Yeshua always gave glory to God and that the miracles he was performing were to fulfill prophecy. Like Moses, there was no trickery, no deceit, no self-glorifying patting on his own back, and certainly no wizardry which is often taught or thought of by skeptics! New Testament, John 10:25 NJB: "The works that I do in My Father's name, they bear witness of Me."

Water into wine. New Testament, John 2:1–11.

Calming the storm. New Testament, Matthew 8:23–27, Mark 4:37–41, Luke 8:22–25.

Feeding five thousand men *plus* the women and children using only five loaves of bread and two fish. New Testament, Matthew 14:14–21, Mark 6:30–44, Luke 9:10–17, John 6:1–14.

Walking on water. New Testament, Matthew 14:22–32, Mark 6:47–52, John 6:16–21.

Amy showed us that the Messiah walking above the water was actually prophesied by Daniel! Tanakh, Nevi'im, Daniel 12:5–7 NIV: "Then I, Daniel, looked, and there before me stood two others, one on this bank of the river, and one on the opposite bank. One of them said to the man clothed in linen, who was above the waters of the river, 'How long will it be before these astonishing things are fulfilled?' The man clothed in linen, who was above the waters of the river, lifted His right hand and His left hand toward heaven, and I heard Him swear by Him who lives forever, saying, 'It'll be for a time, times and half a time. When the power of the Holy people has been finally broken, all these things will be completed.'"

Feeding four thousand men plus women and children using seven loaves of bread and a few fish. New Testament, Matthew 15:32–39 and Mark 8:1–9.

Jesus told Simon to go catch a fish so he can take four-drachmas out of its mouth to pay the taxes for both. Simon did and it happened as Yeshua said. New Testament, Matthew 17:24–27.

A fig tree withers instantly after Yeshua cursed it for not having any fruit on it. New Testament, Matthew 21:18–22, Mark 11:12–14, 20–25.

Huge catch of fish. New Testament, Luke 5:4–11.

Healed a man with leprosy. New Testament, Matthew 8:1–4; Mark 1:40–44, Luke 5:12–14.

Jesus healed a Roman officer's servant who'd become paralyzed. New Testament, Matthew 8:5–13, Luke 7:1–10.

He healed Peter's mother-in-law. New Testament, Matthew 8:14–15, Mark 1:30–31, Luke 4:38–39.

Jesus cast the demons of two men possessed with devils into a herd of pigs. New Testament, Matthew 8:28–34, Mark 5:1–15, Luke 8:27–39.

He healed a woman who'd bled for a twelve years. New Testament, Matthew 9:20–22, Mark 5:25–34, Luke 8:43–48.

Healed two blind men. New Testament, Matthew 9:27–31.

Devil-possessed man who couldn't speak was healed. New Testament, Matthew 9:32–33.

The Canaanite's daughter was demon possessed until Jesus healed her. New Testament, Matthew 15:21–28, Mark 7:24–30.

He healed a possessed boy who couldn't be healed by the disciples. New Testament, Matthew 17:14–21, Mark 9:17–29, Luke 9:38–43.

Two spiritually blind men were healed to see the way, the truth, and the light. New Testament, Matthew 20:29–34, Mark 10:46–52, Luke 18:35–43.

A demon-possessed man in the synagogue shouted, "What do you want with us, Yeshua of Nazareth? Have you come to destroy us? I know who You are; the Holy One of God.' Yeshua rebuked the demon saying, 'Be quiet!' Yeshua refused to accept the witness of a demon even if it was true. Then Yeshua commanded the demon to come out of the man and it caused him to convulse and scream as it left the man. New Testament, Mark 1:21–28 KJV, Luke 4:31–37 KJV.

Blind man at Bethsaida was healed. New Testament, Mark 8:22–26.

A bent-over woman in the synagogue had suffered for eighteen years. Yeshua spoke the word and touched her without being asked. Her spine straightened. New Testament, Luke 13:10–17 KJV.

Yeshua healed the man with dropsy [accumulation of water in the tissues, like congestive heart failure,] New Testament, Luke 14:1–4.

Yeshua from a distance healed ten men with leprosy, New Testament, Luke 17:11–19.

The nobleman's son from Capernaum was healed without going to his home to do so. New Testament, John 4:46–54.

The invalid at the pool of Bethsaidar was healed. New Testament, John 5:1–15.

A man born blind was healed. New Testament, John 9:1–14.

Man with palsy, a paralytic was healed by Yeshua after being lowered into the room through a roof. New Testament, Matthew 9:2–7, Mark 2:3–12, Luke 5:18–26.

Jairus's daughter had just died. Yeshua went to the girl's room healed her and said she was just sleeping. New Testament, Matthew 9:18–26, Mark 5:21–43, Luke 8:40–56.

Drew feels this could mean she wasn't literally dead but was in that critical stage when an ill person's breathing is so shallow it cannot be detected by sight. It'd explain why Yeshua was honest and not taking credit for raising a dead person when he took her by the hand and restored her back to good health.

A funeral was taking place for a widow's only son. Yeshua touched the boy's carrier and told him to rise. The boy sat up. New Testament, Luke 7:11–17.

Lazarus had been dead and in the ground for four days before Yeshua arrived. He ordered the stone to be removed which freaked Martha out as she visualized a smelly decomposing body. Yeshua prayed aloud, "So they may believe it was You who sent Me." Then Yeshua yelled, "Lazarus, come out!" Lazarus came out with his hands, feet, and face, wrapped in clothe. Yeshua then instructed them to unbind him and let him go free. New Testament, John 11:1–44

When the high priest's servant's ear was cut off Yeshua touched the ear and healed it. New Testament, Luke 22:50–51.

- Provided food for a multitude

Moses prayed and God fed the Israelites manna and quail while they escaped to the desert.

First, Jesus prayed and fed a crowd of five thousand men plus women and children with just five loaves of bread and two fish, and then three days later he fed the crowd of four thousand men plus women and children with seven loaves of bread and a few fish.

- Not liked by the governing officials

    The Pharaoh towards Moses at the time of his birth since he was born a male Hebrew.

    The Pharaoh towards Moses when freeing God's people from Egyptian slavery.

    King Herod towards Yeshua at the time of his birth.

    The High Priests, chief priests, and elders, Sanhedrin, an ancient supreme court, and Jewish council towards Yeshua.

    Pontius Pilate, the Governor of Roman Judea, and Herod Antipas towards Yeshua.

- Interceded for his people

    Moses interceded with God when God threatened to kill His chosen people for worshipping the golden calf. Tanakh, Torah, Ekev, Deuteronomy 9:13–29

    Moses interceded with God when God wanted to destroy the Hebrews for being ungrateful in His meeting their needs. Tanakh, Torah, Shelach Lecha, Numbers 14

    Yeshua interceded with God for our sinful natures by becoming the perfect sacrificial lamb.

    Yeshua interceded for the two criminals hung on crosses next his.

- Brought people out of bondage

    Moses freed the people of slavery in Egypt.

    Yeshua freed all of humanity from the bondage of sin.

- Provided a way to the Promised Land

   Moses led the Hebrews to the Promised Land.

   Yeshua provides all of humanity a way to eternal life in heaven, the ultimate Promised Land.

- He'll be a prophet

   A biblical prophet isn't just a person who can predict an event that'll happen in the future. It's also a person who can speak for God. Both displayed these abilities.

   Moses prophesied the ten plagues of Egypt. I call it "Moses warns the Pharaoh if he doesn't free the Hebrews then ___ is going to happen and it does."

   One—...water will be turned into blood. Tanakh, Torah, Va'ayrah, Exodus 7:15–24.

   Two—...your whole country will be plagued with frogs. Tanakh, Torah, Va'ayrah, Exodus 8:1–15.

   Three—...Dust will become gnats. Tanakh, Torah, Va'ayrah, Exodus 8:16–19.

   Four—...Tanakh, Torah, Va'ayrah, Exodus 8:20–32: The Lord told Moses, 'Confront Pharaoh saying, "The Lord says, 'Let My people go…If you don't, God will send flies. The houses of the Egyptians will be full of flies, even on the ground. BUT, God will deal differently where the Hebrew live; no flies will be there; so, you'll know God's in their land. God will make a distinction between His people and your people. This miraculous sign will occur tomorrow.'" Moses obeyed and it happened. Pharaoh agreed to let the Hebrews offer sacrifices to God in the desert if Moses prayed the flies away. Moses kept his end of the deal; but, the Pharaoh didn't.

   Five—...terrible plague to Egyptian livestock, horses, donkeys, camels, cattle, sheep, and goats but no animal belonging to Hebrews will die. Tanakh, Torah, Va'ayrah, Exodus 9:1–7.

Six—...boils will break out on men and animals. Tanakh, Torah, Va'ayrah, Exodus 9:8–12.

Seven—...the worst hailstorm that's ever fallen on Egypt. Tanakh, Torah, Va'ayrah, Exodus 9:13–35.

Eight—...locusts will devour what little you have left after the hail. Tanakh, Torah, Bo, Exodus 10:1–20.

Nine—...total darkness [like everyone was blinded completely] that could be felt where the Egyptians live but light where the Hebrew live. Tanakh, Torah, Bo, Exodus 10:21–29.

Ten—Passover...Every first born Egyptian son will die. Tanakh, Torah, Bo, Exodus 11:1–30.

Later, Moses prophesied how long it'd take to reach the Promised Land, forty years, after God's people became faithless and were ready to stone Moses and return to slavery in Egypt. Tanakh, Torah, Shelach Lecha, Numbers 14:28–34.

Moses prophesied the coming of the Mashiach. Tanakh, Torah, Shoftim, Deuteronomy 18:18–19.

Yeshua prophesied the Temple's destruction. New Testament, Matthew 24:1–2.

Yeshua prophesied his own death, three days of death, and resurrection. New Testament, Matthew 12:39–40.

Jesus prophesied His resurrection in three days. New Testament, John 2:19–21.

He prophesied he'd be delivered into the power of men; they'll put Him to death; and three days later He'll rise again. New Testament, Mark 8:31, Mark 9:31, and Mark 10:32

- Baptisms

Rachel taught us that Moses originated the "cleansing," a Mikveh, so the Israelites would be cleansed for God. "It wasn't something your John the Baptizer created. It wasn't something the Christians started either. God's had it in place for a long time. The purpose of the Mikveh, according to the Jewish Law back then and is still true today was for the forgiveness of sins into a right relationship with God."

John the Baptizer stirred the Return to God movement with his baptisms, Mikveh.

Some baptize their eating utensils in the Mikveh to make them kosher, so they're pure in what they're eating.

Sarah explained how in the Protestant faiths being baptized is a declaration of your faith amongst Yeshua's believers to become unified with the followers. New Testament, 1 Corinthians 12:12–13 NIV: "The body's a unit, though it's made up of many parts; and though all its parts are many, they form one body. So it is with Christ. For we were all baptized by one Spirit into one body—whether Jews or Greeks, slave or free—and we were all given the one Spirit to drink."

Jessica explained being Catholic you're baptized as a baby into Christ. New Testament, Galatians 3:26–29 NIV: So in Christ Jesus you are all children of God through faith, for all of you who were baptized into Christ have clothed yourselves with Christ. There is neither Jew nor Gentile, neither slave nor free, nor is there male and female, for you are all one in Christ Jesus. If you belong to Christ, then you are Abraham's seed, and heirs according to the promise.

I've always been taught that identification with Yeshua's also a part of the Christian Baptismal process. He died. We die by acknowledging we've sinned and repent. He was buried. By immersing in the water we bury our nature with Christ. He arose from being dead. When we rise out of the water it's our identity of being with Christ in His resurrection. His resurrection becomes our resurrection.

Amy added in addition to water baptism, Yeshua brought baptism by the Holy Spirit and baptism by Fire.

The Library Room

Baptism into the Holy Spirit enters into your soul giving you new life when you accept Yeshua into your heart and with faith believe he's the redeemer. Baptism of fire helps purge out the sinful ways or sinful people in your life once you begin your walk with Christ. The temptations will still be there. However, you'll know them as temptations and the baptism of fire as well as the Holy Spirit will give you strength to overcome temptations.

- Both were tended by God at the event of their deaths

    Tanakh, Torah, V'zot Habracha, Deuteronomy 34:5-6 NIV: And Moses the servant of the Lord died there in Moab, as the Lord had said. He [God] buried him in Moab, in the valley opposite Beth Peor, but to this day no one knows where his grave is.

    New Testament, Luke 23:44–46 ESV: It was now about the sixth hour [noon,] darkness came over the whole land until the ninth hour [3 p.m.] for the sun stopped shining. And the curtain of the temple was torn in two. Jesus called out with a loud voice. 'Father, into Your hands I commit My Spirit.' And then, He breathed His last.

Twenty

Sarah watched Jessica make her way to the elevator. She didn't bother keeping up since she saw a new friend coming down the hall to check his mailbox. She lingered by reading her mail by her mailbox.

Sarah initiated the conversation. "Hi, Mike."

"Hey, Sarah!" Mike replied. "I didn't see you all weekend. Did you go home for the weekend?"

"No." Sarah smiled upon hearing he'd looked for her. "I had a typical weekend with friends—a little drama, a little research, and a little eating here and there. How about you? What did you do?"

"Typical weekend avoiding drama, avoiding research, memorizing data for quizzes, and searching out free food and beverages at parties," Mike answered.

"Really? My friends and I attended a couple of parties on Saturday. I didn't see you at either, although they were crowded. Perhaps I missed seeing you amongst the crowd?" Sarah wanted to sound cool but not like a party girl, so she added, "One party was too loud and concentrated more on drinking than eating. We didn't stay for that one. If you can't talk over the music what's the point?"

"I agree," Mike said. "That was cool in junior and senior high school, and the last time I attended college."

"Junior high? Isn't that a bit young to be drinking?" Sarah asked.

"Yes it is, and I'll kill my kids if they do what I did when I was that age," he agreed with a wink.

"You have kids? How old?" Sarah asked.

"Ha! No! I meant, when I grow up, get married, and *have* kids!" Mike laughed.

"This is your second round of college?" Sarah dug for details.

"Yes, it is." He explained, "I attended two years at OSU and then took one off to pay debts not covered by my scholarships. I hate debt to the point of obsession. I'm studying our sick economy. I like this college. It's quieter and more focused on my major, global economics. I want to be the chairman of the Federal Reserve. It's better than a weatherman's position. The salary's higher, and I don't even have to be two percent right for people to *still* trust me. Oops! Did I say that out loud? I won't bore you with my views on the economic mess. What's your major?" he asked.

"I'm a lab-rat girl. I love chemical engineering. I want to work in pharmaceuticals," she answered.

"Woah! I didn't see that one coming. She's beautiful, personable, *and* has a brain!" He made Sarah blush. "I'm sorry. I didn't mean to offend you. Money people aren't always known for our tact and social skills. We're pretty much geeks."

"None taken. Chemistry women are geeks too," she admitted.

"If you're free, would you like to go out Saturday?" he asked.

"Sure! What do ya have in mind?" Sarah asked.

"I was thinking…Heck, I don't know what I was thinking, but I'll think of something by then." He searched the ground for something clever to say to no avail.

"Okay, that sounds like a great unplanned idea. I like it. Give me a call Friday?" She pulled a pen from her purse and wrote her number on the back of his hand.

"Wouldn't it have been easier for you to just call my phone so I could capture it?" he said, looking at his hand.

"That seemed anti-geeky to me. I'm old-fashioned in other areas too. Good night. Talk t'ya later," she said, walking to the elevator.

<hr>

The next morning, Sarah awoke with a jolt. Something felt odd. She got out of bed and went from room to room, making sure everything was all right. The microwave clock showed four o'clock in the morning. She returned to her warm bed.

As she fell back asleep, she was awakened again. She lay in bed, listening hard to the sound of air. Not a sound could be heard except the hum of the furnace. She looked at her phone and saw it was now 4:16 a.m. She tried sleeping again.

The nudge to wake her up made her understand something supernatural was trying to get her attention.

Is it God or one of his angels? Pray? I'm being asked to pray? Father, what do you want me to pray? For whom shall I pray for?

She saw all their faces and her own flash before her eyes. *Everyone? Lord, I plead the blood of Jesus over everyone! I pray, dear God, for your protection and almighty hand of authority to crush evil plots, destroy wicked words, and bless each of my friends, their families, and me. Guide our group through this project. Help us to overcome obstacles of discouragement. Bless us with your grace and mercies in Jesus's name, amen.*

She pulled the covers over her shoulders with a parting thought. *I love you, my friend. Now, can I get some sleep?*

She was fast asleep until the strongest jolt hit her. Her eyes flew open. She again stared into the quiet darkness. Her mind searched for what was going on.

She recited the same prayer she'd said twenty minutes earlier and then got out of bed.

"I see it's going to be one of those mornings," She said looking upwards towards Heaven. "Everyone had better thank me later since I've saved their lives. I know it's a thankless job, but someone has to do it…even at 4:30 a.m."

She made coffee and surfed the news channels. *Maybe a meteor's going to hit the earth or a bad storm or a solar flare's about to fry us. Perhaps that's why God wants me to pray for everyone?'* The news provided nothing meaningful, so she turned the negative biased election noise off. She couldn't wait for the elections to be over! *They're all corrupt with their own evil agendas!*

Without the noise of the television, she prayed again.

She went to the kitchen for a bite to eat. *Prayer and fasting.* Her hand pulled away from the refrigerator. *Well, that's never crossed my mind before!* She went to her bedroom to get dressed. *Perhaps, I can get in a good workout at the gym since I'm not allowed to sleep or eat.*

The apartment lobby was empty of people except for the sleeping security guard. The gym was empty too. The lights in the gym turned on before she entered. She located the detector inside the door.

"Pretty clever," she said under her breath.

Sarah chose an old style treadmill because it required little concentration. After a few minutes of finding her pace, she repeated the prayer. *Where are those words coming from this morning? Those aren't my typical words of prayer. What is it, God? Is it something big? What are we in for today? Or by faith have we avoided what could have happened as a result of the prayers? What are you telling me? Thank you for what you're doing, preventing, or about to show us. Praise your holy name.*

People filed into the room for their workouts as she left.

⚜

Jessica looked at the clock and realized it was much earlier than she'd thought.

The Library Room

She picked up the phone and began dialing her mother's cell phone to pay her back for the late night call.

Karen answered, "Good morning, sweetie."

"Are you sleeping with your phone?" Jessica asked.

"I have since the first day you started college."

"That weirds me out."

"Too bad. It's what mothers do. You'll understand someday. Don't rush it though." Karen yawned.

"I was so tired last night, I couldn't keep up with our conversation, and this morning, I'm up an hour earlier than I'd planned," Jessica admitted.

"What's your plan for the day?" her mother asked.

"A couple classes, lunch, an early afternoon class, and then off to the library to help on the project. That's the part of the day I'm looking forward to the most," Jessica answered.

"So tell me once again about the stumbling block you've encountered putting you and your friends at odds. We didn't get a chance to go over that last night." Karen kept her head on her pillow.

"Well, we researched prophecies pertaining to Jesus then drafted a Moses comparison. Then, Drew and Rachel threw in what I'll call The Old Covenant Clause."

"What do you mean by that?" Karen asked.

"God gave the Hebrews a covenant on Mount Sinai. Jewish people feel they have their laws and if they obey them God will bless them, if they don't obey the laws they ask for forgiveness and try harder. They feel they don't need a Messiah. Although, some feel Jesus is a Messiah *but* for Gentiles only. Jewish people don't believe in the New Covenant or scriptures written in the New Testament."

"But," Karen stated, "they weren't capable of upholding *their* end of the Old Covenant. It was an *if* you do that, *then* God will do this. They continually failed with their carnal nature. The Holy Spirit wasn't known to them yet. God wouldn't send his

Spirit down to dwell in the hearts of humans until Jesus was glorified, which came after his sacrifice, burial, resurrection, and ascension."

"But what if they're obeying their laws and asking for forgiveness like the Jewish people do today?" Jessica asked.

"Too late, the old covenant was broken. It wasn't broken by God, for God would never go back on his word. It was broken by his people. They didn't want to keep the laws. He also knew they could try, but it wasn't in their hearts. When Moses and Jeremiah prophesied about the upcoming Messiah, God told them the new covenant 'would be written in their hearts' instead of on stone."

Karen continued, "At some point in a person's growth, the Holy Spirit comes into your heart and you've the power, free will, to choose if you *want* to be obedient to God. Before there was never a *want* in the hearts of man except for a few God chose to be leaders like Moses, David, Joshua, Samuel, the prophets, and the patriarchs—very few."

"Thank you so much, Mom! This makes total sense to me. Now, how do I go about proving or showing them what you just said? Is it in the Bible? Is it in the Old Testament?" Jessica had renewed strength and felt joy at the revelation of what had just been explained.

"It sure is. I'll do some searches on a few studies I've done over the years and send you what I find." Karen yawned.

"Thanks, Mom, it's been nice talking to you this morning. I love you and give Stewie a big sloppy kiss on his cheek from his favorite sister."

"One more thing, about your purpose," Karen interrupted. "Keep in mind, there's more to life than the here and now. God put us here on purpose and we're to achieve a goal. Our goal is to live in heaven with God. Life's a long series of tests from God, and in the end, he's going to ask everyone, 'What did you do with my Son, Jesus?' With that perception to think about, how's this

The Library Room

a part of your purpose? Don't answer it now. Just think about it. Okay? I love you too, sweetheart."

"Okay," Jessica answered.

They gave each other a noisy air kiss and hung up.

Loren's phone rang as she was eating a bowl of cereal in front of the television set. She watched flames engulfing the restaurant where Giles and Mellissa worked on the news. She answered the phone without taking her eyes off of the TV screen.

"Hello?" Loren answered.

"Good morning, Lor-Lor," her mother chimed. "I called to see how your project's coming along. I hadn't heard from you. You seemed pretty salty last week."

"Oh, morning, mom," Loren said.

"Well?" Diane could tell she was up against something else for Loren's attention. "Are you busy? Do you have time to talk?"

"Um, I'm watching the restaurant Giles works at go up in flames on the news," Loren answered. "They're not sure if anyone was inside yet. I don't know where Giles slept last night. I kicked him out over the weekend. I think he may be staying at his friend Mellissa's house, but I don't know that for sure."

"He's having an affair?" Diane sounded surprised.

"I don't think he was having an affair with her at the time we were living together, Mom."

"What's going on? What aren't you telling me?" Diane pushed. It was typical of Loren to shut out Diane and Mitch when she was hurting, in trouble, or struggling with life.

"After talking with dad the other night, I decided Giles was not the man for me. When I tried explaining that to Giles, he became a bit mad." Loren continued, "He did his best to convince me we were meant to be together and my friends stepped in and helped him understand he needed to leave."

"And…" Diane knew it wasn't that cut and dry.

"He had his friend Mellissa come to the house and move stuff out while I was at the library," Loren paused before continuing. "And she had to bring the truck back so I could get *my* stuff that didn't belong to Giles. The landlord changed my locks. I'm safe."

"Did you feel like you wouldn't be safe?" Diane blurted.

"Mom, sometimes things happen differently than we plan. The police had him under control, and I felt safe when they were called in to help. That's what they're for—to help and protect."

"The police?" Diane questioned.

"Don't blow it out of proportion. He wasn't beating me. He just wanted me to sit, eat, and listen as to why we should stay together. I'd already made up my mind it'd not be that way."

"So why were the police called?" Diane questioned.

"Because he wouldn't let my friends see me and I couldn't leave. He held me in the apartment," Loren blurted.

"Why didn't you call us?" Diane asked.

"Because it was all taken care of and I didn't want you to freak out like you're doing now. I hate drama. I needed some alone time with God to sort it all out. I'm sorry I didn't call," Loren explained.

"I have to tell your father, you know. We don't keep secrets from each other," Diane stated.

"I know. Just don't go crazy in thinking my life was in serious jeopardy. Or just have him call me and I'll tell him." Loren envisioned her mother's frantic recapping.

"What are you doing for dinner tomorrow night? Do you and your friends want to come over? I want to see your face. I love you," Diane threw out.

"Ha! You just want to pick their brains to see if there's more I'm not telling you!" Loren laughed, trying to lighten the mood. "And when you offer free home-cooked food, it might work. I'll ask them. I doubt if Amy will be able to make though. Mrs. Rosenberg, her favorite patient at the nursing home, is about to die, and she'll want to be near her. Or if Mrs. Rosenberg dies,

Amy may be mourning and not up to it. I'll ask her anyway, though."

"Aren't *all* patients in nursing homes dying?"

"No, Mom, not this one. This is more like a country club for older people who can't take care of themselves, don't feel like cooking anymore, don't want the responsibility of maintaining their own home, or can't drive anymore. Some of them reside there for years without being sick or bedridden. Most of the nicer homes are like that now. They have game night, field trips, and do fun things. Amy loves working there."

"Great! Sounds like you've already picked out my next home," Diane joked.

"Now see? The jury's still out. This is why you need to be nice from here on out because *I'm* the one who picks your nursing home," Loren teased. "I love you, Mom. See you Wednesday night."

"Love you too," Diane cooed. "What should I make for dinner?"

I'm craving your old-fashioned chicken and dumplings, the real fluffy ones sprinkled with salt and pepper!"

They said good-bye to each other again and then hung up.

Loren's phone buzzed with text messages. She read through them as each inquired about her location and asked if she was safe. She typed up a message and sent it as a blast to everyone who'd inquired. "Safe at home. Mom wants all 4 dinner Wed PM. Watching news. C U at library."

She heard a knock at the front door.

So help me. It better not be Giles crying for sympathy over that restaurant. I'll call the police. I'm not in the mood for his drama. Please, God, don't let it be Giles. Please, God, she prayed as she approached the door. She thought she saw a shadow go across the living room window and brushed it off as being paranoid. At the door, she was surprised to see Officer Jones. She opened the door.

"Hey there, Loren," Officer Jones greeted.

"Hey, what's up?" Loren asked as Officer Gordon came from around the side of the house. *Well that'd explain the window shadow*, she thought.

"We're just checking in on you. The restaurant Giles works at caught fire this morning, and no one's been able to make contact with him or Mellissa," Officer Jones announced. "Has he contacted you since posting bail?"

"Not at all," Loren said. "You think they're in the restaurant?"

"Not sure." Officer Gordon glanced sideways at Officer Jones.

"What do you mean?" Loren saw the look they gave each other.

"We have reasons to believe *he* may have been sleeping in the manager's office last night," Officer Jones explained. "Listen, we shouldn't tell you this, but we were called to Mellissa's apartment last night. He seemed fine when we got there, and Mellissa said they'd worked out their differences. He asked if he could get a ride to the restaurant to let Mellissa cool down. So we drove him there."

"Okay, it's nice to know he hasn't violated his restraining order against you," Officer Gordon added. "That was our worry and to see if we can locate him before making assumptions regarding the restaurant."

Loren replied, "I'll be going to the library within the hour. However, they've a nice secure room there so I'll be safe."

"I can't talk to you about it." Officer Jones winked. "But I know that room you're speaking of very well." He turned and walked away. "Don't forget to lock your door, just in case. Although, I don't think you'll have anything to worry about if he hasn't bothered you by now."

She locked the door as soon as she shut it.

While packing snacks to take to the library, she reminisced over Giles and hoped he hadn't burned to death in the fire. As much as she no longer liked him, he'd always hold a spot in her heart and wished him no harm. She said a quick prayer for his safety. When she picked up the bag laden with all the snacks, the weight of it astounded her. She thought out loud, "I'd better double bag this, or it'll never make it across the street, let alone to the library."

As she walked to the library, she smelled the fire.

The library seemed dark from smoke clouds darkening the windows on the overcast day. Very few people were there. She speculated most students were at the fire scene, watching something exciting in this sleepy little town. The area of her secret room entrance seemed to be even darker, and she couldn't wait to be safe inside to conquer the gloomy atmosphere by opening the sky dome.

Using her key swipe, she opened the door and stepped inside. As the door closed behind her, she breathed out anxiety. *Why am I nervous? Is it because Officer Jones came to my house asking questions? Is it because no one knows where Giles might be after a bad night? Is it the thought of Giles being in the fire?*

She was staring up at the sky dome when the door opened and startled her.

Sarah had a panicked look on her face as she entered the room.

"Hey, girlfriend! What's up?" Loren asked. "Don't you have classes this morning?"

"All classes are canceled. Mellissa was found dead in the restaurant," Sarah informed Loren. "You didn't have the television on? They're searching for Giles. They haven't released his name or picture, but I'm sure it's a matter of time if they don't find him."

Loren sat hard in her leather chair and shook her head in disbelief. She couldn't move, couldn't speak, and couldn't breathe. "Giles? Giles would do something like this? I had the television on, but I wasn't paying attention. Mom called, Officer Jones showed up, and then I walked here."

The door opened again. Collin, Drew, Rachel, and Jessica knew Loren had heard the news based upon her expression.

No one moved an inch or said a word. They all watched Loren as she stared at the smoky clouds above sky dome.

Loren defended Giles. "He didn't do it on purpose."

One by one, they moved from their statuesque positions to their seats around the table.

"He's an atheist, not a murderer. He believes in peace, not war, and being accountable to society, not a god. It doesn't make sense," Loren cried.

Everyone rose from their chairs to comfort her. Collin kneeled beside her and held her head on his shoulder.

Everyone's phones rang as relatives called to see if they were all right. They all looked to Loren, "Might as well face the families."

Loren's mother was frantic. "Where are you?! Why didn't you tell me it was this bad?"

"Mom, calm down! I didn't know until Sarah told me here at the library because I was on the phone with you. Then Officers Jones and Gordon stopped in to see if I was safe or if Giles had contacted me since he posted bail. Has he contacted you or Dad since Sunday? I put you two on the restraining order list too."

"Restraining order? Posted bail? Loren Marie what's going on! And don't you try your skirting talents to get out of telling me everything! Out with it now!" Diane sounded the maddest she'd ever been at Loren.

Loren took the phone to a bean bag chair to calm her mother down. She knew her mother deserved the full story. She didn't want to leave the security of the room, nor did she want any of her friends to leave either.

Loren saw Drew heading for the door to leave while he was on the phone. Loren called out to him while interrupting her mother's ranting and concerned rage. "Drew, please, we should all stay in here together until Giles is found. It's safe here. Officers Jones and Gordon know I'm here and Officer Jones knows about this room."

Drew stopped in his tracks, gave her a thumbs-up, and walked to the refrigerator where he grabbed water for himself. Then he made hand signals, asking everyone if they'd like him

The Library Room

to bring them a drink. He noticed the big bag of snacks Loren had dropped when Sarah had delivered the news to her. He took it over to the cabinet and put things away while listening to his concerned parents doing all of the talking.

Rachel was on the phone with Amy. She stood in front of the paintings, rocking back and forth like a mother rocks her child. It was a coping motion she'd developed as a child and never outgrew. She longed to talk to her mother. It was hard to stay focused on Amy's conversation because of all the conversations she could hear around her. She assured Amy they all understood why she wasn't there with them.

Collin was on the other bean bag, talking to his father. He promised him he was safe. And he said, "Yes, it's a tragedy, but don't believe everything you hear in the media." Then he described the room to him and the security system for added measures in easing his mind.

As soon as Jessica heard her mother's voice, she cried. She sat at the table opposite Sarah. At one point, Jessica said, "No, Mom, please don't come out here. We're all safe in a private room in the library with a state of the art security system...No, it's not in the main part of the library. It's a hidden room used for the project we're working on...No, only people who are working on the project have access keys to the room."

Sarah avoided eye contact with everyone. She didn't want them to see her shaking. She whispered to her mother, "We all need to pray, Momma. I knew I needed to pray. We need to keep praying." Judy recognized her daughter was in shock. She asked to speak to Jessica, but Sarah said, "She's on phone talking to her mom, and we need to pray."

Judy prayed into the phone. "Lord Jesus, come down and bless those affected by this tragedy. Lord, heal the hearts of your saints and the parents of the girl found in the fire. Give the students a sign of your everlasting love and mercy. Thank you, Jesus for your amazing grace and protection. Thank you, Father. Amen"

Sarah continued praying, "I plead the blood of Jesus Christ over myself, friends, and family. Keep us safe in the palm of your hand. I pleaded the blood this morning just like you wanted. I did it, and I prayed. Keep us safe, Lord. I obeyed and prayed. Keep us safe." No one noticed her irregular behavior and shaking.

"Honey," Judy said, "it'll take me a few hours to drive up there, but I'm on my way. Okay? Keep your phone on and call if you need to talk or pray some more."

"Okay, Mom," Sarah said. "I'll keep praying."

Judy hung up the phone and packed an overnight bag. She was scared. She knew Sarah needed her.

Rachel hung up the phone with Amy. She headed to her seat at the table and noticed Sarah shaking. Rachel went to Sarah.

Collin hung up with his father, climbed out of the beanbag chair, and headed to the snack cabinet.

"Collin, would you mind if we take over the beanbag chair?" Rachel asked him.

He saw Sarah shaking and breaking out in a cold sweat while Rachel led her to the beanbag.

"I think she's in shock!" Rachel assessed.

"We must pray," Sarah demanded as she sat next to Rachel who grabbed her like a child and held her.

"Okay, we'll pray," Rachel said in a calming voice.

"God wouldn't let me sleep. I had to get up and pray, so I did," Sarah explained.

"Okay, we'll pray," Rachel reassured her again.

"I pleaded the blood of Jesus to keep us safe. God warned me and I knew what to pray." Sarah insisted while shaking.

"Sh. Let's just pray now." Rachel held her tighter.

Collin stripped off his football jersey and placed it around Sarah like a makeshift blanket. Jessica stopped crying, Drew cocked his head to the side in question, and Loren used the opportunity to break off her conversation with her mother.

While comforting Sarah, Loren's phone rang.

The Library Room

"Hello?" she answered.

"Just checking in with you to make sure you're in the library room," Officer Jones's voice sounded concerned.

"Yes, I'm in the room and so are my friends, all of whom you've met," Loren reassured.

"I should've guessed you were the lucky group this year to be a part of that project," Officer Jones told her.

"Seriously? Why?" Loren scowled.

"The room's security is there for a reason—spiritual warfare. Everyone needs to plunge into your research today instead of worrying about what's happening outside. The chaos Satan's causing is his best effort to keep you sidetracked from learning about God's grace," Officer Jones explained. "By the way, what does everyone want from Ganzo Subs? Precinct's treat while keeping you under secured protection."

"Ooo! We love Ganzo's! Hold on, I'll ask." Loren pulled the phone away and asked everyone to write down what they wanted so she could scan it and e-mail it over to Gonzo's for Officer Jones. "Umm...Are we in danger?"

"We have reason to believe Giles is looking for you. We've had your house under surveillance for the past half hour. However, earlier the neighbors saw him checking both doors with his old keys. Fortunately, the key under the flower pot's an old one too."

A chill ran down her spine. "He knows about the secret room."

"Does he have a key swipe?" Officer Jones asked.

"No," Loren said.

"You're safe. Don't leave the room. If you need to leave, go in pairs. He's less likely to make a move if you go in pairs. We've alerted the school to monitor the cameras in and around the library. Now, get to work on the project. It's important."

"Yeah yeah," Loren said. "Spiritual warfare."

Loren hung up the phone and filled out her part of the Gonzo order. Collin scanned it and e-mailed it in.

Twenty One

"They haven't found him yet," Loren said. "My neighbors saw him trying the new locks. Officer Jones wants us to say in this room as much as possible. If we need to leave, use the buddy system."

"Loren," Drew said, "I'm sorry for what's going on. I'll speak for everyone. We're not blaming you in any way."

"Thanks, Drew." Loren's eyes watered. "I feel it's somewhat my fault for not seeing Giles as the person he's become."

"People change," Collin offered as comfort.

"Everyone's innocent until proven guilty," Drew reminded everyone. "We've no proof he killed her or caused the fire. We're letting our imaginations run wild because of his recent behavior."

"Spoken like a great future lawyer," Rachel praised. "Drew's right. She could've fallen trying to get out. He could've panicked thinking it's his fault for leaving a grill on. There are too many things that could've happened making him not guilty but running scared."

"We need to pray," Sarah said softly from the beanbag chair. She was no longer shaking, and her eyes registered her return. "I prayed for *our* safety. I pleaded the blood of Jesus Christ over us and our families. But I forgot to pray for Giles and Mellissa. Pray for your *enemies*…I didn't pray for them."

"Sarah," Rachel corrected, "it's not your fault. Besides, it's not too late to pray for them. Pray Giles turns himself in or he's captured gently. Pray Mellissa finds comfort in the Olam Ha-Ba,

The World to Come. Pray for Mellissa's family. Sarah's right, we should pray."

"Back when I attended church," Loren said, "we'd start out in silent prayer. If we felt stirrings inside, we'd speak the prayer out loud."

Drew and Collin donned their yarmulkes while everyone bowed their heads.

Loren prayed, "Lord, please guide us, keep us safe, and comfort the broken hearts. Help authorities find Giles."

Rachel added, "Protect and inspire us to think and act only out of love."

Drew also quoted from the Babylonian Talmud prayer Rachel had used. "Keep far from us all evil. May our paths be free from obstacles from when we go out until we return home."

Jessica picked up the Holy Bible. She opened it in the middle as she'd been taught to do in times of trouble. It always opens to Psalms, and you can always find passages there for help and comfort. She read Tanakh, Ketuvim, Book II, Psalms 46:1–11 NIV: "God is our refuge and strength, an ever-present help in trouble. Therefore we won't fear, though the earth give way and the mountains fall into the heart of the sea, though its waters roar and foam and the mountains quake with their surging…Be still and know that I am God; I'll be exalted among the nations, I'll be exalted in the earth. The Lord Almighty is with us; the God of Jacob is our fortress."

"Thank you, God, for keeping us safe," Sarah added.

Collin ended the session, "Comfort Mellissa and her hurting family. Heal our community. You know us. You know our hearts. We seek your truth. Help us to always search for your truths, your words of wisdom, and your ways of love. Amen."

Loren's phone rang. "Hello?"

"Hello, Loren, this is Professor Finkel."

"Hello, Professor," Loren acknowledged.

"Are you in the library room? It's the safest place on campus. Are your friends with you?" Professor Finkel inquired. "You and your friends are close to figuring it out."

Loren answered, "Yes, we're here. Why do you say that?"

"Since assigning this project, every year, something causes the team to feel threatened. It's always occurred when they were close to realizing God's truths and agreeing to them. Satan has a temper. He doesn't like losing. The more you learn about God the less hold Satan has on you. He'll discourage you from being able to focus on the project." Then the professor said, "Spiritual warfare."

"Spiritual warfare," Loren repeated. "That's funny. Officer Jones said that exact phrase today. Does that mean Satan killed an innocent person to discourage us from finishing this project? I could get salty if that's the case. Why'd God allow that to happen?"

"Loren, it could be a part of something larger than what we can see," the professor said, trying to calm her. "God knows how tragedy ripples. He doesn't want us to hurt any more than a surgeon wants to cause pain. However, sometimes, it's necessary. I don't feel Mellissa died to prevent you from learning more about God. I do worry you and your friends may become distracted by what's happened."

"So like Officer Jones instructed, stay focused and keep moving forward on the project is why you're calling me?" Loren was getting angrier.

"I was also making sure you and your friends were safe," the professor added after hearing Loren's irritation.

"Well, bless those who've risked life and limb enduring spiritual warfare to finish *your* project. Please thank them for anticipating *our* need for protection as a result of *their* experiences. I hope you and the others are enjoying drinks while studying the odds and placing bets on the Christians versus the Jews." Her nerves were shot. The kindness they'd prayed for earlier was lost.

"Loren," Professor reprimanded, "I'm sorry to hear how this is upsetting you. However, don't speak to me that way. Your accusations are off base. The staff and I are in a church basement. We're here to pray for your safety, for our campus, for the resolve of this tragic event, for the family of that poor girl, for the person who caused the fire, and for everything that'll ripple out as a result."

"I'm sorry," Loren apologized. "I'm thankful for the prayers. I don't know why I snapped."

"Apology accepted. Call me if you've any questions or prayers you'd like our staff to pray. We'll be here all day and night," Professor Finkel offered before hanging up.

"What was that all about?" Collin asked.

"You mean," Loren answered, "my idiot rage? Or the professor encouraging us to overlook the spiritual warfare and continue working on the project? Or his humbling me by telling me he and the staff are in a church basement praying for us, Mellissa's family, Giles, and all the ripples caused from the fire?"

"Yep. All of the above." Collin nodded. "Are you okay? It'll be over soon."

"I've never liked being told to go to my room for any reason, even if it's not to punish me," Loren admitted.

"Let's work on the project instead of thinking about what's going on?" Jessica suggested. "Collin, can you display the prayer?"

"Yes," Rachel agreed. "I could use a distraction about now too. What time do you think Officer Jones will be dropping off our lunches?"

"I'll guess any minute now," Loren answered.

"Here we go." Collin led them in prayer.

Loren addressed Rachel and Drew. "How do you two feel about what we've uncovered so far? I mean, does any of this make sense? What were you thinking as we uncovered the information? Are you buying into it? Do you doubt all or most of it? Has this affected your beliefs in Yeshua being your Mashiach in any way? What's your stand on all of this?"

Rachel answered, "I'm not sure how I stand with all the information. I've learned a lot, and I've a list of questions to ask my rabbi when we talk. I can see how it could've been missed by the Hebrews, and I can see why information is withheld from Jewish people to keep them from becoming confused or questioning their faith. I know I don't need Yeshua. I know this being Jewish."

"Why do you feel Jesus isn't the Messiah?" Loren asked.

Drew answered, "If Yeshua were the Mashiach, he'd have led Israel into world dominance with peace. I don't understand how someone so close to the prophesied description of Mashiach could fail the way he did. If he was sent from God, why'd he die before becoming a great ruler? He was a great teacher. He was blessed by God in being able to perform all those miracles. Still, he couldn't pull off the final miracle—world peace. That's why I believe he was a Mashiach of sort, a Mashiach for the Gentiles, not the Jews. God keeps us different. We need a different Mashiach."

"Drew, that makes total sense to me!" Rachel exclaimed. "That's what I was thinking. But I couldn't put into words. This is why they don't teach us about it. It's confusing. Like I said before, why do we need a Mashiach to forgive our sins if we have the Old Covenant?"

Jessica answered, "You need a Messiah because the Old Covenant was broken. Not so much by you or your parents but by your forefathers from Adam to Yeshua's time. They were unable to keep the Mitzvahs, and they didn't have the heart to want to keep them. It's just like Moses and Ezekiel prophesied: He'll write it in their hearts...not on stone like he did with the Ten Commandments. Did you know praying is easier because the Holy Spirit was sent to *all* after the ascension of Yeshua?"

"Jessica, we had The Spirit of God *before* Yeshua came to earth!" Rachel defended. "The Spirit of God in people can be read all over in the Tanakh: Moses, Abraham, Samuel, David, Baalam, etc."

"True, but they were individual people, not everyone. In most cases, it was short-lived, so God could empower them with wisdom or strength to get a job done," Jessica argued. "The Spirit didn't stay with them, except in rare occasions like David and Moses. Now, since the ascension of Yeshua, The Spirit of God, also named the Holy Spirit, can indwell in *our* hearts. Not just people of power."

Loren spoke, "Okay, this sounds like something we need to research. The Spirit of God in the Tanakh and the Holy Spirit in the New Testament are they one in the same? Do they behave the same? What effects or changes took place after Jesus ascended to heaven?"

Collin typed the questions into different Internet search engines. He found references to a few books and wrote them down to collect later. He also made a list of different references found in the Tanakh and in the New Testament.

"I spoke to my dad last night," Collin spoke while typing. "After getting the number for Father Tim, he explained the communion/transubstantiation thing to me. It was informative and I'll go over it all later. Anyway, he mentioned something that hit me. We're researching stuff we should already know. Perhaps, we'd been taught but didn't grasp it because we were too young. He feels second graders are too young to make a commitment to God; our first communion age."

"I agree." Drew nodded. "We aren't permitted to celebrate Bar Mitzvah until we're thirteen for boys or Bat Mitzvah for girls at twelve."

"I remember my Bat Mitzvah as if it were yesterday," Rachel gushed. "I felt like a princess who follows God. My parents and I spent months preparing for it."

"I still remember my first communion too," Jessica said. "I still have the pretty white dress my mother gave me to wear.

It's the same one she'd worn as a child. I'll have my daughter use it if she wants. I hope she does. All of our family and close friends came for dinner at our house afterward. I received a lot of religious presents and money. My mom made me put the money into savings bonds which helped pay college expenses my freshman year."

"And how old were you?" Rachel was intrigued.

"I want to say eight or nine," Jessica answered.

"Did you have any idea what was going on at the time?" Sarah asked. "Being Southern Baptist, we don't have a first communion ceremony. They just keep asking kids if they're ready to accept Jesus into their hearts. Once they accept, they're considered saved or born again. I guess it depends upon the maturity of each kid as to when they accept. I know, I accepted Jesus into my heart a few hundred times because I didn't know for sure if it took place the other times. Once I was older, I learned you need to do it once, and then you're in good with God." She laughed as she visualized how many times she'd gone up to the alter to accept Jesus into her heart and then later watching kids grow up in church doing the same thing and watching the older pious ladies roll their eyes.

"You don't have a party and celebrate such a momentous event in your life?" Rachel sounded appalled. "We celebrate taking that step in life as much as we celebrate for our wedding! It's a commitment worthy of a Simcha! We're told as soon as we hit that age—twelve for a girl, thirteen for a boy—we've become spiritually mature enough to know our bodies and its needs. We become multilayered, realizing our appetites and needs of our physical nature as well as seeking meaning, and inspiration, through a connection to our spiritual side."

"What's a Simcha?" Loren had been taking notes.

"It's a party, a celebration," Drew explained.

"We send out invitations. We have a grand entrance into the hall where family and friends are waiting. We dress in formal attire. There's a band or DJ for dancing. We have a candle lighting ceremony honoring those who've helped us in our spiritual growth, and an awesome candy buffet for dessert!" Rachel explained with enthusiasm.

"Wow! I feel ripped off! I didn't get anything like that," Loren said to Rachel. "I'm Protestant, so I didn't have a first communion party either!"

Drew asked Rachel, "Did *your* parents hire the bottle dancers?"

Rachel replied with a slight laugh. "No, I've heard about them, but I've never seen them."

"The bottle dancers?" Collin asked with a smile.

"Yep," Drew said. "And I've already promised to hire them to perform at my wedding. So I hope you don't mind." He looked at Rachel, blushing. "Collin, look at videos posted on the web. I think you'll agree."

"Ah!" The girls ran to Rachel.

Loren's phone rang. It was Officer Jones.

"Hello, Loren! Hey I'm standing outside the secret door. Can someone let me in?"

"Sure can!" Loren said. "Drew, open the door for Officer Jones, please? He's right outside the door."

As soon as she hung up, she hugged Rachel. "Tell us everything! When did you decide? How have you been able to keep this from us? Where's the ring? Have you set a date?" The questions spewed from the girls while Drew and Collin greeted Officer Jones with the food.

"Am I missing something?" Officer Jones asked.

"Rachel and Drew are engaged!" Sarah exclaimed.

"Oh!" Officer Jones proclaimed. "Mazel Tov! I should've brought champagne too."

"Thanks," Drew said. "We must keep it hushed. I can't ask her father until her parents return. Since I haven't asked her father and she hasn't told her mother, no plans have been made yet."

The sandwiches were distributed.

"Officer Jones, any luck finding Giles?" Loren asked.

The Library Room

"He's vanished. Does he own a bike?" Scott asked. "And please just call me Scott."

"None, I'm aware of," Loren answered.

"Mellissa suffered trauma to her temple area." Scott pointed to his temple, suggesting a gun shot. "The fire damage to her happened postmortem. Does Giles own a gun?"

"He's never mentioned one to me," Loren answered.

"Where do his parents live? We're having trouble locating them," Scott inquired.

"His parents are divorced. He doesn't talk to them. His mother lives in St. Louis, and his father's in Blaine, Minnesota," Loren added.

"Loren, his mother is *buried* in St. Louis. Didn't he tell you his mother died?" Scott watched her. "When I asked, I meant his father and stepmom."

"No, he never indicated his mother was dead. He just said he'll never talk to her ever again." Loren's head spun, grasping the dead mother and stepmother information. "Do you think he killed her?" Loren questioned.

"Who? His mother? No," Scott said. "He was just a toddler."

"How long must we to stay in this room?" Sarah asked. "I'm claustrophobic."

"I'd appreciate it if you'd all stay in here until he's apprehended," Scott requested. "Hopefully, I'll have information on his whereabouts soon."

After everyone finished eating, Scott excused himself.

"He didn't bring up the new sky dome being added," Loren stated. "Think he's been to the room recently?"

"Yep," Collin agreed. "Okay, the Spirit of God research. I'm going to take this list of books to Amida. Anyone else want to step out?" Collin asked.

"Me!" Sarah jumped up. "If ya don't mind standing outside the ladies room for a couple seconds."

"Let's do it." Collin walked toward the door.

Amy worried about her friends but knew they were safe. She worried about Ms. Roses Are My Favorite Flowers too. She'd not stirred, even with visitors talking around her bed. It was the last phase of the process. There were orders to contact Amy if she woke up. As the day dragged, no one alerted her of such news.

Mrs. Rosenberg's family brought Amelia and Alec food, so they didn't have to leave the facility. The air in the room was stale from too many people in it at one time.

Amelia found Amy in the staff lounge eating lunch. She apologized for interrupting with a hug. Amy welcomed the distraction. She sensed something was on Amelia's mind. "You okay?"

"Maybe, I'm not sure," Amelia started. "I've been reading over your notes on Yeshua."

"And..." Amy urged her to continue talking.

"I read the Moses comparison," Amelia wavered.

"The comparison showed both are quite unique compared to you and me yet the same with God guiding them as paralleled lives. Don't you think?" Amy concluded.

"Yes, and *then* I read the prophecies regarding the birth," Amelia admitted. "At first, I wasn't sure. I'd believed all the stories were made up by leaders trying to control people's behaviors or offer them hope. Now, I read your notes, and it's like I'm reading them for the first time. They're real. God's real. You can't have those types of miracles and prophecies witnessed by thousands and not believe in God. He exists, doesn't he?"

Amy was surprised by Amelia's confession of not believing in God. "Yes, he exists."

"God must be so disappointed in me. I'd be ticked off at me if I were him!" Amelia said. "How'll I ever make it up to him? How can I ever be forgiven? I've led people away. My children doubt God's existence because of me."

"You confess your sins and ask Yeshua to forgive you. You do realize Yeshua is God incarnate. Right?" Amy wasn't sure how much Amelia understood other than God exists. "He came down to be a living sacrifice, so we don't have to go to a temple to sacrifice a lamb. He became our lamb. Every time we sin we ask Jesus for forgiveness. It's wiped away *and* it's *forgotten* by God. He'll never use those sins against you. Here, let me get a poem my grandmother wrote to our family a long time ago." Amy handed Amelia a card from her purse.

Before Amelia read the card, she asked, "So do I still need to recite the Teshuvah?"

"What's that?" Amy replied.

"It's what you do to confess your sins to God. It takes you through a process of atonement called Vidui. As you're going through this process it takes you back in time to past iniquities. It helps make your confession come from your heart with meaning. Then, you ask God to forgive your sins and heal the results of your failures," Amelia explained. "There are two different confessions a short one called Ashamnu and the long one which is said at Yom Kippur called Al Cheyt."

"Without knowing the words of what you're saying, I can't say for certain, yes or no. However, based upon the way you've described it, I don't see anything wrong with continuing to do that as long as you're requesting Yeshua's blood to cleanse away your sins. Failures to God are considered sin. Sin prevents us from being able to communicate with God. I like asking for forgiveness as often as possible because I tend to sin a lot in my thinking. I like talking to God like I do a friend, often and about everything. If I've sinned I don't want to talk to God as much. I can tell in my attitude. So doesn't it make sense God's sacrifice can be used any time instead of storing up all the sins and doing it once a year?" Amy explained.

"Oh, saying the Ashamnu can be said any time. Most don't wait to do it once a year." Amelia corrected her. She looked at the card. "I can't take this. It's your only copy."

"I have more copies in my drawer at home, and I even have it on my computer, so I can send it to friends when they've questions like yours," Amy assured her.

"Thank you so much." Amelia hugged Amy. She opened the card and read the poem out loud.

How Can You Love Me?

I say to Him, "How can you love me?
I am so small and full of fear."
He says to me,
"I'll send you courage for every prayer I hear.
I am full of grace."

I say to Him, "How can you love me?
I have sinned so many sins."
He says to me,
"I made a way for you to begin again.
I am full of grace."

I say to Him, "How can you love me?
I have used your name in vain."
He says to me,
"I love you so much; I was able to rise again!
I am full of grace."

I say to Him, "How can you love me?
I've done such evil deeds."
He says to me,
"Have I ever failed in supplying your needs?
I am full of grace."

I say to Him, "How can you love me?
I've deliberately gone against Your will."

He says to me,
"When children defy their parents, do they love them still?
I am full of grace."

I say to Him, "How can you love me?
My past is tarnished, rough, and wild."
He says to me,
"Your future is bright; have faith in Me my child.
I am full of grace."

I say to Him, "How can you love me?
I've done nothing to deserve such grace?"
He says to me,
"No need to be super human; I've already won that race.
I am full of grace."

I say to Him, "How can you love me?
I don't even know where to start."
He says to me,
"It's simple my child, ask Me into your heart.
I am full of grace."

As Amelia read different points, she'd become emotional. It's what she'd felt due to her flesh denying her mind the peace from knowing God. The flesh's power was broken, and she now knew the truth. The truth set her free from fear, and sin. Her new life was beginning.

"Do you think Alec gets this?" Amelia wondered.

"I don't know. He's hard to read, but I get the impression he believes in God," Amy said.

"I'll make copies of the materials you've brought in and share them with my family. I'll leave the decision up to them. If they take the time to read it God will work in their hearts." Amelia shined and hugged Amy. "You've done well for God, and you've done well for me and my family. You've blessed us and may God bless you."

An aide, Amy works with entered to let her know Mrs. Rosenberg was failing now. She wouldn't be waking up in earth. Her next awakening would be seeing the face of God.

Amy and Amelia ran to the room together.

"It's time to say good-bye and show everyone how to send someone off with love," Amy coached Amelia.

"Ms. Roses Are My Favorite Flowers, I love you. I'm so happy you get to see the face of God today. Give him a kiss from me. I've been blessed for having him put you in my life." Amy surprised herself in being able to give permission without crying. She felt joy for Mrs. Rosenberg's new journey.

She watched Amelia hug her mother and say, "I love you, Mom. Kiss Yeshua's face for me and give Dad a hug from me too."

Amy left before Alec said his good-byes.

Mrs. Rosenberg saw the face of God within the hour.

Three aides had figured the nursing home would be short staffed due to the local schools closing as well. They came in to see if they could pick up a few hours. They were greeted with happiness.

Amy took the rest of the day off. She decided to go home to nap before going to the library.

She grieved over Mrs. Rosenberg. Her tears caused her to stumble on the sidewalk. She'd regained her balance before falling.

Alec needed fresh air. While his family mourned together, he chose to mourn outside. He saw Amy stumble on the sidewalk as she cried. He decided to follow her from a distance to make sure she arrived home safely. Both needed alone time, so he didn't approach her.

When she turned the corner, an angry man grabbed her arm. They walked arm in arm.

Alec continued following her. He felt Amy was in some kind of danger, but since the man on her arm showed no other signs of aggression, he held off calling the police. He didn't want to embarrass Amy if it was a lovers' quarrel she needed to work

The Library Room

out. Nonetheless, he wasn't letting this man get away with manhandling her either. If he saw her trying to pull away, Alec decided it'd be game on.

After a couple blocks, Alec realized the two weren't talking to each other. Then he saw it. There was enough distance between their bodies for him to see a pistol aimed at her side.

Alec called 911. He had to whisper, so the man with Amy wouldn't hear his conversation. Alec didn't know the street names. He gave house numbers. He didn't want to alarm her captor in any way. The dispatcher asked him to describe the subjugator.

"He's over six foot tall, maybe six five, wearing a green denim jacket and dark black jeans. He's holding a gun under his jacket into the side of Amy. He looks like a body builder, stocky and well over two hundred pounds. I'm guessing he's in his late forties."

"We have an unmarked car on Hasbro Street. It's dark green. Do you see it?" the 911 operator asked.

"No. You have the wrong street," Alec barked.

"Okay, they're turning down Mayfield do you see them now?" the operator asked.

"No. I don't. I'm coming upon a corner. I think I see a street sign. Please hurry, they're starting to walk towards a car," Alec huffed in panic. "Water Street!" Alec yelled in a whisper, "Water and Pearl—hurry up!"

A car came from behind him and drove past Amy.

"You just passed them up!" Alec exasperated.

"We have to get back up now. We know the location. Hold on, help's on its way," the voice assured.

Within seconds, four cars surrounded the car Amy was being pushed into.

"Put your hands in the air!" yelled an officer.

The man concluded he was surrounded. He raised his hands, still holding on to the gun.

"Drop your weapon!" An officer ordered, and he did. A second police officer kicked the gun out of his reach. Amy was taken to safety by a third officer. "Get on your knees!" As soon as he knelt, an officer handcuffed him.

Alec rushed toward Amy. Officer Jones stopped him. "Thank you for staying with the girl all the way through."

"Anyone know what that was all about?" Alec asked.

"I think the man planned to use her as bait," Officer Jones theorized.

Alec tried explaining why he was following Amy. "I'm a friend of Amy's. I was following her home to make sure she didn't fall while crying. My mother just died. She was special to her."

"Alec!" Amy ran to him. "How'd you know and how did you get here so fast?"

"He called for help," Officer Jones told Amy.

"You followed me after I left the nursing home?" Amy looked at Alec.

"You almost took a nose dive. I didn't want any inheritance money being spent fixing an already perfect nose," Alec joked.

"I should've known." Amy half-smiled.

Collin and Sarah found Amida putting books away.

"Amida." Collin startled her. "We're not supposed to leave the room, but we're in need of a few books. Can you help us find them so we can return?"

"Certainly, I'll bring them to you," Amida offered. She took the list from Collin and signaled them to return to the room.

They didn't see Giles behind the bookshelf until it was too late. "You're going to help me get into that room to talk to Loren." He pulled out a small pistol. "Give me your phones."

They handed him their phones. Collin spotted the camera on the ceiling. He stepped into view and put his hands to the top of his head hoping the person monitoring the cameras would send help.

The Library Room

"Put your hands down! I didn't tell you to put your hands up!" Giles demanded and then noticed the security camera bubble on the ceiling. "Let's go now!"

"We can't," Collin said. "We forgot our keys. Amida's coming back to let us inside with the books she's picking."

"You're a liar," Giles accused. "Clear your pockets."

Collin slowly pulled items out of his pockets while smiling.

When Giles looked to Sarah for a key, she smiled, saying, "I thought he brought his. I came along because I have to go the bathroom."

Giles said, "We'll wait for Amida or for one of your friends to come out to save you."

"Why do you need to see Loren? You'll lose your bail. Why aren't you running away to Minnesota to your dad?" Sarah tried distracting him. She saw movement a shelf away.

"I just wanted to say good-bye and apologize for the mess I've caused. I don't want to hurt her," Giles said.

"Like Mellissa?" Sarah snapped at Giles.

"I didn't hurt Mellissa!" Giles snapped. "There's more to what's going on than any of you know. Look, I owe people money…I'm in trouble. I just wanted to say good-bye before leaving town. I love her. I need to know she understands. I need to know someone believes me."

"Then put the gun down," Collin instructed. "No one's going to believe you when you're flashing the gun that shot Mellissa."

"I didn't hurt—Mellissa's been shot?" Giles's breathing stopped. "They shot Mellissa? How do you know?"

"They found her body in the fire." Sarah faked a gun to her head. "With a bullet in her temple."

"I didn't know. I didn't do it. They're looking for me. They want their money. Loren will give me money to pay them off." Giles shook his head in disbelief. "Loren loves me. I know she does."

"Giles, ask your dad for the money! You've wiped Loren clean." Collin was stalling. He too saw rescuers sneaking into place.

"I can't," Giles sneered. "The old man hates me over the death of my mother. It's my fault. I'd developed scarlet fever from strep throat. They couldn't afford a doctor, but my mother took me anyways. She didn't tell the doctor she was sick too. I got treatment, and she didn't. Her strep turned into spinal meningitis. If there's a God, he would've healed her. She'd prayed for God to heal me. He couldn't because he doesn't exist. So she snuck me to a doctor. Dad told me if there was a God, he'd have healed us *without* the expensive costs of a doctor."

"Giles, I'm sorry about your mother," Sarah offered, "and your cruel father. However, he's wrong. There is a God. God grants us wisdom to know when to take your child to a doctor. God gives doctors wisdom to know what medications to give patients to fight off diseases."

"Listen, put the gun away," Collin said. "We understand where you're coming from. We'll take you to see Loren as soon as Sarah goes to the bathroom." Collin felt the need to get her out of the way. Her words stirred up feelings of contempt with Giles.

"No, we wait until I'm through that door, and then she can go," Giles insisted. "And *no* more God talk." He pointed the gun at Sarah.

"Giles, you're surrounded. Put the gun on the floor and kick it away," Officer Jones demanded.

The officers revealed their positions through the bookshelves. Giles tossed his gun aside.

Collin and Sarah were pulled behind shelves in case Giles had a hidden weapon.

Giles fell to his knees, anticipating their next moves. "Tell Loren I love her and always will."

Collin and Sarah were glad she didn't see the pathetic act.

"Why do you think he owes people so much money that they'd kill to get it back? And how much do you think he owes?" Sarah asked Collin.

"I don't know. Nevertheless, he's made some bad choices," Collin said. "I fear they'll come after Loren knowing they'll never get it from Giles. We need to tell Scott."

"Let everyone know they're free to leave if they want," Scott assured. "I'll be by later to check in on and update Loren."

"Okay, she'll be pleased to know," Collin said with a smile and a wink.

"What was that all about?" Sarah asked.

"Officer Scott Jones has a crush on Loren and wants to ensure she recuperates from her ordeal," Collin explained.

"Typical," Sarah said in disgust, "Men all think we need saving. Does it ever occur to a man a woman may need time to heal after going through something like that?"

"No," Collin said.

They entered the room and Drew questioned, "Didn't you go after books?"

"Yes, Amida's bringing them," Collin answered.

Sarah explained what had happened and that "Scott would be back later.

After a long discussion about Giles, they felt blessed being brought up with their families.

"It's interesting to know God uses the unfortunate to show us how blessed we are in life." Rachel expounded on the topic of gratitude.

"But why *does* God let it happen?" Jessica asked.

"I'm not God," Drew speculated, "but I see pride being a culprit. Pride causes you to turn against God. God will allow things to happen to you as a result of pride. We read earlier God abhors pride. If you're humble, you'll trust God, and he'll give you good things. Pride prevents us from asking God for help. Pride kept his father from trusting God to provide healthcare costs. Later, his pride corrupted him from admitting he was wrong."

A knock on the door caused everyone to freeze.

"That must be Amida with our books." Collin went to answer the door. It was Amida, but she wasn't alone.

"There's someone here. She says she's Sarah's mother and needs to see her daughter," Amida announced.

"Mom!" Sarah ran to the arms of a woman with chestnut shoulder length hair and puffy brown eyes.

"Honey, I had to come. I heard you this morning. It scared me. Are you okay?" Judy didn't stop hugging after Sarah's stopped. Her high cheekbones feigned a smile as her forehead showed wrinkles of concern.

"She's had a rough morning," Jessica said.

"It was horrible." Sarah's eyes watered. "My mind said to pray. So I prayed. Then, I saw the news and understood why I needed to pray. Do you think it was God or my guardian angel?"

"At this point, does it matter?" Judy questioned. "Even if it were your guardian angel, who do you think told your guardian angel?"

"Right." Sarah calmed down. "You always make me realize what's real."

Another knock on the door startled everyone. "We need a peephole in this door," Rachel suggested.

Cautiously, Collin opened the door. Loren's parents rushed in and hugged her before she could stand up. Amida stood in the doorway ensuring they were who they'd said they were before leaving.

"Mom, I didn't know you were coming," Loren said.

"Sweetie, I didn't know either. I told your dad what was going on. He had the car packed before I could change outfits," Diane said, blaming her husband, Mitch. "There was no stopping your father."

"It's all true," Mitch admitted while hugging Loren.

The noise level elevated as the room's details were shown.

"So how's the research going?" Judy asked.

"We're at the Spirit of God in the Tanakh and the Holy Spirit of the New Testament." Collin displayed the work on the SMARTboard.

Twenty Two

Loren's Notes Part VI—The Holy Spirit

Tanakh, Nevi'im, Jeremiah 31:31–35 NIV: "The time is coming," declares the Lord, "when I make a new covenant with the house of Israel and with the house of Judah. It won't be like the covenant I made with their forefathers when I took them by the hand to lead them out of Egypt, because they broke my covenant, though I was a husband to them," declares the Lord. "This is the covenant I'll make with the house of Israel after that time," declares the Lord. "I'll put my law in their minds and write it on their hearts. I'll be their God, and they'll be my people. No longer will a man teach his neighbor, or a man his brother saying, 'Know the Lord,' because they'll all know me, from the least of them to the greatest," declares the Lord. "For I'll forgive their wickedness and will remember their sins no more."

The Old Covenant given to the Hebrews at Mount Sinai had been broken not by God but by the people. God doesn't go back on his word. It was an *if* promise, meaning *if* you do this, then I'll do that. Tanakh, Torah, Yitro, Exodus 19:3–5 NIV: "Then Moses went up to God, and the Lord called to him from the mountain and said, 'This is what you're to say to the house of Jacob and what you're to tell the people of Israel: "You yourselves have seen what I did to Egypt, and how I carried you on eagles' wings and brought you to Myself. Now *if you obey Me and keep My covenant*, then out of all nations you'll be My treasured possession. Although the whole earth's mine, you'll be for Me a kingdom of priests and a Holy nation." These are the words you're to speak to the Israelites.

"If you obey Me and keep My covenant." God's heart was broken. He offered to make them great, the nation of all nations, *if* they obeyed The Ten Commandments—the primary commandments used to make other laws throughout the Torah.

Diane described how God tells us 'I'll put the law into their minds and hearts' as a way of giving them an excuse. God didn't excuse their behavior. However, God being the God of creation understood why it was impossible for mankind to keep the laws. It wasn't in their minds or hearts.

Judy explained that throughout the pre-Yeshua times, God used His Spirit on certain people such as Moses, Jeremiah, David, and a few others. His Spirit was gifted to those whom he needed to teach, prophesy, or get a certain job done. Most of the time, The Spirit of God didn't reside in the person for their entire life. David, of course, was an exception.

God used several prophets to announce the coming of The Holy Spirit. Tanakh, Nevi'im, Isaiah 44:3 NIV: "For I'll pour water on the thirsty land, and streams on the dry ground; I'll pour My Sprit on your offspring, and My blessing on your descendants."

Tanakh, Nevi'im, Ezekiel 39:29 NIV: "I'll no longer hide My face from them, for I'll pour out My Spirit on the house of Israel,' declares the Sovereign Lord."

Tanakh, Nevi'im, Joel 2:28–29 NIV: "And afterward, I'll pour out my Spirit on all people. Your sons and daughters will prophesy, your old men will dream dreams, your young men will see visions. Even on my servants, men and women, I'll pour out My Spirit in those days."

Mitch clarified that The Holy Spirit wasn't indwelling in everyone. Today, we've a hard time relating since the Holy Spirit dwells within us and encourages us to please God. Imagine having a goal so unobtainable you gave up trying? Most turned to instant gratification, working to obey the laws wasn't their desire.

In order to grasp how The Spirit of God changed in world presence we need to take a look at when and how The Spirit of God was used in the Tanakh.

In Part III, of my notes, we learned about Balaam, the sorcerer, called upon by Balak to curse the tribes of Jacob. Balaam tried, but God told him, "Nope, not going to happen. Go against your boss and bless them instead." As hard as he tried to curse the tents of Jacob he could only utter blessings.

The Holy Spirit changed his words *and* his thinking. He knew he was incapable of going against God. He tried explaining this to Balak who'd felt betrayed. Tanakh, Torah, Numbers 24

Judy explicated how God appointed judges in Israel to help get them back on track. The Israelites would go through phases of worshipping idols. God would send a judge when they'd cry out for help after being captured by an enemy. Then, they'd obey God for a while but eventually would fall back into worshipping idols again and need rescued again.

Rachel agreed and brought up Othniel. He was known as Caleb's little brother. She summarized Tanakh, Nevi'im, Judges 3:7–11 NIV. The Israelites stopped worshipping God and served the Baals and the Asherahs. The Lord turned against Israel and He sold them into the hands of Cushan-Rishathaim, king of Aram Naharaim. The Israelites were slaves for eight years. When they cried out to the Lord, he sent a deliverer, Othniel. The Spirit of the Lord came upon him, so that he became Israel's judge and went to war. The Lord gave the king of Aram into the hands of Othniel. So the land had peace for forty years, until Othniel died.

Drew gave us another example: Jephthah the son of a prostitute. He summarized Tanakh, Nevi'im, Judges 11:27–32 JPS: The king of Ammon, ignored the message Jephthah sent him. Then the Spirit of the Lord came upon Jephtah. Then Jephthah went over to fight the Ammonites, and the Lord gave them into his hands.

Judy told us the story about Gideon the farmer and the least amongst his family. She summarized Tanakh, Nevi'im, Judges 6:12-34 NIV. Then the Spirit of the Lord came upon Gideon, and he blew a trumpet, summoning the Abiezrites to follow him.

Samson violated his vow and God's laws several times. And yet, The Spirit of the Lord came upon him with power three different times Tanakh, Nevi'im, Judges 14:6 Samson was filled with the Holy Spirit and was filled with superhuman strength. He tore a lion apart with his bare hands. Tanakh, Nevi'im, Judges 14:19 He struck down thirty men in Ashkelon, and in Tanakh, Nevi'im, Judges 15:14 he ripped new ropes off of his bound hands and still had the strength and endurance to fight and kill a thousand men with a donkey jawbone.

The Holy Spirit would indwell and then leave when God was done using that person for a mission.

Diane gave us another example; Saul after Samuel poured oil on his head and prophesied. Tanakh, Nevi'im, 1 Samuel 10:1-10 NIV: The Spirit of the Lord will come upon you in power, and you'll prophesy with them; and you'll be changed into a different person. Once these signs are fulfilled, do whatever your hand finds to do, for God's with you." As Saul turned to leave Samuel, God changed Saul's heart and all these signs were fulfilled that day. When they arrived at Gibeah, a procession of prophets met him, the Spirit of God came upon him in power, and he joined in the prophesying.

God changed Saul's heart to the point of being able to prophesy; he'd never been a prophet before. If you continue reading the story you'll read Saul later committed evil acts and even committed suicide. How could he after being filled with the Holy Spirit and God changing his heart? Throughout the Tanakh you'll read how the Spirit "came upon" a person temporarily.

But the Holy Spirit never left David. Tanakh, Nevi'im, 1Samuel 16:12–13 NIV: So Samuel anointed him and from that day on the Spirit of the Lord came upon David in power.

David was a shepherd. He liked to write poetry and write music on his harp. He had a heart for God and God had a heart for David too. David wasn't perfect. However, when David sinned, he'd ask and trust God to forgive him of the sins knowing there'd be consequences. God would forgive him and let David suffer the consequences.

Diane showed us the different effects to be experienced through His Spirit. Tanakh, Nevi'im, Isaiah 11:2 KJV: The Spirit of the Lord shall rest upon him, the spirit of wisdom and understanding, the spirit of counsel and of power, the spirit of knowledge and of the fear of the Lord.

Tanakh, Nevi'im, Isaiah 44: 3–5 ESV: I'll pour water on the thirsty land, and streams on the dry ground; I'll pour out My Spirit on your offspring, and My blessing on your descendants. They'll spring up like grass in a meadow, like poplar trees by flowing streams. One will say, "I belong to the Lord." Another will call himself Jacob; still another will write on his hand, "The Lord's," and will take the name Israel.

The Spirit of the Lord will pour out over generations and they'll *want* to be known as the Lord's. The Spirit of the Lord will be in their hearts and minds.

Tanakh, Nevi'im, Isaiah 61:1–3 NIV: The Spirit of the Sovereign Lord's on me, because the Lord's anointed me to preach good news to the poor. He's sent me to bind up the brokenhearted, to proclaim freedom for the captives and release from darkness for the prisoners, to proclaim the year of the Lord's favor and the day of vengeance of our God, to comfort all who mourn, and provide for those who grieve—to bestow on them a crown of beauty instead of ashes, the oil of gladness instead of mourning, and a garment of praise instead of a spirit of despair.

They'll be called oaks of righteousness, a planting of the Lord for the display of his splendor.

Recapping, the Holy Spirit gives words of encouragement, teaches, heals brokenness, frees captives, releases us from darkness, brings comfort to mourners, replaces ashes for the grieving with a crown of beauty, brings gladness, self-confidence, and righteousness. The Spirit of the Lord also proclaims the good news.

So no one knew or felt any of these spiritual gifts except a few before Jesus? Sad when you think about it. They must have been miserable. No wonder they were all about instant gratification.

The Spirit of the Lord, the Holy Spirit, grieves when we turn away from him. The Spirit of the Lord will also humble you if you do so too. He'll allow you to fall into captivity if you turn your back on The Spirit of the Lord. And yet the Spirit of the Lord gives rest.

All these verses on the Spirit of the Lord show you, God and the Holy Spirit are one in the same.

Collin read Tanakh, Nevi'im, Zechariah 12:10 NIV: "I'll pour out on the house of David and the inhabitants of Jerusalem a Spirit of Grace and supplication. They'll look on Me, the One they've pierced, and they'll mourn for Him as one mourns for an only child, and grieve bitterly for Him as one grieves for a firstborn son."

Amy said she'd read that verse a thousand times over the years. But today she understand it as, "They'll look on Me, God, the one giving the prophecy to Zechariah. The one they've pierced, is God telling us He'll be pierced which is crucified Yeshua, which is God incarnate. And they'll mourn for Him as one mourns for an only child is God's flesh of Himself called the Son of God, Jesus. And grieve bitterly for Him as one grieves for a firstborn son, is Yeshua the son of the Virgin Mary, God's only Son."

As we've noted throughout this report, Yeshua's birth and life were foretold by many different prophets. We also see how

The Library Room

the Holy Spirit has worked and how God used his Spirit to help people accomplish missions by guiding their wisdom and strength. Additionally, we've read prophecy pertaining to the coming Spirit from God which will dwell in the hearts and minds of everyone. The above scripture from Zachariah also tells us when God becomes his *only* son and is pierced we'll have in our hearts and minds a Spirit of grace and supplication.

Jessica looked up grace and supplication. Grace is "a favor undeserved." Grace is given unconditionally, not a reward for hard work or a condition of works. Supplication is seen when one has an attitude to pray humbly requesting something from God in a bowed down position with emphasis more on the attitude than the physical position of prayer.

Mitch put it in laymen's terms. "God will pour out his Holy Spirit offering undeserved forgiveness, undeserved love, undeserved mercy, undeserved favor, and undeserved eternal life to us. And we'll want to be humble and ask God for forgiveness and salvation. Now look what happened as soon as Jesus ascended and how it fulfills an important piece of a new covenant—Pentecost."

Rachel argued Pentecost. We already had it. Pentecost, The Day of the First Fruits, comes fifty days from Passover. Described in Tanakh, Torah, Mishpatim, Exodus 23:16. It's one of the three annual festivals—Feast of Unleavened Bread, Feast of Harvest with the first fruits, and Feast of Ingathering at the end of the year when the crops are gathered.

Mitch explained the day the Holy Spirit came and indwelled in the hearts of believers happened on The Day of First Fruits, thus began the Christian church.

Let's read what *The New Testament* says and promises us about the Holy Spirit.

Luke understood the power of the Holy Spirit better than anyone and wrote about the Spirit of the Lord in the books of Luke, and Acts.

John the Baptizer was indwelled with the Holy Spirit during his entire life, Remember the prophecies concerning John's birth we read earlier? In New Testament, Luke 1:15–17 NIV: "...for he'll be filled with the Holy Spirit even from birth. He'll bring back many people of Israel to the Lord their God. And he'll go on before the Lord, in the spirit and power of Elijah, to turn the hearts of the fathers to their children and the disobedient to the wisdom of the righteous—to make ready a people prepared for the Lord."

John, the disciple, also understood the importance of writing what Jesus promised and prophesied about the Spirit of the Lord. New Testament, John 7:37–39 NIV: "On the last and greatest day of the Feast, Jesus stood and said in a loud voice, 'If anyone's thirsty, let him come to me and drink. Whoever believes in me, as the Scriptures say, streams of living water will flow from within him.' By this He meant the Holy Spirit whom His believers later received. Up to that time the Spirit hadn't been given, since Jesus hadn't yet been glorified."

Jesus was referring to the three following scriptures. Tanakh, Nevi'im, Isaiah 12:3 NIV: With joy you'll draw water from the wells of salvation." And in Tanakh, Nevi'im, Isaiah 44:3 NIV: "For I'll pour water on the thirsty land, and streams on the dry ground; I'll pour out my Spirit on your offspring, and my blessing on your descendants." Lastly, in Tanakh, Nevi'im, Isaiah 58:11 NIV: "The Lord will guide you always; He'll satisfy your needs in a sun-scorched land and will strengthen your frame. You'll be like a well-watered garden, like a spring whose waters never fail."

Diane feels by referring to these scriptures Yeshua was announcing himself as the Mashiach since the Messiah would be the only one who could promise to fulfill such prophecies.

In New Testament, John 14:1–30 NIV: "In my Father's house are many rooms; if it weren't so, I'd have told you. I'm going there to prepare a place for you...I'll come back and take you to be with me that you also may be with me. You know the way to the place

I'm going...I am the way, the truth, and the life. No one comes to the Father except through Me. If you know Me, you know My Father. From now on, you know Him and have seen Him."

Philip said, "Lord, show us the Father and that'll be enough."

Jesus answered, "Don't you know Me, Philip? Even after I've been among you such a long time? Anyone who's seen Me has seen the Father...The words I say to you aren't just my own. Rather, it's the Father, living in Me who's doing His work. Believe Me when I say I'm in the Father and the Father's in Me; or at least believe on the evidence of the miracles themselves. I tell you the truth, anyone who has faith in Me will do what I've been doing. He'll do even greater things than these, because I'm going to the Father. And I'll do whatever you ask in My name, so the Son may bring glory to the Father. You may ask Me for anything in My name, and I'll do it."

"He'll give you another Counselor to be with you forever—the Spirit of truth. I'll not leave you as orphans; I'll come to you. Before long, the world won't see Me anymore, but you'll see Me. Because I live, you'll also live. On that day you'll realize that I'm in my Father, and you're in Me, and I'm in you. Whoever has My commands and obeys them, he's the one who loves Me. He who loves Me will be loved by My Father, and I'll love him too and show Myself to him."

"All this I've spoken while still with you. But the Counselor, the Holy Spirit, whom the Father will send in My name will teach you all things and will remind you of everything I've said to you...You heard Me say, 'I'm going away and I'm coming back to you.' If you loved Me, you'd be glad I'm going to the Father, for the Father's greater than I. I've told you now, before it happens, so when it does happen you'll believe."

Yeshua's stating he's leaving his disciples and yet he'll remain with them. The only way for it to be possible is by indwelling them with the Holy Spirit which is promised by Yeshua.

Additionally, Yeshua makes it clear the *only* way to live in heaven with the Father is by believing and loving Yeshua who's the way, the truth, and the life.

Earlier in New Testament, John Chapter 12:27–33 KJV: Yeshua tells us why he has to die for us and that his human flesh dreaded it. He knew he'd be taking on the sins of the world, present and future, and this would separate him from the Father just like we are before asking for forgiveness in Yeshua's name. Yeshua being the Son of God, the Father, didn't want to be separated; but, knew it'd be necessary in order to be glorified. Yeshua said no to his earthly desires and obeyed the Father, God.

Those same verses say Jesus says we'll be drawn to him, to want to know him more, this is what happened when he was lifted up and ascended into heaven.

The Holy Spirit was present while Jesus was being put to death on the cross. Evidence was seen as he took his last breath after he cried out. New Testament, Matthew 27:50–54 NIV: And when Jesus had cried out again in a loud voice, he gave up his Spirit. At that moment the curtain of the temple was torn in two from top to bottom. The earth shook and the rocks split. The tombs broke open and the bodies of many Holy people who'd died were raised to life. They came out of the tombs, and after Jesus' resurrection they went into the Holy City and appeared to many people. When the centurion and those guarding Jesus saw the earthquake and all that had happened, they were terrified, and exclaimed, "Surely He was the Son of God!"

Mitch made clear the importance of how the curtain of the temple was torn in two from top to bottom! There were three different sections of the temple: the courts were for anyone, the Holy Place was for priests only, and the Most Holy Place could only be entered once a year by the High Priests for atonement of sins for the nation. The curtain divided the Holy Place from the Most Holy Place. It was a heavy duty structure of thick material;

a hands breadth thickness [about four inches]. The size was forty cubits long [sixty feet] and twenty cubits wide [thirty feet].

Drew agrees that the strength of the Holy Spirit tearing it from top to bottom would have been incredible! It'd be impossible for a super human to tear it into two going from the bottom to the top; let alone, from top to bottom. Only the Holy Spirit could've had the strength to tear it in half like that!

Judy further explained the significance of the Temple Veil being torn was God letting us know Yeshua's sacrifice for our sins so *all* people could have access to God.

As prophesied, Yeshua was crucified, put into the tomb of a rich man, conquered death, resurrected Himself, and then walked the earth before ascending to heaven. Jessica summarized New Testament, Luke 24:13–49 NIV: "Two men were walking and talking with each other about everything that had happened. Jesus came up and walked along with them; but, they were kept from recognizing Him. He asked them, 'What're you talking about?' They stood still, their faces downcast. Cleopas asked Him, 'Are you a visitor to Jerusalem and don't know what's happened?'

"'What happened?' Jesus asked.

"'Jesus of Nazareth,' they replied, 'was a prophet, powerful in word and deed. The chief priests and our ruler handed him over to be sentenced to death, and they crucified Him; but, we'd hoped He was the redeemer of Israel. And now, it's the third day since all this took place and some of our women went to the tomb early this morning but didn't find His body. They came and told us they'd seen a vision of angels, who said He was alive. Then some of our companions went to the tomb and found it just as the women had said, but Him they didn't see.'

"Jesus said, 'How foolish you are, and how slow of heart to believe all the prophets have spoken! Didn't the Christ have to suffer these things and then enter His glory?' And beginning with Moses and all the Prophets, He explained what was said in all the Scriptures concerning Himself.

"As they approached the village, Jesus acted as if He were going farther. They urged Him strongly, "Stay with us, for it's nearly evening; the day's almost over." So He went in to stay with them.

"When He was at the table with them, He took bread, gave thanks, broke it and gave it to them. Then their eyes were opened and they recognized Him, and He disappeared from their sight. They asked each other, 'Weren't our hearts burning within us while He talked with us on the road and opened the Scripture to us?'

"They got up and returned to Jerusalem. There they found the Eleven and those with them, assembled together saying, 'It's true! The Lord's risen and appeared to Simon.' Then the two told what had happened, and how they recognized Jesus when He broke the bread.

"While they spoke, Jesus stood and said, 'Peace be with you.'

"They were startled and frightened, thinking they saw a ghost. He asked, 'Why are you troubled, and why do doubts rise in your minds? Look at my hands and my feet. It is I, Myself! Touch me and see; a ghost doesn't have flesh and bones, as you see I have.'

"When He'd said this, He showed them His hands and feet. And while they still didn't believe it because of joy and amazement, He asked, 'Do you have anything to eat? They gave him a piece of broiled fish, and He ate it in their presence. He said, 'This is what I'd told you before: Everything must be fulfilled that's written about Me in the Law of Moses, the Prophets, and the Psalms.'

"Then He opened their minds so they understood the Scriptures. He told them, 'This is what's written: The Christ will suffer and rise from the dead on the third day, and repentance and forgiveness of sins will be preached in His name to all nations, beginning at Jerusalem. You're witnesses of these things. I'm sending you what My Father promised; but stay in the city until you've been clothed with power from on High.'"

The Library Room

Amy points out He proved he'd physically resurrected not just his spirit, but his flesh and bones as prophesied. Eating with them also showed his human flesh still craved food, a spirit no longer needs food.

Yeshua spent forty days instructing and teaching. It wasn't an evening as some assume when reading this passage. It's better defined in New Testament, Acts 1:3–5 NIV: "After His suffering, He showed Himself to these men and gave many convincing proofs that He was alive. He appeared over a period of forty days and spoke about the kingdom of God. On one occasion, while He was eating with them, He commanded: 'Don't leave Jerusalem, but wait for the gift my Father promised, which you've heard Me speak about. For John baptized with water, but in a few days you'll be baptized with the Holy Spirit.'"

Collin summarized New Testament, Luke 24:50–53 NIV: "When He'd led them to Bethany, He lifted His hands and blessed them. While He was blessing them, He left them and was taken up into heaven. Then they worshiped Him and returned to Jerusalem with great joy. And they stayed continually at the temple praising God."

New Testament, Acts 2:1–4 NIV: "When the day of Pentecost came, they were all together. Suddenly a sound like the blowing of a violent wind came from heaven and filled the whole house. They saw tongues of fire that separated and came to rest on each of them. All of them were filled with the Holy Spirit and spoke in other languages as the Spirit enabled them."

Imagine being able to speak a language without tedious hours of classroom lessons. In the next few verses of Acts, it says there were God-fearing Jews from every nation and pagans in the area speaking different languages. It even lists the different languages: Galileans, Parthians, Medes, Elamites, Mesopotamians, Judeans, Cappadocians, Pontusians, Asians, Phrygians, Pamphylians, Egyptians, Libyans, Romans, Cretans, and Arabians."

Mitch summarized New Testament, Acts 2:6–12 NIV: "When they heard this sound, a crowd gathered in bewilderment, because each one heard them speaking in his own language. Utterly amazed, they asked, 'Aren't all these speakers Galileans? How're we hearing them in our native language?' 'We hear them declaring the wonders of God in our own tongues!' Amazed and perplexed, they asked one another, 'What does this mean?' There were some in the audience making fun of those speaking in different languages as they didn't know that language but knew the men knew how to speak their own language. They accused them of being drunk. Peter with the help of the Holy Spirit put an end to the rumor and misunderstanding. He then delivered the first sermon concerning the risen Lord Jesus the Christ."

Peter quoted Scriptures found in Tanakh, Nevi'im, Joel 2:28–29, which we've read above prophesying about God pouring out his Spirit on all people. Then Peter told the people about Christ being put to death on the cross and how God raised him and freed him from the agony of death "because it was impossible for death to keep its hold on Him" just as David prophesied in Psalms.

Tanakh, Ketuvim, Book I, Miktam of David, Psalms 16:8–11 ESV: "I've set the Lord always before me. Because He's at my right hand, I'll not be shaken. Therefore my heart's glad and my tongue rejoices; my flesh also dwells secure, because You won't abandon me to the grave, nor will You let Your Only One see decay. You've made known to me the path of life. You'll fill me with joy in Your presence, with eternal pleasure at Your right hand."

With the Holy Spirit upon them, the people of all languages understood Peter wasn't speaking of David who was in a ground grave but of David prophesying about Yeshua who didn't decay in the grave. Many people that were there that day were also present the day Yeshua was crucified, buried, and arose from the tomb.

New Testament, Acts 2:32–41 NIV: "God raised Jesus to life, and we're all witnesses. Exalted to the right hand of God, He's received from the Father the promised Holy Spirit and has poured out what you now see and hear. For David didn't ascend to heaven, and yet he said, 'The Lord said to my Lord: "Sit at my right hand until I make Your enemies a footstool for Your feet."' Therefore let all Israel be assured of this: God has made Jesus, whom you crucified, both Lord and Christ.' When the people heard this, they were cut to the heart and asked, 'What shall we do?' Peter replied, 'Repent and be baptized, every one of you, in the name of Jesus Christ for the forgiveness of your sins. And you'll receive the gift of the Holy Spirit. The promise is for you and your children and for all who are far off—for all whom the Lord our God will call.' With many other words he warned them; and he pleaded with them, 'Save yourselves from this corrupt generation.' Those who accepted his message were baptized, and about three thousand were added to their number."

Three thousand were converted the first day of Pentecost! The Holy Spirit blessed the apostles with the gift of different languages, so all nationalities present had converts and felt the Holy Spirit. This was how the good news grew in all nations. It's since grown to what it is today. In later verses, in Acts, you'll read, "The Lord added to their number daily those who converted."

The Holy Spirit indwelled all mankind. This was a new sensation for everyone. Many discredited it and taught against it. They feared the change. Elders conspired to stop the apostles but failed since they were no match against the Holy Spirit. When asked to stop preaching about Jesus, the apostles would say, "How can you stop God from speaking? You can't and it won't happen."

Over the years, many Christians have been persecuted and even put to death clinging to the Holy Spirit and the promises.

Mitch testifies that the benefits are life-changing. He summarized New Testament, Acts 16:7–9 KJV: "The Holy Spirit prevents us from going to wrong places He doesn't want us to go to at certain times. Have you ever missed an accident by seconds because you stopped to do something? Have you ever been invited somewhere, couldn't find a way there, and later learned it turned out to be a bad event?"

After Collin read New Testament, Acts 22:30, kjv, he concluded, "He makes witnessing easier and increases the opportunities to do so.

Sarah read New Testament, Romans 8:26–27, kjv. She surmises the Holy Spirit helps us in our weakness. He helps us to pray when we don't know what to pray. He intercedes for us in accordance of God's will.

After Amy read New Testament, Romans 8:2–8, kjv she concluded, "He gives us the power to be Christians. Remember before the Holy Spirit there wasn't a 'want' in the hearts of mankind. Mankind followed his fleshly nature. Now, with the Holy Spirit all over the earth there's a strong calling to be close to God and to know God. If you live in the Spirit you'll desire the things the Spirit desires."

Jessica found and read New Testament, 1 Corinthians 2:6–16 kjv. She believes, "He gives us wisdom; His own thoughts can be heard in our hearts or minds."

New Testament, Galatians 5:22–23, kjv: "But the Fruit of the Spirit is love, joy, peace, longsuffering [patience,] kindness, goodness, faithfulness, gentleness and self-control…"

Judy added, "That in New Testament, Ephesians 4 you'll read the Holy Spirit brings a unity in the body of Christ."

Twenty Three

The stars glistened above the glass sky dome as Collin turned off the lights for the parents' experience. A shooting star blazed across the sky, and everyone exclaimed in delight at seeing it together.

It was late in the evening by the time they'd finished researching the Holy Spirit. They felt satisfied with the notes they'd added.

Loren's parents invited everyone to dinner for helping Loren.

Loren left a note for Officer Jones at the front desk, saying they'd gone to dinner at Jacque's Fruits de Mer and then called Amy.

Amy answered, "Hey, is everyone still at the room? I had to come home and nap after Mrs. Rosenberg passed and I was kidnapped."

"Wait! What?" Loren asked in confusion. "Kidnapped?"

Amy calmed her down. "I'll explain when I see you. I'm okay thanks to Alec, Mrs. Rosenberg's son. They caught the guy."

"We're going to Jacque's for dinner. My parents are in town and treating. Want to come along?" Loren begged. "We'll swing by and pick you up in about ten minutes."

"Wow! Ten minutes! I fell asleep in my scrubs, so I need to change my clothes."

"We have a lot to catch you up on too! Including Giles and our latest research information," Loren told her. "We'll see you in a few."

Amy ran to the bedroom closet and picked out three different outfits as soon as she heard "ten minutes." They were thrown across the bed before they hung up from each other. She found the last pair of clean knee highs and slid her feet into an uncomfortable pair of red stilettos and rummaged through her jewelry box for the right earrings and necklace.

She still felt chilled every time she thought about being forced into a car by a stranger at gunpoint.

While applying her makeup, she thought, *Ms. Roses Are My Favorite Flowers is now resting.* Her eyes turned red.

A horn tooted outside and then, there was a knock at the door.

She was happy to see Collin standing at her door ready to escort her to the vehicle with Loren and her parents. A second car pulled up behind theirs. She saw Drew, Rachel, Sarah, Jessica, and some other lady driving.

"Who's the lady driving the other car?" Amy climbed into the back seat with Loren and Collin.

Collin answered, "Sarah's mom, Judy. She came after hearing Sarah freaking out this morning."

"Sarah freaked out?" Amy questioned. "What do you mean?"

"Well," Collin explained, "sort of, yes. It started with the Holy Spirit waking her up a few times prompting her to pray. Then she learned about Mellissa. It threw her a bit. She went into shock. I gave her my shirt. I was more afraid for her being in shock than dealing with Giles."

Loren's mother asked, "She was shaken up that bad?"

"She kept telling us to pray, Mom," Loren added. "She said the same prayer over and over."

"Pleading Jesus's blood over us," Collin clarified, "over and over while rocking, and then, she started shaking."

"That's when Judy called. She knew something was wrong," Loren said. "It's why she's here."

"That poor kid," Mitch said to Diane. "To have a premonition from the Holy Spirit wake you up to pray and then discover why."

Amy's voice cracked as she asked, "Do you think she'll freak out again when she hears how her prayers kept me from getting into a car at gunpoint today?"

"You were led at *gunpoint*?" Loren shouted. "Does Scott know? I mean, Officer Jones?"

"Yes, Officers Jones and Gordon showed up when Alec called it in. If Alec hadn't seen me trip while crying, he wouldn't have followed me. And if he hadn't followed me, he wouldn't have seen the man come up to me at gunpoint, which led him to call for help and saved me from being forced into that car." Amy struggled to remain calm.

Mitch watched Amy's face in his rearview mirror. He nearly hit a construction barrel in the road blocking a large dug out square of pavement. He swerved causing the car to hydroplane a few yards. Luckily, there were no cars in the oncoming lane.

"Mitch! You're going to get us killed! Pay attention to what's in front of us!" Diane yelled.

"Sorry, everyone," Mitch apologized. "I was watching Amy instead of the road. Everyone okay?"

Everyone nodded while processing the day's events. It occurred to them Amy's kidnapper may have been Mellissa's killer.

In the other car, Drew and Rachel sat hand-in-hand in the back seat with Jessica while Sarah and Judy chit-chatted about Giles.

"I believe he didn't know about Mellissa," Sarah stated. "He looked remorseful and scared when we told him she'd been shot and burned. I believe him when he says he loves Loren. I'm sure she's the first person he's allowed into his life as someone he could trust enough to love. He's carried a lifetime of displaced guilt."

"Do you believe Giles is a part of God's design, his big plan, or even Giles' evil father?" Drew asked everyone.

Judy answered Drew, "Yes, I do. Everyone's here for a reason. No one's an accident or a mere phenomenon due to Mom and Dad having sex. We're all given opportunities to discover our purposes, to learn what God wants us to do. However, if a person disengages, God will use them to show us how not to behave."

They all held their breath as they watched Mitch's car swerve.

Sarah panicked. "Did you see that?"

"They're okay, Sarah," Judy assured. "It's okay. You know, every day we're in some sort of danger. Sometimes, we recognize it, and other times, it happens without us knowing about it. Sometimes, we're the victim of a ripple, and other times, we send ripples. We're never without danger. Even while you're sleeping, you're in danger of something. Earthquakes or satellites falling from the sky or heart attacks, etc. Sarah, God instructed you to pray for everyone's safety. You obeyed and he's kept us safe. You have to trust God answered that prayer. Give God credit for what he's done and let him work. Your worries expose your lack of faith in his abilities. Your agitations over the events tell God you know what he wants from you, but your fears are outweighing his assurances."

"Mom, I don't know if I was more frightened, knowing God told me to start praying because something bad was happening or knowing I didn't include Giles and Mellissa," Sarah confessed. "I should've included them. It's my fault they weren't protected."

"Honey," Judy said and placed a hand on Sarah's shoulder, "you did what you were told to do, and you did it well. You felt led to pray for family and friends. It's not your fault. The people you were to pray for are still safe. God had different plans for those two."

There was a large-sized crowd for a Tuesday night. People were sitting in benches near the door with coaster pagers in their hands. Rachel walked to the stand and gave her name. She'd called in a reservation.

The Library Room

They were escorted to a private room in the back with a lit fireplace. The room felt eloquent despite the old nicked chairs.

The three men helped the women to their seats. The server handed out menus while informing them of the specials.

Once the orders were placed, Mitch stood to address everyone. "Diane and I thank everyone for joining us tonight. It takes true friends to do the acts you've done over the past week: from helping Loren with a project in the harsh studying conditions of your library room,"—he paused for the laughs—"to notifying the police when you felt something was wrong, to staying by her side today making sure she stayed safe and protected. We thank you for your love and time. We're pleased with the friends Loren chooses to be around. We're proud of Loren. Diane and I consider you family. You're invited to visit us at the farm any time. Cheers!" He lifted his glass of water and took a sip.

Everyone raised their glasses, "Cheers!"

Loren pitched. "I think we should all go to the farm for a long weekend sometime. We have tons of space for everyone: horses, four-wheeling, hiking paths, bonfire for marshmallows…"

Amy raised her hand. "I vote we head to the farm tonight!"

"Unfortunately," Drew spoke up, "some have classes, football practices, or art galleries to work."

Rachel leaned forward and said, "Thank you for the invitation. Our group will have to come out to the farm. It sounds lovely, and I look forward to the bonfire. There's nothing more intimate than a bunch of friends talking around a bonfire."

"Or a restaurant fireplace," Jessica pointed out.

"Yes, a fireplace is good too," Mitch agreed. "Loren, after tonight, your report's pretty much complete, or the research part at least. Right?"

"I'm not sure," Loren said. "I'm waiting for Rachel and Drew's feedback as to whether or not they agree with everything we've researched. I need to know their views of it and how it affects them."

"I think before casting any group votes, Rachel and I need to speak with our rabbis first," Drew explained. "I'm sure they'll have Talmud commentary on a few things. Just using the Tanakh and your Bible alone doesn't incorporate the conversations and conclusions of the sages. In school, we learned the interpretations of what certain things meant by reading what the sages, or Talmud, and Mishnah, have to say. They provide additional insight."

"What do you mean?" Diane asked. "And what are Sages and Talmud? I'm not familiar with Judaism.

"Chazal, it's not the name of a person but of a collective group of opinions of authority. They're like the Supreme Court of Jewish Law. Maybe you've heard the names Baal Shem Tov, Maimonides, and Hillel, extraordinary scholars and teachers ranging from before the Common Era to about four hundred years ago." Drew taught. "So those are sages."

Rachel added, "The Talmud is oral commentary of the Torah. It formed in the days of Moses since someone had to explain what God was saying to the people. The Mishnah was what they called it once they wrote the commentaries. Together, they're called Gemara."

"And then you've Midrashim!" Drew exclaimed. "I like these better than the Talmud and Mishnah. They're easier to grasp since a lot of the other could be a word or two with no other explanation. On the other hand, the Midrashim, I find to be more engaging. It lends insight to the occurrences, consideration of conditions, explanations in Jewish law, moral lessons, etc. It's ingrained in our way of life. I embraced our faith because I love how the laws can be interpreted. I love studying law and hope to practice law. Rabbis are teachers of the law. 'We live by the law. You have to have law or all will go wrong left up to man's free will.' That's what our rabbi cited when we'd question our faith and traditions."

"I find this all fascinating. Thanks for sharing," Mitch said.

Drew shared more, "My favorite Mishnah teaching came to me when I was ten. It was before my Bar Mitzvah, yet I understood it. 'Don't be a servant who does things to gain something from your master; instead, serve without expecting rewards from your master, and let the favor of God be upon you.' This is how Jews feel about our 'purpose' in life. We follow mitzvah not because we want a bigger crown in heaven as I've learned Christians aspire. We do it because it's a privilege, a sense of duty out of love to God regardless of him choosing to supply our needs according to his plans. To have a God, such as he, *is* a privilege since he's much greater than us and yet guides us. It's our duty to please him."

The food arrived and was placed in front of everyone. After everyone was served, Mitch held his hands out to his sides as a sign to join hands in prayer over the meal.

"Drew, would you do us the honor of praying over our meal this evening?" Mitch requested.

"Certainly," Drew obliged. "Blessed are you, HaShem, our God, king of the universe, who brings forth bread from the earth." He picked up a dinner roll, tore a small piece off, and placed it in his mouth to start the dinner feastings.[2] Rachel also picked her dinner roll up and tore a small bite off before putting it in her mouth. Everyone mirrored the act and began eating.

"Rachel," Loren said, "when are your parents returning?"

"They'll be back the last week of October," Rachel answered. "Dad will miss building a Sukkah this year." She laughed with Drew. "He loves the righteous fight with our superintendent over being allowed to construct three walls on our rooftop deck for seven days. He was happier with the last superintendant. He understood our traditions and even helped Dad. Unfortunately, the newest one isn't Hebrew and fights Dad every year."

"What's a Sue-Kah?" Diane asked. "I'm assuming it's for a seven day event?"

Rachel explained, "Yes, the fifth day after Yom Kippur, a very solemn holiday, begins Sukkot, our Season of Rejoicing, or the Festival of Ingathering. During Yom Kippur, we fast. It's a day of atonement, and we think about and repent our sins. We don't allow ourselves any form of pleasure to keep us in a state of humility.

Sukkot celebrates the harvest season by building a small hut like they used while roaming the desert for forty years. We love decorating it like some Christians love decorating a Christmas tree. When I was younger, mother and I made elaborate drawings of events in the Torah using fabric paints on canvas. Now, she uses strings of lights, gourds, and other fall themed ornaments on the walls. You spend as much of your living hours as you can inside the hut during the week. There are holes in the roof so you can see the stars at night. I can't wait until Drew and I have our own place for our yearly Sukkah."

"I think we should build one here on campus in your back yard!" Jessica volunteered. "It sounds like a great traditional celebration! Why don't Christians celebrate that festival anymore? I think we should bring it back!"

"Now hang on there, Jessica! Don't get so excited, and we should watch what we share with you," Drew teased. "My father once told me his firm hires Gentiles because we Jews have so many days a year we're not allowed to work due to holidays and festivals. Someone's got to work and I tend to agree with him." Everyone laughed at his humor.

"Tell us more about your faith," Collin said, maneuvering the conversation back to Drew and Rachel.

"I'm not sure what to say. It's always been. Just as you assume everyone understands the faith you live, we do too," Rachel said. "Our faith is about traditions, rituals, and how you live life."

"Right. We've thirteen principals of faith written by Maimonides."[2] Drew pulled out his phone and looked up information. "Ah, here we go.

The first one is God exists. That's an easy one to accept and understand for most religions.

Two: God is one and unique. This is where you, as Christians, believe in the Holy Trinity. The Holy Spirit and Yeshua being a part of God is foreign to us. It goes against our beliefs. God is God. Yeshua is Yeshua. The Spirit of the Lord is God himself but isn't separate. Prophets are prophets not gods and not Yahweh. Moses wasn't God. You can't have three different things be God in Judaism.

Three: God's incorporeal. He has no body or materialistic form. Therefore, for him to be Yeshua is impossible in our minds. He's a spirit.

Four: God is eternal. That's easy to accept like he exists.

Five: Prayer is directed to God alone and no one else. Why anyone would want to pray to anything or anyone else is beyond me. I don't understand why people pray to saints or Yeshua's mother. It's wrong. You only pray to God!

Six: The words of the prophets are true."

Drew paused and looked at Rachel as if his belief had been pinged and he repeated for her knowing it'd be something they'd discuss further in private. "Six: the words of the prophets are true.

Seven: Moses's prophecies are true, and Moses was the greatest prophet of all prophets. That one's pretty self-explanatory.

Eight: the first five books of the Tanakh, the Torah, were given to Moses. This one's easy to justify too.

Nine: there'll be no other Torah. This one to me just seems like *duh*. I mean, who could create a different beginning or five books?

Ten: God knows the thoughts and deeds of men. Collin you'd be in trouble if it weren't for me keeping you in line."

"Yeah right, Mister. I've got a cramp in my left knee from saving you from the mugging last week," Collin retorted with a half-laugh.

"True." Drew smiled over the heads-up game they'd created.

"Eleven," Drew said, "God rewards the good and punishes the evil. As I mentioned before, God's more concerned about actions than beliefs. It's all about relationships and how we get along in life. Do we get along with God? Do we get along with our family? Do we get along with our fellow Jews? How do we treat our relationship with the land of Israel? This is what it means to be Jewish. Sometimes, it doesn't appear God's punishing evil people. However, we don't know what God's doing to their peace on the inside. Twelve: the Mashiach will come. The thought of Yeshua as being the Mashiach wasn't and still isn't accepted in Judaism. And thirteen, the dead will be resurrected. We believe in the messianic age the good people will be resurrected to Olam Ha-Ba, the World to Come. Bad people won't be resurrected." Drew finished his lecture on the Rambam's Thirteen Principals of Faith.

The server cleared the empty plates and offered coffee. Everyone declined dessert from being too full.

"Well, understanding what you believe," Judy spoke, "I can see where a conflict of accepting the new information you've been studying would be uncomfortable. I do feel, however, our beliefs aren't far off from each other. I hope the talk with your rabbis will be frank. I predict, however, the decision will be what God speaks in your souls. Just keep asking God to reveal the truth. Based upon those principals, the rabbis will justify their beliefs as they've been taught."

"I appreciate all the information. It's believable when matched with the prophecies. It even makes sense to me, a skeptic." Rachel sounded as if she were apologizing. "However, I'm not sure I *want* to give up Judaism. I love our traditions and rituals. It makes me feel like I'm who I'm supposed to be in this world. That's not saying I don't believe Yeshua's the Mashiach now that I've researched the information. I just don't know what to do with the transformation. I mean, accepting Yeshua as the Mashiach, to me, would mean giving up my Jewry to become a Christian. What sect would I want to become or how would I even know

The Library Room

where to begin? I'd miss, to the point of depression, the life God blessed me with today."

Amy spoke up, "God makes it easy. You ask Jesus into your heart, ask him to forgive yours sins with his blood, and ask him to guide you to the right church. There are several Jewish Messianic Synagogues springing up for people in your situation. I'd love to attend one. I've fallen in love with your traditions, and rituals, I've learned about through you. Maybe you should speak to their rabbi?"

"My parents will kill me if I convert!" Rachel declared.

Mitch watched Rachel's face take on different expressions: frightened, bewildered, and overwhelmed. He asked her, "Is that your fear? You're parents disowning you?"

"I fear failing God," Rachel confessed. "If I'm wrong, I'll offend him. I also fear displeasing my parents. Yes, they're a concern."

"Do you feel you're being pressured by any of us here?" Sarah spoke from the hearth. She'd moved to the fireplace after the server had cleared the dishes. "I don't want you to feel like we're pressuring you. This has to be your resolution only, not our mission."

"Thanks, Sarah," Rachel accepted. "I suppose as I look around the room I see by your faces I'm not being pressured by any of you. However, I feel a pressure in here." She thumped her fist to her chest. "Something deep inside. I need time to digest it."

Rachel turned to Drew to bring attention off of her and back onto their faith by reminding him of the after meal prayer. "Drew, would you mind saying the grace after meals prayer for us?"

Drew understood her request. Drew recited the Birkat[3] he'd learned as a kid. "Certainly. Blessed are you, our God, Creator of time and space, who feeds the entire world through your goodness, with kindness and graciousness. You give bread to every creature, for your beneficence is unending. And through your great goodness, never have we been and never shall we be in need of food. Great is the glory of your name. For you, God, feed the world bringing goodness to all preparing food for all your creations. Blessed are you who feeds the world."

Mitch thanked Drew for the prayer and added, "Thanks again everyone for joining Loren, her mother, and I for dinner this evening. I enjoyed the stimulating dinner conversation."

"Thanks for dinner" was said as everyone got up from their seats and shared hugs and handshakes with Mitch and Diane.

It was decided in the parking lot to have Mitch and Diane drive Amy and Rachel home before stopping at Loren's apartment to pack before going to her parents' hotel.

Drew rubbed Rachel's shoulder before taking her hands in his and giving them a squeeze as they said good night.

"They didn't kiss," Sarah whispered to Jessica. "They hugged and didn't kiss. Don't they know they're engaged?"

It didn't go unnoticed by Collin either. "Dude," Collin addressed as they pulled out of the driveway, "you don't have to be shy about kissing Rachel in front of us."

"Have I ever been shy?" Drew smirked. "There's a reason."

"Onions?" Sarah joked.

"No." Drew smiled. "She has cooties. Girls have cooties, Sarah."

"Cooties never stopped you before," Sarah said.

"True," Drew agreed. "But those cooties didn't inspire me."

"So," Collin challenged, "it was okay to dog around before, but you're not kissing Rachel because you're marrying her?"

"My relationship with Rachel's different than past girlfriends," Drew explained. "I've been serious about a few girls I've dated. I wasn't using them for practice as you may be insinuating. Rachel inspires me to be a better man. We aren't kissing until we say our vows."

"Dude," Collin said, "you're a better man than me. I couldn't do it. I mean, when you're alone with her, how do you keep from

The Library Room

kissing when you hug? It's like a natural instinct for me to want to kiss a girl when I'm holding her or kiss her neck when I smell her clean hair."

"Take a cold shower!" Jessica offered, sitting between the two. "Collin, I find what they're doing to be genuine. If they refrain from kissing the entire time they're engaged, it shows they've a commitment to each other. That'd be sacred. I've heard about this before. It's nothing new. It's a good tradition being brought back to life again."

"Crazy," Collin said. "Hey, it's your game. Good luck."

"It's not a game," said Drew. "It's real. Many Judaic people practice it. Some have never kissed before getting married. I've already ruined that with my past. However, with Rachel, we've not kissed yet, and I want to keep something that intimate for our vows."

Judy remained quiet during the conversation. Being a mother, she prayed for God to send someone like Drew to her daughter.

Sarah pointed the way for Judy to Drew and Collin's place.

The other car remained quiet since everyone was full and exhausted. Rachel was dropped off first and then Amy.

Mitch walked inside Loren's house with her as she gathered items to take to the hotel. He was still concerned about her being alone. Without words, she went to the bedroom and filled a backpack with pajamas and clothes. As soon as she'd finished, they left for the hotel.

---

1. beautiful traditional Judaic prayers can be found at: http://www.jewishvirtuallibrary.org/jsource/Judaism/Brachot.html Bard, Mitchell *Brachot (Blessings) Before Eating* Jewish Virtual Library.org, 2013

2. To easily find more information, visit the website, *Judaism 101*, put together by Tracey R. Rich. This site was helpful in citing 13 Principles of Faith on web page http://www.jewfaq.org/beliefs.htm

3. beautiful traditional Judaic prayers can be found at: http://www.jewishvirtuallibrary.org/jsource/Judaism/grace.html Klein, Rabbi Isaac *Grace After Meals* Jewish Virtual Library.org, 2013

Twenty Four

Rachel had just finished her morning prayers when her mother called.

"Good morning, princess," her mother sung.

"Mom! I miss you!" Rachel exuberated at hearing her voice.

"I read the news on my phone about your college. I needed to hear your voice and make sure you were okay," her mother declared.

"I'm okay, Mom," Rachel assured. "There've been intense moments, but it's over now."

"Moments?" her mom questioned. "You were in danger?"

"No, there's a secured room in the library," Rachel explained. "My friends and I were all safe inside that room. What's the news saying? I haven't turned it on yet."

Rachel's mother recited, "Well, the headlines read, MURDER AND FIRE SHAKES SMALL COLLEGE TOWN. Did you know the people involved?"

"I'd met the murdered girl," Rachel admitted. "But I didn't know her well." She tried sounding nonchalant to not worry her mother.

"Did you know the guy who caught the restaurant on fire?" Rachel's mother asked. "They think it was the chef who did it. Isn't that where your friend, Loren's, boyfriend works?"

Rachel knew her mother was hinting around and wouldn't give up until she knew the whole story.

"Yes, Giles worked there. No, he didn't catch the place on fire nor did he shoot the girl found in the fire. He was set up. He owed someone money. He must've owed them a lot of money to kill for it. I think the same person kidnapped Amy at gunpoint. He was caught, so we don't have to worry about him anymore. It's been stressful and weird."

"Is everyone okay? How's Amy?" Rachel's mother did little to hide the fear in her voice. "How are you? Why did Giles owe someone so much money? Loren must be heartbroken!"

Rachel explained the details of the Loren and Giles drama and then Amy's story. "I need a day of staring at paintings to a point of being disassociated. I don't want to think today, but I've a lot to sort out."

"Oh? What kind of sorting out?" her mother asked.

"All kinds of stuff, from God and the research I've helped with, to Drew, to where I want to open an art studio, to just about everything. I feeeeeel overwhelmed."

"What's wrong with Drew?" Her mother picked up on that point. "He likes to argue. It's in his blood, just like his father, that one. Does his mother know he's not well? Tell him to eat chicken noodle soup. He'll feel better by morning. It always helps me, Jewish penicillin."

"No, no, nothing's wrong with Drew." Rachel half laughed at her mother. "He's healthy. We're in love. He's waiting for Dad to come home so he can ask for my hand."

Rachel held the phone away from her ear as her mother screamed with joy. "Drew! I knew it'd be Drew! I told your father years ago I wanted Drew to be my son-in-law. You two will make me beautiful grandchildren. Will you live in New York City? Rachel, I'll call Shelly! She'll be able to schedule you with a bridal dress designer. Oh no! How soon are you getting married? I'll need to reserve a hall. The best rooms have a long waiting list. I'll call Marci to start searching real estate for you too."

The Library Room

"Wait! Slow down, Mom! We haven't picked a date. You can't call anyone, or it'll be posted in the *New York Times* before Drew asks for my hand! It'd be embarrassing for me if one of his aunties called to congratulate him on his engagement! Mom! You must keep this just between us!" Rachel pleaded.

"Oh fine!" her mother conceded. "By the way, the bombings over here are freaking me out. They seem to be coming more often now. I think we're in for a real bad time here in Israel. Keep our promised land in your prayers. We're cancelling the rest of our trip due to the unrest, so we'll be home sooner. Looks like Dad's building a Sukkah."

"They're bombing Israel? I'm not hearing about it in the media. How bad? How often? Are you safe?" Rachel inquired.

"I'd say thirty to fifty bombs a day. It scares me. I hate seeing the smoke clouds after they hit. A nice couple on our trip went home already. We've noticed a few more have cut their trip short. My heart cries for our fellow Hebrews enduring this kind of life."

"Well, hurry home and be safe. Text your updated itinerary, so I'll know how to pray each morning. I love you, mom. When can I expect to hear from you again? I'd love to talk to you about the research we've done. It's quite eye-opening."

"I love you too, princess. I'll text you the updated itinerary as soon as our guide confirms our arrangements. I'm sure your research project is interesting. Just don't believe everything you read or hear."

"Thanks, Mom. I believe this information. It's from God. His words never lie," Rachel defended.

"Okay, I'm proud of you, baby girl. And I'm so happy about your news I'm not allowed to tell anyone about yet. You're killing me though. You're going to be responsible for your mother having a heart attack from trying to keep this one under wraps." Rachel's mom laughed.

Drew and Collin awoke before the sun rose. It was warmer than the previous days as they walked to the gym.

Drew checked his phone again to see if he'd missed a call. After the seventh time, Collin rolled his eyes and asked, "Are you expecting a call from the president?"

"No, I haven't gotten a text back from Rachel and my mom hasn't called back either." Drew informed.

"Rachel's probably busy planning your life now that her ball and chain's attached to your ankle," Collin teased.

"Hardly," Drew commented. "Everyone knows she's planning her art gallery first unless you consider planning babies. *I* plan to have her pop out a few. We'll make fine-looking boys."

Figuring it impossible to ruffle Drew's feathers, Collin matched his seriousness. "Are you ring shopping? Do you have funds set aside?"

"I've an heirloom ring. Well, my mother has it in the home safe. It was my great-grandmother's ring. She was able to sneak it into the states when she and my grandmother, who was just an infant at the time, escaped by foot to a mansion in Siena, near Tuscany. My great-grandfather promised to catch up to them later, but he didn't make it. He died at the hands of Nazis."

"I didn't know your great-grandparents were in Europe at the time of the Holocaust, Drew. You've never mentioned it before to me or any of our friends." Collin kept his pace on the treadmill.

"I'm not one who has to bring it up all the time." Drew's eyebrows burrowed together as he mimicked a relative giving him a lecture. "The ones who survived taught us to be strong, grow with wisdom, expect God to make you prosperous by keeping his mitzvahs and move forward when a life's not fun."

Drew changed the subject. "I couldn't ask my mother yesterday. I'd like her to bring the ring when she comes this weekend. She's going to flip. She loves Rachel. We've known each other for a long time, in case you didn't know. She'd make me play 'let's get married' as little kids. That's what makes it kind of funny. Now, we're playing 'let's get married' for real. Then her dad was transferred to New York City. I've always liked her as a friend. And then—*bam!*—it hit me I'm in love with her. Since when? I don't know. Possibly, since the day we met as kids."

Amy kept her eyes closed as she answered her phone.

"Rise and shine," Amelia's voice chimed on the other end. "We're on our way to pick you up for breakfast. Alec and I don't want to eat alone. We figured you're the helpful type who'd join us if we asked."

"You two are ridiculous." Amy yawned out her answer. "How long do I have? Where's the rest of your family aren't they hungry too?"

"Well, that's the thing about family reunions. They stay up late and then want to sleep until noon," Amelia said. "You have about ten minutes to get dressed or we're coming in to dress your butt for you."

"Your mother always said you were the bossy one of the family despite what everyone says about Alec," Amy teased. "Okay, give me twenty."

"Fifteen, and you're pushing it. I'm hungry and losing weight as we speak. See you in fifteen. Bye." Amelia hung up.

With a few minutes to spare, she opened a devotional her mother had given to her. *Experiencing God Day by Day* by Henry T. Blackaby and Richard Blackaby. She'd read the message of the date when she'd time. Today, it covered spiritual enemies. She barely had time to skim through it but knew it held meaning to her life over the past couple of days. She placed it face down on the end table as a reminder to re-read it when she returned.

The knock on the door startled her. She opened the door ready to greet Amelia or Alec. Instead, she faced Officer Jones.

"Oh, I was expecting Alec. We're going out to breakfast this morning," Amy blurted.

"I'm sorry to bother you, but I have a few questions I need to ask about yesterday's events. There've been a few twists in the case, and I wanted to know if you could help us piece things together." Officer Jones pointed to Officer Gordon talking on the phone.

"Will it take long? Can I stop by the department after breakfast?" Amy asked as Amelia and Alec pulled up.

Alec stepped out of the car and rushed to Amy's side. "Is there something we can help you with, Officer?" Amy felt protected by Alec.

"Actually, I'm glad you're here too since you saw everything from a different angle." Officer Jones addressed Alec. "We've been going over the forensics. There are a few pieces of the puzzle we're trying to put together. We're hoping you or Amy may have heard or seen something. I have a few questions. I promise they won't take long."

"I'm not sure how much I can help, but we can spare a few minutes. Should we go inside? I need to let Amelia know," Alec said.

"Inside would be great. Thanks for cooperating." He nodded.

Alec went to the car for Amelia.

Amy was glad her apartment was tidy for the unannounced company. She waved her arm around for everyone to find a seat.

Once settled, Office Jones requested, "Amy, would you mind walking me through what happened again?"

"Sure," Amy answered. "I'll do my best."

"Did he come up to you and ask questions? Or did he just walk up and tell you what to do?" Officer Jones asked.

"I don't remember," Amy confessed with a look of panic on her face. "I believe he told me to just keep walking and not make a scene. And then, I felt the cold tip of a gun."

"Do you, Mr. Rosenberg, remember any talking between the two of them?" Officer Jones asked.

"I thought there was talking done by the assailant, but I don't remember seeing Amy reply back. That's why I stayed behind. I didn't know if it was a boyfriend or a person intending to hurt her or if it was someone she needed to talk to clear some things up. I had a gut feeling something wasn't right by the way she didn't look at him and kept walking. Then I saw the gun," Alec stated.

Officer Jones wrote their answers and then asked, "Did either of you see anyone else working with him?"

"No," both answered.

Officer Jones continued, "So he didn't talk at all once he told you to keep walking and don't make a scene." Officer Jones stated, "Did he use his phone or did it ring while you were walking?"

"Oh!" His phone vibrated while we were walking because it startled me. He didn't answer it. He kept one hand on my arm and the other on his gun. I remember him hesitating. I sensed he wanted to answer it." Amy sat up straight recalling this piece of information.

"Good girl! Do you remember what he did with the phone when we surrounded him? Do you remember where the phone was placed on his body when it vibrated?" Officer Jones encouraged.

"No," Amy said. "I think it may have been in a shirt or jacket pocket. It felt high and not in his pant pocket."

Officer Jones looked to Alec to see if he remembered seeing the assailant tossing a phone during the arrest.

"I saw him toss the gun, but I don't recall seeing a phone," Alec recalled out loud.

"We feel he wasn't acting alone. The restaurant was burned to send a message to Giles. The guns collected from Giles and the man who'd held you at gunpoint don't match the bullet recovered from the victim, Mellissa," Officer Jones informed. "We've searched the car for another gun or a sign of another person without luck."

"Do you know where Loren stayed last night?" Officer Jones showed concern on his face. "We didn't see her come last night. Her house is under twenty-four-hour surveillance until this case is closed. Surveillance saw her and two other people arrived at her house at 11:36. An older gentleman went into the house with her and then both left her house after nine minutes."

"The other two people are her parents. They arrived yesterday afternoon when they'd heard everything that had happened with Loren and Giles and the restaurant. She stayed at the hotel with them." Amy watched Scott's face relax when she told him the information.

"Thanks. If you remember anything else, call this number right away. You'll be receiving a subpoena for court regarding the kidnapping. You'll need to come in to testify. It won't be until next week." Officer Jones instructed Amy first and then turned to Alec, "You'll be getting one too. If you're no longer in town, we'll need to set up a video session for the hearing. You'll report to your nearest courthouse and be sworn in there to testify via live video. We find that's much more economical than paying for your trip back into town. Thank you both for your time. I'll be in touch, and we'll be searching for the missing cell phone." Officer Jones stood and shook everyone's hands before leaving.

"I'm starving," Amelia declared. "And you two have some explaining to do. Alec, why didn't' you tell me what happened to Amy yesterday? When you came back all shaken up, I thought it was because of Mom. Come on you two, get in the car. Alec, you're driving now."

Sarah, Jessica, and Judy sat in the coffee shop eating pastries and sipping coffees. Sarah and Jessica were ready to head to their classes when a student came in announcing all classes have been cancelled for the day. The emo-looking boy dressed in frumpy black clothing did his best to convince everyone how

The Library Room

disappointed he was to not take a test he'd studied for all night. No one bought it.

Judy let them know she was more than willing to postpone her trip back home since they've the day off.

Word spread fast as incoming texts announced the free day.

"I'm texting everyone to meet at the library, and we'll decide what we want to do," Jessica exclaimed. "I don't care what we do as long as it's fun. I don't want to do research. I don't want to talk about what happened yesterday. I don't want to think about stuff I need to address once I graduate. I just want fun. I need fun."

Judy set her coffee cup down and stared at Jessica who was almost in tears demanding to have fun. She knew the signs of depression. "You're right. We need to have fun today."

Everyone responded back with times ranging from ten minutes to two hours. Since the two-hour window was the farthest out Jessica posted everyone to meet at noon.

"Hey, Mom, how about the three of us go back to my place to bake a batch of cookies? Jessica, are you in?" Sarah stood up and grabbed her purse to make sure the other two knew she was serious.

"Heck yah, I'm in!" Jessica smiled at the thought of chocolate chip cookies and a tall glass of milk.

"Sure, that sounds like a yummy off of my diet plan. Do we need to stop at a grocery store to get ingredients?" Judy inquired.

Sarah smiled. "I'm not sure what we need now that you've mentioned it. Chocolate chips for sure. What else do you put in cookies?"

"Flour, eggs, sugar, brown sugar, vanilla," Judy said.

"Okay, yeah, I have none of those things, so we should stop by the store. Isn't it easier to just buy the already mixed stuff in the refrigerated section?" Sarah asked.

"Yes, but it's more fun by scratch," Jessica asserted.

"But we don't have all day," Judy reminded the girls.

"So we'll buy the cookie dough tube things and make them faster and less cleanup in my kitchen," Sarah decided.

Judy smiled at the plans knowing the "we'll buy" would actually end up being mom will buy.

Loren's parents went to the hotel lobby for breakfast. Loren was still asleep, and they wanted her to rest. They had no intentions of letting her participate in classes today. They also discussed taking her home for a few days. They'd go to the dean's office to explore their options.

Loren was first awakened by a text from Amy letting her know Scott stopped by and was concerned over her whereabouts. Loren texted her back with one eye open, "OK." The second text came from Rachel letting everyone know all classes were cancelled. The third text was from Jessica about meeting at the library to decide what fun activity they could do together. With irritation, she replied, "Okay, in couple hours, trying to sleep!" The last text was Jessica telling everyone to be there around noon. She did her best to doze off again, but the tranquility was lost, and she was hungry.

She showered, got dressed, and then headed out to find her parents at the breakfast buffet.

"There she is!" Diane smiled.

"Good morning, Best Parents in the World," Loren said, kissing her parent's cheeks before walking to the buffet.

Loren returned with a waffle, scrambled eggs, sausage links, and orange juice; she loved when her parents came to visit her.

"I received a text saying 'no classes again' today," Loren informed her parents. "I need to see if I'm to work this afternoon. I doubt it. It seems any excuse to close up shop they'll use."

Loren's parents were relieved. A battle they'd been dreading had been avoided.

"Everyone's meeting at noon for something fun," Loren said.

The Library Room

"Sounds great!" Mitch accepted. "What's fun?"

"I have no idea. However, knowing Rachel, I'm sure she's a list of things. *And* knowing Rachel, she'll figure the parents into the mix so we can have two cars for hauling us there." Loren laughed.

"Count us in, kiddo." Mitch said. "I'll drive if Judy can drive too. Just tell us where."

Noon arrived with cookies! Once they saw how many different kinds were available, they decided to try them all: sugar cookies, double chocolate chunks, chocolate chip, and marshmallow.

As predicted, Rachel had a list of places. She was great at thinking of places to accommodate any sized group and how to persuade them to all to agree on a single choice.

The zoo won the pick of the list. Loren left a note for Officer Scott Jones at the library's front desk.

The sun was shining, and it was a warm fall day, a perfect day for the zoo. There were very few cars in the parking lot which meant no crowds and no lines.

They stopped for a snack near the elephants. One walked to the railing nearest the picnic tables and took a trunk full of water and squirted it into his mouth. Everyone delighted at the elephant and the useful trunk. Collin stood closer to the railing after finishing his snack to admire the greatness in size. The elephant again filled his trunk with the cool refreshing water and released a blow at Collin.

The uncontrollable laughter brought tears in everyone's eyes, including Collin. No one could believe what they'd just witnessed.

"Well, the elephant thinks Collin should be baptized as an adult!" Sarah announced.

"I've already been baptized! I'm Catholic. It's done when we're babies," Collin defended.

"We call that a dedication of faith from your parents," Sarah chimed. "When you get older, as in you understand the commitment you're making to God by accepting Jesus into your heart and asking him to forgive your sins, you get baptized by immersion in water."

"I'm sure Protestants need to be baptized twice!" Collin said.

"Didn't you get baptized to show your faith? We do it as part of our conversion to Christianity," Amy explained. "It's what John the Baptizer taught. It even tells us to do so in the Bible, both parts."

"Yes, it does," Diane confirmed. "We hold a baptism service at the farm in our lake every spring. Of course, it takes the blood of Jesus to remove your sins. Baptism isn't just a confession of faith, but for believers, it's also a sign of repenting from sins, and then, you confess your sins to Jesus as you go along doing your best to live in the light."

"Nope, it's done when we're babies, and that's all the church says we need," Jessica agreed with Collin.

"We have a mikveh," Rachel explained. "It's at our synagogues. It's a tradition that's been around long before John the Baptizer. It's a way of repenting and washing away the sins of our past *and* for healing. You must be clean before entering the pool. You can't wear jewelry nor have any scabs; nothing should come between you and the water. Your hair must be combed and straight with no tangles. You enter the mikveh by yourself for a complete immersion. Oh and no dirt under your nails. However, we do it often. A woman does it before getting married and after her menstrual cycle for healing. Men do it after holidays, before marriage, after relations with wife, after healing, or any other life-changing effect. We also use the mikveh to bless and make our dishes, pots, pans, and eating utensils kosher. The kitchen in my apartment isn't big enough to keep it kosher."

"I love hearing about the differences in beliefs and traditions. They're not that different," Judy said. "I'm glad the professor gives this assignment out every year. I wish every student had to research it. Surely, the Holy Spirit spoke differently to each. I'd love to have a copy of Loren's report when it's done if it's okay with everyone?"

The Library Room

"Speaking of this project," Loren said, "I feel it's time to submit the report. The only thing, I'm not sure how everyone feels about the outcome of the research we've done. I don't want to discuss it in heated arguments as it became a personal journey for each of us. What if everybody writes a letter to God telling him how it's affected our beliefs? I'll submit the letters with my report. From there we'll live according to how the Holy Spirit directs us."

Everyone felt this was a great idea. As they walked throughout the zoo, they became lost in thought. Some walked conversing in their minds with God, and some walked off alone to pray at a quiet bench.

Jessica found a quiet bench to sit and meditate Judy felt led to stay near. In less than two minutes, Jessica was unable to control her crying. Judy let her cry for a while and then sat by her and prayed.

"No offense, Judy, but you've a hundred acres in this park and you must to sit down and pray at this bench?" Jessica moped.

"Yes," Judy said. "It's time."

"For what?" Jessica asked. "My public breakdown?"

"If that's what it takes, yes. I've been watching you for two days. Your heart's broken, and you don't know how to fix it. I've been there. When Sarah was around six years old, I felt lonely and helpless."

"I'm not lonely. I have friends," Jessica defended.

"Friends can make you feel lonelier if you see them being happy and having a future while you're struggling."

Jessica shot Judy a quick glance exposing her heart even more. Until it was said Jessica had been unable to look at Judy in the eyes. Judy hugged Jessica. Jessica gave way to the tears again.

"I'll tell you what happened to me when I turned thirty." Judy held Jessica. "We lived on the coast. Sometimes after Sarah was in bed, I'd walk the break-wall and stare at the rocks far below.

I'd allowed myself to wallow in depression. I could have jumped many times. However, my beliefs and my daughter kept me from doing it. I knew to commit suicide would be damnation upon my soul. If I'd felt badly here on earth, I didn't want to spend eternity in a place far worse. I'll even admit, my religious upbringing kept me alive more than my daughter. I'd convinced myself she'd be better off without me. I know that's not true today. Praise the Lord! I've met people who've lost a parent to suicide and have never recovered. I was running from so many things back then. I needed to forgive people for things they'd done to me. I also needed to forgive myself for things I'd done to others.

"Every night, I stared at the rocks below forcing a decision to jump or go home. The Holy Spirit kept walking me home. It wasn't easy. I had day after day of discouragement. It seemed the more I tried to focus on Christ, serving others, and my family, the more I felt disappointment. Looking back, I've decided it was spiritual warfare. Satan knew I was depressed enough to jump. He was doing everything he could to keep me focused on negative thoughts. I'd cry myself asleep. My husband never noticed, or if he did, he never leant comforting words or touches. One night, I met my guardian angel."

Jessica gave a "humph" laugh at that thought.

"Don't laugh," Judy reprimanded her attitude. "It happens to people more often than you realize."

Judy continued, "It was winter and dark when I'd started out. I was overwhelmed with grief. I sat at the edge of the wall at the darkest part where the houses are boarded up for the winter, and there are no street lights illuminating the way. You can hide in the shadows. Anyone walking the wall cannot see you until they're close to you.

"Reflecting back, it wasn't the safest place. I could've been mugged. However, at the time, I didn't care. I heard the door slam at the house behind me. A woman in a flannel parka came and sat beside me. She asked me if I was okay. I told her yes. She

The Library Room

told me not to lie. She then told me she'd been watching me cry and feared I was going to jump or die of hypothermia. I looked at my watch and was amazed at the time.

"What would my husband be thinking? Would he come looking for me? I should go, I thought to myself. I looked at her and cried again. She held me like a mother. She told me, 'After tonight everything will be much better for you. Cry and get it all out and then don't cry about it again.' I cried harder than I'd ever cried in my life. When I was done, I was done. I made a decision to obey the woman and never cried over those things again. I accepted the things I couldn't change and took courage in God to help change things I could change. She knew I'd gotten over the hurdle. 'You'll be okay now. Go home, and rest.'

"She walked back across the street. I got up and walked home. The next day, I baked chocolate chip cookies for my daughter and husband. I hadn't been able to perform such an effort in months. I thought it'd be nice to take some to the woman and thank her for her guidance. I went to the house I'd heard her come from and it was boarded up. Then I thought I had the wrong house. All the houses on that block and the next were boarded up for the winter. I never saw her again."

Judy let Jessica think about what she'd just told her.

"So you cried and forgot about all the things bothering you?" Jessica was choked up.

"I stopped crying over the negative things consuming my mind," Judy clarified. "There were things I had to deal with instead of crying over them. I had to remove my self-pity in order to make plans. I had to get out of God's way. In holding on to stress, I kept it to myself. Even if you pray for God to deal with the stress if you don't let go of it he can't work on it."

"Mom says I need to find my purpose, and then I'll be able to find happiness," Jessica added.

"Yes, I understand what she's saying," Judy confirmed. "Our purpose is quite simple, it's not about a career, making money, or finding our soul mate. Our purpose is to have a relationship with God, period. He put us on earth to have a relationship with him. He'll give us tests throughout life to see if we're ready to handle the tasks we'll be in charge of in the afterlife. When you're in a relationship with God, everything falls into place: finances, career, raising a family with your mate, friendships, and finding the right church." Judy paused and then asked, "List your things bothering you, cry them out, and then move forward."

"I'll try. May I call you if it doesn't work?" Jessica asked.

"Absolutely." Judy hugged her.

By the end of the day, everyone was ready to go home.

Drew and Rachel were dropped off at Rachel's house by Mitch and Diane. Judy dropped off Collin and Amy and then drove Jessica and Sarah to their apartments.

Judy gave Jessica a hug good-bye. And then took a seat in the lobby with Sarah for a while.

There was a handwritten letter addressed to Loren at the front desk of the hotel from Scott saying,

> *"I didn't want to interrupt your much needed break with your family and friends today. I want you to know I've been working this case all day and night to get it solved. I look forward to seeing you tomorrow and going over all the details if you're up to it. We've had a huge break in the case and it's all done; you're safe. I'm going home to get some sleep now.*
>
> *Sincerely, Scott*

Loren read the note out loud to her parents to let them know everyone was safe and all the loose ends were tied up. It didn't go unnoticed by her parents the way the note sounded personal to Loren from an admirer. They smiled, a conversation between the two of them for the ride home.

"The letter to God is a great idea," Mitch changed the subject. "It forces everyone to be honest."

"That's my hope," Loren said with a nod.

"So how do you feel about coming home for a rest from everything you've been through?" Diane offered Loren to consider. "I'm sure we can make arrangements through the Dean's office since you've been on the Dean's list every year."

"I'm feeling good," Loren defended. "I'm a little sad as I should be under the circumstances, but I'm leaning on God through this one. I feel confident whatever happens to Giles or the man who tried to take our Amy away will be prosecuted. I don't feel like I'm in any danger. I'm protected by the blood of Christ. If it's my time to go, I'm ready. If it's not my time to go, God will see to it I'm not harmed. Isn't that what you've taught me?"

"Yes," Mitch agreed. "However, you don't have to be prodigious either. It's okay to take a brain rest after trauma."

"I know, Dad." Loren sighed, "But I'm okay."

Loren stayed at the hotel again with her parents for the night.

Rachel and Drew sat on the couch eating a bowl of popcorn.

"Drew," Rachel initiated, "do we need to discuss how we feel about the research results? I know how I feel."

"I know," Drew admitted. "Do you want to discuss this after talking to our rabbis?"

"Aren't you afraid they'll spin what we've learned irrelevant? I mean, I know what I've read. I know it in my soul. I know my parents will be disappointed if I go in the direction I'm feeling led." Rachel left no mistake where she stood. "I'm afraid how it'll affect our relationship."

"I'm not agreeing with you to keep from losing you. I agree with where you're at on this. So it's not an issue. I don't feel a rabbi could twist it around to dissuade our hearts if it's true," Drew encouraged. "Which leads to this. If our hearts are telling us we need Yeshua, then we need find a synagogue supporting our new beliefs along with the traditions we know. We need to read more of The New Testament to know where we go from here. I know God will guide us together in the direction He wants. I trust God. I trust his plans for us."

The popcorn was finished, and it was time for Drew to leave. They were happy being able to discuss the matter without dissention, a sign of a good, lasting relationship.

After Drew left, Rachel thought about writing her letter to God. Then she thought she'd wait until after speaking to her rabbi.

She donned her prayer shawl and recited her prayer. When she'd finished, she replaced the shawl on the holding rack.

After an hour of trying to fall asleep, she resolved her mind wasn't turning off until she obeyed the Holy Spirit and wrote her letter.

Twenty Five

Dear HaShem,

How am I supposed to sleep? I've so much on my mind, and it's all about you, Yeshua, the Holy Spirit, and my future with Drew.

I'm scared, God. I don't know how to move some hours. I'm in panic mode. What am I going through? Why do I find myself in a quandary after being kind and helping a friend with an assignment?

Two weeks ago, I knew what I knew. I knew about You, our heavenly God, my Lord. I've studied the Torah, and in a way, it actually prepared me for seeing what's been forbidden.

My parents will be disappointed! They'll feel my conversion of faith is their failure. Their hearts will break, and they won't understand.

Help us, HaShem. Keep Drew and I focused in exploring Yeshua as the Mashiach. As we discussed earlier, we get it; however, it does little to calm my frightened heart.

My heart breaks over this, Lord! I loved being Jewish. I love my Hebrew friends and going to synagogue. I love our traditions and rituals. Must I give it all up to follow Yeshua? In this way, I feel my parents named me appropriately! Rachel had traditions she loved, yet she needed to trust you in her converted walk. I'm Rachel.

Holy Spirit, soften the sting when loved ones ridicule our conversion. Those who love us should support our beliefs, but reality tells me some won't. Please work in the hearts of our families as we explain your truths.

Yeshua, thank you, for your saving powers. Thank you, for the ability to call on your name for healing, protection, and forgiveness of sin. It's liberating knowing I can call out your name, Yeshua, for forgiveness. Bless you, God our Father, for coming down to earth as Yeshua to save us. Glory to God in the Highest.

Yeshua, as my shepherd, guide my heart, guide my life, guide my thoughts, and bring peace to all I speak to through my days on earth.

Hear O Israel: HaShem is our God. Yeshua is Mashiach. We have victory for the asking through the Holy Spirit. Claim it.

I understand Yahweh is one, my God, my Father, my Yeshua, my Mashiach, and my Holy Spirit.

Hear my prayers, Yahweh, and comfort my troubled mind as I begin a new chapter with the help of Your Holy Spirit.

Your loving child,
Rachel

Rachel fell asleep. She'd released her worries to God.

Amy entered her apartment and threw her purse on the sofa. She was tired but felt satisfied with the events of the day. She'd laughed when Collin was sprayed by the elephant. Recalling the scene made her laugh again.

She looked at her purse and remembered the sympathy card from Alec and Amelia. She felt awkward since she didn't have the time or the funds to do the same for them. She pulled out the card and opened it. A check fell to the floor along with a letter.

The Library Room

Dear little sister,

We've grown to love you as much as Mom loved you. We'd like you to be present at the funeral Friday morning. We've secured your airline ticket for Thursday evening. You'll need to show your ID at the ticket gate. Alec will meet you at the airport and take you to wherever you decide to stay. We've made a hotel reservation for you. However, we'd be honored if you'd consider staying at the family home instead.

The gifted money is from the both of us. It's not a part of the monies you'll be receiving from mother once the will is read. We'd like you to use it to do something special just for yourself. You aren't allowed to use this money to pay a bill. It must be used for something fun. You deserve it, kiddo.

Keep your chin up. As your mind wonders and makes you think you've lost yet another mother, know this time God blessed you with a brother and sister.

We'll see you Thursday night!

Love you!
Alec and Amelia

Amy wept over Mrs. Rosenberg being gone. The card reminded her to thank God and Mrs. Rosenberg for sending a brother and sister. She now had a brother and a sister to talk to, plan vacations around, celebrate mile markers in life, love, and be loved in return.

She drew a bath, lit candles, and played a CD her mother had purchased when they attended a Women of Faith event together. The water, harmonies, scented candles, and God's love brought her peace.

Before climbing into bed, she went to her desk to write a letter to Alec and Amelia. She surprised herself by writing to God first.

Dear God,

I'm grateful for the friends you've placed in my life. Thank you for Mrs. Rosenberg and her lessons during our short but meaningful relationship.

It seems self-absorbed to believe Loren's project could be thrown into my life in such perfect timing. I know it wasn't just about me or even about Mrs. Rosenberg although the project affected us both as well as her family. Mrs. Rosenberg's decision was between you and her. I'll never know for sure her decision in her final hours until it's revealed to me in heaven. I'm holding to my optimistic personality you've placed in me and believe she made the right decision in your eyes.

The journey of this project with the different layers of research brought value to my beliefs. As I read countless acts of love and mercy for your people, I hold to your promises to see me through my problems in the future.

As for my beliefs, I never once doubted your existence. I'll admit my faith may have doubted the need of a Messiah for my Jewish friends. Their teachings and traditions put at odds factual history from political fiction. This, however, is just my opinion, and I blame no one—no rabbis, no high priests, no parents. The truth has been at odds with mankind before Christ was born.

It's my belief upon thorough investigation Jesus is the Messiah for *all* including the Hebrews. Thank You, Holy Spirit, for guiding us on this journey. I pray more professors assign this project. Thank You, God, for Jesus's sacrifice to us who don't deserve such grace. Thank you.

Sincerely,
Amy

"*Collin!*" Collin's two roommates shouted as they muted the television.

"Hey, dudes, anything going on?" Collin inquired.

The Library Room

"No, dude, we were hoping you'd fill us in," Ray said. "There's talk about your friend, Loren's boyfriend, going nutzo."

"First off," Collin said, "Loren had broken up with Giles before anything turned crazy. Secondly, Giles has always been coco. It just took my trusting friend a while to see it. Thirdly, Giles isn't as guilty as everyone thinks, but it'll all come out. There were bad people who wanted to harm him for monies he owed them. Lastly, thou shalt never gossip nor condone it. I'm telling you information that'll be public. But I can't tell you anything personal beyond that. Just as I'd never tell anyone personal stuff about either of you."

"I appreciate the respect and protection," Ray said

Collin change topics in an upbeat nature. "I've been working on a project with my friends. When you two have time I'd like to go over what we've discovered. I'm not sure where you're at spirituality, but I feel you'll find it interesting. It'll make for great discussions."

"Wow!" Ray laughed. "It sounds like you drank some Kool-Aid."

Adam laughed at Ray's attempt at humor.

"Uh-huh." Collin smiled. "Go ahead and laugh, but we'll see who laughs last. This research was interesting and leaves a lot of areas open for discussion and debate. I have copies of the notes we wrote while doing the research here. If it seems interesting to you, Drew and I, are up for questions or conversations. Since we were both involved with the project, you'll hear us talking about our findings. I didn't want you two to feel left out when we do. We welcome your input as well as friends."

"I'll look at it and see what you two missed," Ray volunteered.

"Yeah," Adam agreed. "I'll take a look too. Thanks."

"Cool, thanks," Collin said. "I'm going upstairs to work on homework. Drew will be home shortly from Rachel's. You two know they're an item now don't you?"

"Whoa!" Ray shouted. "She's like a super model! She hooked our Drew? She captured the big fish?"

"Hook, line, and sinker." Collin laughed walking to his room.

In his room, he stripped to his underwear, turned the table lamp on, took out a notepad, and sat at his desk. He always felt he could concentrate better with little to no clothes binding him up.

He'd been thinking about the letter he needed to write to God ever since Loren indicated this was how she wanted to end her report. Pen in hand, he addressed his letter to God.

> Dear God,
>
> I've never been one to write a letter to anyone beside my mother for Mother's Day at the insistence of a school teacher. As I begin this letter with awkwardness, help me to put into words what my soul's feeling so it's honest.
>
> God, you've always been a part of my life. I've always known you as Jesus, the Father, the Son, the Holy Spirit, and my friend. I was asked to be brought into this world by my parents before you placed my soul into my mother's womb. Therefore, you were a part of my life before I was even conceived.
>
> As a child, to question your existence never occurred to me. Growing up knowing firsthand miracles you've performed in my family, church family, and patron saints we studied as children, I've known you existed and are here for everyone.
>
> And yet, with that said, You and I know I've had questionable thoughts.
>
> To question Jesus's reason for our lives never crossed my mind either. I've felt deep inside since my first communion Jesus is real and in my heart. Thank you for your love, sacrifice, and guidance.
>
> I'm humbled to know how the Holy Spirit's guided my thoughts, kept me craving your blessings, inspired me to want to know you more, and instilled a want of doing right instead of doing wrong.
>
> I know Jesus is the Messiah for all mankind.

The Library Room

I'll confess to you. I'm disappointed in a few of the church policies and traditions concerning transubstantiation and water baptism.

As our All-Knowing Father saw, Sarah was humiliated for taking sacrament at our church even though she's a Christian. Upon further research on my own I found the reasons and explanations. I'm a Roman Catholic, and therefore, I should believe without question what I'm being told to believe concerning transubstantiation. And yet, I can see how it could be looked upon as mystical or even political in believing only our priests are able to pray well enough to transform the sacraments. I find it offensive to reject or deny another Christian communion. It's our faith in Christ and remembrance of his love for us he requested, not to literally consume his flesh and drink his blood. Right? See, I don't know, but this is what I've felt I was doing since I was young enough to partake.

I'm confused about the water baptism. I know as a child my parents baptized me. I appreciate what they did. However, I had no say at the time. Should I have a say?

There so many different church practices confusing your believers. Why make it complicated and confusing, God? Do you see how Satan uses these as tools to discourage and place distrust amongst your flock? Of course you, all-knowing God, see this. It must break your heart watching something important be abused or misused.

In doing research, I'm led to believe in some cases man and his cravings for power had a hand in warping what You'd put into place. Now I ask You, Holy Spirit, to guide my heart in discerning what you want me to believe. I ask my beliefs come from the Holy Spirit, and not my interpretations or influences from my past. If I need to become baptized in water, lead me to the stream. If transubstantiation needs to be real to me bring my soul to be at peace with rejecting those who wish for communion and cannot partake due to their different belief.

Father, I'm glad I can talk to you in my mind.

With all of my heart and soul,
Collin

As Sarah and her mother were saying good-byes in the lobby, Mike walked over. Quick introductions were made, and Judy asked questions about his major and how he'd invest if he had spare change.

Mike advised, "Take your money out of a commercial type bank and put the least amount you need to work with into a credit union instead. Any leftover money you don't want it in any bank, even a credit union. You need to invest it in food supplies, storage supplies for food, gold, silver, and colored diamonds. Between our corrupt government and the world economy collapsing, food will be scarce."

Judy was intrigued by this young man's insightfulness. He was passionate in what he believed although it wasn't a positive forecast.

"Did you decide what we're doing Saturday?" Mike teased Sarah as a reminder.

"Um, I'm pretty sure *you* committed to figuring out what we're supposed to do." Sarah laughed.

"Oh, I see how this relationship's going to go. I do all the work in keeping it interesting." Mike rolled his eyes. "What type of things does she like to do? Help a guy out here."

"Fishing!" Judy laughed.

"No!" Sarah scowled at her mother. "I hate fishing and my mother knows it! I never catch fish. I've tried. They hate me, and it's not fun watching everyone catch fish when they don't even bite my line."

"She can't sit still long enough to give fish a chance to bite," Judy explained. "How about mountain biking on trails. She loved biking when she lived at home. You brought your bike to school?"

"Yes, I have it hanging in my bedroom," Sarah said.

"Biking! That sounds great! I have a bike upstairs too," Mike said excitedly. "Why don't we plan that?"

"Sure," Sarah answered. "But, we'll need to pump my tire first. I think it was low the last time I used it."

"No problem. We'll plan on leaving here around noon if that's okay with you," Mike said.

"It sounds like our date's now planned," Sarah said, flirting.

"Yep, I'll let you two ladies finish your conversation and I'll see you Saturday," Mike said, stepping away.

"Okay, see you Saturday," Sarah said.

"Hey, he's cute and smart," Judy commented.

"Yes he is," Sarah agreed.

Sarah walked her mother to her car, giving her a hug.

Once Sarah was in her apartment, she collapsed on the couch with her feet on the coffee table. It was good to be off of her feet. She'd worn the wrong shoes to the zoo, but she'd not had time to change them.

"Okay, God, what am I supposed to be writing? Where do I start on this one?" Sarah thought while grabbing paper from her book bag.

> Hello God,
>
> It's me again. I know you're used to me talking to you every night or when I need your help or like yesterday when you put it into my brain to pray. By the way, I'm flattered you chose me for the prayer task, but you freaked me out. I nominate Loren for that task the next time... Yeah, like you'd take directions from me.
>
> Well, if I were you, I wouldn't take directions from me either. Anyway, your plan worked, and we're all safe, and you showed us how you were in control and kept us safe. Thank you.
>
> Okay, about this assignment Ms. Loren gave us. Bless her heart.
>
> What did I learn and how did it affect my beliefs?

Ha! This project for me was humbling. God, you know as soon as Loren told me about the assignment I thought to myself, "This'll be a slam-dunk." After all, I grew up in a Holy-Roller church, we're evangelists, and we know what we believe. You humbled my butt! I think I even heard you laugh a few times as I learned new things about my faith, Drew and Rachel's faith, Collin and Jessica's faith, and Amy's faith. Then we watched Loren's lack of beliefs grow back into the faith she'd had when she was younger but with a more mature Spirit inside of her. It was humbling because it brought me to basics I never took the time to learn. I was always told I knew the answers, but I didn't. I sort of knew what to say but, never knew how to prove it or show it.

You, my Lord, made it personal. I never thought about how important lineage is—where, when, or how it all needed to be done in order to fulfill prophecy. I remember hearing a preacher proclaim the prophecies had been fulfilled, but I never knew what prophecies and how they were fulfilled. I never knew how to find what was prophesied and compare it to how it turned out. It was eye-opening.

I've never doubted your existence, and have never doubted Jesus being our redeemer.

On the same token, I've never understood the job of the Holy Spirit and why we even need that part of the Holy Trinity. So the part about the Holy Spirit was enlightening.

The Old Covenant versus the New Covenant's another great concept I've never considered. I don't recall it ever being defended, taught, or discussed in any of my Sunday school classes. Or perhaps my ears and eyes weren't open enough? Thank you, Holy Spirit, for allowing me to hear and see your truths.

As a result of all the different avenues of research, I understand why it's confusing for Jewish people. It confused me when defending the need for a Messiah for the Jewish people. They believe they're still covered by the Old Covenant. I wonder how Drew and Rachel feel now we've revealed the truth?

For the record, I believe Jesus is the Messiah for *all* mankind.

Thanks for your guidance in this project with my friends. It's been an incredible journey. I'm grateful I was a part of it.

I love you God.

Sarah

PS. Remember how I used to make fun of the people on TV or in churches who prophesy, receive the gift of laughter, speak in tongues, or lay in a euphoric trance on the floor? I won't make fun of them anymore. Although I don't believe all of them have been touched as they claim, I'll not criticize them ever again. Who am I to judge which ones are of God and which ones wish it were true for themselves? I do pray someday I'll be blessed enough to experience a full body baptism of the Holy Spirit and not just a strong desire to pray for intervention.

Drew found Adam and Ray sitting in their recliners reading papers with the television muted. They looked up at Drew as he entered the living room.

"What're you two up to tonight?" Drew asked.

"Not as much fun as you." Adam smirked. "I hear Rachel and you are an item. Good job. She's nice, smart, and beautiful."

"Yes, she is." Drew nodded to both. "And my mother says *I'm* a catch too."

"Hey," Ray said, "Collin gave us the notes from the research you've been doing. Some of it seems far-fetched, but I've just started reading it. Interesting read so far."

"I take it you've never studied a Bible or the Tanakh to know it's not as far-fetched as you think?" Drew asked.

"No, I've never had an interest. My parents spent quality time with my brothers and me on the weekends, and it was study, study, during the week," Ray confirmed.

"How about you Adam?" Drew asked. "Did you go to church or grow up believing in God?"

"We went every once in a while—weddings, funerals, Passover, or when my Bobeshi would visit," Adam said.

"You're Jewish?" Drew asked.

"Well, I guess I'm nothing like Ray. I grew up knowing we were Jewish but no bar mitzvah. Never learned it," Adam stated.

"So the notes must seem foreign to you both?" Drew guessed.

"Sometimes, it makes total sense, and other times, it's way out there." Ray rolled his eyes

"Keep reading it with an open mind," Drew suggested. "It'll start clicking and you'll see. After a while, you'll believe because it'd be too farfetched not to believe. Trust me, I've tried denying God's existence or even God having someone write a Bible. I'd put all the emphasis on the man who wrote it not who told the man what to write. Once I aligned the miracles to the prophecies, I couldn't deny God."

"That came from researching this stuff?" Ray asked.

"I'm ashamed I've doubted God's existence over the years," Drew admitted. "I did have a bar mitzvah. I should've known better."

"So are you changing to Christianity now you've done this research? How does Ms. Rachel feel about the results?" Adam asked.

"I'm not commenting on either. Research the notes and tell me what you think when you're done. Do it with a Bible and look at the verses with our notes. It speaks differently to different people, and you'll feel something speak to your mind while you're doing it. It's not witchcraft or voodoo or anything of a dark source, but you'll feel a supernatural guidance in your thinking. The whole

The Library Room

team experienced that." Drew poured a glass of milk and drank it down. "With that, I leave you two to begin a new educational adventure. Good night."

"Okay, good night," Ray said

"Thanks for your opinion," Adam said. "I'll keep reading it and let you know what I think. Good night."

Drew went to his desk, picked up the notepad he'd used the day before in the library, and read his note: "Ezekiel 36:26—I'll give you a new heart and put a new spirit in you."

He looked up, "Thank you, HaShem, for my new heart."

He took his notepad and kneeled at the side of the bed. He glanced at the tefilah on his desk he'll use in his morning prayers. He began his letter to God.

> HaShem,
>
> It's been an amazing journey you've put us through this past week. I'd doubted we'd be able to agree on anything, feared watching my friends become let down in their beliefs, and now I see the truth. You knew I'd be changing my beliefs.
>
> Where do we go from here? This new relationship with you, Yeshua, and the Holy Spirit all one God in nature? How do I pray? To whom do I direct my prayers to after I eat, wake up in the morning, and go to bed at night? Does it change in what I've been doing? Do I need to change other than accepting the fact Yeshua's indeed the Mashiach? Where do I go to find my answers?
>
> How we've for generations prayed and prayed for the blessed Mashiach. I've memorized verses of the prophets in longing with my people for the arrival to discover they missed it, and I could've missed it too if it weren't for a professor's assignment.
>
> What happens to my friends back home who don't know? How do I tell them? They need to know. Right? What if I'd never had the opportunity to discover the truth? What would've happened to me? To Rachel? She

was even more devout than I could ever have been. What happens when we tell our parents? How'll this affect my job at the law firm? They think I'm still a part of their Jewish club. Did they hire me more on my religious beliefs or my school scores? It's confusing and terrifying; yet, at the same time liberating and clear.

I'm glad you're real to me now. I used to cringe thinking I was being forced to believe in something or some being I wasn't certain existed. Now I know beyond any disbelief you are God and exist. I'm ashamed for doubting your existence. I'm embarrassed I didn't pick up on the prophecies of Moses with the plagues you'd controlled. I'm sorry for my doubts and ask for your forgiveness.

With that written, I'm now a man of God—not a rabbi, by any means—but a man who believes in You. I know you exist and this is a life lesson I'll never forget.

I know you exist and you give people prophecies. I trust your prophecies. Since I trust your prophecies, I trust the prophecies have been fulfilled by Yeshua as the Mashiach. Since I trust Yeshua's the Mashiach, I trust him when he says he's also God the Father. Since I trust you're the Father, God of the heavens and earth, I believe in heaven. Since I believe in heaven, I believe it's where you long your people to reside, in Olam Ha-Ba. Since I believe it's your heart's desire to gather your people in Olam Ha-Ba. I trust and believe you provided a way for us to do that through Yeshua just like you'd prophesied all along.

I think of all the sin in the world and know Yeshua took it on himself. I believe he was sinless. He couldn't have been around so many people all the time without someone hearing or seeing him fail in keeping a law. He was blameless. You took the fall and showed us it could be done perfectly only by you, God. You sacrificed yourself as a perfect lamb for all mankind's sins: sins of Israel, sins of the world, and my personal sins. It must have broken your heart feeling all those transgressions.

The Library Room

Yeshua, I ask as your child for you to forgive me of my sins. I know I have many. My thoughts alone have been impure and wicked. My actions often fail your expectations. I'm sorry for the sins. I'm sorry for needing Yeshua's blood to cleanse my soul. It does make it different for me knowing Yeshua's blood had to be shed for my own sin as well as others. It makes a difference knowing a perfect human being was sacrificed and not just an ox or a lamb, but you as the Son of man, Yeshua, perfect, God himself incarnate, willing to die so we can become closer to you and not have anything between us.

I'm ashamed for all the times I criticized you, your people the Christians, their beliefs, and their traditions. My heart cries for all the times I made fun of baby Yeshua in manger scenes at Christmas time. It must hurt you hearing and seeing the mean things people think and say. I repent from those evil deeds. I get it now. Forgive me, HaShem.

Help me to seek my friend's forgiveness for ridiculing their beliefs. Help me to ask Loren for forgiveness in thinking I knew all the answers to her project and planned to throw it in everyone's faces. Forgive my haughty eyes. May they never surface again.

Thank You, Holy Spirit, for guiding our group. Thank you for keeping peace amongst friends during a sensitive and personal adventure as a team.

Thank You, God, for my upbringing. I, in no way, feel slighted or misguided. I view the lessons I'd learned as a preview of my life with Your Holy Spirit gracing me with more wisdom.

Help my future wife, Rachel, and I adjust to the new ways of living according to your new laws and love. Help us to raise our children to be God fearing and Yeshua loving.

Give me courage to face the parents and teach them what we've learned. Open them to allow the Holy Spirit to discern your truths.

All these things I ask of You, Yeshua, and the Holy Spirit. Bless You for your love of this world so much.

Very Truly Yours,
Drew

Jessica sat in her apartment. She still hadn't turned on the lights. She kept thinking about the depth of Judy's depression, and it scared her. She'd never thought about killing or hurting herself. She thought about the words Judy had used: *self-pity, hopelessness, depressed, constantly crying, self-absorbed*. It was forcing Jessica to take a personal inventory of her feelings and the causes.

Judy suggested making a list of her worries and disappointments so she could face the demons. As she walked to the kitchen to find a pen, she wept over having to perform such a task in order to stop crying.

She sat in the dark with a small nightlight plugged into an outlet illuminating just enough light to be able to read what she'd written.

To most, her list wouldn't seem like the types of things to be upset over; however, to her, they were real fears and disappointments.

"Now," Jessica heard Judy's voice in her head, "I want you to cry over those things as hard and as loud as you can to get it all out of your system. I want you to cry so hard over these things you can barely get up and walk to the bedroom to go to sleep."

Jessica cried so hard and loud at one point she heard a neighbor standing outside her door. In her mind, she screamed, *"Just go away! I just want to cry it all out!"* It took hours to stop crying over the things listed on her paper. In the end, she wrote at the bottom of her list. "I'm done. God, take it from here."

She was exhausted and climbed into bed with her clothes on.

In the morning, she saw her puffy eyes and tangled hair. She thought to herself, *Looks like I did it the right way. I feel good.*

The Library Room

She saw the list lying on the floor. There were several spots smeared from watery tears. As she read the list, she thought to herself, *I'm so over it all*. She tossed it in the wastebasket next to her desk.

She checked her phone for messages and saw none. The clock on the wall told her she must forgo the coffee shop ritual with Sarah. She texted her.

Sarah texted back. "Are there classes today?"

Jessica texted back. "I hope so. I'm bored. Call me if we don't since you'll be at the school first."

Sarah texted back. "Okay."

A few minutes later, Sarah texted her, "Classes resume 2morrow. Media everywhere. CU@ library."

Jessica was the first to arrive at the library. She looked around the room as if it were the first time she'd seen it. All the spiritual ornaments, paintings, symbolisms, and the wonder of the sky dome felt new to her again. She reread the donations from previous teams. What will her team come up with and how are they going to pay for it?

She grabbed a tablet and pen. She plopped into a beanbag chair to write her letter to God.

> Dear God,
> Thank you for loving me and sending Judy to help me get over my personal hurdle. Thank you for waking me up to acknowledging my depression before it got out of control.
> Thank you for my friends.
> Thank you for sending Jesus to forgive our sins.
> Thank you for sending the Holy Spirit down to keep me safe from my thoughts.
> Thank you for the four years in school to learn how to teach. I pray you use this skill to help others find you.

Thank you for choosing Loren as Professor Finkel's student to be assigned this project.

Thank you for giving a professor the courage to challenge students with this assignment each year.

Thank you for gifting us with this journey.

Thank you for opening my eyes to all the differences which aren't so different between Judaism, Catholicism, and Protestant beliefs.

Forgive me, Jesus, for my sins so I may converse with you without anything being wedged between us.

Forgive me, Jesus, for my worrisome nature. Heal the brokenness that creates fear.

Help me, Lord, to know the right paths to follow.

Help me, Lord, to feel you in every heartbeat.

Help me, Lord, to forgive those who have disappointed me.

Help me, Lord, to I always feel you in my decisions.

Help me, Lord, to toss fear aside as I know you're in control of my life, this country, Israel, and my future.

Help me, Lord, to glorify your blessings so others may see a prosperous Christian.

Thank you, Holy Spirit, God my Father, and Jesus, for all the blessings you give. Praise you Father.

Hallelujah!

Jessica

Loren woke up alone in the hotel room again. "My parents feel it's okay to get up and go down for breakfast without inviting me." She laughed to herself.

Sarah texted her, letting her know there were no classes until Thursday. She also let Loren know she and Jessica were meeting in the library and that her letter to God was done.

"Well, that puts a different spin on today's events," she said out loud. She'd forgotten her own letter needed to be written.

The Library Room

Knowing her parents would stay downstairs eating breakfast until she came down to meet them, she decided to use the time to write her letter. On a piece of hotel stationery, she began.

Dear Father in heaven,

To say you picked the perfect imperfect person to be assigned this project may be the understatement of the year. My questioning your existence at the beginning of the project proved how much you were calling me back to you.

Thank you, Father, for your saving grace, mercy, and having a "come to Jesus" talk with me, not to mention the work you've done in my friends. Praises to you, Father.

I've asked myself after everything I've learned how could I've thought of you as merely amongst the trees or just a Higher Power or a Spirit I emit into the world? Thank you for your patience as I worked through that phase. Thank you for humbling me. I'm embarrassed of all the belittling thoughts I'd had of a God so great. I'm humbled and ask you, Jesus, for your forgiveness.

You've made me new again! I'm back. I feel the strength of the Holy Spirit in my veins. You've made us more than conquerors through the blood of Jesus Christ. We have victory over death; therefore, I fear nothing, not even death or persecution. I lean on you and look forward to walking with you every day.

Help me, Lord, to find a church to your liking. Keep me from being burned out like the last time from volunteering too much and allowing jealousies to take the joy out of serving you.

Help me, Holy Spirit to grow more mature in the Lord so I may use the knowledge you've placed in my heart to help others see you.

Yeshua, Jesus, Christ, Messiah, Mashiach, blessed are you for sacrificing your perfectness for us sinners. The mitzvahs, laws, commandments were too hard for us without you replacing our stone hearts with one that desires to please you. Help me to always please you before pleasing myself.

As I just wrote, "Help me to please you before pleasing myself," I had flashes of what my flesh thinks is fun and know it's not of your liking. It'll be hard to overcome my fleshly nature. So I ask you again, a second time, with a genuine and sincere heart to help me overcome my own pleasures in order to please you first. Thank you for the pleasures you do send my way. Bless me to feel satisfied with those blessings.

Forgive me of all of my sins, Yeshua, with your blood.

Protect my friends and family from harm as we move forward. Help everyone to stay close and connected to you. I've watched us grow.

Thank you for your protection and sending guardian angels to watch over us during our spiritual warfare. Apparently, Satan forgot the battle's already been won. Just remind him to read the last chapter of the Bible called Revelations in the New Testament.

At a time in my life when I should be sad for having to end a relationship, scared from all the drama, and worried about my future employment and students loans, I'm elated in your Spirit. I'm happy and confident your plan's going to work for me just fine.

Thank You Father for your love, mercy, and grace.

Loren

Loren went down to the lobby and ate breakfast with her parents, letting them know it was time for them to take her to her library room. They offered to take her home for the remainder of the semester. She declined their offer by assuring them God was on her side.

By the time Loren arrived at the library room, Drew, Rachel, and Amy had arrived and stood with Collin, Sarah, and Jessica. They were all there—her friends for life.

One by one, they handed their letters to God to her. One by one, each asked for forgiveness if they'd ever done or said anything that offended each other. One by one, all were forgiven by each other and all past matters were settled.

The project was complete. The room was theirs to use for the remainder of the school year. The project would be assigned again next year to an unsuspecting student who'd involve friends in a life changing journey.

Conclusion

Loren's Final Report

Thank you, Professor Finkel, for this assignment and the ability to allow my friends to participate. It's been an eye opening experience.

I won't bore you with all the scripture verses you've memorized over the years from assigning this report. I will, however, include the notes we wrote down as a group in doing our research, as well as the reference materials we used in completing the research.

I passed the different sections of notes onto my pastor from the church I used to attend. He helped explain a few areas that seemed clear to the team at the time but became muddied after doing more research per his instruction.

We learned some Bible scholars who accept the virgin conception as a matter of faith are still reluctant to base it on Isaiah 7:14. They've no problem using the other verses, but this one's touchy because of questions about the linguistic linkage between the Hebrew Old Testament, the Septuagint, and the Greek New Testament. In other words, the interpretation of wording isn't strong enough. The other verses, however, we pulled from the messianic prophecies were strong enough. I'm keeping the reference in my notes as it does go well with the other verses we discovered and in a way lends support regardless of saying "virgin" or "maiden" when going through the translations.

As you mentioned in an earlier review, "any Jr. High or High School student can pull together the Messianic Prophecies to make a biased case." I agree. I also feel they're necessary in finding the truth or in finding the purpose and/or reasons for our determinations.

It was obvious from the start the Holy Spirit was influencing our findings as well as increasing our desires of wanting to know the truth. Going from a semi-non-believer, to a full believer is proof positive the Holy Spirit indwells in the hearts and minds of mankind when they seek the truth. Having two Hebrews, two Catholics, two Protestants, and one New Ager, work in peace through the process and all come to the same conclusions can only be explained as divine intervention.

"Open your hearts, open your eyes, open your ears, open your minds, and open to Me, the Spirit of the Lord." God called to each of us.

The Spirit of the Lord kept our hearts longing to know the truth as a team. It occupied our thoughts throughout our days. This prodding from the Spirit became a vital part of making our decision. We learned through researching the Tanakh that there wasn't always a longing in the hearts and minds of mankind to seek and obey God. Even today, amongst the Judaic religions, the Holy Spirit calls to his people who chose to follow and seek his approval. It's in the hearts of all mankind regardless of religion. The Spirit of the Lord resides in everyone now if you want to become closer to God.

Today, I know God is real. There are too many prophecies in the Tanakh alone with prophets like Moses, Daniel, Samuel, etc., to prove God exists. The prophecies of the plagues, the prophecies concerning Abraham, Isaac, etc., prove God's more than a thought in the back of a person's mind. The predicted miracles are evidence that God is real.

Therefore, *all* of his prophecies are real and not part of someone's embellished stories to create meaning, laws, or explanations of how, or why, we're here.

God's words became alive as we read about his history, his desires, and his love for us. The Spirit of the Lord often led us to read whole chapters instead of a small referenced verse to gain better understanding of the meaning or condition in which they were written. The characters throughout the Tanakh and Brit Chadashah (New Testament) became alive in our minds as we read and were led. It's this project team's opinion God's word becomes an essential tool; therefore, it's a part of God and becomes alive in the hearts of mankind as it's read.

John 1:1 NIV: "In the beginning was the Word, and the Word was with God, and the Word was God."

Because God's word is alive, it feels as if God's words can have many meanings, just like his prophecies can be interpreted and used in different ways too. God's word is never wrong. He spoke it to encompass all changes with timing, and generational differences.

With that said, God is our purpose for living. He's everything, our reason, our drive, and our everlasting goal. He created us individually and leads us individually, for if not individually, we wouldn't have been led to read the chapters and verses we've read in searching for the truth. Without God we've no accountability, no guide, no sense of purpose, and no desire to please anything but ourselves. We cannot be our own God. If we were our own God, what'd be our purpose or end result of a self-absorbed life? Nothing. It takes a living God to make sense of our reason for being here on earth. Our purpose is to know God personally so we can be with him for all eternity.

Since God's word is true, we can believe it's for us today as it was yesterday and will be tomorrow. He did this on purpose. There are no accidents with God. Nothing spoken by the prophets is coincidental.

We know God's word to be true; therefore, when the Spirit of the Lord gave words to a prophet concerning the future and the need for a Mashiach, God meant it. He also explained why and how it'd happen so we don't miss out on his opportunities, even if it means researching for yourself despite all the teachings you've been taught about Yeshua being the Messiah.

The Covenant God gave Moses to tell all of the Hebrews when they were ready to return to God was that he'd take them back. (Deuteronomy 30) God knew they'd stray again and again. He's a God of mercy. Some people turn away from God before realizing the importance of having God in their life. Some people suffer total destruction of property and family before turning to God and asking for forgiveness and help. God promised he'd always be there for those who turn to him. He'll love and forgive by giving an inward spiritual circumcision of the heart. *If* you follow God's laws with all your soul, you'll become prosperous in the works of your hands in the fruit of your womb, livestock, and crops of your land. This was a promise of grace, forgiveness, and materialistic prosperity. This wasn't a promise of eternal life with God.

Resurrection was assumed to be accomplished by obeying God's laws.

As further research was required toward the end of this project our group needed to find out what happened to humans after death prior to Yeshua's proposed covenant. The Tanakh is clear about how or what happens. Job was one of the first to talk about resurrection. In Job's time, Israel didn't have a clear doctrine of resurrection, heaven, or Olam Ha-Ba. However, our team believes, his confidence in God through the Spirit of the Lord, gave him the "knowing" of an afterlife with God. Tanakh, Ketuvim, Job 19:25–27 NIV: "I know my Redeemer lives, and in the end He'll stand upon the earth. And after my skin's been

The Library Room

destroyed, yet in my flesh I'll see God; I'll see Him with my own eyes—I, and not another. How my heart yearns within me!"

Isaiah prophesied about it in Isaiah 26:19 NIV: "But, your dead will live; their bodies will rise. You, who dwell in the dust, wake up and shout for joy. Your dew is like the dew of the morning; the earth will give birth to her dead."

Daniel also prophesied about being asleep in the dust, resurrected, being judged, and eternally living with our life choice with multitudes at one time. Tanakh, Nevi'im, Daniel 12:2–13 NIV: "Multitudes who sleep in the dust of the earth will awake: some to everlasting life, others to shame and everlasting contempt. The wise will shine like the brightness of the heavens, and those who lead many to righteousness, like the stars forever and ever...Many will be purified, made spotless and refined, but the wicked will continue to be wicked. None of the wicked will understand, but the wise will understand...As for you, go your way till the end. You'll rest, and then at the end of the days you'll rise to receive your allotted inheritance."

David gave us his belief in a verse found in Tanankh, Ketuvim, Psalms Book 1, Psalms 17:15 NIV: "And I—in righteousness I'll see your face; when I awake, I'll be satisfied with seeing your likeness."

Yeshua, we feel as a team, is the Mashiach for not only the Gentiles but the Jewish people as well.

In keeping the project personal and allowing the Holy Spirit to speak to the hearts of each person individually, I requested from them a letter to God as I felt it'd be more honest and less intimidating should their opinions differ from the others. Along with the research notes, you'll find their letters.

In each letter you'll read everyone agrees Yeshua fulfilled the prophecies of birth, and what a Mashiach would be like while Yeshua was here on earth. Additionally, Yeshua was like Moses only better; he exceeded the miracles and as a result of Yeshua the Spirit of the Lord was written in the hearts and minds of all mankind.

We, as a team, agree it was God's own seed implanted into the Virgin Mary which he did to become flesh. The miracles Yeshua performed could only be done using the Spirit of the Lord. Only God would be able to keep the entire mitzvah and live without sinning. Only God, himself, in the form of a human could resurrect himself and then ascend to heaven.

Since Yeshua is God, and the Spirit of the Lord is God, it's clear to us, as a team, God, Yeshua, and the Holy Spirit, are indeed one in the same, yet all three have different roles or forms in one nature, equal in power and glory.

One of the hardest problems for humans to comprehend is God. Prior to God coming down to earth as Yeshua people saw or related to him as a spirit or ghost. Satan too can produce spirits, demons, and ghosts. Additionally, Satan could convince people idols could perform immediate miracles. The people needed something solid they could relate to knowing and seeing. They needed the Holy Spirit to guide them and give them a sense of discernment. The people needed concrete physical evidence God loved them despite hearing or seeing the miracles and history of God freeing the Israelites from bondage and the miracles prophets had performed in the name of God. Jesus became the bridge. He became the physical redeemer, a vessel to deliver us to God.

If you believe God's a loving Father to us, then you must believe he'd be willing to come down in flesh to prove he's almighty. Denying Yeshua is denying God, therefore, you must accept Yeshua as God if you're to bring God into your heart and mind.

Yeshua's covenant promises eternal life; our ultimate goal. Yeshua provides a way to accomplish that goal without the tasks of taking a perfect animal to temple for a sacrifice. God knew we'd never uphold the mitzvah. Yeshua became the sacrifice for mankind. God allowed his own sinless flesh to die as a sacrifice for our sins. He then showed us Yeshua, being God, was greater than death and resurrected himself before ascending to heaven.

These things were done publicly, nothing was hidden, thousands testified to seeing Yeshua resurrected. If it weren't true, it'd have been written and told from generation to generation of a great deception and it'd have ended. Instead, we've written documentation as proof as well as Yeshua's history told from generation to generation throughout times when illiteracy was the normal way of life. Of course, there were those who disputed Yeshua's miracles despite seeing them with their own eyes just like the magicians did with Moses. They claimed deception or hocus-pocus; however, they were always proven to be miracles indeed of God. Thus the power of the Holy Spirit grew amongst the nations. Again, with the help of the Holy Spirit, the need, craving, and desires to know God in a personal way is in the hearts and minds of those who seek the Truth.

Several times during our research, we'd wonder, "Why didn't the Jewish people accept all these Messianic Prophecies and see the compelling likeness of Yeshua being 'like Moses' or any of the prophesied descriptions back when they were being fulfilled?"

Actually, many did! For someone to fulfill just one of them is a miracle or even if only two or three were fulfilled let alone as many as Christ fulfilled. However, we still wonder and ask why didn't they all see it?

Collin's theory. Look around a house or church and tell me how many Bibles do you see? How many do you think they had back then? Keep in mind, they only had scrolls of the different books of the Tanakh back then too so they couldn't readily do a comparison of the prophecies and of Christ's life. Most didn't memorize scripture. Again, there was no "want" to know them since they didn't offer instant gratification in their eyes.

Drew and Rachel educated us about the jobs of the scribes. Keep in mind they didn't have printing presses, and it wasn't proper to have them printed. Scribes had to copy the Tanakh and they were always placed in a safe place like the temple, synagogues, or once they aged more than seven years old in a genizah (storage room or cemetery that was created for retiring worn out documents including letters containing the name of God). Because of this, most people didn't know the Tanakh very well.

Jessica did side research and discovered a lot of priests and rabbis didn't know scriptures very well since they were caught up in the traditions, sacrifices, and everyday teachings of living life according to the six hundred thirteen Mitzvot (God's laws) more than studying and memorizing entire chapters on prophecies. However, as Yeshua fulfilled them, some were caught and noted by scribes, rabbis, and high priests. But not all, thus the teaching at the temple when Yeshua revealed himself to the Jewish people "many came to believe in Him" then.

Again, because of the lack of written scrolls concerning the upcoming Mashiach, the verses they did dwell upon and kept in their hearts were the partials of Mashiach being a King and ruling over all of Israel. Like Tanakh, Nevi'im, Jeremiah 23:5 ESV: "…He shall reign as king and shall prosper." They in their minds conjured up a larger than life image of a man coming to rule over Israel and bring back world peace—a strong, handsome, being. They were looking for a king to be born in a palace, not a manger. There were centuries and generations of romanticizing over the upcoming Mashiach combined with lack of memorization of scripture He became what we'd think of today as a superhero. We feel many Jewish people are still led astray by these images fancied up from lack of personal study today, relying too much on the rabbis and synagogues picking and choosing what to teach them instead of learning it all themselves.

They'd long forgotten (and conveniently so in some cases) the parts of Tanakh, Nevi'im, Isaiah 53, which described just the opposite of what they'd anticipated their Mashiach King should be like. Isaiah 53:2 & 53 KJV: "He hath no form nor comeliness; and when we shall see him, there is no beauty that we should desire him...He was despised, and we esteemed him not." Perhaps the scribes who copied the scrolls knew this verse and they were the ones who then later became disciples and followers as described in John 8:30. "As He was saying this, many came to believe in Him."

Amy's pastor also brought to light that besides the lack of physical resources, another reason for their disbelief was simply that their hearts were hardened.

After Yeshua ascended the Holy Spirit fell upon the people—*all* people, Hebrews and Gentiles. There became a longing in the hearts of men to seek God. It was a time of Pentecost. Even today Jewish people who aren't Christian are still seeking God in their hearts and want to focus on the Laws (not all but most.) It wasn't like that before Yeshua.

Yes, Yeshua's the only way to accomplish forgiveness and enter into a union with God the Father and secure eternal and everlasting life in the presence of God.

Yes, Yeshua's the Mashiach for all of mankind.

I'm grateful for being assigned this project. May you shine as bright as the stars in heavens after we're all resurrected for bringing me and my friends to a heart and mind of righteousness.

—Loren P. Boyer
Project Team Leader 2012

Your Chapter

Now, go ahead and write your own letter to God below…

References

Different Bibles Used in research, quoting, condensing, and summarizing.

    JPS—Jewish Publication Society
    ESV—English Standard Version
    NIV—New International Version
    KJV—King James Version
    NJB—New Jewish Bible

The Jewish Virtual Library. http://www.jewishvirtuallibrary.org. This site became my favorite web site for seeking information on customs, etiquette, tradition, definition, and admiration, for the Judaic faith. May God deeply bless the persons who developed that site for all to explore!

(5) the prayers recited by Drew and Rachel as well as other beautiful traditional Judaic prayers can be found at: http://www.Jewishvirtuallibrary.org/jsource/Judaism/bedtime.html

Eisenberg, Ronald L. *The JPS Guide to Jewish Traditions.* PA: Jewish Publication Society, 2004; "Prayer Kriat Sh'ma"

Bard, Mitchell *Brachot (Blessings) Before Eating* Jewish Virtual Library.org, 2013 http://www.jewishvirtuallibrary.org/jsource/Judaism/Brachot.html

The Coming Prince. written by Sir Robert Anderson You may download and/or read this entire book at http://philologos.org/__eb-tcp/

To easily find more information regarding the Judaic faith, I found a website called Judaism 101 put together by Tracey R. Rich to be helpful and educational. This site was helpful in citing and simplifying the 13 Principles of Faith on web page http://www.jewfaq.org/beliefs.htm

The Purpose Driven Life by Rick Warren—Although no quotes were directly extracted from this work, it is and has influenced my beliefs since reading the book.

Believer's Bible Commentary by William MacDonald

Jewish Encyclopedia http://www.jewishencyclopedia.com/

The Oxford Companion to the Bible by Bruce Metzger and Michael Coogan

A History of the Jews by Paul Johnson, p. 91, Phoenix, 1993 (org pub 1987), ISBN 1-85799-096-X Cushing's address—New York times Sept 29, 1964; see also John Oesterreicher, The New Encounter Between Christians and Jews (New York; Philosophical Library, 1986) 197-98; see also Rabbi James Rudin, Christians and Jews Faith to Faith, (Woodstock, VT; JEWISH LIGHTS Publishing) 99-100

The construction and size of the Temple Veil—The sources Gill cites are: (w) Misn. Shekalim, c. 8. sect. 5. Shernot Rabba, sect. 50. fol. 144. 2. Bernidbar Rabba, sect. 4. fol. 183. 2. (x) Vid. Bartenora & Yom. Tob. in ib.

The BibleWay Online http://www.thebiblewayonline.com/Active/Life%20of%20Christ-Humble.html

Saltshakers—Where Jews and Gentile can meet in peace in Messiah Jesus. http://www.hebrewroots.com/node/231 Messianic and Hebraic Christian community website. #24

Baptism of Yeshua, Submitted by saltysteve on Sun, 05/31/2009—16:54

The Israeli National News—© Arutz Sheva, All Rights Reserved http://www.israelnationalnews.com/News/News.aspx/140251#.UJQQFIZP9ut

Copyright Disclaimer Under Section 107 of the Copyright Act 1976, allowance is made for "fair use" for purposes such as criticism, comment, news reporting, teaching, scholarship, and research.